FIGHT WE MUST

K'LUMA BOOK 1

HEIDI ALERT

Summary: A powerful force brings together an unlikely pair: a small-town girl from the islands and a crown prince of the K'Luma Empire, who is currently on the run. Together, they must save the reclusive Mountain Kingdom from the emperor's latest conquest.

Cover by Grayson Alert

www.behance.com/graysonalert

Editing by Sara Coombes

www.saracoombes.com

First Edition

ISBN: 979-8-9866267-0-3

BOOKS BY HEID ALERT

<u>K'Luma Series</u>
Fight We Must
Win We Shall

PRAISE FOR FIGHT WE MUST

AMAZON REVIEWS

"A great read and story about hope and destiny in the face of darkness."

"Strong themes of trust, faith, and friendship. Excellent for teens and young adults."

"If you're looking for something to read that is uplifting and thought provoking, but still engaging and action packed, this is the perfect choice."

"This book was an absolute delight! The storyline was captivating, the message uplifting, the characters well developed."

To my family.
Gordon, my greatest champion;
Zakyla, my inspiration; and,
Zhaun, my dream-setter.

Chapter 1

I T WAS ONLY ONE hour before the proudest moment in Charlotte's life. It was less than two hours before her world would fall apart.

"How do I look?" Lily twirled, the embroidered flowers in her short skirt dancing like those in the field behind their house. Her brown eyes sparkled against the mint green of her top, her soft brown curls bouncing with each twist.

Charlotte smiled from where she reclined on the edge of the bed, trying to match her older sister's enthusiasm. "Amazing." Her artistic sister truly was the image of spring and all things joyful.

"It was brilliant to include metal threads for the tops, Char." Ava stood, smoothing out her long, midnight black dress, the thin shavings reflecting the sunshine that streamed into the room of the inn. Ava's dress was covered in small, glittering stars, with a crescent moon over her heart. Her hair was pulled up into a tight bun, in usual form, accentuating her high cheekbones.

Their mom had spent the weeks leading up to the ceremony making the dresses by hand, and they couldn't be more perfectly suited to the twins.

For her part, Charlotte was happy to be in her comfortable dark tights and high boots. She double-checked to make sure her red undershirt and black jacket were clean and stain-free. Thankfully, her family had given up on questioning why she wore a jacket when it was always so hot out—they did live on a tropical island after all. But the material was light, and nothing could ever replace the usefulness of the myriad of pockets her jacket had.

All three sisters were radically different, but joy washed over Charlotte as she looked at her older twin sisters. She may not be the one receiving a prize, but she couldn't have been prouder of her family. Everything was going according to plan.

Their family had traveled from a poor fishing village on the outskirts of the island to Kinstun, the biggest city on Jamroq, for the special prize-giving ceremony. Every year, top students from the conquered isles would be honored through an event that was broadcast live throughout the K'Luma Empire.

Jamroq rarely won anything, let alone two prizes in the same year, and never from some remote, unknown village at that.

Ava won the top academic performer based on math and science marks. Lily had flourished with a paintbrush for as long as Charlotte could remember and was to be awarded the top prize in the arts.

"You two realize the impossible expectations you've placed on Jamroq students for years to come, right?" Charlotte chided her sisters with a grin. "Not to mention, me."

Lily fluttered to Charlotte's side on the bed, wrapping an arm around her. "Don't worry, lil' sis. By the time you reach your last year, I'm sure they'll add a prize for... making stuff."

Charlotte's cheeks warmed at her sister's attempt to compliment her unusual skills. But she doubted that much would change in the next three years before her own graduation.

"It's called tech," Ava corrected Lily. "And yes, dear Char, unfortunately, the value of such is highly underrated in the isles. The Sahemy in Pergamum keep it way too secret, and what's not understood is often brushed aside." She sat on Charlotte's other side, and the three sisters shared an embrace.

"I'll just be happy when you two take important posts here in Kinstun, and I can get back to working on my inventions," Charlotte said.

Lily leaned forward and narrowed her eyes at Ava. "Remember, even if the head of the Sahemy comes to offer you a position in the science guild, we're sticking to the plan and staying right here in Jamroq. No leaving."

"I know, I know. Change things from our own backyard, first. Most important." Ava nodded. But then she paused and sighed, allowing her eyes to glaze over. "Even though studying with the Sahemy would be such a dream."

Charlotte's mouth dropped open, and she nudged Ava in the ribs, worried her sister might have a change of heart.

"Don't worry," Ava laughed. "I'm not leaving."

"We're not leaving," Lily added.

Prize winners were often given opportunities to work or further their learning in the capital of the K'Luma Empire, Pergamum. However, once students left, they were never seen again—only heard from in reports; sometimes by packages sent to their families.

The girls' parents, or perhaps more so Dad and Gran, always talked about bringing better education and access to their village of Mina, and Jamroq as a whole. The twin's success helped to prove each person had potential, regardless of status.

Charlotte was happy—no, proud was more accurate—of her sisters and what they now symbolized for other villagers in Mina, and throughout the island.

The door to the room opened, and their dad stuck his head in. His dark skin glistened slightly from the heat. The tavern they had spent the night in lacked proper ventilation and the sea breeze they were accustomed to in Mina. "Mom's about ready. How are you three beauties doing?"

Lily jumped up and walked over to embrace him. "Ready as ever to make the best teacher in all of Jamroq, proud."

He smiled and adjusted his glasses. "I think your creativity comes more from your mom than me, but yes, all three of you make my glad-bag buss."

Charlotte laughed at his rare use of local dialect.

"Or maybe I should say, the three of you cause my bag full of gladness to burst wide open." He grinned, putting on a more proper air. "But seriously, you all shine—whether working on a canvas, solving an equation, or getting a discarded piece of tech to work." He looked at each girl in turn, and when he mentioned tech, he looked at Charlotte's wrist where her gazer was safely hidden beneath the sleeve of her jacket.

Yet another reason to love her jacket. Last year, Gran had found the thin, bracelet-like device discarded in the trash as she cleaned the Imperial guards' offices and brought it home for Charlotte.

A part of Charlotte wondered whether it had actually been discarded, but it was definitely broken when Gran handed it over. It had taken Charlotte a few months to restore it to proper working order. It recorded and stored videos and images which could then be projected via hologram. She had disabled any tracking or communication capabilities, even though she knew the gazer could do much more.

Every time she tried to explain how she got it to work, her dad's eyes would glaze over. She had never been taught about tech—no one outside the Sahemy knew how to build or operate tech. But to her, how the parts worked together, and the language used to instruct the devices, just came naturally. Now, she couldn't be parted from the device.

"Okay, let me see my girls." Their mom waltzed into the room, looking radiant with her flowered top, black leggings and boots, and a star-lined twill skirt. She somehow had managed to pull representation from each daughter into her ensemble. Her light skin and long blond hair practically glowed with excitement.

After examining Ava and Lily's dresses, smoothing Lily's headband, and nodding approvingly at Ava, their mom turned to Charlotte. She licked her palm and tried to tame the loose curls that were always popping out from her bun no matter how hard Charlotte tried to pull her hair into order.

"You all look perfect," she declared. "Let's go before the stars of the show are late."

They bustled out of the tavern and down the stone-paved street to the main square where the ceremony was to be held.

Charlotte loved the stone streets in Kinstun, much more than the single, packed-dirt main street that ran through Mina.

A loud buzzing noise from the sky pulled her gaze upwards. "Is that... a K'Luma Carrier?" Charlotte stared in awe as a small, hover-tech powered aircraft landed behind some nearby buildings.

"Looks like Jamroq has caught the notice of some important people from Pergamum," her mom said, smiling.

Only nobles from the capital city, or in some cases, high-ranking Imperial guards, had access to flying hovercraft. And nobles had never come in person to any academic prize-giving before. Then again, Jamroq had never had two perfect scores at one time before either.

Charlotte caught the crease that formed on her dad's forehead, but he didn't say anything, just led their family forward.

They reached the main square, where a platform with a large screen had been erected. People dressed in their best garments packed the rows of chairs that flowed to the very edges of the square. Little lights strung overhead for the dinner which would follow reminded Charlotte of Feast Day celebrations, which would be held in a few weeks' time.

The mayor himself, an Imperial figurehead Charlotte knew only from photos hung in Mina's official buildings, came running over to her parents. "Ah, Mr. King, Mrs. King, it's a pleasure to host you. You must be so proud. Miss Ava and Miss Lily, congratulations!" He pumped each of their hands in turn. "Come, come. We have a place of honor set up."

The pudgy, overzealous mayor didn't even acknowledge Charlotte, but she kept any scowl from her face. This was her sisters' night. Her dad draped an arm around her shoulder as they followed the mayor through the packed crowd. Her mom walked ahead; arms interlocked tightly with the twins.

"Miss Ava and Miss Lily will be seated on the stage," the mayor explained when they reached the edge of the platform. "Mr. and Mrs. King, you'll be seated right here." He pointed to two chairs with special padding in the front row.

Her dad cleared his throat, his arm still around Charlotte.

Charlotte detected a fleeting look of annoyance as the mayor made eye contact with her for the first time, but he quickly schooled his features.

"Oh yes, of course. Miss?"

"Charlotte," her dad answered with a defensive edge to his voice.

The mayor motioned for some of the nearby guards to squeeze another chair into the row. This involved shifting some very important people who darted glares at Charlotte and her parents.

Her cheeks warmed, and she kept her eyes downcast. Thankfully, the mayor had disappeared behind the stage saying something about a VIP visitor.

Charlotte sunk into her seat and crossed her arms.

Ava and Lily were all smiles from where they sat on the stage, and Lily gave a small wave to her family.

Charlotte uncrossed her arms and tried to relax; for the sake of her sisters.

The humongous screen on stage came to life and showed a split-view of a similar stage set up in Kimwaki and Salan, the two other conquered isles.

A tanned, muscular boy with long, dark, wavy hair sat stiffly in Kimwaki. Charlotte squinted to see if she could make out the details of the tattoos that reached up the side of his neck.

Normally she wasn't so close to the front, or near a screen, but their dad had once shown them a picture of an old chief from Kimwaki. Lily had been fascinated with the tattoos, drawing tribal patterns throughout the house for weeks. While the black ink on the boy's neck was visible on screen, what really caught Charlotte's attention was the boy's narrowed, fiery eyes and unsmiling mouth.

Why does he look so upset? Charlotte wondered.

On the other half of the screen, the girl on stage from Salan shared a glow and smile similar to Charlotte's sisters. Salan people had distinctively blonde hair and light skin, and in this regard, the twins took much more from their mom.

Charlotte's mom and Gran had moved to Jamroq from Salan right before the Emperor, *may he be forever cursed*, assumed the throne of K'Luma almost twenty years ago, and threw the isles into chaos. She shuddered at the memory of the history lesson.

In his later years, the previous ruler of K'Luma had issued a decree that the Imperial who brought him the greatest prize would be named his heir. This was after all his children had mysteriously died in quick succession.

When a young Elite, a member of the prestigious inner guards, brought back the head of the Chief of Kimwaki, he was named successor and given the Chief's daughter as a bride.

Within a year the old ruler had died, and the Elite rose to power. Rumors swirled about the old ruler's sudden death, but no one questioned the new Emperor. At least, no one questioned and lived.

A trumpet blared, and the mayor stepped up to the podium, pulling out a handkerchief to wipe his brow before speaking. He leaned in and pulled the mic down, seeming much more nervous than he had previously.

Where is the VIP guest he had mentioned going to greet? Charlotte thought.

"Welcome to the special tenth anniversary of the academic prize-giving ceremony of the great K'Luma Empire. May the Emperor be blessed and live forever." The mayor droned on, reading from a long-winded script touting the greatness of everything Empire related.

As he was talking, a tall, pale woman with raven-colored hair strutted onto the stage. She wore an elegant, jewel-encrusted, black, and ruby-colored dress. Her hair was done in a style that was half tied up in intricate braids with the other half running straight down her back. She wasn't the Empress, Charlotte knew, but the way she carried herself, the wealth she exuded, and the security detail that followed in her wake, all screamed important Imperial noble.

Charlotte's dad tensed beside her.

Even the mayor seemed a little shaken by her presence, and he cleared his throat. "Let us jump straight into the program."

"Who's that?" Charlotte's mom whispered from her dad's other side.

Charlotte leaned over.

Her mom had a look of wonder and awe on her face. Whereas her dad's eyes were narrowed and matched the lump in Charlotte's throat. Surprises from the Empire were never good.

"In this historic year, our awardees are particularly stunning," the mayor continued. His eyes shifted towards the mysterious woman who stood near the podium with her hands folded in front of her, deep red lips pursed. "Please allow me to introduce Mrs. Elisa Wumi, wife of Commander Uzoma Wumi. She will name the prized students... er, the students who won the prizes... the awardees."

Charlotte gulped.

The mayor was stumbling all over himself, but now she understood. Commander Uzoma, head of the Imperial army, was the right hand to the Emperor. He was undefeated in battle and had earned his ruthless reputation starting with the conquest of Kimwaki.

But what is his wife doing in Jamroq? Charlotte glanced at her sisters on the stage who shared a look of confusion and were now holding hands.

On the screen, the boy from Kimwaki was gripping the arms of his chair, his head turned to the screen behind him showing the feed from Jamroq.

Elisa walked over to the podium, barely casting a glance at the mayor, who was bowing as he shuffled out of the way. She raised the mic, keeping her back straight and looked directly into the camera set up in the center aisle.

"The Emperor of the great K'Luma Empire, may he be blessed and live forever, has in his wisdom and glory, issued a new decree." She paused to look over the crowd. "Effective this year, all academic awardees who represent the best and brightest of the students in these conquered isles, will be brought to serve in the Legacy Towers of Pergamum."

Charlotte grabbed her dad's hand, her heart squeezing.

Murmurs rang through the crowd, and Charlotte's mom gasped. The Legacy Towers were effectively a prison system set up by the previous Emperor to hold hostage the former leaders and influential persons from conquered territories. *Her sisters would be sent there?* Charlotte gasped.

"The Emperor will allow no good thing to come from Mina. I should have known," her dad mumbled under his breath, muscles taut.

"These lucky students include Ava King, top in both math and science, Lily King, top in artistic endeavors..."

Tears blurred Charlotte's vision as Elisa continued to read out the students from Kimwaki and Salan.

Charlotte's dad stood and moved towards the edge of the stage.

Elisa held two fingers separated by the stub of her thumb, across her heart, a signal of allegiance to the Emperor. "K'Luma forever," she trilled, and moved towards the exit.

Ava and Lily sprang from their seats and raced towards where their dad was approaching the edge of the stage.

The audience exploded in loud chatter, everyone talking at once. Charlotte and her mom got up, following in her dad's wake.

The K'Luma anthem started blaring over the loudspeakers, and the live feed on the big screen went dark.

Guards in black uniforms with a crisscross of crimson intercepted the twins on stage before they could reach their dad.

Lily froze and shot a look of panic toward her family.

"Dad!" Ava shouted from beside her.

Guards grabbed hold of the twins and dragged them in the direction Elisa had gone.

"Ava! Lily!" her dad called out, racing to scramble up the stage. He was caught by two other guards in the same black uniforms.

Her mom screamed, trying to weave through a wall of guards who had blocked the exit.

Charlotte was falling behind in the crush.

"Mom! Dad! Char!" Ava and Lily shouted as they were pulled further away. Their voices competing to be heard over the growing chaos of the crowd.

Charlotte caught a glimpse of Lily's bright dress and madly tried to claw her way to her sisters.

A guard grabbed her by the arm and pulled her away. The harder she fought, the tighter the guard squeezed her arms behind her back. Tears of fear and frustration ran down her face.

The area near the stage cleared as everyone tried to get out of the square.

Charlotte's dad lay in a heap on the ground not far away. Her mom huddled over him protectively, still looking around frantically, calling out for the twins.

A guard with gold stripes on his uniform held out a stick, and a burst of electricity crackled at the end. As soon as it touched her mom, her eyes went wide, and she dropped in a similar crumpled heap over her dad.

Charlotte pulled again at the guard holding her, screaming for her parents, and her sisters. She tried with all her might to wriggle free. But his grip was ironclad, unmoving. Tears streamed freely down her face as helplessness overwhelmed her.

The last thing she remembered, with haunting clarity, was a voice in her ear as the guard leaned in. "Learn well from this, young one. No one fights the Empire and wins."

Chapter 2

Three years later...

CHARLOTTE BIT HER LOWER lip in concentration, ignoring a drop of sweat that rolled down her forehead.

Just a little more, she thought.

She pushed the reflective panel into the grooves she had spent the night trying to align. A soft click sounded as it slid into place.

Does that mean—?

A few seconds later, gears whirred to life. Two blue-white lights flashed on, giving the flyer-board lift.

"It works!" Charlotte shouted a little more loudly than she had intended.

Jax rubbed his eyes from where he had fallen asleep in the corner of the dimly lit cellar.

A flood of relief and joy rushed over her. She ran a hand over the engraved brass board, enjoying the hum and vibration of its movement.

A big grin had replaced her best friend's sleepy face by the time he stood beside her, draping an arm over her shoulder. "Hey! You did it, Char. You're truly a genius." His slate eyes shone with pride.

Charlotte flinched a little though at the word *genius*. That's what everyone used to call Ava, who was much more deserving of the title.

I'm getting closer, dear sisters, she thought. *I won't let you down for much longer.*

Pulling her focus back to the cellar, Charlotte stared at the floating board and shook her head in disbelief. "Three years of scrounging discarded parts and pieces to put this baby together." She leaned against Jax's arm, trying to process that she could finally put their rescue plan into action.

"I still can't believe Gran found that sun collector yesterday," Jax said, shaking his head.

Charlotte did worry about some of these "finds" her grandmother had while working for the Imperials. Gran had a rebellious streak to her that most people overlooked, but Charlotte knew better. Gran would do everything possible to fight the Empire, especially after it had taken so much from her.

"Ready to take it for a test spin or do you want to tell your dad first?"

Charlotte cringed. "Let's make sure it's really working first. I don't want to raise his hopes. You know how he's been since mom..." She couldn't finish the sentence. Even for Charlotte it was still raw two years later.

"She'd be proud of you for not giving up," Jax said softly.

Charlotte took a deep breath. *What else could I have done but keep moving forward?* Even though it pained her to think about how fearful her dad had become.

She tapped the gazer on her wrist. "Sunrise was an hour ago. Let's go try it out before breakfast."

Smells from the kitchen already wafted down from the trapdoor in the ceiling. It was Feast Day, so Gran would have come over early to help with preparations.

Jax grabbed the small bag that he used to collect herbs and roots in the forest. Charlotte was convinced he'd become a healer one day. He was already well known in the village for his collection and knowledge of bush medicine.

Charlotte carefully pulled the hand-held sun collector out of the board, wrapped it in cloth, and slipped it into one of the many pockets of her cargo pants. She then collapsed the board to half its extended size and hooked it to a strap on her back.

She followed Jax as he crawled into the tunnel that would take them closer to the forest. Dust and dirt pressed into Charlotte's hands and knees as she made her way in the darkness of the tunnel.

The house was built on a small hill, and while most homes in Jamroq didn't have cellars, her dad had dug one out three years ago. Back when their whole family—mom, dad, Gran, and her—would spend every night trying to work out a plan to get to the mainland, and then on to Pergamum to rescue the twins.

How things had changed.

Two years ago, after a particularly frustrating night of hopeless ideas, her mom had set out before dawn. She had hitched a ride with Jax's parents, who ran the biggest fishing operation in the village.

Charlotte still wasn't sure what her mom had planned. Unfortunately, she would never know. A swift, ferocious storm had hit after daybreak, and only pieces of the ship had been found by other fishermen days later.

Since then, Gran had taken Jax in to live with her in the cottage next to Charlotte and her dad.

Sunlight and humidity assaulted Charlotte as she crawled out of the tunnel and into the field just before the tree line. She didn't bother to dust off her clothes but ran up to Jax and embraced him tightly.

His body tensed at first, but then he returned the hug before running a hand to brush some dirt from Charlotte's hair. "What was that for?"

Charlotte stepped back to look him in the eye—this took some craning of her neck as Charlotte was shorter than most, and Jax was taller than average. "No matter how things turn out with this flyer-board, I just want to thank you for being there for me. These past two years—"

"Hey," Jax interrupted, placing a hand on her shoulder. "I don't know what I'd have done without you and your dad, and of course, Gran. So, it should be me thanking you. In fact, I wanted to tell you—"

A part of Charlotte picked up on Jax's softened tone, but she was distracted by something else she noticed. "Jax! What did you do to your arm?" Charlotte stared at the word *Freedom* that was inked on his left forearm.

He smiled and rubbed a thumb over the word. "Don't worry, it's not permanent... yet. I drew it last night with some ink I found while you were working on the board."

Over the last year, Jax had started training with a group of young men their age. They called themselves Freedom Fighters, which Charlotte thought was a bit too on the nose, but they were proud of the name.

"If any of the Imperials see that..."

"I'll wear long sleeves to the feast tonight, don't worry. Plus, the ink is barely visible against my skin." Jax winked and flashed a toothy grin.

"Be careful, please."

"Says the one who wears a gazer all the time?" He made a point of staring at her wrist.

"I—" Charlotte stuttered.

Jax laughed and shook his head.

"Hey, you two!" Gran shouted through the distant kitchen window. "Fresh cocoa tea! Come!"

The forest tugged at Charlotte from a short distance off, and she could have sworn the board vibrated on her back.

But Jax did an abrupt about turn and gave Charlotte a pleading look. "Quick breakfast first. You know your Gran makes the best cocoa tea in all of Jamroq."

Charlotte smirked. "You make *all of Jamroq* seem like such a big place. Let's just agree it's the best cocoa tea in this tiny village, on this tiny island."

"Whatever. I'm never turning down Gran's cocoa." He bounded up the hill.

Charlotte followed reluctantly, wishing she didn't have to face a Feast Day breakfast without her mom and sisters.

She sighed as she stepped through the back door and slid the flyer-board strap over her head, leaning it against the wall in the entryway.

"Hey, kiddo," Her dad poked his head around the corner. "Hungry? Gran's had me cooking up a storm for breakfast."

The smell of sizzling bacon and eggs wafted in behind him.

Charlotte could tell he was trying extra hard this morning. It was progress, and she didn't want to ruin it by talking about the rescue plan he had all but forbade after the shipwreck.

He must have noticed her downcast face because his charcoal eyes softened, and he stepped into the small hallway. He pulled her in for a proper hug. "I'm glad I still have you." After a moment, he stepped back, and his mouth fell into a familiar frown. "And the Emperor be damned for taking them all away from us."

Charlotte glanced at the transmitter near the door. Thankfully, her homemade cover was in place. She had put it on last night before they had gone down to the cellar.

Every home had an Empire-commissioned transmitter installed—one of the only pieces of tech authorized in non-Imperial homes.

Back when things were normal, one of the first inventions Charlotte made was a device to cover the transmitter so that her dad could give small groups of students unsanctioned lessons after school in peace.

Her dad put on a smile and led her toward the kitchen. "But for now, cocoa tea awaits."

The kitchen was a flurry of activity. Jax was helping set the table while Gran was at the stove barking orders.

"There you two are." Gran raised an eyebrow as she stirred a big pot on the stove.

The last three years had taken their toll on everyone. Gran was even more slender than before, with perpetual dark circles under her eyes.

Charlotte put an encouraging arm around her and stuck her nose over the pot of cocoa tea. Cinnamon, nutmeg, and bay leaf mixed with freshly grated cocoa simmered in a pot of milk. She closed her eyes, allowing the powerful scent of chocolate and spices to fill her soul.

"Okay, okay, you get the first cup," Gran assented, using a ladle to fill a mug.

Everyone squeezed around the small table and filled their plates.

"I got the board working," Charlotte said.

All eyes turned on her, and silence fell for a few seconds.

"At least, I think it's working. Jax and I are taking it for a test run after breakfast."

"Really?" her dad's eyes hardened.

Charlotte gulped and nodded. "I... I'm not giving up." She wasn't trying to take an accusatory tone, but her dad's eyes flooded with guilt or sadness, Charlotte wasn't quite sure anymore. He pushed back his chair and walked out of the room.

Gran reached for Charlotte's hand. "He's hurting."

"We are all," Charlotte said a little more forcefully than she intended. "But I *will* rescue Ava and Lily and bring them back. I can do that much."

"Everything in its time," Gran said. "You'll know the right path when it opens up. And until then, just keep searching and trying. None of us have given up, and your dad will come around."

Charlotte didn't want to argue. She just wanted to get out of the house. She downed the rest of her cocoa tea and nudged Jax. "Ready?"

Jax grimaced as he looked at his plate of food, shoving it in his mouth as quickly as possible.

Charlotte stood and promised to be back in time for the mandatory feast in the town square that afternoon. She kissed Gran on the cheek. "See you later."

Charlotte was halfway across the field when Jax finally caught up.

"You certainly know how to give a guy indigestion," he grumbled.

"Sorry." Charlotte took a deep breath of warm, fresh air, trying to clear her head.

They reached the forest, and she unstrapped the board and slid the sun collector back into place.

For a moment, nothing happened, and her heart fell. But then the board whirred to life once more.

She exhaled and stood next to Jax. "Okay, thankfully this is one of the older, clunkier models. Which means that it's sturdy enough to hold two people. But let me try it first."

Charlotte held on to Jax's shoulder for balance and stepped onto the board.

It was surprisingly stable. She shifted her weight to her front leg, thrusting forward towards a nearby silk cotton tree. She shifted to her back leg and jerked to a stop barely avoiding a collision with the tree's massive trunk.

The board held steady, though, and Charlotte stayed upright.

Jax let out a whoop and ran to catch up. "That was great!"

Charlotte wiped a drizzle of sweat from her brow that was already forming in the heat. "Let's keep going."

Jax reached a hand to her shoulder. "We're in this together, remember?" He stepped up behind her on the board, his massive form adding significant weight. But again, the board balanced itself. Keeping upright was surprisingly easy.

"Whoa, this is amazing," Jax said.

"Yep. These boards have a self-balancing gyroscope inside. I admit, I didn't think it would work as well as it does." Charlotte laughed but was again relieved.

She wasted no time and shifted to speed forward. Jax squeezed her shoulders and cried out in delight.

They continued practicing, taking turns riding together and separately. After an hour or so, a few near-crashes and one tumble, Charlotte stopped for a break.

Jax hopped off and dropped to the ground, resting his back against a tree. "Ahh, solid ground once more," he let out a sigh.

Charlotte couldn't wipe the wide grin from her face. She slid the sun collector out and turned it over in her hand. "Everything looks great! And the sun collector self-charges in the sunlight, just like I'd hoped."

Charlotte plopped next to Jax and pulled a portugyal fruit out from a pocket. She peeled the citrus and offered half to Jax.

"I don't know how you always manage to carry fruit with you," Jax teased, but took the half offered and shoved a piece in his mouth.

"Always be prepared. Plus, portugyal season is my absolute favorite." Charlotte closed her eyes in deep satisfaction as the sweet juices exploded in her mouth; the last bit of stress from breakfast finally dissipating.

"I still can't believe you were able to retrofit that sun collector to the flyer-board," Jax said. "I would have sworn it was too big or busted."

Charlotte turned her head towards Jax, a hint of worry passing through her mind. "In all the excitement, I never really asked. Where *did* Gran find the collector?"

"She said she was called in to clean the Imperial guard's office. Something about a special group coming in today for the feast. She said the small panel was tucked away in a dusty corner and no one would miss it." Jax shrugged.

Charlotte groaned. Not that she had any love for the guards, but she didn't want Gran getting in trouble because of her. Especially if Gran needed to look after Dad while she was gone.

"Don't worry," Jax said. "You know how much she wants to help. I'm still not exactly sure how this board plays into rescuing Ava and Lily though. Aren't they imprisoned in the Legacy Towers? Surely, you're not going to ride the board the whole way there."

"The idea is to have something valuable enough to trade at Portemore when we make it to the mainland. Dad heard about an underground network that can help us get into the capital and to the Legacy Towers."

"And you're sure you can trust an underground network? How will you even find them?" Jax shifted to face Charlotte and scrunched up his eyebrows.

"One challenge at a time," Charlotte said.

A rumble from the sky sounded in the distance.

"Is it supposed to storm?" Jax shielded his eyes as he looked up at the cloudless sky.

"No, look. It's a K'Luma Carrier." Charlotte's jaw hung slack as the airborne pod flew overhead. The carriers used two sets of rotating blades, one on top of the pod and the other attached to a tail of sorts, which Charlotte assumed helped with the steering, like on a boat.

"You don't think the Emperor would be coming here, do you?" Jax asked.

"Nah, no way. He always gives his Feast Day speech from the Legacy Towers. But certainly, someone important." A pang of worry formed in Charlotte's stomach, remembering the last time an Imperial VIP had visited, but she refused to dwell on what-ifs.

Whatever Imperial had landed, she would find a way to get off Jamroq and to the mainland. Her sisters had been captive in the towers for long enough. *All for what? Because the Emperor wanted to hold the best and brightest hostage? Rubbish,* Charlotte thought.

"Ow," Charlotte cried out in pain and rubbed her head where a rock or something hard had struck her.

"What's wrong?" Jax asked.

"Something hit me." Charlotte scanned the trees above, and a furry little creature sat looking right at her. Its face and shoulders were white, the rest of its body covered in brown fur.

"A monkey?" Jax's tone seemed to share Charlotte's wonder.

"I've heard of some Imperials bringing in exotic pets, but I've never seen one in the wild," Charlotte said.

The monkey made a series of grunts, then swung down to land right next to Charlotte.

"What do you think it wants?" Charlotte asked, entranced by the boldness of the little creature.

In a flash, the monkey reached out to Charlotte's wrist, then jumped back up the tree.

"What the—" Charlotte was momentarily confused, then horror set in as she realized the monkey had stolen her gazer.

"Thief!" Charlotte cried out as she jumped to her feet.

The monkey swung to a neighboring tree, and full-fledged panic set in. That gazer held all the plans and information she had been gathering over the past year.

"C'mon. Quickly, before we lose him." Charlotte restarted the board and climbed on even as the monkey continued to swing at surprising speed.

"Are you sure this is a good—" Jax's question cut off as Charlotte raced forward, trying to keep up with the monkey.

"Keep an eye on it," Charlotte shouted. "Don't lose sight."

Jax called out directions as Charlotte navigated the board around towering trees, bamboo patches, rocks, and other forest debris. Colors of green, orange, brown, and pink flashed by as they sped along. *Wait, pink?*

"Stop!" Jax cried at the same time Charlotte slammed her back foot hard in order to not crash into a grove of blossoming cannonball trees.

The monkey swung to the ground, glanced back, and disappeared into the thick grove.

Charlotte and Jax jumped off the board and followed on foot. From the moment Charlotte passed the first tree, a tingling charge ran down her body.

Large vines covered the trees. Huge, bright fuchsia flowers opened with yellow stamens protruding from the center. They looked like underwater seaweed floating in the air. A few of the flowers had dried and turned into large brown balls, from which the cannonball tree derived its name.

"Is it just me, or does this place feel a little strange?" Jax asked.

Charlotte reached a hand to touch the petals of one of the flowers. "Something is different," she said engulfed in her own awe and wonder.

The monkey grunted from a short distance away, its deep-set black eyes glistening. It waved its arm wide in a beckoning fashion, then walked deeper into the grove.

Charlotte gave a moment of pause and bit her lip.

As if picking up on her hesitation, Jax grabbed her hand. "You need your gazer. Plus, there's only one way to see how far this mongoose trail goes."

"Let's keep going," Charlotte agreed.

After a short distance, they entered a clearing, and in the center, stood a massive samaan tree. Its wide canopy extended well over a hundred feet, like a large symmetrical umbrella, and it was almost as tall as it was wide. The little monkey looked like an ant where it stood on the ground at the base of the tree.

Charlotte's heart beat faster as they approached the monkey. There was a hollow in the trunk of the tree, and the monkey stepped inside.

No turning back now, she thought.

Charlotte ducked her head and followed inside. Her breath caught in her throat. Inside, she stood up straight in what looked to be an ancient library.

Jax let out a low whistle after he came in behind her.

Shelves had been intricately carved into the trunk of the tree, and each was lined with books of all different shapes and sizes. Some were leather-bound, some were sheets of paper tied with twine, and some even looked to be ancient scrolls.

"What is this place?" Charlotte wondered aloud, goosebumps rising on her skin.

"Perhaps more importantly, *where* is this place, is the question you should be asking," said a soft, mellow voice.

Charlotte turned around, her hand instinctively reaching for the pocketknife that was strapped to her thigh. She tried to find the source of the voice, but it was only her, Jax, and the monkey in the hollow.

The monkey jumped onto a shelf eye-level with Charlotte and held out her gazer. She reached to grab it back but froze midway, jaw slack, as the monkey spoke.

"Sorry about that temporary act of mischief, Miss Charlotte, but I needed to ensure you followed me here."

Chapter 3

S ONOS GAZED OUT AT the massive Ti're River from his personal balcony in the palace. Surrounding lights on the outside slowly winked out as the sun rose, and the air was filled with a warming dawn-glow.

Today's the day. Sonos exhaled audibly. *The day I am finally free from my lockdown.*

He glanced at his bare wrist, wondering if he'd be allowed his gazer back—or any tech for that matter. At this point, he'd be happy to even be allowed to read a book again.

The door to his bedroom banged open, interrupting his thoughts.

"Sonos! Know what day it is?" Taine's excitement was palpable as he crossed the large room carrying a tray laden with food and drink—an awkward task for a tall, muscular bodyguard.

Taine made a show of bowing to Sonos as he placed the tray on the small table, then unstrapped the hooked sword from his back and plopped down in an unoccupied chair.

Sonos reached for the coffee gratefully. "No, I have no clue what day it is." He rolled his eyes. "Only that I've counted, let's see... three hundred and sixty-five days stuck in this room."

Taine laughed and held out his hand towards Sonos' mug. "I think that deserves a joint celebration."

Sonos shook his head then relented, handing it over for Taine to sip.

"Ahh, the coffee they make for you royals is so much better than the sludge they pour us in the kitchens! I don't know why Seena Sweethand won't simply give me two cups for you every morning."

Sonos smiled, reflecting on his bodyguard's companionship. "I don't know what I'd have done without you over this past year."

Taine's light-hearted humor had been a lifeline. Sonos hadn't seen his family, or anyone other than Taine and the weapons trainer, since the fiasco last Feast Day.

"I admit it's pretty boring protecting someone who's barely allowed to leave his room. I had to make myself useful somehow." Taine gave a cheeky grin.

"It's true. I think I've begun taking on the color of these walls. If it's one thing Father accomplished, I finally learned to love training in the practice fields."

Daily weapons training was the only time Sonos was allowed to leave his room. Supposedly, focusing on weapons technology would help him appreciate what made the Empire and its rule impenetrable.

"And I admit, I do have a new admiration for the weapons tech the Sahemy have developed." He looked at Taine's sword, which lay propped against his bodyguard's knee, never out of arm's reach.

The hooked sword was imbued with tech that allowed the handle to extend or shorten as needed, charge with electricity, and even transform into a small electrical-based shield. The weapon was exclusive to royal bodyguards and Elites. It was amazing in both design and function.

He had to admit that learning how to use the weapons in the heat of training built an appreciation beyond theory.

Sonos picked up a warm roll and a slice of cheese from the plate, while Taine popped some grapes into his mouth.

The door to the bedroom flew open once more and Ade waltzed in. Taine jumped up from the chair, grabbed his sword, and stood at attention against the nearest wall.

Ade flashed his eyes towards Taine with a look of disapproval.

Sonos' older brother worked hard to keep an immaculate appearance which aligned with his intense preparations to become Emperor one day. His wavy black hair was slicked back, his informal tunic steam-pressed, along with his white linen pants. If anything, after a year, Ade looked more like their father.

Sonos ran a hand over his own close-cropped hair as he stood, a style he had taken to while in isolation. He had shaved his head as a small act of rebellion and one of the few things he had control over, but being around his brother always made him a little self-conscious.

Today, though, Ade approached with a relaxed smile on his face. The two shared a quick embrace.

"Happy Feast Day, little brother."

"Little?" Sonos cocked his head. "You do realize I turned sixteen last week, right?"

Ade looked Sonos up and down. "Perhaps the focused training this past year did some good for you after all. It does look like you've put on some muscle, finally."

"Focused training, you say? How about outright overreaction from Father?" Sonos worked to keep the anger that popped up at bay.

"The Emperor showed you great mercy after what happened," Ade's voice dropped, and his eyes narrowed. "He could have easily had you killed."

The two brothers stood; eyes locked.

Sonos relented first. Starting a fight with his brother first thing did not bode well for the rest of the day. He shifted his eyes to the warming sky. "It's a new day. Come, join me for breakfast." He waved his hand to the seat Taine had occupied a few moments earlier.

Ade sat next to Sonos and picked through the fruit, selecting a ripe plum. He then slid a book across the table. "For you."

A cautious smile spread across Sonos' face as he picked up the book. The weight and feel of the pages were almost overwhelming. It was leather-bound with a gold embossed dragon in mid-flight on the cover. He ran a hand over their family crest.

"Sorry you're still not allowed to have a gazer or any tech, but Emperor has granted permission for a journal," Ade said. "He thinks it would be good for you to capture the lessons learned from your year of reflection."

Ade always referred to their dad as Emperor. Not Father—always 'Emperor'. Just the way the Emperor liked it. In fact, his father had forbidden use of his given name, Dracul. Sonos had only heard the name whispered once by his mother. But now, his father had his identity and power wrapped up in his position, and he insisted on being called Emperor and his wife to be Empress; nothing more, nothing less.

Sonos held the journal to his nose and inhaled the scent of fresh paper and leather. "Thank you," he whispered.

As he thumbed through the blank pages, a small origami tree fell into his lap. His heart warmed, knowing it was from his mother. Even though time with their mother had always been limited, she'd find ways of leaving him these origami trees as reminders of their talks.

"For my tiny seed. One day you'll become a mighty tree," she always used to tell him.

Ade's voice broke his memory. "Of course, your tutor will be required to inspect your writing regularly and report to the Emperor any... *radical* ideas that may emerge. But for your sake, I hope you've stopped—"

"I get to have a tutor again? Who? When?" Sonos interrupted his brother's attempted warning. Truth be told, this past year had only stoked the questions that got him in trouble in the first place.

"I don't know the details," Ade said. "Given Sah Timur's disgrace, I'm sure the Order of the Sahemy will be much more selective in who they send."

A wave of hurt washed over Sonos at the mention of his former tutor's name. His mother had chosen Timur personally for Sonos, and Timur was the first tutor who had truly encouraged Sonos' curiosity about society, rulership, and the wider world.

However, General Baku, head of the Imperial Guard, had uncovered Sah Timur as the source of the whole fiasco. Shortly thereafter, Sonos had received his former tutor's cut-out tongue and thumbs on a platter for breakfast. Sonos didn't eat breakfast for a full month afterward.

Sonos set the journal in his lap and took another sip of coffee. "How are Mother and Father?"

Ade shifted in his seat to face Sonos directly. "Sonos, you need to understand the seriousness of our situation."

"Our situation?" Sonos asked, confused.

"Do you not remember Emperor telling us many years ago the truth of what happened to the previous ruler's heirs?"

Sonos rolled his eyes. "He only said that to scare us into being good. No father, Emperor or not, would deliberately murder all his kids because they were weak."

Ade's gaze held.

"Really? But how do you know?" Sonos racked his brain sorting through the rumors that had been told throughout the years of how all the heirs had died. Health, accidents, one sent to the warfront and died in battle.

"The weapons trainer was working at the palace back then and can verify it is true," Ade said. "There is no place for weakness in the Empire. Even more so in its ruler."

Sonos took a moment to digest what his brother was saying. "Even if it's true, you're perfect. Father should have no worries handing you the throne at the appropriate time."

Ade looked off into the distance. "Who's to say, really?" He shifted his gaze back to Sonos. "But that is why you must understand the mercy he showed you and not take it for granted."

Sonos looked down and placed the origami tree gently on top of the journal. It was a lot to process.

Ade suddenly grabbed the origami tree from Sonos' lap and crumpled it in his fist, then threw it on the floor.

"Hey! What are you—" Sonos grabbed it back up.

"And do not let Empress corrupt you. She is a trophy to show Emperor's lasting victory. Nothing more." Ade's voice grew harder as he spoke.

"We are scheduled to be at the baths early today," Ade said, rising to his feet. "Emperor is likely already down there, and he wants to see you."

Sonos groaned, still feeling defensive over what Ade had said about their mother. But there was no good in keeping their father waiting.

As Sonos walked beside his brother down the open-aired hallways, he caught himself studying Ade's bodyguard who walked in front of them, leading the way down to the baths.

Similar to Taine, the tattoos were mesmerizing. The geometric patterns started behind their earlobe and ran down the right side of their neck, covering their shoulder, chest, and arm to the elbow. All warriors from Kimwaki were similarly marked.

Sonos had finally coaxed Taine into explaining the markings a few months ago. The tattoos were unique to each individual, representing their community, heritage, personality, responsibilities, and even their future. Taine had bristled at going deeper into the explanation, for reasons Sonos didn't quite understand yet. But Sonos was determined to figure out the pattern and meanings one day.

Sonos inhaled a deep breath of the warm spring air as they crossed a carefully sculpted garden on their way toward the river.

The baths were shaped by large rectangular pools, fed from a small channel connected to the Ti're River. Trees and shrubs bordered each pool, one for males and one for females, providing privacy and separation.

The brothers entered the men's side and, true to word, the Emperor was already soaking in the far end of the bath. They both bowed from the waist.

Their father barely cracked an eyelid to acknowledge their presence.

Similar to Ade, his father took pride in physical strength and kept his body in top form. His skin was paler than the boys', who took more after their tanned mother. However, he kept his hair long and dark, like all the nobles.

Sonos knew many of the Imperials resorted to dyeing their hair black, but their mother had naturally passed down this quality others craved.

Despite all the vanity, dark circles were visible under the Emperor's eyes, along with more lines etched across his forehead.

After undressing, Ade and Sonos slipped into the pool where Sonos tried to pick the absolute furthest spot away from the Emperor.

The water was cool but refreshing. Servants rushed to add scented oils to the water, and the smells of lily, myrrh, and cinnamon soon flooded Sonos' nose.

A servant boy came bearing a tray with spiced wine. He could not have been more than ten years old. His pale skin and blond curly hair marked him from one of the southern isles—Salan, if Sonos remembered correctly.

Unfortunately, as the boy leaned to set the tray next to the pool, he tipped it too far, and the mug splashed into the water.

Sonos yelped in surprise but moved quickly to help when he saw the deep level of fear creep into the boy's face. He tried to place the mug back on the tray and act as though nothing happened, but it was too late.

Two of the older servants had already come over. One to clean up the mess and the other to pull the young boy away.

The Emperor made eye contact with the servant holding the boy and signaled with his hand.

Sonos cringed as he recognized the Emperor's instructions. The boy would be given five lashes. *A bit excessive, but it seems some things never change.* Sonos didn't argue, as it would likely only bring the poor boy more trouble.

The servant started to lead the boy away, but the Emperor stopped him. "Here," he commanded.

The older servant bowed and pulled out a leather-braided, hand-held whip that had been laced to his belt. The boy bravely stuck out his arms.

Sonos looked away.

"Sonos, you will watch." The Emperor's voice was cold enough to bring back the freeze of winter.

Sonos narrowed his eyes and reluctantly turned back to the boy about to receive lashes for what? Accidentally dropping a tray that was too big for him? Boys his age should be out playing in the streets with their friends, not being punished for work they shouldn't be doing in the first place.

Whack. Pause.

Whack. Pause.

Whack.

It seemed to continue forever. Sonos' anger boiled stronger with each lash. *Did oppression of people and excessive harshness build an Empire's strength? Was rule based on fear truly sustainable?* He thought about the questions he had dared to write last year.

To the boy's credit, even though tears streamed down his face, he did not cry out once. The final two lashes finished, the older servant took the boy back towards the palace.

"I see you have shorn your hair." The Emperor gave no further regard to the servant boy and kept his eyes fixed on Sonos.

"Easier to manage this way." The cheeky response flew off Sonos' tongue while he worked to keep his anger and frustration in check.

"This year has not done much for your temperament, Sonos. Perhaps more time for reflection is required?" The Emperor remained perfectly calm and still in the water but raised an eyebrow as he asked the question.

Sonos paused, composing himself before answering. "No, Father, I'm sorry."

"I trust you will resume a proper appearance now that you are out of isolation, but perhaps it is a befitting statement for the feast. A visible showing of the consequences our choices bring us."

A hundred words of retort and defense bubbled in Sonos' chest, but he forced them all down, maintaining a silent, calm demeanor. He couldn't manage another year of lockdown.

"Mmm. Your words have finally slowed. Good. After we enter the feast tonight, you will remain seated at the head table and limit your interactions with others. We do not need any stir like last year."

Like what happened last year was my idea, Sonos thought. Heat crept up his neck. Broadcasting the private words and musings of his journal entries on the big screen had been mortifying. That Sah Timur had chosen the climax of the Emperor's speech as the point at which the images were shown, only worsened the effect. Sonos hung his head, but even as shame of the memory and everyone's gasps and subsequent stares came rushing back, the questions still nagged at his brain.

The Emperor lifted himself from the bath, and servants streamed over to dry and dress him. "Ade, you will join me to go meet with Baku and discuss the security in place for tonight."

Ade jumped out of the water immediately. He gave a brief smile to Sonos. Was it sympathy? Encouragement? Arrogance?

Sonos didn't care. His father and brother gone, he closed his eyes and sank deeper into the fragrant water.

After a while, Taine stooped close to the water's edge. "Sonos? Anything you need?"

Sonos sighed. Every interaction with his father left him deflated. It was like battering against an ancient stone wall. Pointless. And Ade was more than happy to carry on the same legacy.

He lifted himself out of the water. As he was dried off, Sonos thought back to the questions he dared to ask before. Many nights, he had stayed up typing entries into his gazer. Forming words that matched his discontent with the way things were.

His mother kept a neutral stance, but Sonos knew her Kimwaki roots, and the fact that she had been kidnapped as a prize to the Emperor from his first conquest, made her different. They never spoke overtly, but over the last few years, they had developed a code of sorts—the origami trees being one symbol of hope.

Despite the despair created by the Emperor, a flicker of resolve sparked inside Sonos' heart again. As Taine led the way back to his room, his mind was stirred.

"Taine, find me something to write with."

His father wanted reflections from his past year? Yes, he would write.

Perhaps catching the fire that burned in Sonos' eyes, Taine responded, "With pleasure, Highness." He then added under his breath, "Glad they didn't stop you today."

Sonos paused at the entrance to his room, then squared his shoulders and lifted his chin. "Some things are worth fighting for, always."

Sonos still wasn't sure what exactly he was going to do to generate any real change, but the most important thing for today was simply *knowing* that he wasn't defeated.

Chapter 4

"I'M DREAMING, RIGHT?" Charlotte stared at the monkey.

"If you're dreaming, looks like I'm dreaming with you." Jax scratched his head while looking around the hollow.

"Neither of you are dreaming." The statement came from the little monkey's mouth, but Charlotte still shook her head in disbelief.

"You can talk, you little thief?" Charlotte crossed her arms, keeping her eyes locked on the monkey. She was ready to pounce if he made a move to run.

Soft morning light shone into the hollow through small holes, like windows that had been carved into the tree.

The monkey focused its intelligent eyes on her and placed its hands akimbo in a very human-like way. "I understand this is coming at you quite suddenly, Charlotte, but yes, I am speaking." He held out Charlotte's gazer again, which she snatched back with a glare.

"How do you know my name? And who—or *what*—are you?" Charlotte asked as Jax stepped beside her.

"I've had many names, but you can call me Rapha." The monkey jumped onto a slightly higher shelf.

"RAFF-a?" Charlotte repeated the name while snapping the gazer back on.

"Yes. It's an old name meaning healer."

"How can you talk?" Jax asked.

Rapha crossed his arms. "I can always talk. It's only here you can understand me."

"And where exactly is *here*?" Charlotte asked.

"Ah, now you're asking an interesting question." Rapha grinned and bobbed his head. "We're in a temporal portal." He waved his arms wide open. "Please, take a look around."

Charlotte furrowed her brow, a thousand questions running through her mind. She tapped her gazer, trying to pull up a map of the area. It beeped out an error code stating that no location could be found. She tapped again, frustrated. They had to be *somewhere*.

"Is something humming?" Jax asked, walking slowly around the hollow. He stopped, cocked his head, and stood on his toes, reaching to one of the highest shelves. He patted around, then pulled down a dusty scroll.

Two rods protruded through the parchment, with midnight black rocks on the ends of each rod.

Jax blew off some of the dust and turned the scroll over in his hand. He sat on the floor and tried to wipe it off gently. "I could have sworn this was humming a minute ago. But now I'm not hearing anything."

Charlotte knelt beside him and touched one of the rocks which emitted a light vibration.

"I *feel* the vibration. Are these rocks obsidian?" Charlotte asked, leaning closer. She remembered a geology class her dad taught—obsidian had something to do with volcanoes, if memory served correctly.

"Oi!" Charlotte jumped in surprise when Rapha climbed up her body to perch on her shoulder.

"Very interesting," Rapha said, eyes fixed on the scroll.

"Uhm, sure, you can sit on my shoulder." Charlotte let sarcasm fill her words as she turned to look at Rapha.

Rapha patted her head. "Good. Because we have a long journey ahead. And yes, those stones are obsidian." He then turned back to Jax. "Go ahead and unroll it."

Jax held one rod steady while pulling the other rod slowly.

Charlotte leaned in behind him, thankful that the parchment didn't fall apart as he opened it.

"*This is written for a future hero of El,*" Jax read aloud.

A bright glow flared in Charlotte's periphery, distracting her. She took her eyes from Jax's scroll and turned towards the light.

The glow emitted from a leather-bound journal in the middle of a stack of other books.

"Give me a second." She patted Jax's shoulder and walked over to the shelf. She pulled the journal out, its light already fading as she held the ancient-looking book.

"Found something?" Rapha asked, still perched on her shoulder.

"You didn't see it glowing?" Charlotte asked, turning the book over.

"The texts in here call out in many different ways," Rapha said, jumping down to rejoin Jax on the floor.

"*El...* isn't that one of the old gods your dad told us about once, Char?" Jax asked.

"Yes, that rings a bell, but I don't remember a lot about it," she admitted, still turning the journal in her hands.

Religion had been banned by the Emperor, who declared himself to be the only god the people needed. However, Charlotte's dad often gave non-authorized lessons at home to supplement the Imperial curriculum he was forced to teach at school. Usually, these lessons talked about the history of Jamroq, its contributions, leaders and world perspective—which often differed from what the Empire wanted people to learn. *"Don't let the conquerors rewrite our story,"* he would say.

A twang of guilt ran through Charlotte as she remembered the firebrand teacher her father once was. These past three years had changed him. Broken him.

"El is not just one of the old gods or religions," Rapha interrupted her thoughts. "He is *the* God. Even over your Emperor."

"I don't suggest telling the Emperor that," Jax muttered under his breath, still studying the scroll.

"Speaking of the Emperor, we need to head back to the house," Charlotte said. *What are we doing here anyway?* "We can't be late to that feast." She tried to pull up the time on her gazer, but it gave the same error as when she tried to find the map. "What time is it?" Worry started to seep into her mind.

"El operates outside of time, and thus this portal of his does so, too," Rapha said calmly. "It's true the feast will wait for no one, but have no fear, the Emperor's time is passing."

"What is that supposed to mean?" Charlotte asked, annoyed that her tech wasn't working. She didn't understand anything that was happening with this talking monkey and strange place. She glanced towards Jax, but his eyes were transfixed on the scroll. He ran his hand gently over the words; muttering under his breath.

Rapha ignored her question and swung down to join Jax on the floor. He laid a slender hand to touch the scroll. "I often wondered when this prophecy would come to light. I remember when the hero heard those words during a particularly perilous journey. That's why it's only a few sentences long."

Was that a sad look that passed over Rapha's face? Charlotte was not used to monkey expressions.

"Wait, this scroll looks to be hundreds of years old, if not more. How can you remember when it was written?" Charlotte asked.

Rapha smiled. "A good question, young one. I have taken many shapes and forms over time, but the short answer is yes, it's possible. I have been around since the Beginning."

Charlotte sank against the wall, or the trunk of the tree. Whatever. Her head was spinning. A talking, immortal monkey. An old God. Prophecies. Journals. Heroes. A *portal* in a grove of cannonball trees. If only Ava was here. She'd know what to do. Her analytical mind was always able to piece things together. Or even Dad, before...

Charlotte closed her eyes, trying to find a single thread of thought to follow. When facing complex problems, her dad would tell her to focus on one thing at a time. *Don't focus on the tangle, find one thread to trace at a time.*

She opened her eyes and turned the journal in her hand. The leather was in perfect condition, and it gave off an earthy, slightly sweet smell. She opened to the first page, the handwritten letters feeling extremely personal.

'Be strong and very courageous. I will be with you to the End.' These were the words of promise told to me before leading the former slaves turned warriors to fight our greatest enemy.

Something stirred inside of Charlotte. She couldn't quite explain, but it was as if the words were more than just a historical text. Slaves turned into warriors? Kind of the opposite of what happened to the Kimwaki warriors who were turned into slaves for the Empire. But what if slaves could become warriors once more? She closed her eyes and leaned her head against the wall.

"Charlotte? You okay?" Rapha asked the question, but Jax's eyes were also fixed on her, a slight frown on his face.

"Sorry, it's just a lot to process. But there's this niggling feeling of familiarity." Charlotte narrowed her eyes at Rapha, searching for something she couldn't put her finger on.

"Let me explain it this way. You know tuning forks?" Rapha asked.

Charlotte nodded. Her dad used one in his science class.

"When you strike the fork, it produces a frequency that causes other items that are tuned to that same frequency to resonate. The same principle applies to the spirit realm," Rapha said.

"The spirit realm?" Jax asked.

"The unseen realm..." Rapha spread his arms outwards. "...that is sometimes seen."

Charlotte cocked her head. She had a lot to talk through with her dad and Gran later. She needed figure out what was really going on and not be further confused by a talking monkey who never answered a question straight. She stood up, ready to head back to the house.

Rapha stepped in front of Charlotte and folded his hands behind his back. "I'm very sorry, but you cannot take any of the texts outside of this portal."

"What? Then why bring us here?" Charlotte asked, annoyed.

"In times past, heroes would copy the texts into their own notebooks. However, if you don't want to take that long, I recognize that you have some technology to help speed up the process." Rapha tapped his wrist and indicated to where Charlotte wore her gazer.

"Fine," Charlotte sighed, disappointed she wouldn't be taking the physical journal with her. But she took off her gazer and tapped a pattern to turn on the capture function. She held the gazer carefully over the journal as she turned the pages and took an image of each one.

After she finished, she walked over to where Jax sat near his scroll, deep in thought.

"Unfortunately, taking a photo won't help you much with this scroll," Rapha said. "You can only understand the words because of the magic here. When you view it outside the portal, it will just look like very strange symbols."

"My gazer captures sound too, why don't you read it and we'll have a video capture instead?" Charlotte suggested.

"Great idea." Jax smiled and cleared his throat.

"*This is written for a future hero of El. Open your eyes! The one who created the world from nothing is doing something new. Are you seeing it? It's springing forth even now. He causes a river to flow in the badlands. What is impossible for him?*" Jax looked up from the scroll. "The end."

Charlotte tapped her gazer again, stopped the recording, and slid it back onto her wrist. Time to go. She closed the journal and walked back over to the shelf.

"Who wrote these texts?" Jax asked as he carefully rolled back the scroll.

"Ordinary people, just like you two, who served an extraordinary God. For various reasons, they are remembered and celebrated by followers of *El* to this day. Even if *El* and his people are forbidden by your Emperor, their contributions and the Truth of what they did is undeniable," Rapha said.

"Sounds like something my dad would say... used to say," Charlotte said. Her dad's depression since her mom's disappearance only seemed to worsen over time.

Jax squeezed her shoulder. "Don't worry, he'll come back around."

"There's one more thing before we go," Rapha said.

Charlotte turned from where she had placed the now-dim journal back onto its shelf.

"Breath is required for your mission," Rapha said.

"What mission?" Charlotte asked.

"What breath?" Jax asked.

"Breath marks you as one of *El's* and allows you to see beyond what your natural eyes can grasp," Rapha answered. Behind his white fur face, his dark eyes glimmered.

"You're speaking in riddles again," Charlotte said, growing impatient. "Plus, I already have a mission, I'm not looking for another one."

"I know about your sisters," Rapha said. "But to save Ava and Lily, you must first save the Mountain Kingdom."

"The Mountain Kingdom?" Charlotte racked her brain for details of the recluse kingdom. Her dad had an Empire-approved map of the mainland of the K'Luma Empire. The islands, including Jamroq, lay to the South, little dots in the sea. To the far west of the mainland, she remembered a grayed-out area that her dad had said was the Mountain Kingdom.

"What's the Mountain Kingdom have to do with my sisters?" Charlotte asked. She didn't bother asking how the monkey knew about them—he was his own enigma.

"And what or who are we saving the Mountain Kingdom from?" Jax added.

"All good questions, but first I must have your acceptance of the mission. As you have already read in the journal you found, Charlotte, the promises made to the author are also made to you. *El* will be with you and protect you. And Jaxtyn, in the words you read, you can be assured that the way is being created to lead you even now."

"Sorry, Raph," Charlotte said, "But as I said, my focus is on Ava and Lily who need my help now. Is *El* willing to help me with that or not?"

"I don't set the order of things, I'm sorry." Rapha folded his hands in front of him.

"Well, I hate to break it to you, but *El* has this thing wrong. If you really want to save the Mountain Kingdom, Ava and Lily are your best bet. They're as smart as they come, and they may even bring Dad back from the dark place he's in. Then you'll really have the team you need. But not me." Charlotte wiped her eyes and walked towards the exit.

She stepped outside but when Jax wasn't behind her, she stuck her head back in the room.

"Are you coming?" Charlotte asked.

"I... I can't quite explain it," Jax fumbled over his words. He looked at the scroll, then at Rapha, and back to Charlotte. "I have this strong sense that saving the Mountain Kingdom is the right thing to do. I mean, all of this can't be coincidence, can it? A talking monkey in a temporal portal? And the texts did call out to us..."

"You have a sense? We've been planning for three years to get Ava and Lily back." Charlotte felt betrayed that he'd jump ship on her now. All she wanted to do was leave and get home. "But please, by all means, follow your *sense.*"

Charlotte didn't wait for his response. Anger began to burn, along with disappointment that Rapha, or *El,* or whoever wouldn't help her. What a waste of time. A whole magical realm that cared nothing for what mattered most to her.

She grabbed her flyer-board and sprinted out of the cannonball grove, wanting to put some distance between her and the monkey.

Inside the cannonball trees, the sun shone bright as at midday, but as she made her way back into the more familiar forest, strangely it was more like late-afternoon sun. She sighed. The last thing she needed was to be late for the feast, especially with the important Imperials who arrived in the K'Luma Carrier earlier.

She gave a last glance towards the grove but decided Jax would have to figure out how to work with his monkey-friend to find his way back. She pulled out the sun collector to restart the board.

As she slid it into place, a sickening *crack* sounded, and the panel broke in two.

Charlotte let out a gut-wrenching cry, dropping her head against the now defunct board. Just when everything was coming together, all her plans seemed to slip through her fingers.

A thought struck her, and she wondered if Rapha had somehow caused her panel to break. She gritted her teeth and stood up, tucking the board under her arm. Well, Rapha would fix it. Especially since he caused Jax to abandon her—she at least needed a working board. She stomped back in the direction of the cannonball trees.

After a few minutes, she looked around in confusion. Charlotte had an excellent sense of direction, and she was sure she backtracked correctly. But she should have already come to the grove.

"Jax?" She shouted. "Rapha?"

No answer.

She called out again, and again—silence.

She closed her eyes and took in a calming breath. *Let me just get back to the house and sort this out.*

"Home," Charlotte said aloud, allowing the steadiness in her voice to fix her mind on the next step. She tapped her gazer, pulling up a map of the area. She was a lot further into the forest than she thought. It would take her a couple of hours to get back, which meant she would definitely be late for the feast.

"Great. Just add it to the list of what went wrong on this cursed day," she muttered.

After sliding the panel pieces back into her pocket, she strapped the board to her back. *Maybe there's a way to repair the panel*, she thought.

Charlotte refused to give up hope, and she would never give up on her family. She just needed to get her dad and sisters back together again. Then they could heal and figure things out.

She set a quick pace towards home.

It was full dark by the time she exited the forest and caught sight of the house. Thankfully, the sky was clear, and the moon was full, giving pale light to see.

She quickly put the flyer-board back in the cellar, then jogged toward the town square where everyone would be gathered.

She approached the entrance to the square, slightly out of breath from the jog.

Out of nowhere, a pair of gruff hands grabbed her. "There you are!" a guard said, a dark edge to his voice.

Charlotte vaguely recognized the guard as one of the Imperials who had been assigned to Mina over the last year.

He dragged her towards the stage at the far end of the packed square. The whole place was quiet, which was strange for the feast.

She fought the guard's grip, looking for her dad, wondering how her absence had caused such a stir. Yes, attendance was mandatory, but this seemed a bit dramatic.

As they drew closer to the stage, Charlotte stared in horror as she saw Gran huddled in a corner, strange guards on either side of her. But that wasn't the worst of it.

In the center of the stage, a tall Imperial she didn't recognize, in a strange black uniform with gold and red stripes, stood over the kneeling forms of Jax and her dad. Two bulky guards towered over them on either side.

"Ahhh," the leader with the fancy uniform said while looking at her. "The infamous Charlotte King has finally arrived."

<h1 style="text-align:center">CHAPTER 5</h1>

S ONOS PAUSED AND TOOK a deep breath of the early evening air. Being outside the palace had never tasted so sweet.

"Sonos, come on." Ade was already ahead of him, trying to stay close to the procession carrying the Emperor and Empress.

With a quick glance to Taine, who faithfully kept by his side, Sonos jogged to catch up. He pushed aside the nagging fears of returning to the same event where everything had come crashing down last year. *Besides, what more could possibly go wrong this year?*

The blue-white glow and hum from the hover-platform which carried his father and mother buzzed ahead.

The Emperor loved to embrace ancient traditions and imbue them with technology developed by his own secretive Order of the Sahemy.

His father had once boasted how the platform was a perfect reminder of the superior hover-tech that had spurred the K'Luma Empire to greatness. At the same time, he insisted that a base-board be carried on the shoulders of men, harking back to ancient palanquins.

Vanity, Sonos thought. Especially given that on Feast Day, the men used to carry the base were brought from the four conquered territories: the islands of Kimwaki, Salan, and Jamroq, alongside the harbor city of Portemore.

"Remember, keep your head down, and don't leave the head table." Ade insisted on rehearsing the instructions given by the Emperor.

"Head down, head table. I think I got it," Sonos muttered. He had no interest in conversing with the nobles anyway.

He did, however, look forward to seeing his mother again. He strained his neck to see if he could glimpse her even now, but the back of her cushioned futon was too high. He could only see the top of her head, black hair flowing, and small braids intricately woven around her golden crown.

A shiver ran down Sonos' back as he considered the upright form of his father next to her. The Emperor's gaze never shifted from facing straight ahead. Even the wind seemed too intimidated to ruffle his slicked-back, raven-colored hair, or his crimson cloak with its high collar.

The stiffness of his own cloak scratched at Sonos' skin. He was in formal attire tonight, which meant a pure white tunic with puffy sleeves that he hated, a black vest, and a crimson cloak with the gold-embossed flying dragon. The only part of the outfit he enjoyed was his comfortable high, leather boots. That, and his cloak which had a few secret pockets woven in. Sonos tapped one of those hidden pockets which held his newly minted journal.

The walk through the inner city to the Legacy Towers was not long. It was a smooth jaunt along asphalt-paved streets, thanks to material sequestered from one of the conquered isles.

Sonos looked up at the dusk-filled sky.

"Do you remember the first time Father took us up on one of the K'Luma Carriers?" Sonos asked his brother.

Ade smiled. "He allowed us to accompany him to watch the final battle and capture of Salan."

"Yes," Sonos cringed. "But I was actually thinking about how the city looked from above: circles within circles within circles. *Order from chaos, strength from weakness*, as Father would say," Sonos mused aloud.

"Get through tonight, and tomorrow your life gets back on track. That's the order you need," Ade said.

Back on track. And what does that look like? Helping continue Father's ruthless legacy? Continue to conquer other nations and prove the Empire's never-ending strength? The questions ran through Sonos' mind, but he kept his tongue in check.

The procession stopped at the entrance to the courtyard, and the hover-platform was lowered to the ground.

The men who had carried the platform, prostrated themselves fully while the hundreds of nobles in the square dropped to their knees in unison as the Emperor walked in.

The Empress gracefully lowered herself, and Ade and Sonos also took a knee. To the Emperor, everyone signaled their submission; no exceptions.

Sonos glanced at his mother, who held her bow like everyone else. Ade's earlier comment about her serving only as a visible, living trophy for their father caused a spark of anger to rise. He swallowed it down with all his other questions though. Sonos wanted no trouble tonight.

Once the Emperor reached the stage which had been erected on the far end of the courtyard, he nodded, and everyone stood to resume the feast activities.

Commander Uzoma and General Baku, the head of the army and the Imperial guards respectively, joined the Emperor and the three took seats at the head table next to the stage. Sonos made his way there, head down, and took a seat as far as he could from the Emperor.

The feast was held in the courtyard of the Legacy Towers, which served as a backdrop to the stage. The location was symbolic, as every structure built signified a conquered territory. *Living temples*, his father called them.

Each tower was built in the same tiered, symmetrical, six-level design. Each tier had a hexagonal outcropping with five sharp points that angled upwards.

A small group of older noblewomen walked by the head table, whispering.

Sonos didn't catch what they said, but as soon as he raised his head, they averted their gaze and dropped their voices even lower. Sonos sighed. He needed a distraction. He pulled out his journal and pencil. A few sketches couldn't hurt.

Sonos scanned the area. It didn't take long for him to find who he was looking for. His mother stood with her handmaidens, attended to by a swarm of servants.

Tonight, the Empress was a symbol of K'Luma's power and wealth. She wore a stunning dress of midnight black with a crimson, stiff-lace collar that ran up her long neck and flared, framing her jawline. The same crimson lace started at her elbows and ran out past her fingertips. Her golden crown was noticeable but not overstated. The soft lighting strung across the courtyard danced in her fierce blue eyes.

Is that sadness in her gaze? Sonos wondered.

Her mouth twitched ever so slightly as she mouthed the word "sorry" before turning her back and walking towards another group of nobles.

Sonos sighed. She wouldn't risk talking to him or going against the Emperor's wishes.

The lead from his pencil began to take shape on paper as Sonos sketched. He was not a great artist by any stretch, but he had an eye for detail that allowed him to accurately replicate real life or images that he saw. The Emperor could not keep everything from him.

"It is good to see you have traded rebellious words for sketches of your family this year," a nasal voice said from directly behind him.

Sonos jumped in his seat, not realizing he had attracted any attention. The lanky form of Baku stood with his hands folded behind his back, his face as pale as the moon.

"And let's hope for stronger security this year too, shall we?" Sonos couldn't help returning the jab.

A flash of anger sparked in Baku's eyes, but his demeanor remained perfectly calm otherwise. "It is good to see you out of isolation, Highness. Please, enjoy your evening." Baku turned and headed back to his seat at the other end of the long table.

A trumpet sounded from the stage, and everyone made their way to their respective tables. Sonos slipped the journal and pencil back into his cloak as Ade took the seat next to him.

The Empress nodded towards Sonos and smiled as she sat on Ade's other side.

Once everyone in the courtyard was seated, a second trumpet sounded, and the Emperor rose and took his place on center stage.

Spotlights shone on him as the cameras started to broadcast his speech throughout the Empire. Similar to hover-tech, anything that ran on solar or wind power was a closely guarded secret.

The Emperor began speaking with a low, but fierce voice. "People of K'Luma, as you celebrate this Feast Day, you celebrate the greatest Empire this world has ever known."

The platitudes about the history and greatness of the Empire continued and Sonos' mind wandered. His gaze was drawn towards the Legacy Towers behind his father. Had he seen a flash of light in one of the windows? Sonos squinted, trying to see into the darkness beyond the light shining on the stage.

There it was again! From the second tier of the closest tower. The light was more of a flicker, like a hand waving in front of a candle, causing a specific pattern to repeat. To most people, it might seem like normal, random candlelight, but Sonos was sure it was deliberate.

One, two, three seconds of light, two seconds of darkness. Five seconds of light, one second of darkness. Two seconds of light, three seconds of darkness. Then the whole sequence repeated.

Sonos looked around to see if anyone else noticed the light. Ade was engrossed in what the Emperor was saying, like everyone else at the head table.

Sonos remembered a line he had jotted down in his notebook earlier. A line of an ancient poem that had run through his mind more than once over the past year.

To those who were called, who were destined
to see,
A Light shone through darkness,
shimmering, pleading.
A travesty that for all who have eyes,
so few can see.

Sonos leaned towards his brother. "Did you see that light from the towers?"

"What? No. I am listening to the Emperor, as you should be, too." Ade whispered through gritted teeth.

Their mother turned her head ever so slightly, one eyebrow raised at the brothers.

Ade grunted, never taking his eyes off the Emperor.

Sonos was bursting with curiosity, but for the sake of his mother, tried to focus on his father.

There, again.

Sonos was almost certain it was coming from the Salan tower. He itched to make some notes, but deliberately squeezed his hands together and refused to pull out his journal.

"In this year of the dragon, I have commanded a new conquest to be led by Commander Uzoma." The Emperor's voice rose with excitement.

Sonos' attention snapped back to center stage. *What did I miss? Year of the dragon? New conquest?* It had been at least a decade since the last conquest when Salan was taken.

A hulking figure joined the Emperor on stage. Unlike the Imperial guards whose uniforms were trimmed in bright gold and red stripes, the army uniforms were dark as midnight. Combined with the dark tones of Uzoma's skin, he created a huge and menacing shadow that seemed to magnify the Emperor's stance.

"Our fearless and undefeated Commander Uzoma has been tasked to subdue the Mountain Kingdom and return with the fabled gold that fills its treasure house."

Cheers and shouts erupted from the audience.

"There will be much to celebrate this year." The Emperor's mouth twitched upwards but there was no mirth in his gray eyes. "For now, I bless you in the name of the dragon. May it be a year where the eternal K'Luma Empire continues to grow in strength, power, and wealth."

The Emperor finished his speech as the nobles banged mugs against the tables and cries of "*All hail the year of the dragon!*" erupted across the courtyard.

The night sky filled with bursts of lights and colors, great booms echoing from near the river. The Sahemy used special cases like Feast Day to show off new feats of light and fire.

Food, drinks, and music came in abundance. Throughout the meal, Sonos kept glancing at the Salan tower, trying to catch sight of any flickers, but the towers were once again dark.

"I wonder how Uzoma plans to attack," Ade asked, his mouth full of meat, eyes gleaming. "I mean, the last true challenge was Kimwaki, but he can't burn the ships this time."

Sonos glanced back to where Taine stood at attention, guarding his back.

The battle against the warrior tribes was brutal and bloody, even as told by the Empire's recount. When supplies were running low and Kimwaki held strong, their father had ordered the burning of all the army's ships. There would be no return, or survival, without victory, the commander had declared.

In the end, their father had brought the disembodied head of the Chieftain of Kimwaki to the then-ruler of K'Luma. He was named heir and given the Chieftain's only daughter as a prize.

Sonos leaned forward and stole a glance at his mother, her eyes scanning the courtyard. She may wear the wealth of the Empire, but Sonos knew her Kimwaki roots ran deep below the surface.

"I've heard rumors that the Sahemy developed some kind of chemical weapon," Ade continued to talk through possible scenarios for how Uzoma would attack the Mountain Kingdom.

Sonos lost his appetite.

After the meal was finished, Ade left the table and made his way back to the other young nobles. Laughter, dancing, and lively music filled the courtyard.

A young voice made Sonos turn. "Excuse me, Highness, would you care for some spiced wine?"

Sonos recognized the same serving boy with the blonde curls from the baths earlier. The boy held onto the tray tightly with two hands.

"They have you working again already? How are your arms, boy?"

The boy gave a half-smile. "Everyone is required for Feast Day, Highness. Mother said the lashes should not scar. I was quite brave." In a rush, the boy let go of one hand to raise his sleeve and show Sonos his arm.

Sonos watched in horror as the glass started to topple.

Out of nowhere, Taine rushed in with his lightning-quick reactions and caught the glass right before it hit the ground. With a wink, Taine placed the glass back onto the tray. Even though the contents had spilled, at least there was no clamor, and hopefully no one else noticed.

"Need to be more careful, young one." Taine patted the boy on the head, then moved back to the shadows.

The boy's look of relief switched to panic again when he turned back to Sonos. "Highness, your cloak! The wine spilled on you. I'm so sorry. Let me put this down and come back with a rag." He rushed towards the servant entrance but tripped not far from the head table.

This time, the glass fell to the ground. As the banished gods would have it, the lively song playing had just ended and, in that pause, the crash echoed.

It happened quickly, but Sonos caught Baku's smirk as he stepped away from the boy.

Was this some kind of test to see how I'll respond? Sonos wondered. He was certain that Baku was aware what had happened at the baths, and surely the boy's placement to serve Sonos again was not mere coincidence.

Two older servants grabbed the boy by his arm, and a yelp escaped the boy's lips.

As they walked away, they passed behind the Emperor, who made a motion to the older servant.

The boy turned his head to glance back towards Sonos with a look of pure fear.

Sonos closed his eyes and tried to think. What good would defying a command from his father do if he tried to save the boy? How could he possibly enact change if he was locked away, perhaps permanently this time. Or worse. But how could he stand by and do nothing?

Sonos rose from the table in desperate need of some fresh air and distance from all the nobles; his father in particular.

Taine followed close on his heels.

Sonos didn't want to cross through the lively courtyard to reach the street, so instead, he walked towards the towers.

Taine broke the silence after they passed out of sight from the courtyard. "It wasn't your fault what happened to the boy. I will check on him tomorrow."

A cry sounded from nearby.

As they rounded a corner, the scene triggered the pent-up anger Sonos had been trying to suppress all day.

The young servant boy stood shirtless facing the building, legs spread with his hands pressed against the wall. Blood was running down his back.

The master-servant with a crimson sash watched cross-armed as another man stood over the boy.

The man held a full-size bull-pistle whip, which had long strands of leather strips, each with a sharp piece of stone tied at the end. Grown men usually cowered after a few lashes.

"Stop!" Sonos rushed towards the group.

The master-servant moved to block Sonos from reaching the boy. "The Emperor has deemed this young one unworthy after both indiscretions today. He will be punished fully."

The boy whimpered and something cracked in Sonos. Unjust cruelty must stop somewhere and must be stopped by *someone*. He pulled the dagger from his belt and held it to the whip-wielding man's throat.

"I command you to stop."

The man flinched with this unexpected move.

The master-servant stepped closer and answered with a calm and arrogant voice. "Highness, I'm sure you know that Emperor's word is final. May I suggest having another drink at the feast?"

Ugh. After Father's harsh punishment this past year, even the servants feel empowered to speak against me, Sonos lamented.

Out of the corner of his eye, Sonos confirmed that Taine's hooked sword was already drawn and ready.

Even though a small thought entered his mind to stop and think about what he was doing, Sonos pushed it far away and focused on the task at hand. He wrapped his foot around the servant's ankle and simultaneously shoved against his upper body. The servant fell backward to the ground with a force that surprised even Sonos.

Sonos readied for a continued fight, but the servant was completely still. *I must have knocked the wind out of him,* he thought.

Taine had the master-servant pinned against the wall and swiftly used the blunt end of his sword to knock the man unconscious.

Sonos looked down at the servant he had knocked over. A pool of blood grew steadily under his head. *What in the gods...*

Taine knelt and rolled the man over. A huge gash showed on the back of his head. Somehow, he had fallen directly onto a sharp rock that was protruding from the ground.

"No pulse," Taine confirmed. "We need to move quickly."

Sonos nodded, his mind reeling in shock. He hadn't meant to *kill* anyone. His father would have his head for this latest interference with the Empire's authority.

"Sonos?" Taine called his attention back to the present.

Sonos' voice cracked as he said, "The boy..."

The young servant had collapsed to his knees during the scuffle. His back was bleeding from the whipping he had already received before Sonos and Taine had arrived.

Taine bent and picked up the boy.

"Follow me."

Chapter 6

Fireworks flashed on the large screen, broadcasting live from Pergamum. The Emperor's speech must have already finished.

Charlotte grimaced as she stood at the end of the stage, inwardly cursing the monkey for making her so late. *But how did Jax arrive on time,* she wondered.

"I admit, I'm a little torn." The bulky Imperial with the unfamiliar uniform paced the stage. "Now that you've finally arrived, I've no need to coerce the information on your whereabouts from these two." He waved his hands towards where her dad and Jax knelt between the guards.

Charlotte stood frozen in place, held at the edge of the stage, the hairs on the back of her neck rising. She glanced at Gran, huddled in the corner of the stage.

Memories of her dad's crumpled form after their last encounter with Pergamum guards replayed in her mind. Charlotte's heart started racing.

She blinked her eyes, trying to confirm that her dad was still okay and upright, even if kneeling. Was Gran moving? Was she okay?

Charlotte's breathing came faster and faster.

Is the guard trying to say something to me? Charlotte tried to focus her thoughts. Her ears were ringing.

Charlotte gasped for breath. She fell to her knees, haunted by the screams of her sisters. *Are they here? At the feast?* She heard her mom's cries. It couldn't be real.

She tried to shake her head and clear her thoughts, but it came out as convulsions. She crumpled on the stage, the world going black.

Her last fuzzy memory was of a little monkey coming and grabbing her gazer once again.

"Char!" A deep voice was shouting. "Let me help her!"

Charlotte squinted and tried to sit up. Her head was pounding, her ears still ringing.

The voice came from her dad. He and Jax were still restrained on the stage.

Charlotte sat up and tried to give him a reassuring smile. She didn't want her dad or Jax hurt on her account. Well, hurt further. She cringed inwardly.

She looked around the stage for sight of Gran.

"If you're looking for your grandmother, we had to escort that feisty one off stage," the head Imperial said.

The anger that burned in Charlotte got her blood flowing in all the right places. She stood to her feet, scanning the crowd.

Gran called out from a nearby exit of the square. She was held by two guards, but otherwise looked unharmed.

"Now," the guard next to Charlotte said loudly, then cleared his throat. "Would you care to explain what just happened here?"

Charlotte furrowed her brow. What right did he have to come in here and traumatize her family, then ask what happened? She kept her lips in a tight line.

The Imperial speaking wore a uniform she had only seen once before, three years ago on the guard who had protected Eliza Wumi, a high-ranking noble. Those were Elites, Charlotte forced her brain to think and remember. The Elite's red and gold criss-crossing stripes glimmered down the left side of his body, offset against the black of his impeccably straight uniform.

"Silence," the Elite said. "Silence when I asked these two where you were." He gestured towards Jax and her dad. "Silence when I asked you a question. Is your whole family so resistant to simple questions?"

The Elite narrowed his slate eyes at Charlotte, and she dropped her gaze. She felt her heart starting to race again.

"Let's try to widen this net." The Elite stepped forward to the edge of the stage. "Would *anyone* care to speak up and tell me what is happening? Surely, this is the first place I've visited, not to mention a backwater village on a long-conquered island, that refuses to cooperate with simple instructions and answer simple questions."

For some reason, Gran's voice echoed in Charlotte's mind. She would always talk about how even though the Emperor had in-vaded their land, they would never be conquered, not where it mattered most—on the inside.

The crowd must have felt the same anger at the Elite's words. No one answered his questions.

Charlotte glanced out at her fellow villagers, people she had grown up with all her life. Some of the cocoa-toned and sun-kissed faces had downcast eyes. Others had tight-drawn lips and eyes that shone with fire. But no one spoke up.

"I see," the Elite muttered under his breath. He turned towards Charlotte and grabbed her arm. "Well, if you can't catch Quackoo, catch his shirt."

Charlotte's stomach knotted. The Elite was convinced something was wrong, but since he couldn't find what he was looking for exactly, he'd take her all the same.

"You're coming with me, young one. And we will get to the bottom of what is happening in this town." The Elite pulled her towards the edge of the stage.

"Wait," Charlotte's dad cried out.

"Too late," the Elite said, ice coating his words. He turned once more to the crowd in the square. "Everyone, go home immediately. And no one is to leave the village."

Tears streamed freely down Charlotte's face as he pulled her off the stage. *He just has a few questions,* Charlotte thought as she tried to calm her rising anxiety. She wasn't being taken like her sisters.

The Elite handed her off to another pair of guards who led her around the perimeter of the courtyard and down the street to a large, two-story building that served as the Imperial guards' quarters.

Before the occupation, it was a bustling inn and gem of Mina. Now stripped of its previous glamor, it had become a dormitory and base of operations for the Empire in Jamroq.

Charlotte was put into a small room with a single table and a few chairs. She focused her breathing as she waited, not wanting another anxiety attack to set in.

A moment of panic shot through her mind as she pulled up the sleeve of her jacket. The gazer was gone. Did it somehow fall off? Did one of the guards confiscate it when she was unconscious? She remembered the last fuzzy image before she blacked out on the stage: seeing Rapha swipe her gazer once more. She hoped that was the case, and that she could find him again once more.

Time passed excruciatingly slow. Charlotte sat in a hard-backed chair. She tapped her foot. She bit her nails. She loosened her hair and tied it back again a million times.

A guard stood inside the door watching her every move, making her even more unnerved.

Finally, the door swung open and the tall Elite with tanned skin and a perfect uniform walked into the room. For the first time, Charlotte noticed a hint of tattoos creeping out from his high collar.

He carried a steaming mug of tea—Charlotte caught a whiff of ginger and lemon. Her stomach rumbled in protest, and she remembered the last time she ate was some fruit on her ill-fated hike back to the village.

The Elite sat opposite Charlotte and took a loud slurp of the tea. His slate-colored eyes seemed to miss no detail. His full lips were pulled tight, set above a square jaw. He radiated strength, but it was overlaid with anger.

"What bad manners. I forgot we haven't been properly introduced." He inclined his head slightly, but the intensity of his eyes never wavered. "I am Captain Diekololaluwa, leader of the Imperial Elites, special forces of the Imperial Guards, protector of the blessed and most honorable Emperor, may he live forever."

Die- what? The first syllable of the captain's name echoed in Charlotte's brain.

"Die-kolo-la-lu-wa," the captain said more slowly, enunciating each syllable. He must have caught her confused look. "Most people miss it the first time, but you'll learn it soon enough."

A shiver ran down Charlotte's spine. She had no intention of sticking around long enough to learn anything from him.

"I would offer you some tea," Captain Die said, "But first, you must earn it. Nothing in the Empire comes free."

Charlotte kept her mouth shut. At this point, she didn't trust what might fly out if she even tried to answer or respond.

"Do you know why I am here?" Captain Die asked.

Charlotte shook her head.

"The Shadows," he said. "Do you know the Shadows, girl?"

"No." Charlotte racked her brain for any scraps her dad may have shared. Something about old magic?

"They are the power of the dark realm." The captain stared as if *she* was about to turn into a Shadow. "And particularly strong leading up to the year of the dragon."

Why is he telling me this? What do Shadows or the dark realm have to do with me?

"Why were you late to the feast? Your family doesn't teach you discipline and respect for the Empire?"

"I... I'm sorry. They do. It was my fault, I got lost in the woods." She had to defend her dad and Gran. And she was speaking the truth.

"Was Jaxtyn with you?"

Charlotte swallowed. One answer requires another. She should have kept her mouth shut. "Yes, for a time. But I ran off and we got separated."

"He left you in the woods by yourself?"

"He probably thought I went back separately."

The captain grunted and took another sip of tea. "Are you planning to kill the Emperor?"

"What? No! I... what on earth makes you think *I* could kill the Emperor?" *Where had* that *question come from?*

"You *want* to kill the Emperor?"

"No. That would be madness."

"You want to *fight* the Emperor?"

Charlotte hesitated.

"Hmm. Truth, at last." The captain leaned forward.

"I want my sisters back," Charlotte admitted, realizing that outright lying would be too risky. "But it is foolish to desire anything other than what the Empire wants." Charlotte hoped the truth of that statement was enough to cover the defiance that still fought inside of her.

"One of the Mina guards told me that they were taken to the Legacy Towers three years ago. You should be proud," Captain Die stated matter-of-factly.

Charlotte bit her bottom lip, knowing that anything she said would work against her.

"And yet, I was also told that your mother died at sea trying to reach them... to rescue them." Captain Die's gaze bore into Charlotte.

She was horrified that this Imperial-whatever knew so many personal details about her family. She supposed it was no secret, but shame on him for flaunting those details in front of her now.

"I simply don't understand why you, or anyone in your family, would try and chase after them. Why defy the Emperor's wishes?" Captain Die said.

"What choice do we have?" She forced herself to hold the captain's gaze, unflinching.

Finally, he sighed and stood. "Go home. But do not leave town for any reason, including any trips into the forest. Am I understood?"

"Yes." Was she really getting to leave and go home? There was surely a deeper game at play. Why was he so calm?

Captain Die left the room, leaving the door open. Charlotte waited a minute, then peeked her head out the door. An Elite stood at the end of the hallway. Charlotte straightened her shoulders and walked down the hall. Games or no, she'd be happy to play them on her own turf.

Once she was outside, she broke into a run towards home.

The moon was high in the sky, giving plenty of light to see. Once she left the main square, there were no more lamp posts. The streets were deserted, and a cool ocean breeze cooled her as she ran.

It was about a mile until she reached the outskirts of the town and the dirt path towards her house. Gran's house was dark, but lights were on in Charlotte's wooden home.

Cheerful cries and tears of joy greeted her as soon as she walked in the front door. Jax, Gran, and her dad all pulled her close in a huge group hug.

Charlotte had to literally wrench herself free from her dad's embrace, but it was a happy moment.

She caught sight of a white, furry face seated calmly on a stool, and breathed a sigh of relief.

Gran cleared her throat. "This little guy followed us home and has just been sitting there. I think he has something of yours, Char."

Sure enough, Charlotte's gazer rested on Rapha's lap. She walked over and grabbed it, snapping it back on her wrist. She still wasn't sure that she trusted the little monkey, but she dropped to a knee, eyes level with the fur-ball. "Thank you, Rapha."

He made a series of grunts and patted her head.

Gran chuckled. "A lot of personality, that one."

The events of the day swam through Charlotte's mind, nearly drowning her in exhaustion now that she was finally home. She wanted to tell them about the broken flyer-board and Captain Die's line of questioning, but she could barely put two coherent thoughts together.

Gran pulled her to sit next to her on the couch, and Jax offered to make some lemon balm tea.

Dad paced but didn't leave the room.

Charlotte was just about dozing off, joining Rapha's snores from where he lay curled up in Gran's lap, when a loud *thud* sounded on the roof.

"What was that?" Jax stood, eyes wide.

A series of *whoosh* followed by *thud, thud, thud*, followed.

Jax and her dad exchanged a glance.

"We're under attack," Gran gasped.

CHAPTER 7

S ONOS FOLLOWED TAINE AS they darted from one shadowed wall to another, away from the courtyard and towards the Legacy Towers.

The young servant boy was heaped on Taine's broad shoulders.

Sonos shoved down the emotions threatening to flood his brain. *Did I really just kill a man?* He closed his eyes for a few seconds, forcing himself to stay in the moment.

Sonos stumbled as Taine made an abrupt turn into an alley. He jogged to catch up.

"Give me your cloak," Taine said, one knee on the ground.

Sonos slipped his journal out from the hidden pocket and handed the cloak over to Taine. He then tucked the journal into the back of his pants, under his tunic.

The young servant boy was unconscious. His back was bleeding heavily, but thankfully his breathing was steady.

Taine gently wrapped the cloak around the boy's upper body and slung him back over his shoulder.

The boy squirmed a bit, a soft moan escaping his lips.

Taine squeezed the boy's leg. "Be still, young one. We have a long night ahead."

Taine poked his head out of the alley, looking in both directions. He took a step towards the towers, but Sonos tugged him back.

"Taine, we're going the wrong way," Sonos hissed.

"No, it's the only way out," Taine replied.

Sonos was thoroughly confused. Those towers were the pride of his father, trophies of his conquests. "Why are we going into a stronghold of the Emperor if we're trying to escape?"

"Stronghold, you say? More like a prison." Taine held his gaze, eyes sharp. "You've asked some brave questions, Sonos. I just hope you're ready to find some answers."

Sonos flinched. He hadn't exactly planned out how he would find those answers yet, but even if he had, it certainly would not have gone like this. A niggling question grew in his mind. How much could he trust his bodyguard without the protection of the palace?

Shouts erupted from the direction of the courtyard. The servants must have been discovered. Time was running out.

"Make your choice now," Taine said. "Trust me, and we may still make it through the night."

Sonos could barely think, his heart was beating so fast. It was now or never. "Okay, lead the way," he said.

"We need to make it to the backside of the Kimwaki Tower." Taine pointed to the fourth tower in the arching row.

The entrance to each tower was guarded by two Imperial guards. Sonos guessed there were roving patrols in addition.

"May *El* guide and protect us." The words escaped as a whisper from the boy.

Sonos frowned. Maybe the boy was muttering in his sleep? He'd heard about followers of *El* in his studies of religion but didn't realize anyone still practiced—especially as it was punishable by death. There wasn't much time to ponder though because a dark cloud passed in front of the moon, providing a convenient cover of darkness.

"Run," Taine urged.

Without hesitation, Sonos followed Taine's sprint towards the back of the nearest tower.

Even with the extra weight on his shoulder, Taine was lightning quick.

Sonos gulped in air when they reached the back of the first tower. The stone wall felt cool against his cheek as he leaned in a crouch. The outcroppings provided a nice covering and darkness. Thankfully, no sounds of pursuit followed them, yet.

The cloud cover passed, and in the increased moonlight, Taine pointed out their next target wall. This one was closer.

They continued maneuvering from tower to tower until they reached the fourth one.

"What now?" Sonos whispered. There was no sign of life on the backside of the tower.

Taine tapped on one of the wooden shutters. The windows were closed and dark, but soon enough, a soft rapping responded. Taine tapped out another response, which was followed by silence.

Sonos wiped the sweat from his brow and strained to see any movement in the dark. At any moment he expected to see a guard burst around the corner.

There were no sounds from inside the tower.

"What are we waiting for?" Sonos whispered. The adrenaline coursing through his veins made every minute crouched in waiting feel like an eternity.

"Patience," Taine said.

"We're waiting for patience?" Frustration, anger, and anxiety all stirred together inside of Sonos.

"We're waiting for—" The end of a rope fell from the outcropping above them. "This." Taine smiled.

"You've done this before?" The familiarity of Taine's behavior shocked Sonos. Like everyone else, Sonos believed that the tower's occupants were completely shut off from the outside world. That was clearly *not* the case.

Ignoring his question, Taine shifted the unconscious boy to his other shoulder and took hold of the rope. "I will go up first and try to convince them not to turn you over at first sight." He winked before pulling himself up.

"What—" Sonos started, doubt again growing in his gut.

Taine was out of sight and over the ledge of the bottom tier in a matter of seconds.

The rope jiggled a few times, which Sonos took as the signal to climb. He touched the journal secured against his back and reached for the rope, but it suddenly disappeared. Pulled up without him.

Had he just been deserted?

Footsteps sounded nearby.

Sonos dropped to his belly and flattened himself against the wall of the tower behind a jasmine bush. For once, he was thankful for his father's obsession with plants. Aside from people, his father had requisitioned the best native greenery from the lands he conquered.

He slowed his breathing, straining his ears.

The footsteps faded, but a swishing sound came from overhead. Sonos panicked for a second, but then realized it was just the rope dropped back down.

Sonos scrambled over, grasped the rope, took a deep breath, and pulled. His body felt like lead. Mercifully, the rope was knotted to provide grips.

By the time he reached the edge of the wooden outcropping, he was huffing and puffing, muscles burning. He put his arm over the ledge, followed by one of his legs, and heaved himself over.

He tumbled onto the floor of the narrow balcony. Soft light spilled out from the open doorway and illuminated Taine in an intense argument with a tall, young woman. Their hands gesticulated wildly even as they kept their voices low.

Sonos pulled up the rope and sat quietly in the shadows. The servant boy had been propped against the wall. Taine and the girl completely ignored Sonos, talking in a sing-song language Sonos recognized as native to Kimwaki.

The girl wore a dark brown, loose-fitting robe. She had on a wooden and indigo-beaded choker that matched the blue paint that ran in a thick horizontal streak across her face.

She threw her hands in the air and hmphed at Taine. As she shook her head, her long dark hair shifted, and there was no mistaking the tattoos that peeked above her necklace and ran to her strong jawline. She stormed over to where Sonos sat, and he jumped up, holding out the rope as if it were a peace offering.

"Taine may have invoked the warrior's judgment over you for the moment, but you are far from safe, *Royal*." She spat out the last word, as her fierce, dark eyes glared at Sonos. She grabbed the rope and wrapped it around her waist like a belt.

"Follow me." Without looking back, she walked through the doorway.

Sonos leaned in as Taine picked up the boy in his arms. "I take it you know her?" he whispered.

"My sister, Taimani," he answered, eyes hard.

Taimani carried a torch as she led them deeper into the tower. The light flickered over a painted image of the Emperor.

"I never knew you had family here," Sonos inclined his head towards Taine as they walked through the hallway.

"We were both taken five years ago. Mani was too young at the time to serve as a bodyguard, even though she was at the top of her class back home."

"Hence I was sent to this prison to spend every hour cooped up in a blasted tower." Taimani spun around, the light from the torch reflecting the sparks in her eyes. "Forced to take lessons and be *enlightened*, or more accurately *dulled*, by the ways of the Empire."

Sonos gulped. It wasn't like *he* had set up these towers or personally brought her here, but he was a part of the legacy of the system. He couldn't argue that. He decided to take a softer response. "I share your sentiments about those horrid lessons."

Taimani's eyes narrowed, and she studied him, her expression unreadable. After a moment, she turned and opened a door to reveal a wooden, spiral staircase that ran through the center of the tower.

Taimani placed the torch into a slot on the circular brick wall. Each level was marked by two lighted torches. Sonos fought vertigo when he made the mistake of leaning over the wooden railing and looking upwards.

They walked up to the next level, and Taimani opened the door. A man in a matching brown robe stood just inside. He had a chiseled face and cleft chin, and his eyes opened wide when he looked at Sonos.

"Take the boy to the healer," Taimani instructed as if she ran the place. "He needs to be ready to travel as soon as possible. I'm taking these two to the chief."

"*Ioe, tase fa'aaloalo*," the man nodded and reached for the boy.

The servant boy moaned as Taine transferred him to the man. "Where am I?"

Taine rested a hand on the boy's head. "Somewhere safe, for now. Go brave, we'll see you soon."

Go brave? Sonos thought that was more applicable to them heading to the chief versus the boy getting healed. Alas.

"We must hurry," Taimani urged them along. "I'm sure it won't be long before *he's* missed." She used every opportunity to glare at Sonos.

They stopped at the third level. When Taimani opened the door, laughter and the smells of spiced meat washed into the stairwell. Taimani instructed a young man on watch by the door in their tongue, then led them further upstairs.

As they climbed, Taimani explained. "Everyone not on watch is at the feast, but the chief and his advisers will meet us upstairs immediately." She turned and gave a cut-eye towards her brother. "Since you decided to bring a *prince* down on us."

Sonos glanced at Taine, but his expression was stoic. Whatever Taine's motivation, he had been willing to stand up to his sister for Sonos.

They reached the end of the stairs, six floors if Sonos counted correctly, despite his swimming head. Once again, a robed man stood watch inside the door.

Taimani pulled him aside, speaking in soft tones. The man glanced at Sonos with a frown but quickly sprang into action. They drew thick curtains over the shuttered windows, then lit a series of torches to illuminate the room.

Taimani fixed a cover of sorts over a transmitter that was installed on the wall next to the door. *They're blocking the transmitter?* Sonos wondered how such a simplistic idea worked.

Taimani turned and a mischievous grin spread across her face, but she didn't say anything more, and got back to arranging the room.

She had just situated a cushioned chair on a small platform in the middle of the room, when a massive form burst through the door.

Taimani, Taine, and the other robed man immediately dropped to a knee and double-tapped a fist over their heart.

Sonos hesitated, not sure what to do. He had never bowed to anyone except the Emperor. At most, others were only allowed a nod of acknowledgment from the royal family. *But these are not normal circumstances*, he thought.

Sonos bowed formally from the waist to the chief.

A handful of others followed in the chief's wake, all in the same drab robes. The chief stopped before the chair and abruptly disrobed.

Sonos' face flushed, before realizing that the chief had on a tribal print wrap that covered the lower half of his body. His bare torso revealed tattoos that stretched over his whole chest, down his bulging biceps, up his neck, and over his upper back. He wore an intricate necklace made from several sharpened bones.

In a flash, everyone else wearing a robe stood and followed suit. The men all stood bare-chested in wraps, the women in shorter skirts and leather vests. Even Taine stripped off his shirt and sported his tattoos as well.

Sonos panicked, wondering whether he'd be expected to do the same.

Taine turned and gave the briefest shake of his head. He stretched out his arm towards Sonos, then dropped to one knee and spoke in a loud sing-song voice to the chief. "*Tupu fitafita sili, ua tatou oo mai i le filemu.*"

The chief sang back to him, "*O le fitafita ma le lototoa, matou te talia oe i totonu o lo matou fale. Matou te toe foi atu ia te outou i le filemu.*"

Taine stood and signaled for Sonos to join him before the chief. "We are received with peace. The chief will hear our request."

The chief spoke with a deep voice, his accent curling around his words. "We may speak in the common tongue for the sake of time. I cannot imagine a prince who goes missing from the feast will go unnoticed for long."

Taine cleared his throat. "O great one, it is well known what occurred last Feast Day when Prince Sonos' private musings were broadcast to the entire Empire."

Sonos cringed as Taine spoke, wondering if he would ever be seen beyond that event.

"He served a year-long forced and focused effort to re-indoctrinate the ways of the Empire into his mind and spirit." Taine paused and looked at his sister. "But like the honored warriors here in the tower, I can attest that these efforts were in vain."

A bit of pride swelled in Sonos' chest at Taine's defense of him. *The true nature of friendship is revealed in crisis*, his mother's voice rang in his head.

"In the efforts to save a servant boy from brutality, he opposed the Emperor's command and inadvertently took another servant's life. We now stand in defiance of the Crown and are seeking assistance for safe passage out of the capital."

The chief's face remained emotionless and unreadable, but Taimani raised an eyebrow and her mouth twitched upward.

Hopefully, we have at least one ally, Sonos thought.

The chief signaled and drew his advisers close for a council. Taimani walked over to stand on the other side of Taine.

"Directly defying the Emperor, himself? You two aim high." She grinned, the open hostility from earlier melting by the second.

Sonos scrunched his brow and ran a hand through his cropped hair. He didn't know what to think anymore. What if the chief decided to simply hand him over to his father?

"Nervous, Highness?" Taimani chuckled. "Don't tell me you're having regrets now?"

"A few minutes ago, I thought you wanted to shove me off the balcony, so I'm just trying to adjust to the... admiration?" Sonos kept his voice low as they spoke.

"Don't go so far. But if you oppose the Emperor, I acknowledge we're on the same side. So no, I won't throw you to your own wolves. And I imagine Chief will agree."

The advisers backed away from the chief and took their place behind him. "Step forward," he commanded Taine and Sonos.

Sonos followed Taine's lead, and they knelt before the chief.

"Taine O'lauo, you have brought great risk to the people of this tower—your people, your family—by bringing a fugitive royal before me." The chief narrowed his eyes and gave pause before continuing. "But you have both shown great courage in protecting the life of an innocent, especially an enslaved one with no hope for recourse. You defended principles of justice and honor, which are highly esteemed by Kimwaki."

Sonos breathed a sigh of relief. At least it didn't sound like he was about to be turned over summarily to the Imperial guards.

"My ruling is that we will extend the same kindness and protection to both of you in return. History—"

Whatever the chief was about to say was cut off by a distant clamor coming from the stairwell. Everyone sprung to their feet and donned their robes once more.

The chief stood and placed a hand on Taine's shoulder. "Taimani will lead you to the exit. You must take the boy as well, as the tower will most certainly be upturned in the search."

Taine bowed his head, and the chief extended his other hand to Sonos. "Live a life worthy of the honor that has been bestowed upon you. History may be written by those in power, but Truth always finds a way to remain." The chief and his advisors swept out of the room.

Taimani whistled from the door of the balcony, and Sonos' heart quickened. *Surely, they don't intend to take a rope down six stories,* he hoped.

Thankfully, the door was still closed, and she had opened a trapdoor in the floor. Her belt, or more accurately rope, was secured to a lever, and she indicated for Taine to go down first.

"Hopefully you go faster on the way down, Highness." Taimani's eyes gleamed, and she gave a lopsided smile.

Sonos gripped the rope and lowered his body, allowing his feet to slide and find leverage against a knot. He found the floor in quick order, and Taimani was right behind him. She had closed the trapdoor as soon as she was on the rope. From the floor, she flicked her wrist, and the rope disengaged and dropped.

They continued this pattern all the way to the second floor. They heard a commotion in the stairwell, but the floors were mercifully dark, at least the route Taimani led them through.

The last level they entered was a cramped closet. At least it was cramped given the number of people. The warrior with the cleft chin stood next to the young servant boy who was now awake and dressed in a fresh tunic, a brave smile on his face.

Sonos marveled at whatever the healer had done to help the boy get to this level of functionality so quickly.

The cleft-chin man opened another trapdoor, which opened to what looked like a dark tunnel. This time, Taimani went down first. Taine helped carry the boy and Sonos followed last.

By the time Sonos reached the floor of the tunnel, Taimani had lit a torch which she handed to Sonos.

"At every intersection, there are directions scratched in the walls. Follow the Old Tongue to get to the market. It will eventually lead to a wooden door. Use the same protocols I gave you."

Taine nodded.

"I wish I could take you myself, but we need to get upstairs for the headcount." She grasped Taine's forearms, and they touched foreheads. "*Alu ma le toa.*"

The rope jiggled, and Taimani scrambled back up through the hole in a matter of seconds. The torchlight reflected off her brown eyes and blue streak as she smiled one last time before closing the trapdoor.

"My mom is going to be so happy that you saved me, Highness. She's always said that you were different." The boy's smile broke the darkness of the tunnel as it reflected off the torchlight.

Sonos didn't have the heart to tell the boy he may never see his mom again.

It struck Sonos that *he* would likely never see his mother again either.

May he live a life worthy of the sacrifice, as the chief had said.

CHAPTER 8

"CHARLOTTE KING, YOU AND your family are found guilty of conspiring against the Empire. Come out now and face your judgment."

Charlotte peered out the window. With horror, she stared at the mass of guards assembled outside.

Moonlight glinted off their drawn weapons. Some held crossbows and rapiers, those were most likely the normal Imperial guards. The Elites, as Charlotte now recognized, held hooked swords that were charged with some kind of electricity giving off a blue hue.

Captain Die-*whatever* stood proudly, front and center. He faced the house and bellowed, using an amplifier for his voice.

"We have you surrounded," Captain Die continued. "Come out now and you will be shown a merciful death."

Smoke billowed along the ceiling; the sickening sound of the fire's crackle growing stronger.

Tears formed in Charlotte's eyes.

Why does he want my whole family? This is all my fault, putting them in danger like this. If only I hadn't taken the flyer-board out, or stormed away from Rapha... I would've made it back to the feast on time with Jax. The internal questions plagued her mind.

Gran locked eyes with Charlotte from where she stood opposite Jax at the other window. "Time to go. And not out the front door." She grabbed Jax's arm and motioned to the kitchen.

Dad took hold of Charlotte's hand and followed.

Charlotte wasn't sure how they would outrun the Empire long-term, but at least the cellar would buy them some time to think.

A loud *crash* sounded from the corner of the room, and Charlotte jumped. A piece of the ceiling had caved and now burned brightly. She coughed as smoke poured in.

Her dad squeezed her hand, bringing her focus back to their movement.

As they entered the kitchen, Gran was already down the ladder leading to the cellar.

Jax sat near the trapdoor, ready to help.

Charlotte paused to quickly wet some towels in the sink, trying to tune out Captain Die's voice which was getting louder and louder with warnings.

She scurried down the ladder behind her dad, and Jax pulled the trapdoor shut above them.

The cellar was cramped, gadgets and tools scattered all over the place. Half-finished projects lay in corners and on the lone table in the middle of the room. Mercifully, the dirt room was much cooler than upstairs.

Charlotte passed the wet towels around for everyone to cool and have some protection if the smoke started coming in.

"Are you sure they don't know about the tunnel that leads outside?" Dad asked while pacing the small room.

"We made sure to cover the trapdoor on the hillside and blend it in with the field. We're always careful to look around before stepping out. And until those Elites came today, no one seemed particularly interested in us... in me," Charlotte said, dropping her eyes to the floor.

Dad grunted and didn't push the matter further.

Charlotte plopped into a chair opposite Gran. The day had started off so brilliantly but could not have ended worse. Their home was literally burning down above them with Imperials waiting outside to kill them.

A soft humming sound emanated from above. Charlotte scanned the room, and Jax pointed towards the trapdoor that led to the kitchen. Rapha stood at the top of the ladder, a hand placed on the trapdoor, and... *hummed?*

"He's creating a seal of sorts—I think," Jax said in a half-curious, half-sure tone.

"How do you know?" Charlotte asked.

"I see things kind of differently since he breathed on me in the samaan tree. I'm not sure how, exactly. But I just *know* some of what Rapha is doing, and what's happening."

"You have a connection to the unseen realm." Gran leaned forward in her chair.

"Rapha said something along those lines. About an unseen realm," Charlotte said, the terror from upstairs temporarily squelched by curiosity with Rapha. "You *see* something, Jax? How's it work?" It still smarted that Jax had chosen Rapha over her, but now was not the time for grudges.

"Not exactly," Jax said.

Rapha swung down the ladder and jumped into Charlotte's lap. Why was this monkey so focused on her when it was Jax who had stayed behind?

"You guys were at a samaan tree earlier?" Charlotte's dad joined them at the table. "Where exactly were you?"

"First things first," Gran stood. "Rapha has helped create a barrier between us and the fire for now. Jax, run and go find those Freedom boys. About time to put some of that training into action."

Jax nodded. He gave one brief look to Charlotte, then scurried through the small tunnel that would lead to the forest.

As soon as he was gone, Gran turned to Charlotte. "Explain what happened, quickly."

Charlotte gulped. "We got the flyer-board to work. The monkey stole my gazer in the forest. We chased him to a magical grove of cannonball trees, which led to a samaan tree that had this hollow in its trunk which turned out to be a library—well, actually a temporal portal."

Gran leaned in further, her gaze not leaving Charlotte.

Charlotte continued. "Turns out, Rapha can speak. He told us about *El*, we found some really old texts. He said we have to save the Mountain Kingdom. But I told him I had to save my sisters first and ran out. Jax stayed behind, and Rapha breathed on him... or something. I'm not entirely sure."

There was a moment of silence, then the questions flowed.

"The monkey can talk?"

"A magical grove?"

"What about the Mountain Kingdom?"

"A library?"

Charlotte bent down to look Rapha in eyes where he now perched on the table. "Now would be a good time for you to speak up, Raph." But the monkey just grunted in response.

A thread of anger snapped in Charlotte, similar to what she felt in the portal. "You know what? This whole day went to crap because of this monkey. As I said before, I have sisters to save. He and Jax can go save the Mountain Kingdom if they want."

Charlotte stormed over to a corner of the cellar and picked up the flyer-board, pulling the broken sun collector from the cloth.

After a few minutes, her dad came and sat beside her.

Charlotte wiped her eyes. It was time for focus, not emotion.

"Char," he began and cleared his throat. "You know I'd give anything to have Ava and Lily back. To have mom..." He paused and closed his eyes.

She knew. Her shoulders sagged. "I'm so sorry, Dad. I thought I could still make the plan work. Get to the Underground in Portemore. But now... it's just all wrong." The tears were flowing freely.

"I think," Gran said softly from behind her, easing her slim form to the ground on Charlotte's other side, "that it's less about what we thought the plan was or what happened with the sun collector, and more about where things are heading for the future."

Rapha scurried into Gran's lap.

Her dad wrapped his arms around her and Gran.

Chaos swirled around them, death was at their door, but Charlotte savored this brief moment of love and protection.

"Sometimes," Gran continued, "we can have the best well-laid plans, but *El* knows the end from the beginning, and if he's in this thing, you're not going to fail, Char. If Rapha said the Mountain Kingdom will help you save your sisters, I believe him."

Rapha hummed from where he sat in Gran's lap.

Charlotte's eyes fixated on Gran, jaw slack.

"You're a follower of *El?*" Her dad asked the question on Charlotte's mind.

Gran's eyes softened. "There are so many times I wanted to tell you all. I'm sorry. Even before the Emperor invaded, the ruler of Salan tried to pacify the Emperor. He made it punishable by death to worship or follow any other gods, some of us sought refuge in the Mountain Kingdom. Your mother and I chose this village instead." She squeezed Charlotte's hand.

She then turned her gaze to Rapha. "And I'm sorry for not being brave enough to tell anyone before."

Rapha grunted and patted Gran's hand.

Jax climbed back into the cellar, his clothes smelling faintly of smoke. "The team is gathering. We'll meet them in the forest in twenty minutes."

"The guards?" Charlotte's dad asked.

"The house is still burning. They seem to be waiting for things to cool down before coming in." Jax frowned.

"We're running out of time," Gran said, snapping back to her normal vim and vigor self. "Charlotte, you said you and Jax found ancient texts when you were with Rapha?"

Charlotte nodded. Gran's surety and focus were contagious. She tapped her gazer until she found the recording of Jax reading from the scroll. She set it in the middle of the floor and projected the video for everyone to see.

Jax's voice on the recording filled the cellar. "*This is written for a future hero of El. Open your eyes! The one who created the world from nothing is doing something new. Are you seeing it? It's springing forth even now. He causes a river to flow in the badlands. What is impossible for him?*"

When it finished playing, Gran narrowed her eyes at Rapha. "Are you sure he can't talk anymore?"

Rapha grunted and crossed his arms, then jumped down to poke around at some of Charlotte's projects in another corner of the cellar.

"What do you think it means?" Charlotte asked.

"I'm not entirely sure," Gran said. "The words could be a metaphor for unexpected help, or it could be a literal prophecy—especially if you find yourself in some badlands, I suppose."

Her dad scratched the back of his head. "At the feast, the Emperor declared open war on the Mountain Kingdom. The Badlands sit between the Pergamum and the mountains."

Time was ticking and the cellar was starting to feel warm. "Okay, we can figure out all the pieces later. But it's time to agree on what we're doing first. Either the Mountain Kingdom or the twins." Charlotte said, her mind turning. She still thought Ava and Lily would be best suited to save the Mountain Kingdom, but that was an argument no one was listening to... at least not Rapha.

"I don't think it has to be an *or*," Gran said gently. "It's an *and*, but the order is important."

"Okay, fine. Assume I agree to do the Mountain Kingdom first. How do we even get off Jamroq with the Imperials hunting us?" Charlotte asked.

"I still have a few fisher-friends who knew my parents," Jax offered. "I'm sure I can get passage for Char and me to at least get to Salan."

Dad's face twisted in agony.

Charlotte knew how painful thoughts of the sea were—for all of them—but what choice did they have?

The closest neighbor-island was a few hours by a large ferry, it would probably take all night in a small fishing vessel.

"And then what after Salan? Do you have any idea how you'll get to Portemore on the mainland? Or how to locate the Underground Network to move beyond there?" Her dad asked the questions, his voice taut. "We should all go together."

"I think this mission is specifically for these two who got the calling from *El*," Gran said. "Once the Freedom boys can get us to Kinstun, I can find us hiding until things blow over."

"You mean until Captain Die leaves in *pursuit* of Char and Jax?" Her dad's voice raised.

"Surely you didn't think that standing up against the Empire was going to be a dance through a field of wildflowers?" Gran stood, hands on her hips, her fiery gaze locked on Dad. "No matter what, there was always going to be an Imperial or an informer working against us. At least now, we know who the hunter is."

"And that makes it better? The head of the Elites putting a target on us? On Char? I will not allow it." Her dad's voice spilled over with everything he had tried to keep bottled up for the last three years.

Charlotte was amazed at the emotions that finally surfaced after so long. Strangely, it stirred something in her heart knowing that all was not lost. Her dad still cared, he still had spirit inside of him, and most importantly, he was not broken.

Gran was unfazed by Dad's argument. "This path may not be of our choosing, but *El* is in it, so fight we must." She paused and shifted her gaze to Rapha. "But win we shall."

The words carried weight and seemed to drop something like physical resolve in Charlotte's spirit. She took a breath, her heart pounding.

"I'll do it," Charlotte spoke up. "I'll go with you." She looked at Jax and Rapha.

"No," her dad stammered, words unsure. "Not alone."

"Not alone," Charlotte said. "Jax and I are both officially adults, in case you forgot that I turned sixteen last week." She was proud of her steady voice despite her racing pulse. "We can use some of this tech to help pay for passage, and I'll take the flyer-board with me, as planned, to Portemore. It still must be worth something, even with the broken sun-collector. We'll just have to make sure it's enough."

"I swear to protect Char with my life," Jax stood and grabbed Charlotte's hand. "We will find our way to Portemore, save the Mountain Kingdom, then get Ava and Lily back."

"Mountain Kingdom first, then the Legacy Towers," Charlotte repeated.

Rapha squeaked, and ran up to perch himself on Charlotte's shoulder.

Gran grabbed her other hand, and they all faced her dad.

Her dad sighed. "May your mother forgive me if anything happens to you. But how can I withstand all of you in agreement?" His eyes finally softened. "But you must promise to come back to me. No matter what."

"No matter what." Charlotte stepped forward and gave him a tight embrace.

She glanced towards the trapdoor. The fire had to be dying down. Now that the plan was decided, they needed to move.

"Wait, you need the breath first, Char," Jax said. "I think it's how I got out of the forest on time earlier. It gives Raph, or *El*, I guess, access to work with us in a closer, different way."

Charlotte closed her eyes and nodded. Something told her this was an all-or-nothing decision. No halfway commitment. And for her part, no more overthinking things. At some point, she just needed to decide to trust what was in front of her.

She walked over to the table.

Rapha waved her closer, and when she stood mere inches from him, he touched her temples with his tiny hands, inhaled then blew out directly into her face.

"What in the—" Charlotte recoiled, confused.

But instead of foul animal breath, a cool, refreshing mist covered her head. Sweet scents of jasmine invaded her nostrils, and an overwhelming sense of peace and stillness settled in her heart.

When the mist cleared, Charlotte rubbed her eyes. Aside from the initial sensation, there didn't seem to be any lasting physical changes.

"Did it work?" Charlotte asked, looking at Rapha then to Jax.

"I'm no expert, but at least for me, the changes have been subtle. So don't panic if you're not feeling anything major," Jax assured her.

A thud sounded against the trapdoor in the ceiling.

"Time to go," Charlotte said. She glanced at her dad and Gran. She would return with her sisters. She wouldn't fail her family.

"One last thing," Gran turned to Charlotte and Jax. "Out there, don't always believe what you see with your eyes. You have to see *beyond.* Rapha will help, but for every choice, the two of you need to come to an agreement. Use each other's strengths, learn from any mistakes, and most importantly, keep moving forward."

She then crawled into the tunnel, followed by Charlotte's dad.

Rapha pulled two packs across the floor towards Charlotte.

Without thinking, Charlotte strapped the smaller one across her chest and tossed the second, bigger pack to Jax.

She reached for the flyer-board, wrapped it in a blanket, and strapped it to her back. It had to be worth something, surely.

"Hurry," Jax crouched in the entrance of the tunnel.

Charlotte took a last glance around the cellar, the last of her home. *Forward ever*—the thought settled on her heart. She looked at Rapha, who winked, then turned and scampered down the tunnel.

"Forward ever," she repeated aloud, giving a hopeful smile at Jax before crawling into the damp darkness.

CHAPTER 9

— · —

TAINE HELD THE TORCH close to the dirt wall of the intersection. Large stones sporadically lined the walls of the tunnel. Taine studied one that held the instructions which Taimani had promised would guide them to the market.

Outside of the torchlight, the tunnel was pitch black and eerily silent. Even their footsteps were muted on the damp earthen floor.

Sonos wasn't sure if he was glad they hadn't run into anyone else, or worried. Perhaps all the tower residents—prisoners, rather—were experiencing the same shakedown and headcount in the attempt to find *him*. He shivered, the dampness of the tunnel seeping through his thin, formal tunic.

"I'm trying to figure out how far we've come. You'd agree we've been down here about an hour?" Taine asked.

"It feels like we've been walking all night." Sibi, the young servant boy, sat on the floor of the tunnel, resting as he had been at each intersection.

Whatever medicine the Kimwaki healer gave the boy had worked wonders, but he still needed a lot of rest. He had a petite form, even for a ten-year-old, but what he lacked in size, the boy made up for in spunk. One thing that never tired was Sibi's mouth. Once he had introduced himself, his high-pitched nasal accent had filled the tunnels almost non-stop.

"Five-thousand eight-hundred and two steps, so just under three miles," Sonos answered Taine's question.

Sibi's mouth dropped open.

Even Taine raised an eyebrow.

"What? Focusing on details like steps helps keep me calm." Sonos shrugged. "Plus, we know exactly how far we've gone." He grinned.

"Hmm. I knew you had an eye for detail, but I clearly underestimated how much," Taine said.

"It seems we both have much to learn about each other." Sonos couldn't resist the retort.

Taine inclined his head but didn't argue. He focused back on the task at hand. "My best guess is we should reach the market area in about two more miles. But these tunnels test the limits of my sense of direction." Taine looked at the markings one more time, then held out a hand to Sibi. "Let's keep going."

Sonos was still flabbergasted at the extent of this whole tunnel system. The tunnel was wide enough for two persons abreast, and Sonos could walk upright. Taine had to bend his shoulders most of the way, but the tunnel was still at least six feet tall.

Taine held the torch and led in front, setting a quick pace forward. Sonos and Sibi walked side by side.

Sibi eventually fell silent, and Sonos guessed the medicine was beginning to wear off. They'd have to find somewhere safe for the boy as he was a growing liability.

Taine allowed Sibi to ride on his back so they wouldn't slow.

The dark and monotonous environment provided an unwanted space for Sonos' thoughts. He kept having flashbacks of the pool of blood around the servant's head and the eyes that went lifeless in an instant. *How had it happened,* he wondered.

He deliberately tried to focus his mind on something else. Taine's earlier words echoed: *Open your eyes and see.* It reminded

Sonos of a line he had written in his journal: *A travesty that for all who have eyes, so few can see.*

It was as if they were both referring to a realm or something beyond what could be seen with his natural eyes.

Sonos thought again about the flashing light from the Salan Tower during the feast, which no one else seemed to notice. He considered Taimani, the Chief and other captives who held onto their way of life, even in oppression.

One thing was clear, they were venturing into a world that was more connected and different than he could have ever imagined.

They had just crossed eight-thousand steps when the tunnel ended abruptly into dirt stairs that led to a large wooden door.

Sibi collapsed on the bottom step. "Finally!"

"Where do you think this actually leads?" Sonos asked, pressing his ear against the door, but hearing nothing.

"Only one way to find out." Taine pushed the buzzer following the same pattern he used on the shutters at the tower.

Silence.

A few minutes later Taine tried the same pattern again.

"What if no one comes? What if the buzzer is broken?" Sonos plopped down next to Sibi who was already snoring on the bottom step. "Do you think we can break in somehow?" But the door was made of solid hardwood, and there were no visible handles or hinges.

"Someone will come. Give it time." Taine leaned against the door and ran a hand over his hooked sword.

Eventually, a scraping sound came through from the other side, and Sonos jumped to his feet.

The door slid open, and a young boy who looked a few years older than Sibi poked his head through. He had dark hair that tumbled down to his eyes and looked as if he'd been pulled from a deep sleep.

"Kimwaki, right?"

"Yes," Taine said, stepping forward.

"Come in," the boy instructed, fighting a big yawn.

Taine leaned in close to Sonos. "Keep your eyes downcast and don't say a word. With any luck, we'll be able to hide your identity for a bit."

They stepped through the doorway and into a fully stocked pantry. Shelves lined the walls with canned goods and spices. Barrels covered the floor, and dried meats hung from the ceiling.

The young boy slid the door back into place, which fit perfectly into the wall acting as a hidden panel.

What secrets this city holds, Sonos thought, watching the mechanisms of the door.

"My name's Lee," said their young host. "Follow me, and please don't make any noise."

Sibi let out a huge yawn, matching Lee's first greeting. "I hope you're leading us to a nice, warm bed."

Lee led them through a large, empty kitchen and up two flights of stairs through a back stairwell.

Sonos guessed they were in some kind of inn. Given the emptiness of the place, it must be well past midnight. They walked to the end of a hallway, and Lee opened the door to a small room. He set the candle on a table by the barred window. Two beds took up most of the space, and there was barely enough room for them to all stand.

"You'll see the master as soon as he's done with his meeting, but for now, you can wash and rest. Please don't leave the room for any reason, not until you've talked to Master."

Lee exited, and as the door clicked shut, the room filled with snoring. Sibi was curled up in one of the two small beds.

Taine let out a chuckle, a relieving sound after the tenseness of the entire day and night. "Our little pup is clearly tired. Let us get some rest too, while we can."

Sonos sat on the other bed and took off his boots. His white tunic which had been crisp and clean before the feast was now stained with dust and sweat. He washed his face in the small basin in the corner. He took off his shirt and pulled out his journal from where it had uncomfortably been tucked the entire night. The palace already felt a world away.

Taine blew out the candle, then used the base to set an alarm by the door. He slunk down in the chair. "Get some rest, Sonos. I know you would love to stay up trying to figure things out, but we won't know more until we meet this master. On the run, you need to get sleep when you can. I'll hear if anyone or anything tries to enter."

Sonos conceded and dropped into the bed. Despite his own exhaustion, sleep did not come easy. His mind replayed the day—from the hope and freshness of the morning, to last hours spent traversing the dark tunnels.

The memory of Sibi being beaten with the bull-pistle whip. Blood everywhere. Sonos squeezed his eyes shut, wishing he could close his mind as easily.

A particularly guttural snore from Sibi interrupted his thoughts bringing him back to the present. Sonos smiled. Somehow the very normal sound brought comfort, and Sonos finally drifted off.

The door creaked open, and the floorboards rumbled as Taine moved with lightning reflexives.

Sonos gasped, sitting up in a cold sweat. He had been dreaming of his father forcing his head into a noose. His mother had been screaming nearby, even as Ade had helped their father to restrain him.

He steadied his breathing, focusing on Taine.

Taine stood poised with his sword in hand, ready to take on any intruder.

"Whoa there, warrior." Lee held out his hands as he stepped into the room.

Sonos squinted towards the window, his head fuzzy. It was still dark outside and, based on how tired he was, they hadn't slept very long.

"Master is ready and wants to see you immediately," Lee said.

Taine nudged Sibi, who was still sleeping soundly. The boy stretched, then immediately cried out in pain and reached to touch his back. The medicine must have worn off even more.

"Come quickly, please," Lee said, watching Sonos carefully.

Taine strapped on his sword, and Sonos grabbed his journal, throwing his dirty tunic back over his head.

Taine helped Sibi along as they followed Lee back down the steps.

"Do you find Lee is looking at me strangely?" Sonos whispered to Taine.

Taine raised an eyebrow. "How so?"

"I noticed deference towards me that wasn't there last night. Do you think he knows who I am? Is this a trap?"

"Possibly, but I don't see what choice we have." Taine shrugged.

They reached the bottom of the steps, and the sounds of pots clanging spilled through the kitchen. There were no smells of food yet, confirming the early hour.

Instead of taking them back through the kitchen, Lee took them down a narrow, dimly lit hallway. There were no doors or rooms leading off the hallway. Sonos guessed this was a hidden section of the inn, not one traversed by normal customers. *Then again, it's not like I've ever been in an inn or tavern myself before,* Sonos thought. He was forced, once again, to face his ignorance and lack of experience.

The door at the end of the hallway stood halfway open, and Lee led them inside.

Two beefy men sat at a table playing cards, but they barely glanced at the game. There was nothing casual about the way their sharp eyes took in the details of everyone who entered.

"Leave the sword in the corner and any other weapons," one said in a deep baritone.

Taine hesitated.

Sonos knew his bodyguard was strong in hand-to-hand fighting, but leaving the sword was surely a risk.

The other guard stood up, placing his cards on the table and faced Taine. He made no fast or offensive movement, but his gaze was clear. "Is there a problem?"

"No." Taine unstrapped his weapon and rested in a corner.

Lee went to the far wall of the room and pushed an intricate pattern into the wood at varying heights. A lever released, and Lee opened another hidden door. This one led to a staircase which they followed into a large underground room.

Torches mounted on the walls made the room bright. Sonos couldn't help but marvel at the shelves packed full of books. It was an impressive collection.

In the far corner, a small table held beakers and liquids set up in the same fashion Sah Timur used in their lessons years ago.

"Master," Lee addressed a figure sitting behind a desk stacked high with papers.

The master grunted, keeping his head down and focused on the paper he was reading. *Something is very familiar about this guy*, Sonos thought.

When the master looked up a few moments later, Sonos sucked in his breath. "Sah Timur?"

His former tutor looked to have aged a decade over the last year with dark circles under his eyes, sunken cheeks, and pallid skin that made Sonos wonder if he ever left this basement.

Timur's eyes registered none of the shock that Sonos felt. Had they been expected then? That would explain Lee's odd looks earlier.

"Mani?" Taine asked from behind.

Taimani strode forward from where she had been leaning against the back wall. "Brother." She bowed her head towards Taine and went to stand next to Timur.

She was dressed in form-fitting leather pants and high boots, with a soft tunic embroidered with colorful flowers. The blue paint had been cleaned from her face, but she still wore dark liner around her eyes, and her hair was pulled into two braids, which accentuated the intricate tattoos on her neck.

Timur made a guttural sound in his throat and thumped his palm on the desk.

Lee ran forward with a chalkboard in hand, and Timur began writing, holding the chalk between two fingers.

Sonos cringed at the missing thumbs and tongue. Even if he was angry at Timur for exposing him, Sonos couldn't agree that the most brilliant scientist in the Sahemy deserved this.

The chalk-markings were fast and furious shorthand. Lee started to translate, "Things are worse than you think."

Timur erased the board with the sleeve of his robe and began again.

"Taimani will explain," Lee read.

Taimani cleared her throat. "Our Chief is set to betray you."

"What?" Sonos and Taine both said at the same time.

Sibi squeaked and sank down to the floor

"It's a matter of using this... opportunity to find favor from the Emperor. A bargaining chip, as some would say," Taimani said, arms crossed.

"You assume my father would consider me valuable enough," Sonos replied.

"Even if not from love, from pride. The Emperor would surely reward anyone who brought the crown prince back safely." Taimani kept her voice level.

Taine scoffed and started pacing behind Sonos.

Sonos ran a hand through his hair. "But why tell us this now?"

"Because betraying you would jeopardize my brother. The Chief would be forced to have Taine punished publicly for failing his duty. Or if he was returned to the palace with you, I can only imagine what the Emperor might do to him."

Taimani was right.

"How much time do we have?" Taine jumped straight to the point.

"I snuck out as soon as I realized what they were planning. You know how long advisers can argue over details. And no one is faster than me in the tunnels. But all said, only a couple hours head start."

"They'll know you tipped us off," Taine said, holding his sister's gaze.

"Which is why I'm coming with you."

Taine's eyes narrowed, and he grabbed his sister's forearm and pulled her over to a corner where they spoke in their rapid sing-song tongue.

Timur scratched on his board again, and Lee translated. "Master has arranged to get all four of you passage on a river vessel to Portemore."

"All four of us?" Sonos asked.

Lee pointed to Sibi.

"Surely Timur can find hiding for him here?" Sonos didn't like the idea of so many joining him on the run.

Lee read from Timur's board. "The city will be crawling very soon, looking for any clues. Master will make arrangements for the boy to return to Salan from Portemore."

"Salan?" Sibi's eyes lit up. "I've always wanted to see Mama's home."

"And what about us?" Sonos asked.

Timur scratched again. "The less anyone knows, including Master, the better. He'll provide a contact in Portemore who will give whatever resources you need, but you will need to decide your path."

Lee read the last set of scratching, then ran to pick up two packs that were sitting against the wall. "Change quickly, as you must meet the market cart."

Taine and Taimani rejoined the group, and Lee tossed Taine a fresh pair of clothes. The leather pants and linen tunic were similar to what Taimani wore already, minus the feminine flowers. They were also given dark green, hooded cloaks made of remarkably light material.

Taine's eyes sparked, and his mouth was pulled into a tight line, while Taimani was smiling. It was clear who won their argument.

Timur walked to a bookshelf in the far corner of the room and returned with a handful of folded papers. He handed them to Sonos and patted him on the hand.

Sonos opened one to reveal a detailed map of Pergamum. Glancing at the papers, he saw varying levels of scale and detail of the whole K'Luma Empire. He was grateful and tucked the papers into his journal.

But something wouldn't quiet in his spirit. "Sah... I mean, Master Timur. Thank you for all you're doing, but I just need to know. Was it really you last year? You hacked my gazer and put those entries out there for the world to see?"

Timur's eyes softened, and his shoulders fell.

Sonos' stomach dropped. A part of him had hoped there was some big misunderstanding and that his tutor hadn't been the one to betray him.

Timur picked up the paper that he had been looking at when they entered the basement. With the help of Lee, he folded and put it into an envelope, scratching something on the outside. Timur held the envelope out to Sonos.

A buzzer sounded from a small, box-like mechanism on the wall. By this time, Sonos recognized the pattern for the Kimwaki protocols.

Taimani flushed like a warrior about to head into battle. "They're here."

Sonos took the envelope and tucked it, along with the maps, into his journal. He glanced at what Timur had written on the outside.

The Truth is always worth fighting for.

Chapter 10

"**I** DON'T SEE ANYONE." Charlotte tried to keep her voice to the lowest possible whisper as she squinted in the pale moonlight.

She and Jax lay flat on their stomachs on the hillside behind her home. Well, what was left of her home. A section of the house was still burning, and the air was choked thick with lingering smoke.

Anger and deep sadness competed inside of Charlotte's heart as the finality of the loss sunk in.

Jax tapped her arm and pointed to where a pair of guards walked around the corner of the house. A faint charge sparked from their special hooked swords, which Charlotte was quickly learning to identify. They were Elites.

Charlotte's pulse quickened.

Moonlight reflected off their weapons as they turned the corner on the other side of the house.

Whew.

Jax slid back down. "Coast is clear for now," he confirmed to her dad and Gran who were waiting prone nearby.

The forest was not far off, but the open field between the hillside and the trees seemed to stretch for an eternity. All it would take is one glance of the Imperials seeing them cross, and it would be over in a heartbeat.

"We need to keep low and out sight as we cross," Jax said. He dropped to his belly to demonstrate. He propped himself on his forearms and alternated his opposite knee and elbow to propel himself forward.

The training with the Freedom Fighters had clearly been put to some good use.

Charlotte knelt and adjusted the pack and wrapped flyer-board on her back.

As they moved out, Rapha kept close to Charlotte and Gran, Jax led the way in front, and her dad covered their back.

It was slow work, but every time Charlotte wanted to grumble, she stole a glance at Gran. Her frail form must have been un-comfortable belly-crawling through a field. But Gran crawled with determination, her eyes fixed ahead.

The trees grew closer with every pull of the elbows and push of the legs.

This may just work... Charlotte thought. She was so focused on the rhythm of the crawl that she didn't realize Jax had stopped in front of her. She collided face-first with his boot. She almost cried out, but the sound of two Imperials on the hillside froze her in place.

The guards chatted casually, not as ones in pursuit. "Things are going to change around here if that Cap' stays."

"Nah, he's just here to find that threat against the Emperor, like he said."

What are they doing? Charlotte wondered, turning her head with as little movement as possible.

"Hope tonight takes care of it, even though I don't see how that mish-mash family could possibly pose a threat to the Emperor."

Two guards with the old-time spears stood relaxed, facing the forest, and—*Oh!* Charlotte turned her head back in embarrassment, they were relieving themselves. She crinkled her nose as the scent of their urine wafted over.

"Don't underestimate angry and desperate people. I was stationed in Kimwaki shortly after that island was conquered. Even after they lost so much, they never stopped finding ways to rebel. Not looking for that amount of work here."

Charlotte was sure they would hear her heart beating out of her chest. *Please, just finish and leave*, she pleaded silently.

Finally, their voices dropped as they walked back towards the house.

Jax started crawling again, faster than before, but this time Charlotte had no trouble keeping up thanks to the adrenaline coursing through her veins. She didn't bother to wipe the dirt that kicked up into her face. It was all she could do to keep from jumping up and running the rest of the distance.

As soon as she reached the first tree, Charlotte scooted a little further in, then ran and hugged one of the trunks in relief. Her dad and Gran weren't far behind.

"One step at a time, we'll get through this," Charlotte whispered under her breath.

Rapha squeaked as a shadow moved behind one of the trees. No, not *a* shadow. Many shadows.

Charlotte covered her mouth to keep from crying out and backed up to Jax who stood close by.

Jax placed a calm hand on her shoulder.

"Hey, it's just us," a deep voice spoke with the familiar Jamroq clip.

Charlotte let out a breath and forced her shoulders to relax. She now placed the voice to Zeek, a boy who was a little older than Jax.

They walked deeper into the forest and away from the house.

Charlotte counted about ten other faces. She couldn't place every name, but everyone was familiar from the village. "I didn't realize there were so many of you learning to fight," she said.

"We all wanted to help," Zeek said. "I regret we didn't do it sooner at the feast."

Gran made a show of dusting off her clothes and linked her arm through Zeek's. "They would have retaliated even harsher if you had tried. Everything has a time, and I'm glad you're here now."

Zeek bowed his head respectfully. "We have a safe place for each of you to hide out until things blow over and we can get you further afoot. Even the monkey, if you want."

Rapha had perched himself on Charlotte's shoulder.

"About that," Jax spoke up, "Char and I are taking a different path. We need to get down to Robby's place."

Zeek raised an eyebrow but didn't ask for any details. "Respect. We'll help to cover any tracks and ensure that those Imperials can't find two footsteps to match."

Charlotte glanced at her dad and Gran. It was really happening. This was goodbye.

Her dad seemed to have the same hesitation. He stretched one arm to Charlotte and the other to Gran and pulled them both in for a group hug. Jax stepped forward and encircled Charlotte and Gran from the other side. Even Rapha snuggled in close. No one said anything for a few moments and Charlotte attuned herself to her family's strength.

"This isn't goodbye." Gran wriggled a hand free and lifted Charlotte's chin. Her unflinching green eyes that matched Charlotte's own, sparked.

"You can do this, Char." Her dad spoke with all their faces close together. "It may not be the way we planned, but it's the way that's before us. Be brave. You and Jax stick together with that monkey."

Rapha hummed.

"And most importantly, you come back to us. You hear?" he added.

"I will. With Ava and Lily."

Zeek stepped closer. "Sir?"

Her dad nodded, letting Charlotte go and keeping his arm around Gran.

Charlotte put on a brave smile, then strapped the flyer-board and pack on her back.

Jax adjusted his sleeves and the *Freedom* he drew the previous night showed proudly on his dark skin. "See you soon." He bowed his head to her dad, and Gran then led Charlotte deeper into the forest with four of the fighters.

They walked in silence, heading towards the sea. It wasn't far, only a couple of miles to reach the fishing pavilion where Robby was based.

In normal circumstances, Charlotte would have been consulting the map on her gazer. Tonight, she simply followed the others, allowing her mind to chew over what they would do when they got to Portemore on the mainland. She had to find that underground network somehow.

The sound of the waves grew louder. It wasn't long before they stopped at the edge of a clearing, the blackness of the sea ahead of them, and a small smattering of open-air huts on the sand.

Charlotte took a deep breath of the saltwater air, trying to clear the last remnants of the smoke from her nostrils.

"Thanks for everything," Jax told his friend. They clasped hands, and the others turned to go.

"Walk good, my brother," the fighter offered Jax the colloquial salutation for 'good luck'. "We have your back on this side and will keep the family safe." He gave a nod to Charlotte and disappeared back into the trees.

Charlotte was thankful for the tightness of their community. There was not a thread of doubt that the band of fighters, as well as any other villager, would do everything possible to protect and care for her dad and Gran.

"Come, let's hope Robby keeps up his routine even after the big feast." Jax led the way across the dirt track and into the sand.

The smell of the sea and the soft crashing of the waves filled Charlotte with calm. The rhythm was like a steady beat from the earth, from something bigger than the circumstances they faced.

The moon was low in the sky, and she guessed they had less than an hour before sunrise.

A lone figure shuffled about in one of the open-air huts, slow and deliberate. His movements were framed by a small lantern, reflecting off his muscled, brown, bare chest and long dreadlocks.

"Robby!" Jax called out.

Robby's white teeth gleamed as he waved them both closer. "Jax. Charly. And, uh, Monkey Fella." He nodded at each in turn.

Charlotte smiled at the fisherman's nickname for everyone, including her. She leaned against one of the wooden posts, letting Jax take the lead.

"We need some help." Jax got straight to the point.

"Aye. Saw you both got yerselves into some spotlight with the big, fancy Cap' at the feast." Robby's gaze lingered on Jax's arm. "And I see you still keeping the Freedom mark though, eh?"

"Some things are worth fighting for," Jax replied.

"Mmm." Robby nodded. "Done know," he offered his agreement.

"Robs, we don't have much time. Can you get us to Salan?" Jax asked.

Robby looked up and cocked his head, eyebrows raised. "Why I feel you pullin' me into yer trouble? I'm guessing that big fire that was blazing earlier is connected to you, too?"

Jax nodded. "I wish we had more time or another way. But we have neither." Jax spread his hands open. "And honestly, the less you know, is probably for the better. But we need to get off of Jamroq, tonight."

Robby stared out at the black ocean for some time. Charlotte worried about what would happen if Robby refused to help. There weren't many options.

"Your parents saved me, you know?" Robby asked, still staring at the ocean. "They were good people. Knew the sea like nobody's business. Pulled me outta trouble in the city and taught me to fish."

"I know." Jax walked over to stand next to Robby. "They talked about you with a lot of pride. 'No one's lionfish tastes like Robby's,' they used to tell everyone."

Robby turned his head and smiled at Jax. "I'll take yuh and the young gal to Salan. I owe it to them to help their blood."

Charlotte breathed a sigh of relief. *One step at a time*, she repeated in her mind.

In short order, they helped carry Robby's fishing supplies to the small sailboat and pushed off into the pre-dawn waters. They paddled out first, and Robby explained they'd open the sails later when they were out of sight.

There were two small benches on the boat. One in front of the mast, which Charlotte sat on with Rapha curled in her lap.

After ensuring Robby was okay, Jax came and squeezed in next to Charlotte.

Whether he said anything as he sat down, Charlotte wasn't sure. Her mind was swimming, and fatigue had officially set in. She laid a head on his shoulder and fell fast asleep against the surety of his form and presence.

CHAPTER 11

CAPTAIN DIEKOLOLAOLUWA PACED THE tiny office in the run-down headquarters for the Imperials in Mina. No bodies had been found at the house.

He had stayed until after the sun rose, insisting on looking himself. Bones don't just *disappear*. He still couldn't believe that the family hadn't come running out when the house was set on fire. It made no sense.

The decision to kill the family brought him no joy, but after hearing Charlotte's desperation to rescue her sisters, he knew that the family could not be allowed to live. Desperation that is left to fester turns into rebellion quicker than a wildfire.

Die had watched that with his own people in Kimwaki, and neither hope nor rebellion could be allowed to grow. It was futile. The only way to survive was to become a part of the system.

What other choice did we have? Charlotte had asked that question during the interrogation when he had prodded why the mother and her remaining family seemed intent on saving the twins. Well, this was his choice: survival.

He cleared his throat and pulled back his shoulders. He was due for his daily check-in with General Baku, head of all Imperial guards, including the squadron of Elites that Die led. He sighed and tapped his gazer, initiating the call.

As he waited for the connection, he removed the gazer from his wrist and set it in the middle of the table. Soon enough, the holographic image of General Baku projected upwards from the gazer, his lanky form as stiff as it would be in person. Baku held his hands behind his back and looked directly at Die.

"Captain." Baku nodded in acknowledgment. Even through the hologram, the general's sunken eyes seemed to miss no detail. "Did you find the rebels?"

This was the balancing game. He needed to give only the right amount of information required.

"There is a strong lead. A family with a connection to *El*, just as the sorcerer divined."

"Your instincts are usually reliable, even if unconventional. Tell me, now that we are alone, why *did* you pick the backwater island of Jamroq to search for the threat against the Emperor, may he live forever?"

When a sorcerer had warned of a threat to the Emperor's conquest of the Mountain Kingdom, another captain had immediately insisted on leading a force of Elites to Kimwaki, a logical choice if one was looking for strength alone.

"I have never known Kimwaki to harbor followers of *El*." Die resisted the urge to adjust his collar, which still bore the tattoos he had taken as a young man. "Plus, Jamroq has only been part of the K'Luma Empire for one generation. There would be elders who remember unchecked independence and those growing up who may want it for themselves. A perfect storm."

"I see. Perhaps a stronger hand is needed there, even after the threat is quelled."

Die's ambitions lay in the heart of Pergamum, not another island. But now was not the time to argue. "I trust you will treat with Jamroq as needed, General. But for now, all efforts will be focused on the immediate threat."

"Indeed. I look forward to questioning them myself as well. So please ensure they are kept alive... enough."

Die inwardly shuddered at the glint in Baku's eyes. His torture tactics were well known. Those who survived were usually maimed to the point of wishing they hadn't lived.

"Yes, sir. No stone will be left unturned."

Baku nodded and severed the connection, his image faded to black.

Die stared at the table for a moment, then stuck his head into the hallway to shout for someone to bring him the sorcerer who had been sent to accompany his team.

Die usually preferred his strategy to be informed by physical and intellectual abilities, not the dark arts. But this case of the missing family seemed to involve something beyond natural explanation.

Chapter 12

"**R**un!" Taimani used a hushed voice, but the guttural urgency was undeniable.

Taine refused to move and crossed his arms.

They stood in an alley a few streets from the inn, having been rushed out by Master Timur before Lee had let in the delegates from the Kimwaki Tower.

Sonos stood on the balls of his feet ready to move but confused as he looked between Taine and Taimani. He hoped sibling feuds wouldn't follow them the entire journey.

Sibi leaned into Sonos. "Who do we follow?"

Sonos took a step towards Taine.

But Taimani made a set of complicated hand signals to Taine, and then she grabbed Sonos by the wrist and pulled him towards the exit of the alley.

Taine sucked his tongue against his front teeth, a gesture Sonos had learned was used to display high levels of annoyance. With a scowl, he picked up the two packs Timur had provided and took Sibi in the opposite direction.

It was still the wee hours of the morning, the dawn glow not yet visible. Sonos pulled his cloak a little tighter against the chill air, making sure to keep the hood covering his face well.

He followed Taimani onto the main street. They hadn't walked far when a pair of guards on horseback approached.

Sonos' heart raced. Surely, they couldn't get caught so quickly.

Taimani, on the other hand, tossed back the hood of her cloak, shook out her hair, and giggled.

Sonos stepped back in surprise.

She threw her arms around his neck, and then pulled Sonos into her as she leaned against the wall, making sure to keep Sonos' back towards the guards.

Her full lips pressed against his, and his entire body froze.

She whispered in his ear, "You better make this believable."

The clop of the guards' horses came closer.

Sonos was sure Taimani would feel the heat emanating from his cheeks, but hopefully, the darkness hid his embarrassment and awkwardness.

He pressed his hand against the wall where Taimani was leaning and buried his face against her neck. She wrapped her leg around him and giggled some more.

Sonos tried to keep his mind focused on the danger of the guards, but Taimani was immensely distracting. Her skin had a hint of lavender that mixed with the leather of her clothing.

"These two ain't no prince and bodyguard," one of the guards laughed. He drew his horse close enough that Sonos could feel the muzzle of the horse against his back. "Get outta here and go find a room."

Sonos grunted but Taimani pulled him closer. She raised her head and spoke in a coy voice. "Yes, officers. Of course." She then nibbled Sonos' ear and whispered, "Keep your head down."

Stepping away from the wall, Taimani wrapped her arm around Sonos' waist and tugged him in an almost stupor down the street.

Eventually, the guards moved away in the opposite direction.

"I think they're gone," Taimani said, glancing behind and then straightening herself.

Sonos' mind was wet mush, remembering her breath in his ear more than anything. He couldn't even say how many steps they had walked, and those were details he usually tracked without conscious thought.

"Hey, you didn't hear me?" Taimani slapped Sonos' arm away. "They're gone."

He hadn't realized that he had still been draping his arm around her neck.

Taimani narrowed her eyes as she pulled her hair back and tied it with a leather cord, then tucked it back into her hood. "Don't be getting any funny ideas, you hear?"

"Uh, yeah. Of course." Sonos shook his head trying to clear his thoughts.

"Let's get moving," Taimani said. "Taine was quite upset about splitting up, and it's best not to keep my brother waiting." She rolled her eyes, pulling the hood of her cloak up to shadow her face once more.

Sonos worked to keep pace as Taimani led them through the winding, dark streets. Eventually, they neared the market close to the edge of the city. A few vendors moved about, pushing carts and setting up their stalls.

Taimani turned her head sharply.

Sonos followed her gaze and saw a flicker of movement in the shadows.

Taine stepped forward and glared at his sister. "Don't ever separate me from *my* charge again."

She lowered her hood and returned a gaze just as fierce. "Stop underestimating me. I respect you, but when we're moving as a team, you need to learn to trust, too. Besides, you really think that you could've played a lover with him and made it believable?"

"You— What?" Taine stared open-mouthed between Sonos and Taimani.

Heat crept up Sonos' neck once more, and he was glad for the deep covering of the hood.

He was saved from further reply by a bright burst of lightning that broke through the darkness, followed by a loud clap of thunder.

Taimani led them to a spot near the stalls closest to the city wall to wait.

The entire place reeked of fish guts, and Sonos crinkled his nose.

An old cart pulled by a single horse rumbled towards them. A hooded figure sat on the front seat.

Taimani stepped forward and lowered her hood. "Think there's any blue salmon to be caught on the river this fine morning?" she asked the driver.

"Only if you're lucky enough to see some rainbow trout first," a gruff reply came. "Now c'mon, before this rain lets loose."

Taimani signaled for them to climb into the back of the cart.

Sonos was impressed by the level of organization this network clearly had. Codes and all.

There was a low bench in the wagon that ran the length behind where the driver sat.

Taine insisted that Sonos lay on the floor under the bench. One glare from the warrior stopped any protest that may have risen from Sonos. Taine tucked his sword next to Sonos.

Meanwhile, Taimani put one of the packs on Sibi's back and then covered it with the cloak.

Sibi winced with the weight. Timur had provided some more healing balm and medicine, but the boy was still frail. With the pack on, he looked more like a hunchback, especially with the hood pulled up, but he supposed it was better than looking like a child.

Taimani positioned Sibi on the bench between her and Taine, helping to offset any weight on his back.

Rain started falling, and Sonos was glad to be under the covering of the bench. After a few minutes of rumbling down the cobblestone street, they came to a stop. Sonos kept his face well covered but tried to see through Taine's legs. It looked like they had stopped at the city gate.

"Ho there!" A watchman called out. "What's your business?"

"Aye," the driver responded. "Taking out a fishing crew."

"Some kind of morning for fishing," said the guard.

"Mouths to feed, storm or no."

"True, true," the guard said, "Hope you all can find some catfish. My wife's been complaining she can't find any at the market these days." The guard spoke as he walked around the wagon.

Sonos held completely still, hoping to blend in with what remained of the darkness as his heart raced.

Another cart pulled in behind them, waiting to exit.

"What's the hold-up, Joe?" the other driver shouted.

The guard took a last look into their wagon and waved them through.

"Have to take some extra precautions. Seems that prince disappeared or did somethin' crazy again this year." The voices faded as their cart rumbled out onto the dirt track.

The road was bumpy, and Sonos breathed a sigh of relief when Taine finally gave the all-clear for him to come out from under the bench.

Sibi had fallen asleep on Taimani's arm, but the two warriors were awake and alert.

When it became apparent that no one was moving to make space for him on the bench, Sonos sat on the floor of the wagon, his back against the edge, knees tucked in. The cloak was helpful, but the chill already started to seep into his bones.

The sky grew brighter, even as the rain continued to pelt down.

Sonos felt for the envelope he had stashed in his pocket. He wanted nothing more than to rip it open and see what Timur had written. But there wasn't enough light just yet, and with no tech available... *No technology!* Sonos would need to get used to this reality.

Even though he'd lived without personal tech like his gazer for a year, it would be strange to not see lights and hover-tech, or the heating and cooling he'd come to take for granted in the palace and Inner City of Pergamum. The Emperor was extremely controlling of access to technology, considering tech and the Sahemy a key source of his strength and power.

It wasn't long before the road turned sharply towards the riverbank. The driver pulled to a stop near a large, open-air shed.

A scattering of men sat around tables; lanterns hung from corners of the shed providing dim lighting.

Taimani nudged Sibi awake and hopped out of the wagon. "You guys wait here for a minute. I need to find Wylder." She was gone before anyone had a chance to argue.

The driver unhitched the horse and walked it towards a thick bunch of trees with overhead cover.

"Uhm, Highness?" Sibi shrugged out of the big pack under his cloak.

Taine made the sucking noise with his teeth. "We're trying to stay undercover, boy. Use your head and call him something else. Like... Sonny."

"Do *not* call me Sonny. That's horrid. But do drop the formalities. What is it, Sib?"

"It looks like we're going to be taking a boat to wherever."

"Yes."

"Well, I..." His small voice quivered. "I can't swim. And I'm terrified of the river."

Taine placed a hand on Sibi's leg. "Hey, your ancestors are from an island. Hopefully, you'll have some hidden muscle memory that will keep you alive. But if not, well, just don't fall in."

Sibi groaned but said nothing further as Taimani walked back towards them with purpose in her step, unfazed by the steady rain. A man in a long, dark coat and floppy hat followed in her steps.

"Boys, meet Wylder. He'll be our captain."

He was more clean-cut than Sonos would have imagined for a fisherman.

Wylder nodded an acknowledgment to the group. "Let's go," he said in a deep voice that held an unfamiliar lilt.

"We're going out in the storm?" Panic filled Sibi's question.

Wylder had already turned and was walking toward the river. If he heard Sibi, he gave no response.

Taine jumped out of the wagon and held out a hand to Sibi. "Now or never, Sib. C'mon."

Taine leaned into Sibi as they walked, "Lucky for you, Kimwaki warriors are trained for land as well as water. We won't let anything happen to you."

Sonos recognized the soft spot he valued so greatly in his bodyguard.

Wylder stopped by a small, overturned pirogue. Its blue paint was chipped and faded.

Sonos wondered whether the boat would hold all of them, let alone make the journey to Portemore in one piece.

Wylder instructed Taine to grab the opposite end of the small, wooden boat. "We lift on three. You two," he looked at Sonos and Taimani, "grab the nets underneath. One... two... three."

Sonos and Taimani pulled out the heavy nets as soon as the boat was lifted.

"Are we all going to fit in this?" Taimani asked, her voice carrying the same worry as Sonos.

But Wylder didn't allow time for discussion. He called out instructions at all four of them, and soon enough, they had the boat in the river, and everyone safely crammed aboard.

By this time, the rain had slowed to a drizzle and Sonos was thankful. He and Taine sat on the middle bench, Taimani and Sibi squeezed onto the small bench in front, and Wylder was in the back, rowing with two long oars.

They quickly put distance between them and the other fishermen. Once they were out of sight and in a relatively calm section of the river, Wylder called Taine back to take over the oars. He then opened a compartment under the back bench and pulled out a large cylinder. It was the length of Wylder's arm and almost as thick as his waist. From inside his cloak, he pulled out a set of blades and gears.

The rain had stopped completely, and early morning sun rays were peeking through the clouds.

Wylder's hands were sure as he pieced together all the components.

Sonos leaned over the side of the boat, pushing back his hood just a bit, fascinated, as Wylder connected the cylinder to the back of the boat.

Wylder lifted his sleeve and tapped his gazer, a holographic control panel coming to life. After tapping a few buttons, the motor started.

Sonos couldn't hold back his shock. A fisherman with access to a high-end device Sonos had only seen on Empire-authorized shipping boats.

"How? What—" Sonos asked.

"Time to open your eyes, *Highness.* The Empire is not all there is to this world," Wylder said.

Taimani hissed from the front of the boat. "Why do you address him so?"

Sonos flushed, forgetting himself for a moment.

Wylder smirked. "It's not too hard to piece together."

Taine's knuckles went white as he gripped the oars tighter.

"But don't worry. Your secret is safe with me, inked ones," Wylder said, "I have just as much to lose if you are discovered to have passed through my hands."

Taine narrowed his eyes and shook his head ever so slightly at Taimani. They continued down the river in silence, the hum of the motor speeding them along. The sun was soon blazing overhead, drying them out.

Sonos swatted a mosquito, scratching his neck where he felt a bite. Strange that mosquitoes could have bitten him through the cloak.

But Sonos' mind started to feel cloudy. He fought to keep his eyes open, and thoughts straight.

Sibi leaned against the side of the boat in front of him, snoring away. *This kid has a real talent for falling asleep anywhere, anytime.* That was the last thought Sonos remembered, then the world went black.

A rough kick to his gut startled Sonos awake. He coughed and tried to catch his breath. His eyes were heavy and groggy. He was lying on the floor of the boat, water splashing in and people shouting.

"Sonos, get up!" Taine called.

Sonos struggled to sit up. He was between the front and middle bench, Sibi passed out next to him.

Taine stood on the back bench, his sword sparking in his hands. Taimani stood on the middle bench, oar in hand, facing Taine.

At first, Sonos worried that they were fighting each other. But then he saw their focus was on Wylder who was pinned to the floor between them.

"*Sa e fai mai sa faatuatuaina o ia!*" Taine shouted at Taimani.

"*Ou te le iloa le mea na tupu!*" Taimani shouted back.

As they argued, Wylder pulled a contraption over his face and rolled under the bench to reach Sonos. He slapped something hard over Sonos' nose and mouth.

Sonos tried to cry out, but in a split second, Wylder flipped them both into the water.

Sonos' cloak snagged on the bench, pulling off as he went overboard. The cold rush of water reached Sonos' bones instantly. He gasped for air through the contraption Wylder had put on his face. Sonos tried to orient himself underwater as Wylder held on to his collar, pulling him deeper.

But then something else grabbed his foot and jerked Sonos back towards the surface of the water. Sonos turned, and relief flooded his mind when he caught sight of Taine.

In a moment of clarity, Sonos fought off Wylder's grip, and Taine was able to pull him back above water.

Sibi shouted their names, and Taimani's relief was visible as she paddled over to them. She extended the oar to Taine, helping them both back into the boat.

"What in the banished gods happened back there?" Sonos asked when they had finally settled back into the boat.

Taine rowed them downstream, while Taimani kept her eyes peeled on the river.

"Wylder is a traitor," Taimani said, spitting out his name. She tossed a blowgun to Sonos. "He used this to try to drug everyone."

Sonos rubbed the back of his neck. *It seems it wasn't a mosquito bite earlier, but rather some kind of poisoned dart*, he thought.

"Kimwaki warriors are inoculated from poison as part of our training," Taine said.

"Huh," Sonos raised an eyebrow at his bodyguard.

"Some secrets shall remain ours," Taimani glared at Taine.

Taine shrugged. "So, what now?"

"We lost one of our packs when Wylder pulled Sonos overboard," Taimani said. "Thankfully, Sibi was still wearing his, but those supplies won't last long."

Sonos glanced towards the back of the boat. It was noticeably quiet.

Taimani shrugged. "I also had to destroy the motor. There was no way to control it, and I needed to keep the boat near where you two went under."

Sonos nodded. "Thanks. To all of you." The weight of the endangerment he brought hung on Sonos' shoulders.

Sibi grunted, in obvious pain, but he scooted to sit beside Sonos, handing him the cloak that had fortuitously remained in the boat. "We're in this together."

Taimani turned from the river and looked at the two of them. The corner of her mouth twitched up. "Hope is nothing if not infectious."

Hope. Sonos dug through his cloak, ensuring his journal was still there. He let out a sigh of relief when he found it safely tucked in the hidden pocket. "Wylder may have turned on us, but I still trust Timur. I say we head to Portemore as planned and see if we can find his connection. At the very least, a large city will have the resources we need to resupply for wherever we head next."

Taimani nodded. "I'll take the first shift with the rowing while you guys put on some dry clothes," she said.

No one argued.

After changing, Sonos stretched out his legs on the middle bench and pulled out the journal with the maps. He had tucked the envelope safely inside the pages. Time to focus on something else.

Let's see what Truth was worth fighting for, Timur, Sonos thought.

Chapter 13

C HARLOTTE CLUNG TO THE red, wooden mast for dear life. Waves spilled over the side of the ship, mixing with rain that pelted from the sky. Her arms ached as she tried to keep her body upright on the constantly moving deck.

She shouted for help, but the sound was drowned out by the storm.

She squeezed her eyes shut, trying to block out the terror.

A deep voice rumbled from the sky, "Do you trust me?"

What? Trust? Trust who? Charlotte's mind raced.

The voice called out again, deep like thunder. "Do you trust me?"

Charlotte clung tighter to the base of the mast, splinters digging into her hands. The forceful rain made it impossible to see anything more than what was right in front of her, but she felt the voice waiting for an answer. There was something familiar about the sound of it. Is that how to describe it? It was like being tuned into something familiar and safe.

"I... I guess so." Did she really have a choice? "Yes, I trust you."

"Be bold and courageous. I am with you." The words reverberated inside, slowly calming her even while the storm raged on.

She remembered the writing from the journal she had read in the temporal portal—in the hollow of the samaan tree.

Strong arms embraced her shaking limbs from behind. Jax whispered in her ear, "Char, it's okay. It's okay. Wake up."

Charlotte blinked open her eyes and realized she was clinging to the bench of Robby's fishing boat. She must have fallen asleep. The sun was blazing, the sail filled with a strong gust of wind.

She took a deep, calming breath, settling back into reality.

Jax sat next to her on the bench. Rapha was with Robby who managed the rudder from the back of the boat.

"Bad dream?" Jax asked as he rubbed Charlotte's back.

She nodded, suddenly feeling self-conscious. She stretched her sore limbs. The memory of yesterday flooded back into her mind, and she wasn't sure whether being awake was much better than her nightmare. "Where are we?"

"About two hours out from Salan. Thankfully, the winds have been blowing in our favor." Jax adjusted himself to straddle the bench so that he faced Charlotte, resting his back against the side of the boat. "Want to talk?"

Charlotte took a deep breath and stared out at the water. The blues and greens of the sea mixed with the bright blue of the sky. A thought passed through her mind that her sister Lily would do a great capture of the scene with her watercolors. *Soon come,* Charlotte resolved in her heart. *Just have to save a kingdom first.*

Rapha squeaked and jumped into her lap.

She laid a hand on the monkey's head. "I dreamt about a ship. It had a huge red mast, and we were in a crazy fierce storm. It felt like the whole ship was going to be torn apart by the waves and wind."

Jax scooted closer, laying his hand over hers. "It's been pretty calm all morning, but maybe it's the rocking of the boat that threw you off."

"Maybe," Charlotte said. But there was something more to it. "There was this voice. In the midst of the storm. Maybe from the storm, or in the storm? I'm not sure. It asked me if I trusted it."

"It?"

"I... I think the voice was *El*." Charlotte looked at Rapha. The connection to *El* just popped into her head as she was talking to Jax, but as soon as she said it, she knew it to be true. Maybe that breath thing was working? "Rapha, try talking."

Rapha crossed his arms and made a series of grunts.

"Hmph, figures." Charlotte shook her head. It was worth a shot.

"We need to plan ahead for what we're going to do in Salan." She leaned towards Jax, keeping her voice down. The less Robby knew, the better. "We gotta find passage to Portemore. Everything starts from the mainland. The Mountain Kingdom, and eventually Pergamum."

There was still a tinge of doubt, or maybe it was disappointment, that they weren't going to Pergamum first. But a promise was a promise, and she wasn't about to upset the cosmos, or at the very least Rapha, by bolting.

Charlotte looked through her bag to take stock of what exactly Rapha had packed. Her messenger bag held Jax's box of dried herbs, her multi-tool, a few coppers, and a couple of broken gadgets and gears.

Looking through Jax's pack, there was a thick rope, a change of clothes for each of them, and a pile of fruit. *It's a good thing we spent so much time in that cellar that we had a stockpile of essentials*, Charlotte thought.

She peeled a portugyal and popped a few pieces in her mouth. The sweetness of the citrus never failed to lift her spirits.

She tossed a piece of fruit to Jax, and one back to Robby.

"Tenks," Robby said gratefully from the back.

Charlotte adjusted the blanket covering the flyer-board. She imagined that Salan would be similar to Jamroq in restricting tech to Imperials only.

Looking at the sparse items in their possession, Charlotte couldn't help but feel tremors of despair. How would they secure passage to Portemore and pay the underground network with the little they had? What did they really have of value anymore aside from the flyer-board? And even with that, the sun collector was cracked.

She laid a hand on Rapha who had curled up in a ball on the bench. The words from Jax's scroll flowed into her mind. *He causes a river to flow in the badlands. What is impossible for him?*

Rapha stirred under her hand.

"If you can manage to make a river in the unlikeliest of places, let's hope you can get us to the mainland, too," she said under her breath.

Soon enough, the mountainous shape of Salan came into view. Supposedly the island was the remnant of an ancient volcano, but it had been dormant for hundreds of years. The port was easily double the size of Mina's, with roughly fifty vessels of various shapes and sizes in the harbor.

Jax helped Robby pull down the sail, and he rowed them to the furthest dock.

A young boy ran over to help tie the boat. "Need any help unloading?" he asked Robby.

"Not today young'un," Robby answered, flipping a coin to the boy.

The boy waved and ran away down the dock.

Robby reached out a hand to help Charlotte out of the boat. "You and Jax take care of each other, yuh hear?"

Charlotte put on a brave smile as she slung the bag across her body and adjusted the board on her back. "Thank you for everything, Robby." She ignored his outstretched hand and gave him a hug. "You sure you'll be okay?"

"Likkle late for second thoughts, my dear." Robby gave a lopsided grin. "But don't worry. You know we Jammies look after each other. And I'm sure your dad and granny will be all right."

Charlotte smiled and climbed out of the boat, Rapha trailing right behind her and scurrying up to his favorite spot on her shoulder.

Jax and Robby exchanged "walk good" salutations and Jax joined Charlotte on the jetty. He untied the ropes, pushed Robby off, and they waved goodbye.

A sudden, single tear slipped through Charlotte's eyelashes, which she quickly wiped away. Even though their last tether to home was sailing away, it was a time to look forward, not back.

Jax grabbed her hand and led her to the shore. The sun was at its highest point, and Charlotte's stomach grumbled.

"We'll try to find some food," Jax said. "And I'm hoping we'll find a ship leaving for Portemore today."

"A ship who will take a broken flyer-board as payment." Charlotte sighed.

Rapha made a squeaky sound from her shoulder, as if encouraging her to relax. She was still a little unsure about reading Rapha's emotions.

Jax described his connection to the unseen realm as hearing something or just knowing it. But she still felt it as a vibration, a frequency. It just felt right.

Charlotte shook her head. Time for puzzling that out later. More pressing things at hand.

They reached the end of the jetty and spotted a man standing near a small, open fire.

"Fish! Roast Fish! Fresh Roast Fish!" he called out.

The smell of the fresh fish and herbs wafted through the air, and Charlotte's stomach rumbled again.

"Okay, okay, I hear you." Jax chuckled and led them over to get some fish.

The vendor wrapped the fish in some plantain leaves, just like back in Mina. Charlotte looked at the fruits on a nearby table but was reluctant to use more of their few coppers than they had to.

Who knew when they would find a way to get more coin. The coppers felt like a drop in dry bucket. Futile. But restraint provided some measure of control, and after paying for the meal, she only bought a banana for Rapha.

Jax directed them to some wooden crates nearby, and she unwrapped the fish. She took a moment to savor the explosion of flavors in her mouth from the green onions, lemon, and spices. The fish practically melted in her mouth.

Rapha chomped on the banana at her feet.

Jax surveyed the harbor. "I'm glad there are so many ships here. I remember my parents bringing me on a few trips. The sheer number of vessels and buildings made Mina seem so small."

Charlotte paused from inhaling the meal and followed his gaze towards the docks.

People flowed on and off ships, carrying loads in both directions. A steady stream continued to a nearby town.

A part of her wanted to hide in the stream of people and animals on the move. Buy them some time to plan and gather resources. Make sure Captain Die thought they were dead. The thought of Captain Die sent a shiver down her back. No, staying in one place was risky. The only way was to keep moving forward.

"So how do you think we tackle finding a ship?" Charlotte asked. "Do we just go and ask if any captain is willing to accept a broken flyer-board in exchange for taking us to Portemore?" Saying the offer aloud made it seem even more ludicrous.

"Well..." Jax had a playful light to his eyes that usually preceded some reckless decision. "There's only one way to find out."

He folded up his fish bones and jumped up.

Charlotte started to do the same, but Jax stopped her. "It'll be easier for me to talk man to man with the seamen. Stay and finish eating, and I'll be back before you know it." He called out the last part as he was already jogging away.

She rolled her eyes about the whole man-thing, but Jax was probably right. He had spent his whole life around seamen and fisher-folk. Better him to negotiate the impossible.

She stretched her legs out into the sand and looked up at the cloudless sky. At least they should have good weather to start with. She hoped that nightmare would stay as only a bad dream.

The unhindered sea breeze continually tugged strands of her hair loose from her hasty bun as she waited for Jax to return. Eventually, she just let her hair down and shook it out in the breeze.

The smell of citrus floated over from the fruit vendor. Charlotte turned and watched as he peeled an orange. Her mouth watered. She did a quick scan of the docks, but Jax was nowhere in sight.

Rapha was curled up, asleep at her feet. She tapped the small pouch that held their remaining coppers. What if this was her last chance to get some fresh fruit? Who knew what might be readily available on the mainland? And she could buy some extra for the trip to Portemore—they'd need some kind of sustenance for the journey.

Her mind made up, she walked over and asked the vendor how much for the portugyals.

"Portugyals?" He asked with a quizzical look. "What?"

Charlotte pointed to a pile of citrus.

"Oh, tangerines? What did you call them?"

"Portugyals. But yes, tangerines, whatever." This man was annoying her, and Jax could come back anytime.

"Where you from?" the vendor asked.

Charlotte's heart raced. She didn't mean to leave a trail.

"Oh wait, that's what they call tangerines down in Jamroq, ain't it? Portugyals. So weird," he said.

"Never mind." Charlotte put away her pouch and started to walk away.

"Now that I think of it, some of those guards were walking through here earlier. Talking about some message they got from Jamroq, looking for—"

Charlotte didn't hear the rest. Her heart was thumping so fast that blood filled her ears. She ran to pick up her covered flyer-board and pack from the crates.

Rapha squeaked and flailed his arms at being woken up.

"Gotta go find Jax, *now*," Charlotte hissed at Rapha.

She took off running towards the docks, not looking back at the fruit vendor, and too terrified to look around for any guards. As soon as she reached the closest pier, she almost ran smack into Jax.

"Hey, hey. Where're you running? I was just coming to get you." Jax placed two hands on her shoulders.

Charlotte risked a glance back, but the fruit vendor had left his stall. "They know." Charlotte struggled to catch her breath from the sprint.

"Who knows what?" Jax asked, keeping his voice calm and eyes locked on her.

"Guards. They got some message or something from Jamroq."

Jax scanned the area behind her. "Okay, I don't see any guards. But come." He slung his arm over her shoulder and led her down one of the piers, a big grin on his face. "Lucky for you, I am quite amazing at negotiation."

"What?" Charlotte had a hard time walking at a slow pace. She just wanted to run and get out of sight of everyone.

The distinctive sound of boots marching in unison down one of the far docks caused Jax's muscles to tighten. "Uhm, never mind the details. Let's just get on that boat."

They picked up speed, walking as fast as possible down the wooden pier to a ship tied at the far end. Rapha had climbed onto Charlotte's shoulder as Jax held her hand. They followed one of the loaders rolling a large barrel up the plank. It must have been the last one because nothing else was left on the pier.

When they reached the main deck, Charlotte's face grew hot, and not just from the warmth of the sun or fast walking. Everywhere she looked, bare-chested sailors bustled about, shouting at each other in a tongue she didn't recognize.

"Just in time," a big burly man walked up to Jax. He was one of the few who had on a shirt, though it was unbuttoned with a very hairy chest interspersed with his long beard. White teeth gleamed against deeply tanned skin. He shouted a set of orders to the crew. Ropes were loosened, and the plank pulled up onto the deck.

Charlotte stepped from side to side feeling like she was constantly in the way.

Captain Hair, as Charlotte thought of him, turned his gaze directly to her, as if sizing her up. She hoped he didn't expect her to be of much help on the crew. Maybe Jax had offered his services?

"So, this is the little tech genius who is going to get our motor working?"

Charlotte worked hard to keep her mouth from falling wide open. Jax put an arm around her shoulder and grinned. "Absolutely! My girl can fix anything that runs with tech."

The captain grunted. "For your sake, let's hope so." He scanned the waters as the ship hit the open sea. He called someone over, someone with a shirt on, so Charlotte assumed it might be the first mate or whatever the proper term was called. "Take them down to the storage room and give them a cot. Don't let them out until that motor is working."

Charlotte's heart dropped to her stomach. What had Jax gotten them into? As the first mate led them across the deck, her breath caught, and she leaned close to Jax. "Hey, do you see that?"

The paint was faded and chipping, not nearly the brightness she had remembered from her dream, but there was no mistaking the distinctive red color of the mast.

Chapter 14

—·—

*T*IME IS SHORT, AND *these remaining fingers are slow. I will answer the question I know you will ask. Yes, it was me. I wish I could say I was sorry. I know it caused you pain. It also cost me greatly. I think I underestimated Baku's abilities, or perhaps I overestimated mine. But even so, I would make the same choice again. Why? A simple word: Hope! You dared to ask the right questions. Reality can be shaped and changed. Have the courage to see. Follow the Light, it will show the way. Move the mountain without touching it, and you will find what you are looking for.*

Sonos read the letter over and over again and studied the folded origami tree that had been placed in the envelope. The tree had to be connected to his mother... but how?

Deciphering Timur's scratches had taken some time, and the words to the end were rushed. Timur must have written it in the short space of time between hearing the plan of betrayal from Taimani, and Lee bringing them down from the room.

Reality sunk in. His tutor had betrayed him—and wasn't even sorry about it.

Taimani squeezed in next to Sonos on the middle bench on the boat. Taine must have just relieved her turn rowing, which meant that Sonos would be next. He rubbed his already sore arms. They were switching off every hour and planned to go until it was too dark to see what lay ahead.

Sonos folded the letter into his notebook and took out one of Timur's detailed maps. He wanted to look at the Mountain Kingdom once again. The mountains were rumored to hold troves of treasure and gold, but their entrances were hard to access and well-guarded.

His father must feel quite confident to attack the recluse kingdom now.

Timur said Sonos must move the mountain without touching it. It had to be connected to his father's conquest somehow.

"Show me where we are." Taimani leaned close and looked over his shoulder. She had pulled her hair into two tight braids. Sweat and smells of the river had replaced her earlier scent of lavender.

Sonos shifted away slightly.

She just scooted closer.

Sonos sighed and pointed to a dot that lay on the west bank of the river, halfway between Pergamum and Portemore. "We'll soon pass Riverton."

"I vaguely remember when they brought us upriver from Portemore. I think it took us two days to reach Pergamum, but those were Imperial ships that had motors," Taine said from where he rowed.

"We have the currents on our side going downriver. We'll probably make the same time without a motor," Sonos said. "We should be able to get to Portemore before dark tomorrow."

He thought Timur was going to provide a specific contact in the letter, but all he said was to follow the Light. What did that even mean? And move the mountain without touching it? Riddles. But Sonos couldn't take his eyes off the Mountain Kingdom on the map. Everything was pointing there.

"We're not stopping in Riverton, right?" Taimani raised an eyebrow. "The less chance we have of getting spotted, the better. In fact, I'm glad we'll be passing Riverton after dark."

"Agreed," Taine said from behind. "We'll take turns keeping watch tonight, but I don't think we should stop. We don't know who or what may be waiting on the riverbanks."

Sonos had to retrain his brain to being on the run. Even if he always had a knack for details, he needed a filter to see a lot more risk and danger. He didn't want to rely on the warriors alone.

Sibi rummaged through the pack he had been carrying since Timur's. "Looks like we have enough dried meat and biscuits to last a few days. Anyone hungry?" He asked as he stuffed one of the biscuits in his mouth.

"What about water?" Sonos asked.

Taimani smiled and pulled a small tube from a pocket inside her cloak. "It's not exactly tech as you and the Sahemy would classify it, but Kimwaki specializes in tools for survival. Every warrior carries one of these." She handed it to Sonos.

He turned the tube over in his hands, but something was stuck inside. It looked like pulp... or roots? Sonos couldn't figure it out.

"Don't worry, I replace the fibers regularly. The Emperor has quite extensive gardens."

"Fibers?" Sonos asked.

"Yes, this tube can take any water and make it drinkable through the special fibers that act as a filtration system," Taimani explained. "Your father brought the plant from Kimwaki, but I doubt he knows its full potential or uses."

Sonos' admiration for the invention was interrupted by the sound of a motor in the distance. It sounded like it was coming towards them from the south.

Before he had time to think, Taimani had shoved Sonos under the bench and threw his cloak over him. They did the same to Sibi.

Taine and Taimani spoke to each other in their native tongue and Sonos' heart raced. The boat rocked violently from the waves caused by the other vessel.

"They don't seem to be stopping or taking much notice of us," Taimani said just loud enough for Sonos to hear. "But stay down until they're out of sight." A few minutes passed and the sound of the motor eventually faded from hearing, and the rocking subsided.

"All clear," Taine finally said.

Sonos crawled out from under the bench and scanned the river. No other vessels were in sight.

Taine's sword leaned against the warrior's leg.

Taimani held a blowgun and a flat pouch on her lap. She opened the pouch to adjust the feathered darts, then strapped it back onto her thigh.

Sibi was the only one who seemed calm, quite calm in fact, as he stretched after crawling out from under the bench. His movements were slow and pained, but the boy looked unfazed, all things considered.

"It was a shipping vessel, thankfully. Focused on speed and not searching for anything," Taimani said.

"The sooner we get to Portemore, the better. I feel like a sitting duck in this rinky boat." Taine rowed with vim and vigor.

"Why do you look so relaxed, Sib?" Sonos asked.

"I just know we're not going to get caught." Sibi shrugged.

"Uhm, you know this how?" Sonos asked.

"*El* didn't bring us this far just to kill us now. There has to be something bigger going on. Mama always said that *El* is ten steps ahead of the guards." Sibi sat up as tall as he could.

"*El?*" Sonos asked in disbelief. He remembered the prayer Sibi had muttered under his breath when they were running from the feast. But the way Sibi spoke, seemed to indicate a belief system more than just desperate prayers.

"What's *El* have to do with this?" Taimani joined in Sonos' questioning.

"Surely you can't believe it was coincidence that brought us all together? A prince, two warriors, and a hero of Salan?" Sibi grinned at the last part, clearly proud of himself. "There has to be some great plan."

Taimani raised an eyebrow. "Well, it seems that you and *El* have this all worked out, eh?"

"Wait," Sonos said. When Sibi said Salan, it triggered a memory. "I've been meaning to ask you both about the towers. During the feast, while the Emperor was speaking, I noticed some sort of pattern emitting from a light in the window of the Salan tower. Could it have been some sort of signal?"

Taine and Taimani exchanged a glance.

Sibi was quick to answer, likely assuming the question about Salan was meant for him. "I've never actually been to the Salan tower, sorry."

"Taine? Mani? You guys seem to know *something*." Sonos eyed them both.

"I'm not exactly sure," Taimani said after a moment's hesitation. "Each tower has its own codes, signals, and ways of communicating. I admit that as we watched the speech projected in the Kimwaki tower, I noticed the pattern from Salan. I'm impressed that you picked up on it as well. Especially since you didn't know codes existed."

"Details are kind of his thing," Taine said.

"Any idea what they were trying to communicate?" Sonos asked.

"There have been rumors that a new captain of the Imperial Guard has brought a harsh hand to the island. The flow of people, whether refugees or workers sent to the capital, or even to the tower, has all but stopped over the past few months."

Sibi sucked in a breath. "Really? I... I guess it's true. Now that I think about it, we haven't seen *any* new people from Salan recently. And Mama usually welcomes any new workers to the palace."

"Sorry, Sib." Taimani laid a hand on his shoulder.

Sibi flinched and fiddled with the biscuit in his hand. "I know you all may not believe in *El*, but I don't believe my life was spared for nothing." He looked up, his eyes shining. "Fight we must, but win we shall."

"Another Mama saying?" Sonos asked.

Sibi nodded.

"Fight we must—" Taine repeated, still rowing.

"But win we shall," Taimani finished.

It certainly had a ring to it.

The sun was high in the sky on the second day when they arrived in Portemore. Sonos rubbed his sore muscles, even though Taine and Taimani had done a lion's share of the rowing.

It was a little earlier than predicted, thanks to the strong currents. Throughout the journey, there had been a string of ships that passed them heading in both directions, but there had always been enough warning from the motors to find cover behind rocks or brush in the river. When they passed through the narrower channels, it had been mercifully clear.

Even though it was blazing hot, Sonos pulled the hood of his cloak up to cover his face as they exited the mouth of the Ti're and spilled out into the open sea.

The number of ships and movement in the harbor was over-whelming. Vessels of every size and shape jostled in close prox-imity. Shouts in many languages created a cacophony of sound.

"Isn't it beautiful?" Taimani asked. Loose strands from her tied-back hair whipped around her face as she opened her arms and took a deep breath.

Was she seeing the same confusion and craziness that Sonos saw? He raised his eyebrows questioningly. "Beautiful isn't exactly the word that comes to mind, no."

Taimani laughed. "It may look like chaos to some, but to me, it's an intricate dance full of energy and life. City life is so *energizing*."

"How is it that you lived cooped up in that tower for so long?" Sibi asked from where he sat at the front of the boat. He was putting away all their remaining items into the pack.

"Confinement was truly one of the hardest parts of living in that horrid tower. The tunnels were there, sure, but with extremely limited use." She rubbed her arms as if trying to rub out the memory. "I will say this, even if my people sought to betray Sonos and my brother, I understand the reason. It is not good for a warrior's heart to be dulled and constrained for years."

"*Tatau ona tatou fa'asaolotoina o tatou tagata,*" Taine said softly from where he was rowing behind.

Taimani turned and bowed her head towards her brother. "Yes, I agree. We must find a way to free our people." She turned back to look at the docks and the city of Portemore beyond. "But first, let us survive long enough to figure out how."

A boy waved his arms from the docks as Taine navigated the boat closer. "I think we're being directed over there." Sonos point-ed towards the boy.

Taine barely missed a collision with another much larger ship, but they finally pulled up next to the dock. Sonos scrambled onto the wooden platform as soon as they had tied the boat. It was good to be on steady ground again and especially out of the chaotic harbor.

Taimani handed the young dockhand a coin with instructions to watch over the boat. "Where's the best place to get a warm meal and bed for the night?" she asked him.

"Woodyard Square is thatta way," the boy pointed. "Look for Jep's place."

Someone shouted from another vessel nearby, and the boy went running.

"You think the boat is safe here?" Sonos asked.

"Not at all," Taine laughed as he took the pack from Sibi and placed it over the sword strapped to his back. "But we won't be using the river again."

"I'll scout ahead and meet you there," Taimani said as she jogged off in the general direction the dockhand had pointed. The sunlight caught highlights and different shades of her dark hair as she ran.

Taine gripped Sonos' shoulder. "I'll only say this once. Do *not* look at my sister with wandering eyes."

The sudden fierceness to Taine's voice took Sonos by surprise. He didn't even realize that he had been staring off after Taimani.

Taine didn't give Sonos a chance to respond, he simply stormed off in the direction of the square.

Sonos shook his head, and he and Sibi hurried to catch up.

The buzz in the atmosphere of Portemore did not let up as they moved away from the docks and into the streets. For the most part, the roads were paved with stone. But unlike the orderly design of Pergamum, the streets here flowed like a river, taking twists and turns.

In some places, the roads were wide enough to fit two carts or carriages plus vendors on either side. Then they'd turn a bend, and the road would suddenly narrow, and all the people and wagons would bottleneck.

Pure chaos.

The smell of sea and sweat pressed on Sonos from all sides. He closed his eyes for a moment to try and catch his breath. When he opened them again, he caught a flutter of movement from the corner of his eye. *Is that man staring at us?* Sonos wondered. But as soon as he looked in the direction, the man turned and disappeared into the crowd. Sonos adjusted his hood again.

Around the next bend in the road, they came upon a large open square. A platform stood erected in the center of the square, and a large crowd milled around. Two guards stood at either corner, their black uniforms with gold trim identifying them as Imperial guards.

Sonos moved to get a closer look, but a strong hand pulled on his shoulder.

"Wrong way there, Sonny. We stay *away* from anyone in a uniform," Taine said.

Sonos searched the square, again feeling as if they were being watched.

Taimani walked out of the crowd towards them. "I have good news and bad news," she said, leading them to stand against a far wall.

"Good news first," Sibi said with a half-smile, his shoulders sagging. They really needed a place for him to rest and recuperate.

"I found Jep's, and the place is clean. We can get a hot meal and plan our next move. I suggest we get *you* off the streets as soon as possible." She looked straight at Sonos as she spoke the last line.

He adjusted his hood, which was still covering his face.

"You saw Wylder, too?" Taine asked.

"Yes, that's the bad news. But let's talk more inside."

They all moved towards the inn but a yelp from Sibi stopped them short. Sibi stood with his hands over his mouth, eyes wide as he looked towards the platform in the square.

Workers had climbed atop a large wooden frame and were in the process of tying thick ropes—no, nooses—from the top beam.

"What in the Empire is going on?" Sonos muttered.

The only time Sonos had seen a public hanging was when Baku claimed to have found a palace servant planning treason against the Emperor. A shiver went down his spine remembering the terrified young man and the way his body had swung after he died. Baku had left him hanging in the main courtyard of the palace for days, as a warning to other servants.

A large Imperial stepped to center stage where a mic was standing. "People of Portemore, citizens and servants of the great K'Luma Empire." His voice boomed throughout the courtyard, and he paused as chatter stopped and eyes turned towards him. "The most blessed and worshiped Emperor, may he live forever, has declared this to be a Year of the Dragon. It is a year of conquest, and it is also a year of rooting out all dissidents in any form and fashion."

Soft murmurs ran throughout the crowd. Sonos wondered what kind of criminals they would choose to make an example of. He counted the number of ropes being secured, and it seemed like a group of them would be hung.

A collective gasp could be heard as a frightened family was prodded onto the stage. They all had blonde, curly hair, the eldest of the three kids might have been Sibi's age. Two others gripped their mother's hand.

"Illegal refugees were discovered on a ship from Salan," the Imperial continued.

Sibi moaned, and Taimani cursed under her breath. However, the Imperial's voice was unwavering, and he looked with disgust at the disheveled family. "They attempted to abandon their duty to the Empire and show blatant disregard for the laws and rule of this land. An example will be made—"

The words of the Imperial grew distant as a sharp object was pushed into Sonos' back, and strong arms pulled him away from the square.

"Quiet now," a gruff voice said. "We don't want to attract any unnecessary attention."

Sonos was pulled into an alley, then turned to face a group of burly men. Two held Taine, one had a knife to Taimani's throat, and another had a hand on Sibi's shoulder.

The man holding the knife to Sonos jerked down his hood, and in a flash, Sonos was exposed.

The man chuckled and walked around to face Sonos, lifting a dark, floppy hat. "Hello again, Highness," Wylder said with a grin that stayed far from his eyes.

Chapter 15

— · —

"U NBELIEVABLE!" Captain Die's shout reverberated throughout the room. He threw the sorcerer's bowl of liquid against the wall. The small man cowered in a corner.

Die walked over and grabbed the front of the sorcerer's dark cloak, pulling him to his feet.

He spoke with a quiet, menacing voice. "Where did they go?"

"I... I don't see that. I don't know. I can only confirm that those you seek have left Jamroq."

Die grunted in displeasure. "Was it the whole family that left?"

"I can only confirm it's those who pose the greatest risk to the Emperor, the ones the darkness is tracking," the sorcerer squeaked.

"What is the point of dark power if it only shows you bits and pieces?" Die dropped the little man back into his corner.

He paced around the room, speaking to no one in particular. "If they've left Jamroq, the most likely way is by sea. And if they are a threat to the Emperor, they will be heading to the mainland. I'll cut them off at Portemore."

He gripped the sides of the small table in the crowded office the previous sergeant had commandeered. Yes, he still had time to find them. He must find them. Failure was not an option.

Die rubbed the back of his neck, wishing, not for the first time, he could rub off the tattoos. Because of them, he was an outsider, constantly having to prove his worth.

Over the years, he had earned his place as a leader of an Elite squad. But it required him to be ten times better than any other Imperial guard, giving and being more than anyone else.

The Emperor had removed the tattoos from the Empress, his sister. However, it seemed Imperial guards, even Elites, weren't important enough to use Sahemy resources on such things.

He remembered a saying from his father, one of the few memories he had from before he was taken as a young boy. *Whatever doesn't kill you makes you stronger.*

Die made up his mind. He rang a bell, and a young servant boy came running in.

"Yes, sir?"

"Spread the word, we're leaving at first light."

The boy ran from the room, and the sorcerer took the opportunity to run out behind him.

Die smiled. He poured a glass of mulled wine, considering the situation.

"Yes, catching them in Portemore in the middle of their scheme is even better. Then there will be no doubt that these are threats shown by the dark realm, brought down by none other than Captain Diekololaoluwa, soon-to-be head of the entire Elite Force."

Perhaps then, he would finally be accepted by the other Imperial guards. Or maybe he would stop caring. Either way, the answer lay in stopping these rebels.

Chapter 16

C HARLOTTE BIT HER BOTTOM lip, eyes laser-focused on the barely discernible grooves of the motor, as she lined up the sun collector.

This has to work, it's our only shot, she thought.

Jax sat in the corner of the converted storage closet where they had been confined. His hands deftly worked on untying and retying knots in the length of rope Rapha had packed in his bag.

Charlotte took a calming breath to steady her hands. Rapha stood right next to her, gazing intently at the slot she had retrofitted to match the size of her sun collector.

"You want to do that humm-y thing—like when you sealed off the cellar from the fire?" she asked the monkey. At this moment, she'd take any help or miracles they could get.

Rapha ignored her request but continued gazing at the motor.

Charlotte pulled back the sun collector and wiped her sweaty palms on her pants. The captain had checked on them last night after dinner, reminding them they had until the sighting of Portemore to get the thing working, or else.

"Do you really think they'd make us walk the plank if we don't get this going? I mean isn't that kind of drastic?" Charlotte asked Jax.

Jax came over to join her on the floor. "Seamen aren't known to be the most merciful bunch. But even if that happens, at least the mainland would be in sight, and I *would* find a way to get us to shore."

Charlotte loved his confident grin, but she knew they would be tens of miles from shore, and she didn't feel the same level of comfort that they'd survive being sent overboard.

He must have sensed her nerves because he put a hand on her knee and waited for her to meet his gaze. "Char, listen to me. I have *never* seen a piece of tech you haven't been able to bring to life."

"But those things took months. And it takes gathering a million little pieces and gears." She glanced at the flyer-board which was propped against one of the walls. She knew it wasn't working, and they were unlikely to find another sun collector, but she couldn't let it go. It was a last symbol of hope that something she had made could be of worth.

"And I really don't know if that binding chemical we found was enough to hold the sun collector together." She turned the panel over in her hands. There was a discolored, jagged line where the compound had been applied. Early that morning, they had been allowed out for an hour to give the panel a chance to collect power from the sun.

The sunrise had painted the sky red, highlighting the clouds that filled the horizon. *Had there been enough light? Did it have enough time to build charge?* The questions plagued Charlotte's mind.

Rapha laid a hand on her arm and hummed softly. It was only for a few seconds, but it resonated with something inside of her. She remembered her dream and *El*'s voice, *"Do you trust me?"*

"Okay, Raph, I get it." She focused once more on the grooves and slid the sun collector into place. A *click* confirmed it locked in.

A few seconds later she smiled as a small vibration flowed into her hand. When the blue and white lights turned on and the motor whirred, Jax jumped up and pulled Charlotte with him, spinning her in a circle.

"See! I told you! I knew you could do it."

Charlotte's joy turned to panic when she heard the motor grind. There was a small turbine that whirred, but it would need water to work properly. She quickly hit the kill switch, and the motor powered back down.

"I should have guessed it needed to be submerged in water to work properly." She ran a hand over the motor, but it didn't look worse for the wear. It really was a beautiful machine.

"No wonder the Imperials are always ahead, with access to such things," Charlotte muttered.

But then she thought about the tech she had acquired on Jamroq, and clearly, this captain had a knack for getting access to tech as well. *Not as impenetrable as they think they are.* Charlotte smiled at the thought.

Jax banged on the door, alerting their guard to go get the captain.

It wasn't long before Captain Hair opened the door. His eyes went directly to the motor.

"It needs to be submerged in the water or else it will burn out," Charlotte explained.

"If this works—" His eyes gleamed and he looked greedily towards Charlotte.

A wave of dread washed over her. She hoped he wasn't going to try and keep her on the ship. She stepped a little closer to Jax, and Rapha ran up her side to his perch on her shoulder.

The little monkey growled under its breath.

The captain called for a few of his crew and had them lift the motor and carry it to the main deck. "Let's test this bugger out before the storm hits."

Storm? When they got to the main deck, Charlotte understood. The sky was full of dark and menacing clouds. She wished they had grabbed their cloaks from the storeroom. She squinted in the direction the ship was heading. She couldn't be sure, but it looked like the outline of the mainland could be seen in the distance. Maybe it was just clouds.

"We're close," Jax said, leaning in and pointing in the direction Charlotte had been looking.

It was the mainland then. Still too far to swim though, if it came to that.

The captain bellowed instructions for the crew to hurry as they loaded the motor onto a smaller boat that hung suspended on the side of the larger ship.

Charlotte leaned over the side, even as the waves seemed to swell. The red morning had been a sailor's warning for what the day would hold.

The small boat hit the water, and the men struggled to attach it to a frame that had been built on the side of the ship.

"I guess the captain was confident we'd get it working," Charlotte whispered to Jax.

He just smiled.

The sun collector reflected as the ship rocked, only the top of the motor visible. Charlotte reached up and squeezed one of Rapha's legs, hoping, praying that this would work. But how did they plan to activate the motor?

As soon as the lifeboat was out of the water, the captain rolled up his sleeve, displaying a gazer on his wrist. Charlotte gasped as he tapped the device and projected a complex control panel.

"He has a way to control the motor from his gazer? Brilliant!" Charlotte grinned.

With a few spins and pulls of the holographic buttons and levers, the ship lurched forward. Charlotte fell into Jax, who thankfully had better sea legs than her.

The captain let out a whoop and threw his hands in the air. "Ha ha! It works!"

Charlotte pushed her hair back from her face. The strong winds were pulling every last curl free, and the skies darkened even further.

The crew tied down the rest of the sails, but the motor and the swells, or likely both, kept them moving forward.

A flash of lightning lit up the entire dark sky. The actual bolt was close enough to flash for a few seconds in Charlotte's periphery.

Then the clap of thunder came.

CRACK.

The entire ship shook, reverberating from the sound.

The crew jumped into action and shouted instructions. The captain and second mate stood leaning over the railing, arguing.

"We need to get back to the room," Jax shouted over the wind and the next clap of thunder.

Charlotte nodded. She didn't need to be told twice.

Jax helped her keep her balance as they ran for the steps that led to the lower level. Charlotte's heartbeat thrummed in her ears.

The clouds let loose pelting rain moments before they were able to get under cover. All it took were those few moments to soak them from head to toe.

"Where's Rapha?" Charlotte cried out when they reached the stairs. Worry began to mix with her already tight nerves. She couldn't remember when the monkey had left her shoulder.

The ship rocked as they hit another swell, and Jax grabbed her and sat her down on the steps. "I can't see a thing," he said apologetically. "Hopefully, his animal instincts kicked in before ours and he's already under cover."

The ship rose again, then plummeted downward, lurching to the left as it struggled to remain upright in the maelstrom.

Charlotte closed her eyes, trying to keep from vomiting.

Jax led them down the steps, and they made their way back to the storeroom. When they were finally inside, Charlotte dropped to the floor and hugged one of the legs of the now-empty table which was bolted to the floor.

Surely, they couldn't get so close to the mainland just to die in a shipwreck. Her whole body was shaking—a combination of being wet and from fear.

There was a lull in the thunder, and Jax sat up straight from where he had been huddled next to Charlotte on the floor. "What's that sound?" He looked around the room. "It sounds like—"

"Snoring," Charlotte finished. Her head was still pounding, but the sound was familiar. And was it her imagination or was the boat rocking just a bit less?

Jax scooted along the floor towards the sound.

"Rapha!" He called out with a laugh. The little monkey was curled up between two barrels, fast asleep. At the sound of his name, he jumped up, squeaking his displeasure at being woken.

Relief washed over Charlotte, but it was quickly followed by annoyance. She addressed the little monkey through her own chattering teeth. "One, how did you get in here? Two, how in the Empire could you be sleeping in this storm? Isn't there something you can do? I assume the plan was for us to get to the Mountain Kingdom alive!"

Her questions were interrupted by another crack of thunder.

Charlotte sighed and pulled Rapha in for a hug. "I'm glad you're safe though."

Jax found them some dry clothes, and they took turns changing. Charlotte was sure her body would be covered in black and blue marks from being jostled around. Finally, Jax draped their cloaks over them, and they sat at the table for what felt like an hour.

"Things seem to be calm now," Jax said.

It was true, the extreme rocking had subsided.

The captain threw open the door to the storeroom and entered with a huff. His clothes were soaked, but white teeth glistened behind a face full of hair. "Brilliant, just brilliant, my girl. You sure you don't want to stay on? Sail the open seas? A crew full of seamen to protect you?"

She gulped. *How much did this captain know?* she wondered.

Jax stood, eyes narrowed, muscles taut. It wasn't often that Jax grew hostile, but Charlotte knew he would be quick to strike if they were threatened.

"Whoa there, son. I'm a man of my word, certainly one that's promised on the sea. If you two want to exit in Portemore, we're almost there. But you're clearly running from somethin' and I'm just saying—staying is an option."

Charlotte stood and stepped a nudge in front of Jax. "Thanks, but Portemore is our stop."

The captain shrugged. "Suit yourselves. Gather your things and get upstairs though, we're not docking long." He left as quickly as he had come.

Jax let out a long breath. "Remember that saying of Gran's about live-long-enough? She called it L-L-E." An impish grin had returned to his face.

Charlotte nodded, thankful Jax's anger was always quick to fade. "Yes, she always said that things have a way of working out in the end." Though she hadn't used the saying much over the last three years.

"Well, when we live long enough, we're going to have one mighty story to tell our grandkids."

Uhm, did he just say our *grandkids?* Charlotte wondered. She may have just added one more problem to her growing list.

CHAPTER 17

"L ET. US. GO." TAINE spoke the words slowly and in a danger- ously quiet way. Two men restrained him on either side as he stood opposite Sonos in the alley.

Wylder laughed. "You look a little outnumbered, inked one."

Taimani was held by a man twice her size. Another stood near- by.

Sibi was nowhere to be seen.

Though Taimani had a trickle of blood running down from where her captor's knife was held to her throat, she remained perfectly calm, as if she were the one in control. Her eyes burned silent anger, and she made discreet motions with her fingers.

Only because Sonos had spent the last few days in intense proximity to her and Taine together did he notice what she was doing. Unfortunately, he had not learned enough to know what the signals meant.

Taine tapped a response against his thigh.

"Feeling nervous, big guy?" Wylder asked Taine.

Taimani muttered something under her breath.

Wylder turned, "What was that?"

That was the opening Taine needed. He lunged into action, pulling his massive arms together to throw the two men holding him off balance. At the same time, Taimani spun out of the grip of her attacker. With a few well-placed kicks she snatched the knife from the thug. She then turned to ram it against Wylder's collarbone.

The move would have been perfect except for one small glitch. Instead of crumbling to the ground, Wylder stood and simply glared at Taimani. He did not appear to have been affected in the least by the strike, whereas Taimani stood, her hand shaking, eyebrows drawn together in confusion.

"What in the—" Sonos stared, mouth agape, at the bent knife on the ground. Everything had happened in the blink of an eye.

"Reinforced clothing that is stronger than armor, but as light and flexible as a normal cloak." Wylder smiled at Taimani, then stuck out his palm and tapped a button on his forearm. A feathered dart shot out of his shimmering sleeve.

Taimani's eyes rolled up into her head, and she crumpled to the ground.

"Technology *always* wins," Wylder smirked.

"No!" Sonos ran to Taimani.

He heard a struggle behind him and turned to see Taine in a heap on the ground with a feather in his neck too.

Feet pattered behind the thugs as Sibi fled back towards the square with the pack and Taine's sword. He must have been hiding.

One of the men moved to chase the boy, but Wylder stopped him. "The boy is of no consequence. These two..." he pointed to Sonos and Taine "...are everything. She's the cherry on top."

Sonos could see both Taimani and Taine still breathing, though very slowly. Wylder moved closer to Sonos; his palm extended. There was a flash of color. "Sorry Highness, but it's easier this way."

The world went black.

A door slammed in the distance. Sonos groaned. His entire body ached. When he blinked, his head flooded with pain. He squinted and slowly opened his eyes to take in the dimly lit room. He was laying on his side on a hard, stone floor. His arms were bound behind him. He squirmed into a seated position and leaned against a wooden barrel.

"Welcome back to the land of the living," Taine said from the other side of the room.

"Took you long enough," Taimani added. They were seated back-to-back on two wooden chairs.

Sonos blinked in a moment of confusion, his brain working slower than normal. What was the last thing he could remember? *Oh! Wylder!*

"Where's Sibi?" Sonos asked, worried when he didn't see the boy anywhere.

"I was hoping you could tell us," Taine answered.

"I... I remember him running from the alley after the two of you went down." Sonos rolled his shoulders, trying to loosen some muscles. The after-effects of whatever drugs Wylder used were determined to hang on. "He took our pack and the hooked sword."

"Ah, our little hero in the making," Taimani said.

They could certainly use a hero now. Sonos scanned the room. They were in some kind of storage room or cellar. There were no windows and a wooden staircase on the far side of the room. The barrel Sonos leaned against smelled like ale, and the nearby shelves had bottles of what looked to be spiced wine.

"Wait—" Something popped into Sonos' brain. "I thought warriors from Kimwaki couldn't be poisoned? Didn't Wylder's darts have no effect when he tried to use them on you on the river?"

"It would seem our friend has come up with some new kind of concoction." Taimani scowled.

"Okay, we need a plan." Sonos shook his head, trying to focus. "Can't you two use some kind of warrior strength to free yourselves from the ropes?"

"Our boy is finally thinking again." Taimani rolled her eyes.

"They have some kind of sensor under our seats." Taine sighed. "As soon as we move, a loud buzzer sounds, and some goons come running down the steps."

"They had just gone back upstairs before you woke up," Taimani added.

Oh, that was the slamming door that woke me up, Sonos thought.

"Let me find something to cut these ropes." Sonos pulled his knees towards him in an effort to stand, checking to make sure there was no sensor under him. A flashing green light on his ankle caught his eye. "I think we have a bigger problem."

"Oh, joy," Taimani said.

"Yep, it's a tracker." Sonos tilted his head to get a better look at the metal clasp fitted around one of his boots.

"You can get it off?" Taimani asked.

"I can try. But first, I need to get my hands and feet free." Sonos stood and squirmed onto the barrel. He managed to balance and grab one of the wine bottles from the shelf.

"Training this past year has served you well, Sonny." Taine said from where he sat.

Sonos grunted.

A loud boom from outside the room reverberated through the ceiling of the cellar.

"Was that thunder?" Sonos wondered aloud.

A second clap seemed to confirm.

"It seems that red sunrise we saw this morning held true," Taine said.

Sonos hoped the noise of the storm above would cover his next move. He positioned the wine bottle as best as he could and dropped it to the stone floor. He was rewarded with shattered glass, and no one came running down the steps to investigate. He hopped off the barrel and stooped to pick up a large shard of the glass.

"Come, bring it over here and I'll help you, bright eyes," Taimani said.

"Bright eyes?" Sonos furrowed his brow.

"Trying out some different nicknames since you don't like Sonny." She laughed. "Plus, I've heard it described that baby blues like yours pierce the soul. So 'bright eyes' works, no?"

Taine gruffed and turned his head to give Sonos a warning glare.

Sonos grimaced and shrugged. *Awkward.*

He hopped over to the warriors, having to pause halfway across the room to catch his breath and rest his sore muscles. They had been left in their cloaks, and Sonos was now sweating. Finally, he reached Taimani and placed the piece of glass in her hand.

Even with her arms bound against Taine, she moved deftly and had his hands free in no time.

He rubbed his wrists, working out the kinks, then cut his feet free. He paused to check the hidden pocket in his cloak and breathed a sigh of relief when he felt his journal inside. Even though its pages were blank for the most part, it was one of the last remnants of home. Not to mention the maps and letter from Sah Timur.

"Uhm, Sonos?" Taimani raised her eyebrows.

"Sorry, coming." He cut the ropes that bound the warriors.

The storm raged louder outside, booms of thunder reaching the cellar on a regular basis.

"Any suggestions on how to disable the sensor?" Taine asked. Even though the ropes were cut, they couldn't move.

"And that tracker?" Taimani added. "It won't do us much good to escape if we're being tracked."

Sonos sat and pulled his ankle close. Even though he had more interest in chemistry and history, Timur had insisted on exposing him to physical tech like drones, transmitters, and trackers like these-beyond the everyday tech like gazers.

He ran his hand over the metal band looking for the tiny groove. When he depressed the button, a small hologram appeared with a keypad to enter a code.

"Ah, there we go." Sonos smiled, happy to see it was like the ones he had learned.

"Uhm, why are you smiling though? Unless you somehow know Wylder's code?" Taimani asked.

Sonos cast a mischievous grin at Taine. "Remember that time Timur taught us the failsafe way to disable these?"

"When Baku had the brilliant idea of strapping a tracker on every bodyguard?" Taine scoffed. "Yeah, thankfully the Empress convinced your father it was a security risk for the nobles."

"Aye, but I remember the workaround. So, the short answer is yes, I can get this tracker off. But it will likely send an alert to Wylder when I do, so let's do that when we're out of the building."

"Okay, so sensor then?" Taimani asked.

"I may have an idea for that one, too. But first, I need a promise." Sonos said.

The buzzer from the sensor sounded even louder than Sonos expected. It didn't take long for the door to fly open and footsteps to pound down the stairs. Sonos once again lay on the floor, eyes closed holding as still as possible, his hands and feet loosely tied.

"You two trying a thing *again?*" a deep voice asked.

The warriors sat tied in the chairs, but Sonos had loosely strung the ropes back on.

"Your precious prince hasn't woken up, and it looks like he stopped breathing. I think you need to check him out," Taimani said.

A boot nudged Sonos in the gut, but he did his best not to respond. The sound of heavy breathing and distinctly foul breath hovered over his face.

"He's alive—" The guard was cut off and broken glass shattered on the floor.

That was Sonos' signal. He jumped up, shedding the ropes and grabbing a bottle he had placed on the barrel. One guard already lay motionless at his feet.

The buzzer blared incessantly, mixing with the rolling thunderclaps from outside.

In short order, Taine took down the second guard, the element of surprise working in their favor this time.

"Hurry, we need to get them on the sensor." Sonos ran over to help Taimani while Taine hefted his guard to the chair.

Finally, they had both guards seated and the sensor stopped blaring.

"What's taking so long?" a guard shouted from the top of the steps. After no response, the guard came down a few steps.

A colored dart flew past Sonos, but this time it found its mark on the guard. His eyes widened, then he slumped and rolled down the remaining steps.

Sonos turned to see Taimani lower the blowgun from her lips, a smile on her face.

"Tech doesn't always win." Taimani pulled the remaining darts from one of the guards in the chair. "This guy had my collection. Thief." She strapped the pouch around her thigh and covered it with her cloak.

Taine took a knife from one of the other guards and then tossed one to Sonos. Sonos bent over the guard who had rolled down the steps, to ensure he was still alive.

"No mortal wounds, as promised," Taimani told Sonos.

He nodded thankfully. The image of the servant he had accidentally killed still haunted him, and he wanted no further deaths on his conscience.

"Who knows where Wylder is if he hasn't come down already. Let's get moving," Taine said, leading the way up the stairs.

The stairwell opened to the inside of a pantry, and the sounds of an active kitchen were just beyond the pantry door.

"Mani front, Sonos follow, and I'll cover the back," Taine gave the orders.

Taimani opened the door, and the three of them stepped out into a busy kitchen. It was so busy, in fact, that no one noticed them until they were halfway to the back door.

"Hey!" a woman's voice called out. "What are you doing back here?"

Taimani took off running.

Sonos and Taine followed close on her heels.

The door emptied onto a back street. It was pouring rain. Sonos pulled up the hood of his cloak.

Taimani didn't hesitate and led them quickly down the street.

"Taine! Mani! Sonny!" A familiar voice called through the storm from a nearby alley.

They ran into the alley and found a relieved looking Sibi. The young boy squirmed the big pack off his back and handed Taine the hooked sword.

"Ah! My brave, little man. You have made yourself a hero in my book." Taine twirled the weapon in his hands, then strapped it to his back. He took the pack from Sibi as well to place it over the weapon.

"Well done, Sib." Taimani stuck a hand into his hood and ruffled his hair.

Sonos bowed his head to the young boy. "It's good to see you. Well done. But as I told you before, do *not* call me *Sonny.*"

"We'll get you a better name, *Son*, but let's keep moving," Taine said, eying the street.

"One sec," Sonos said, stooping to trigger the tracker on his ankle. He entered the bypass code he had memorized prior, and mercifully it still worked. The tracker clicked, and Sonos was able to unclasp it and toss it aside. "Now we're ready."

"Come. I'll show you how to get back to the proper side." Sibi's head bobbed as he led them through the narrow alley.

"Proper side?" Sonos asked.

It soon became evident though. The Portemore they had entered from the docks had cobblestone streets, a mix of wagons, vendors, people walking, and even the occasional guard zipping by on a flyer-board. Where they were now had basic dirt streets turned to mud with the heavy rain. Many windows had boards covering them, and it was generally more rundown.

Sibi led them through the meandering streets to a large gate, and Sonos' pulse spiked. Guards were not a good thing. But the flow of traffic seemed to go both in and out, unhindered. Everyone had the hoods of their cloaks pulled tightly above their heads or were running to seek shelter.

"They only close the gates after dusk," Sibi explained.

They joined the flow of people making their way to the 'proper' side of the city.

The difference in the road and buildings was immediate. Sonos was glad to be out of the muddy not-the-city side and back to a road lined with stone.

Sibi ran towards the shelter of an outcropping from a nearby building, but Taimani pulled him back.

"We need to keep moving," she said, taking the lead.

An alert buzzed on Wylder's gazer again.

What were those useless guards doing? Or not doing, rather.

The first time the sensor had triggered the guards confirmed they contained the two warriors easily. That didn't sit well with Wylder, and his mercenary instincts were rarely wrong.

At first, he had thought it serendipitous that a high-ranking Elite, none other than Captain Diekololaoluwa, had arrived in Portemore this same day. If he could offer the prince and warriors up to the Elites now in exchange for payment, it would save him the trouble and the risk of trying to transport them to Pergamum himself.

Just as he pressed his gazer to hail the guards at the tavern, a pompous Elite dressed in black with gold and red stripes called him over. "The captain will see you now."

Those guards better have things under control, Wylder thought.

After crisscrossing through streets and alleys for the better part of an hour, Sonos became convinced Taimani was leading them in circles. The rain had finally stopped, but Sonos kept his hood up, as did Taine. Taimani allowed her hood down, but had her hair loose, covering any tattoos. The sun was getting low in the sky, already hidden behind the buildings.

They passed Woodyard Square, where the family from Salan now stood on tall stools, with nooses around each of their necks.

They're still alive? Sonos wondered.

Sibi hesitated, but Taine nudged him forward. "Not now, Sib. Keep up with Mani."

They headed in the direction of the dockyards. She had suggested starting back at the beginning, and no one had disagreed.

The smell of saltwater, fish, and a press of bodies leaving the port reminded Sonos how much he hated the chaos of the area. They were now in the market next to the docks, a few vendors trying to sell the last of their goods for the day.

A nearby light post turned on, then others follow suit as the sun continued its descent. Sonos was glad to see some level of technology at play. He paused at one of the posts to look up at a sun collector that was mounted and caged near the top of the post.

Another flicker of light in the distance caught Sonos' eye. He squinted at the middle level of what looked like a three-story building.

He remembered a line from Timur's letter, *"Follow the Light, it will show the way."*

"I know where we need to go," he declared.

A light from within one of the windows was flickering off and on. It looked like a deliberate pattern.

In fact, it was the same pattern that emitted from the Salan tower at the feast.

CHAPTER 18

WIND WHIPPED AGAINST CHARLOTTE'S face, pulling loose a few rebel curls from the top bun she had worked diligently to pull tight. But nothing could wipe the smile from her face as the ship drew closer to Portemore.

The air held after-the-storm freshness, and the sky was bathed in reds and purples, drawing the last rays of the sun into a painting worthy of her sister's collection.

"None of the descriptions my parents gave of this place do it justice." Jax spoke with a faraway voice, his forearms resting on the side of the ship as he gazed at the harbor.

Charlotte adjusted the covered flyer-board strapped to her back, causing a squeak from Rapha who was perched on her shoulder. She pulled away a bit from Jax. His earlier comment about *their* grandkids had her emotions in a bit of a swirl.

Back in Jamroq, he had been so focused on training with his Freedom Fighters, and her on the tech and plan to get back her sisters... *Since when was Jax thinking about the future—or me—in that way?* she wondered.

At the moment, he seemed transfixed on Portemore though, so she pushed the comment to the back of her mind. She would chew on that problem later.

"Ho! Watch it!" A sailor pushed his way between them to tie a rope to a notch on the side of the ship.

The captain and crew resonated at a similar frequency to the frenzy of passing vessels of every shape and size.

Jax motioned her to where the plank would be lowered as soon as they docked.

Conflicting emotions about Jax aside, energy pulsed through Charlotte as she looked out at the dock. As men scurried on the pier to tie the ropes thrown from the sailors, excitement warmed her cheeks.

"We made it," she whispered to the wind.

The sprawling city teemed with life. Buildings rose beyond the docks; towering structures that were three and floor levels stretched on as far as her eye could see.

"Five dock-hands, fish vendors, market district..." Jax muttered observations under his breath.

Charlotte leaned in, Rapha's small form between their heads. "You know any plan is going to fall apart the moment we land."

Jax turned and cocked his head. "Don't tell me the journey is already turning you into a pessimist."

"No." She hesitated. "At least I don't think so." Charlotte mused for a moment. Over the last few years, she had to be a rock of hope, especially in the face of her dad's depression. No, she wouldn't let her family down by allowing doubt and pessimism to dominate her now.

As soon as the ship was tied and a plank lowered to connect to the dock, Jax grabbed Charlotte's hand and ran off the ship. He didn't stop until they reached the end of the pier and stepped onto land.

Charlotte bent over catching her breath from the unexpected sprint. "What was that about?"

"Sorry, I didn't want to take any chances of that captain trying to keep us on board." Jax looked around as a surge of people, carts, animals, vendors, and all matter of beings pushed and pressed around them. It seemed everyone was in a hurry to get home. It wouldn't be long before the sun disappeared.

Rapha squeaked excitedly and clutched Charlotte's shoulder.

"Ow," Charlotte pulled Rapha from his perch and rubbed where he had dug in. "No need to get violent, Raph. What is it?"

Rapha continued to squirm and wave his arms.

"It looks like he's trying to point us to something," Jax said.

Charlotte looked around but the flow of people on the street continued steadily with nothing in particular standing out.

In fact, she couldn't help but enjoy the diversity of skin tones, clothing, and accents. Her eyes caught on a group of four who stood looking almost as disoriented as them.

Two had the hoods of their cloaks pulled up, but a young boy with blond curls smiled and pointed at Rapha.

A beautiful young woman about Charlotte's age glanced their way. Her dark eyes had a fierceness in them, emphasized by dark liner.

Intrigued, Charlotte made a step towards them, but the woman pulled the young boy and moved their group in another direction.

"Who was that?" Jax asked.

"Not sure, actually." Charlotte chastised herself for feeling pulled in by the first group of random strangers she saw.

Rapha grunted. He pushed Charlotte's chin up, causing her to look towards the top of the nearby buildings.

Frustration was beginning to bubble up. "All I see are tall buildings, a few stars above, lights turning on in windows—" Rapha interrupted Charlotte, squeaking again and nodding.

Wait, is that... Charlotte wondered. "Jax, look! Do you see the streetlamps? Actual lights, not torches? I bet they have sun collectors." Her mind raced with possibilities.

She stepped out to cross the street and immediately collided with a vendor who was rushing by with a fruit tray strapped around his neck. Oranges and apples tumbled all around, and the small man started cussing, angrily shouting at Charlotte.

"I'm so sorry," she said, bending over to help pick up the fruit.

"You'll pay for this," the man grabbed Charlotte's arm, his eyes flashing.

Jax walked over, dropping the fruits he had helped pick up back in the man's tray. He stood to his full height, which towered over the vendor. "She said she was sorry. It was an accident."

The man hesitated, and Jax reached towards the knife strapped to his waist. The vendor gazed at Jax's hand, and finally let go of Charlotte, cursing under his breath. He hastily arranged the fruit on his tray, grabbing the fallen pieces from Charlotte's hands.

"Stupid newcomers. No sense," he muttered and walked away, but not before throwing a menacing scowl over his shoulder.

Charlotte released the breath she had been holding once he was a safe distance away. She adjusted the covered board on her back and turned a grateful eye to Jax. They needed to keep moving.

"Hey, where's Raph?" Worry shot through Charlotte as she looked around for the monkey. Where had he gone? She caught sight of Rapha on the other side of the street, waving his arms and pointing to something in the distance. A flicker of light caught her eye, but a loud shout interrupted her thoughts.

"That's them!" The vendor walked beside an Imperial guard, pointing in their direction.

Jax tensed beside her, grabbed her hand and ran in the opposite direction.

Charlotte turned to look behind her and called out to Rapha, but the guard was gaining ground on them.

As they ran, Charlotte reached under the sleeve of her jacket and tapped her gazer to record their movements. After losing the guard, they needed to make their way back to the harbor to find Rapha.

The main road leading from the harbor twisted and turned like a river. They dodged and ducked around wagons and people alike, trying to put some distance between them and the guard.

After passing a sharp bend, a young boy called out. "Hey, this way!"

Jax paused and looked to Charlotte.

Charlotte glanced behind them, but the bend kept the guard out of sight. "We need to get off the main road." She grabbed Jax's arm and stepped into the alley.

It was dark in the crack between the buildings, with only slivers of lights casting through from the streetlamps.

"I saw the fruit vendor give you trouble," the boy said. His voice cracked mid-sentence, as one at the beginning stages of puberty. "I can help get you to safety," he squeaked.

Jax kept glancing towards the street.

"Just get us away from this guard, then we can talk." Charlotte waved her hand for them to keep moving.

The boy stuck to side streets and alleys, moving deftly through the maze of the city. At one point they passed a big open square and Charlotte paused.

What in the Empire? she thought.

"Is that a *family* standing with nooses around their necks?" she asked.

The boy nodded, dark hair tumbling over his eyes. He wiped his hair back. "Refugee family who didn't know enough to connect with us, and they were caught."

"Us?" Jax asked, skepticism filling his voice.

"Oh, uhm," he hesitated. "My uncle will explain."

Jax frowned, but Charlotte didn't want to be left alone in the city with a guard chasing them. "What's your name?"

"Dayo," the boy answered. "But let's keep moving, the gate will be closing soon."

"Char?" Jax placed a hand on her shoulder.

A part of Charlotte wondered when the boy said "us" if he might be part of the Underground. The network her parents had been convinced could help them get to Pergamum.

"We'll look for Rapha tomorrow, but it's not safe to be out tonight, and at least we'll make some important connections we may need for the future," she whispered back. "Come."

After more twists and turns than Charlotte could count, they reached a gate with large wooden doors that were wide open. There was a steady stream of people heading through to whatever lay beyond.

The guards barely cast a glance at those going through to the other side. However, a young woman was stopped immediately when she tried to leave.

"It's after dark, woman. No passing," the guard gruffed.

"Please, I have urgent business in the city," the woman said.

The guard laughed. "Sure you do. But it'll have to wait till morning."

The woman continued to plead.

Dayo urged Charlotte and Jax along. "Hurry," he said under his breath.

As they entered the other side, everything instantly felt grimier. The road turned from stone to packed dirt which was muddy from the earlier rains. The buildings were smaller, windows were boarded, and people scuttled about quickly with their heads down. There were no streetlamps here, only light that spilled out from rowdy, loud rooms.

Dayo led them down the main road, then ducked into a nearby alley.

Jax hesitated again and pulled Charlotte's arm.

"I don't know about this, Char."

The knot in her stomach agreed with him.

"What else can we do though?" Charlotte replied. "You saw how the guards weren't allowing anyone to leave this side to go back to the city."

Jax sighed.

"Let's just keep moving forward," Charlotte said, trying to put some cheer in her voice. "Besides, I still want to meet his uncle."

"Assuming his uncle isn't a murderer," Jax muttered.

Charlotte rolled her eyes, then hooked her arm through his before entering the alley. She missed Rapha's presence on her shoulder but was thankful Jax was by her side.

Dayo was not far off, standing in an open doorway. He waved them over. "Come, come."

They stepped into a dimly lit room with two candles flickering from a long table in the center of the room. A spindly old man paced around the table muttering to himself.

"Two ounces of iron. No, no, that's not right. Three? Four, maybe."

"Uncle?" Dayo tried to get the man's attention. "Uncle Ned?"

"Huh? Oh. Dayo? Yes, yes, it's you." Ned blinked and looked around the room as if coming out of a stupor.

"Uncle, I brought some friends. They just arrived in the city."

Ned's eyes suddenly became laser-focused and sharp as he looked in their direction. He walked over to Charlotte and stood directly in front of her.

"Who are you?" He leaned closer and sniffed the air around her. "You have a funny smell."

Charlotte scooted back uncomfortably. "I'm Charlotte, and this is Jaxtyn." She cleared her throat, trying not to let her nerves show.

Ned's eyes glazed over again. He looked up at the ceiling. "Three ounces of iron, two drops of venom." He went back to pacing and muttering.

Jax leaned towards Dayo, "Is he okay?"

"Absolutely," the lad said a bit too confidently. Dayo gave pleading look to Charlotte. "He just gets a little—focused—sometimes."

Dayo moved to the far corner of the room where a small cot was set up. He pulled a mat out from under the cot and spread it on the floor on the opposite wall. "Silvey will be back in a while with some food. Until then, you can relax here."

"Silvey?" Charlotte asked.

"She works in one of the taverns. Always comes back late but brings food to share." Dayo looked towards his uncle who was now scribbling in a notebook by the candlelight. "And hopefully Uncle will be finished with his work by then, too."

Jax closed his eyes and exhaled, his hands balled into fists.

Charlotte knew that look of frustration, but there was nothing to do about it now.

She walked forward and sat on the straw mat that Dayo had spread. She lay the flyer-board, still covered, on the floor beside her and opened the messenger bag, pulling out two portugyals. She handed one to Dayo. "Here you go, for you and your uncle."

The boy's eyes lit up as he grabbed the food. "Thanks," he said, peeling off a piece for Ned and filling his mouth with a bite.

Jax sat down next to Charlotte, their backs against the wall as they split the other fruit. "We'll take turns keeping watch. And get out of here as soon as day breaks."

Charlotte nodded, worry already unsettling her mind. "Okay."

Exhaustion from the ups and downs of the past few days set in, and she rested her head against Jax's shoulder. She enjoyed his earthy scent that always seemed to hold a hint of mint or herbs.

"You think we'll be able to find Rapha tomorrow?" She felt her heart sink even as she asked the question. "How did we get separated so quickly?"

"We'll find him." Jax spoke with a quiet confidence. "Remember, he found us in the middle of nowhere when we weren't even looking. Plus, we have a mission to finish for him."

Jax's calmness was contagious, and Charlotte's eyelids felt like lead. Her last thought was of Rapha pointing towards something before they ran. "What had he been pointing at? Something in one of those buildings?" she mumbled.

Chapter 19

"WE NEED TO MOVE," Taimani nudged Sonos, breaking his concentration. "I'm seeing more guards here than yesterday. Something's up."

"Give me a chance." Sonos squinted again at the window with the blinking light. It was like a hand was waving in front of a candle, causing the specific pattern to repeat.

To most people, it might seem like random flickering, but Sonos was sure it was deliberate. One, two, three seconds of light, two seconds of darkness. Five seconds of light, one second of darkness. Two seconds of light, three seconds of darkness. Then the whole sequence repeated—same as before at the feast.

Was it some kind of message? It's a rather short pattern. Maybe it's a call, he wondered.

Sonos considered Timur's letter. *Follow the Light, it will show the way. Move the mountain without touching it, and you will find what you are looking for.*

The only mountains remotely close was the range belonging to the reclusive Mountain Kingdom. And the last time he saw the blinking light it was from the Salan Legacy Tower. Were the two related? His mind swarmed with more and more questions, but he needed to make a choice, and fast, in the gathering gloom. They needed to keep moving forward.

"Do you see that little monkey?" Sibi asked, tugging on Sonos' sleeve.

Sonos looked up as Sibi took a step towards a girl with a white capuchin monkey on her shoulder. The girl looked to be about Taimani's age, but shorter than average. Soft curls spilled out from a messy bun, and she had on a dark jacket, form fitting-pants, and high boots. Captivating green eyes shifted his way.

Sonos caught his breath. But no, surely, she couldn't see his face hidden deep in the hood of his cloak.

A dark, rather menacing guy followed her gaze and looked their way.

"Let's go. Like, *now*. Before we bring more attention to ourselves. Everyone else is moving." Taimani pulled Sibi back by the arm and looked at Sonos.

"Fine," Sonos said. "That way." He pointed at the building and started walking. He chastised himself for being so easily distracted.

After they cleared the harbor, Taimani jogged ahead to scout.

The last of the sun disappeared, but the combination of light from the streetlamps and torchlight that spilled out from the buildings provided more than enough light to see clearly.

Sonos was still getting used to the mix of both Imperial tech used in the streets, and ancient torches and candlelight used in non-Imperial homes and buildings.

Sibi paused to place a hand against the wall, catching his breath.

"How are you holding up, Sib?" Sonos asked. They had been doing a lot of walking, and Sibi had also carried Taine's sword and their pack for an extended period before they had escaped Wylder. They needed to remember that the boy was still healing.

"I'm just... tired, sorry," Sibi answered with a sigh.

Taine stepped closer and laid a hand on Sibi's shoulder. "The rush and excitement of the last few days may be wearing off, young one. We'll take it a little slower."

Sibi took a deep breath and nodded. "Slower," he gasped, his warm eyes losing steam.

Sonos worried about how they would make it to the Mountain Kingdom if Sibi continued to deteriorate, but one problem at a time. First to figure out what was going on in that building.

Soon enough, they caught up to Taimani and crammed together in an alley across the street. A wooden sign with a steaming loaf of bread identified it as a bakery, at least on the main floor. The shop was closed but the flickering light still repeated from a window on the third floor.

"This is definitely it," Sonos said, staring again at the pattern, running through any known codes for what it could mean.

"I'll run a quick security check around the building," Taimani said, then walked out into the street.

"Do you really think the blinking light is linked to what you saw from the Salan Tower?" Sibi whispered to Sonos.

"I can't say *how* they're linked, but it's definitely the same pattern."

After a few minutes, Taimani rejoined the group in the alley. "I'm not seeing anything out of order on the street or around the building. What's your plan of approach, Sonos?"

"Let's start simple, shall we?" He stepped out onto the street before she could argue.

Sonos approached the closed front door of the bakery, Sibi at his side.

Muffled sounds could be heard coming from inside. At least someone was there. The door was made from sturdy but rough wood, and no knocker was installed.

Sonos used the palm of his hand to knock and shouted "Hello!" with a strong voice.

Taimani muttered under her breath, "So much for tact."

Sonos glanced back and noticed Taine had stayed in the alley, likely to keep watch from the street.

Footsteps approached from inside, and Sonos leaned in closer to listen. Out of nowhere, a creature jumped and landed right next to him. Sonos yelped.

"What the—" Taimani already had a dagger in hand.

A brazen little monkey with a white face looked straight at Sonos and seemed to wink.

"Did that hairball just—" Sonos started, then the monkey turned and ran up Sibi's legs to perch on the boy's shoulder.

Sibi giggled with delight. "Hey little guy," he said and rubbed its head.

Is that the same monkey Sibi had seen in the harbor? Something pulled in Sonos' mind.

The door scraped open, and an old lady peeked through a crack, candlelight spilling out to where they stood. "We're closed," she grunted, but then squinted her eyes at Sonos. "Who are you?"

"I'm... uh..." Sonos wasn't quite sure how to answer. His hood still covered his face, but he wasn't comfortable enough to let it down. Maybe this had been a bad idea.

Sibi stepped in front of Sonos with the monkey still on his shoulder. "Hi! I'm Sibi. These are my friends Sonny and Taimani."

The old woman shifted her gaze to Sibi. "Well, at least one of you has some manners." Her eyes flickered towards Sonos, but then back to Sibi. "And I see you brought a little hairy friend, too. Come in, then. Need to get you off the street."

She opened the door wide. Her silver hair was pulled back into a low bun, and she wore an apron over a long skirt and bright red blouse. She wiped her hands as if she had just come from the kitchen.

"What about the last one? The one in the alley? Tell him to get in here, too." The lady looked at Taimani as she spoke, and Taimani returned an unflinching, icy gaze.

The lady sighed but kept her shoulders square. "The one who seeks you is quickly approaching, and I don't think you want to leave your friend outside."

After some hesitation, Taimani finally hmphed and hand signaled to her brother.

A confused looking Taine jogged over, and they all stepped inside.

The old lady closed the door and placed a finger over her lips.

A long, wide window was covered with panels for the night, but the lady pointed to some wide cracks which gave sight of the street. A few moments later, a pair of guards zipped by on flyer-boards. Only Elites had access to that kind of technology. *What are they doing here?* Sonos thought.

"Not them," the lady said in a soft voice. "Although their presence here is... *interesting.*" She paused and continued looking at the street.

A short time later, a man passed through the edges of the nearest streetlamp, and Sonos recognized the unmistakable long, dark coat and floppy hat. Two bulky figures followed in his wake. They paused on the street outside the bakery, turning around slowly. One of the guys with Wylder stuck his head into the alley where Taine had just been.

Taimani cursed under her breath.

After a short discussion, Wylder and the guards kept moving down the street.

"Do you think they saw us come in here?" Sonos looked between Taine and Taimani.

"Don't worry, young man. You came to the right place. You're protected in here." The old lady's gaze drifted to the monkey which still sat perched on Sibi's shoulder as she spoke. "I see you carry a special friend with you, Master Sibi. What have you named him?"

A grin spread from ear to ear on Sibi's face. "Well, actually, he just sort of found us." Sibi rubbed the monkey's belly and it chittered pleasantly. "He came to us right outside— Oh wait, is he yours?" His face fell for a moment.

"Nobody *owns* something from another realm." She paused, gazing at the monkey.

Sonos began to wonder if she was a little bit crazy.

"But I'm jumping ahead, my apologies. I haven't even introduced myself. My name is Miss Gemma." She straightened her apron and smiled warmly. "And you are just in time for dinner. Please, come join us. And hopefully without hiding your face."

Miss Gemma winked at Sonos. She then wrapped an arm around Sibi's shoulder, careful not to disturb the monkey, and she led him around the empty bakery counter towards a curtained doorway at the far end of the room. "Come Master Sibi, you still haven't told me the name of your little friend."

Sonos glanced at Taine, who shrugged his shoulders. "She did just save us from being seen by the Elites and Wylder."

Taimani shook her head. "There's more to Miss Gemma than what she's letting on."

"Agreed, but there's only one way to find out," Sonos said, reluctantly pulling down his hood. As he walked towards the doorway, his stomach growled as the smell of freshly baked bread grew stronger.

The doorway opened into a large room that housed a kitchen on one side with multiple brick ovens and workspaces for the bakers. On the other side was a long table with benches along both sides. Sonos counted six men and two women seated at the table, and another woman and two girls cooking, with a handful of kids running around in between.

Taking in the people at the table, they were a real mix-up. The men's dress ranged from loose cloth shirts that Sonos recognized from the harbor, rough leather used by workmen, one in a button-down shirt that merchants favored, and one in a dirty apron. Both women wore long-sleeved tunics similar to Taimani's.

An awkward silence had ensued when Sonos and the warriors entered the room, but Miss Gemma waved the group to the table. "Make some room for our guests."

She shooed those seated at the table, who in turn, responded as if they were used to these kinds of interruptions and instructions.

Taine and Taimani took the ends of the benches on opposite sides, and Sonos sat between Taine and the rotund man in the apron.

"Henry's my name, and welcome." The cook held out a hand to Sonos. "We were beginning to wonder if y'all were going to show. Sometimes Miss Gemma doesn't always get the details right."

Sonos gulped. *How much did they know?* he wondered.

Miss Gemma huffed. "I don't claim to know *when* all the pieces come together, I just see the picture."

"Didn't you say there were two others coming from Jamroq though?" one of the women asked. "No one here looks to be from Jamroq."

The question surprised Sonos. Maybe they had mistaken them for some refugees?

The little monkey on Sibi's shoulder chittered at something, and Sibi looked at it quizzically.

"Miss Gemma?" Sibi looked up. His earlier exhaustion seemed to be dissipating since their arrival, and Sonos was relieved.

"Yes, dear?"

"I think his name is Kairos," Sibi said rubbing the monkey's head.

"Kairos," Miss Gemma repeated. "That is an old name, young one. Do you know what it means?"

"Not exactly. I can't say if I heard it somewhere before, but it just feels right," Sibi answered.

"It means the right or opportune time. Some would say it means the perfect time." Miss Gemma winked at the monkey then ruffled Sibi's hair. "Yes, you have chosen his name wisely."

"Food's almost ready," the lady from the kitchen said. "Henry, come taste this quickly."

Henry grunted but a smile played behind his eyes as he got up from next to Sonos.

"Emma, run upstairs, and tell Baji to come down," Gemma instructed one of the little girls with bouncy blonde curls. "If the others haven't come yet, they're unlikely to meet us here tonight, and I'm sure he's tired from the hand waving."

Emma nodded and ran off while the remaining girls from the kitchen started passing around steaming bowls of soup and fresh-baked bread.

Sonos' hunger overcame any lingering questions, and he gratefully slurped a spoonful of the thick soup. A rush of flavors from onions, pimento, garlic, and thyme played on his tongue.

"Oh! You made cow heel soup? It's one of my Mama's favorites." Sibi exclaimed between bites.

Sonos almost gagged. "Cow *what*?"

Taine choked down a laugh beside him as Sonos reached for some bread.

Taimani's eyes also twinkled as if they all shared some secret.

Miss Gemma pulled a chair and sat at the head of the table. She looked at Sibi. "Ah, you must have roots in one of the islands then? And if I'm to guess from those blonde curls, I'm thinking Salan?"

Sibi's head bobbed from where he sat across from Sonos. The monkey now sat in his lap, nibbling on a piece of fruit.

Miss Gemma turned to Sonos. "When the Imperials came in and demanded the choicest parts of the meat, we learned how to love what was available. So, things like cow heel, chicken neck, pig tail. And we islanders certainly know how to spice things up, eh?" She grinned at Sibi.

"Hear, hear." One of the women smiled and lifted a glass.

Sonos wasn't trying to stick out like a sore thumb. He dipped the bread into the soup as he had seen one of the men do. *Let me just stay away from anything that looks like a… heel*, Sonos thought. He tried to not dwell on it and focused on the spices.

Emma bounded through the doorway followed by a short, older fellow who sat in the empty space next to Sonos. Henry and the other woman were still over by the ovens.

"Baji, right?" Sonos guessed.

"Mmm," Baji agreed as he took a spoon of the soup.

"Miss Gemma mentioned your hand might be tired. You were the one behind the light?"

Baji nodded. "You're the one who saw it then? Who saw the pattern? It's a good thing too because I was beginning to wonder. Two nights I've been sitting at that window."

That meant he sat there from the time they landed in the harbor. "I'm sorry, but it seems like everyone was expecting us. You knew we were coming? How?" Sonos asked.

Baji's eyes shifted towards Miss Gemma who was talking with one of the kids. "Miss Gemma has a way of… a connection, really, to the unseen realm. Uhm, are you a follower of *El?*"

"*El?* Really?" Sonos was disappointed. This was all about the ancient fables and old religion?

"Sorry, I didn't mean to upset you," Baji said. "It's just a bit easier to explain if, well, there's a baseline. But let's just say that Miss Gemma sees certain things."

Sonos decided to try another angle. "The light signal. It reminded me of a similar pattern I saw during the Feast Day broadcast, coming from the Salan Legacy Tower."

Baji nodded. "Yes, it's a signal used to communicate with followers of *El*. It's a beacon meant to encourage and give hope."

Hope. It's the word that Timur had used in his letter to describe what Sonos had stirred up through his journal. *Two more pieces of the puzzle*, he thought.

Miss Gemma cleared her throat and addressed the table. "Now, for the reason we've all gathered. We received a call for help from one of the northern villages where the army is likely to pass on their march around the Badlands to the Mountain Kingdom."

Sonos was well aware of Commander Uzoma's ruthless reputation, but what could such a small group offer in the way of protection from the army? "Who are you, exactly?" he asked.

"As you would know, your father put a ban on any sort of faith other than that of the great K'Luma Empire and its ruler."

"His *father*?" one of the men exclaimed.

"Be still, warrior," Miss Gemma spoke sternly to Taimani, who had her hands under the table and eyes narrowed at the man who had spoken.

Miss Gemma continued, "We mean you no harm. Quite the opposite. We are followers of *El*, and it is he who has brought you here."

"Our own two feet brought us here," Taimani said coldly.

Miss Gemma chuckled, unfazed. "Indeed. And a riverboat, I would imagine. But I can assure you, purpose is what will drive you forward. Purpose and hope." As she spoke the last word, she looked at Sonos and pulled something from her pocket. She handed him a folded silk cloth.

Sonos lifted a corner of the cloth, and his heart skipped a beat. Inside lay a carefully folded origami tree. The leaves were various shades of green and orange, each delicately arranged just like his mother used to make them.

"A tiny seed—" Gemma said softly.

"Becomes a mighty tree," Sonos finished, then lifted his head to look at Miss Gemma. "How?"

"Your mother is a wise woman, Sonos. And a strong believer."

"She probably *was*," Sonos scoffed, still trying to wrap his mind around his mother being connected to *El*. "But the Emperor doesn't leave a lot of room for any other gods."

Gemma's eyes softened. "Your father can control many things, but hope springs from within, where no man can touch and no sword can strike down. You're more prepared for this quest than you realize."

"Quest?" Sonos' head was swimming again. He was on the run, not a quest. Sure, Timur had told him about finding answers if he could move the mountain, but he barely had time to think through the real questions he wanted to ask.

"Your part in this is not the village, but to head to the Mountain Kingdom. There you will find your answers and save the kingdom."

Sonos' mouth went agape. He couldn't help it. This woman knew so much. She assumed so much.

"Both groups will head north in the morning. Jamin will lead the team to the village." She nodded towards one of the men dressed in leather. "Sonos, you and your warriors will need to go through the Badlands to make it to the Mountain Kingdom before the army."

Sonos was still speechless. Where did he even begin to question?

Miss Gemma continued, "We'll gather all the needed supplies tonight, and I'm still holding out hope for our last two additions from Jamroq."

"Wait!" Sibi stood. "We need to save the Salan family first."

"The ones in Woodyard Square?" Miss Gemma asked.

Sibi nodded. "They're still tied up to the gallows, we passed them earlier on our way here. The guard said they'd stand there as an example until sunrise tomorrow when their judgment will be finalized."

One of the women clicked her tongue. "Imperials are turning to such savagery."

"The family is being used as a living example meant to create terror and helplessness," Taine said with a hint of sadness in his voice.

"While I empathize, I'm still not sure it's our battle to fight," Jamin said. "Isn't it more important to save the village and the Mountain Kingdom?"

"We're just leaving them to die?" Sibi looked at Sonos with pleading eyes, some of his earlier exhaustion showing through.

Something slowed in Sonos' mind as he looked at the folded tree in his hand. Saving the Mountain Kingdom seemed like an impossible task. But this family was right in front of them. And it also seemed like something this group of *El*-followers hadn't planned for ahead of time.

It is a risk to save the family, but didn't my own journey begin with the decision to stand up for one boy? Sonos thought.

"I agree, Sibi. If we cannot care enough to risk ourselves for one family who stands in defiance of the Empire, how can we stand up for an entire village or a kingdom? And what was their defiance against the Empire? To move to a new city in hope of a better life?" Sonos looked around the table as he spoke.

Silence ensued.

"Wise words, my boy," Miss Gemma said, her wrinkled eyes soft and shining. "Once you save the family from the square, I will find a way to protect them here. And I also have a special plan for you, Master Sibi."

CHAPTER 20

CHARLOTTE JOLTED AWAKE. THE room was dark, and it took a few moments for her eyes to adjust enough to make out shapes. Where were they again? *Oh yes, Dayo and his crazy uncle,* she remembered. The realization disquieted her instantly.

Jax's warm body rested next to her. They were sitting on the small mat with their backs against the wall.

Jax leaned over and put a finger over his lips. He then pointed toward a shadowed figure standing near the table in the middle of the room.

"Where is that darn lighter? Nothing ever stays where I put it." It was a feminine voice, probably the mysterious Silvey who Dayo mentioned earlier.

"Ah, finally." The woman managed to light a candle.

"Ack! Who are you?" she shouted, seeing Jax and Charlotte for the first time.

Dayo jumped up from the corner of the room he shared with Uncle Ned, who was still fast asleep on the only cot.

"Miss Silvey, this is Charlotte, and that is Jax," Dayo said quickly. "They're new to town and... uh, wanted to find out more about our operations. Charlotte has a flyer-board, so they have resources."

Charlotte reached to make sure the flyer-board was still tucked behind her, even as her heart started to race. This was feeling more and more like a setup, and she cursed inwardly at ever trusting the boy.

"Oh? How interesting." Silvey stepped around the table and walked towards them.

She didn't look like any cook Charlotte had ever known. Silvey had long dark hair that hung loosely over her slim shoulders. She wore a form-fitting dress that was low cut enough to make Charlotte blush, and her lips were painted red.

Jax stood up as she approached, and Charlotte scrambled to stand up next to him, trying to keep the board safely tucked behind her.

Silvey took her time looking Jax over from top to bottom and back up again.

Charlotte crossed her arms. *Who is this woman?* she wondered.

"Where did you say you were from again?" Silvey reached up and placed a finger under his chin, inspecting Jax as if he were a piece of meat.

"Hey!" Charlotte uncrossed her arms and stomped from the wall.

But Jax was quicker. He grabbed Silvey's wrist and twisted it slightly. His voice was hard when he spoke. "We didn't say. I'm not sure what or who you think I am, but it seems there's been a mistake."

Silvey laughed: a trill, annoying laugh. "I see. Well, no worries. People use our operations for many reasons. I don't need to know them all. I just need to know the risk and ensure that customers can pay."

Ned stirred in the corner, sitting up on the cot.

"We don't need the Underground now," Charlotte said, sticking out her chin. She ignored the uneasiness in her stomach, wanting to ensure she had a plan in place for getting to her sisters. They hadn't worked for the last three years to find the Underground, just to toss it aside because some unsavory people ran it. What else could she have expected? "We have something else to do first. We just wanted to make a connection to get to Pergamum for the future."

"Well, some down-payment may be required, even if it is for a *future* time." Silvey's eyes flashed towards the flyer-board.

The flyer-board was the *only* thing Charlotte had for payment. She couldn't use it for a simple downpayment. And she wasn't comfortable letting it go now, when they may need it to get to the Mountain Kingdom.

"We're not ready to confirm, exactly. I just wanted to find out how things work and how much it would cost," Charlotte said.

Silvey shrugged her shoulders and walked back to the table. "Well, I hope you have more than a simple flyer-board in mind. One of my customers told me about some big captain and his team of Elites who arrived yesterday. It appears they're tracking a couple of young rebels from Jamroq." Silvey raised an eyebrow.

She can't know for sure, Charlotte thought as she swallowed some bile that had risen in her throat. She didn't trust herself to respond to Silvey.

Jax was tense beside her, but also didn't speak.

"For rebels to catch the attention of the Elites, they must be quite smart and resourceful on their own." Silvey opened the container of food, handing a plate to Dayo.

The boy sat next to his uncle in the corner. Ned continued his earlier mutterings between bites about metals and venom and strange herbs.

"What do you think he's up to?" Charlotte whispered to Jax. They remained standing against the wall.

Jax shrugged but kept his eyes on Silvey who was picking at some food herself. "This whole group gives me the creeps," he said in her ear.

"Yes!" Ned shouted, then scribbled something in his book. He laughed to himself, then stared directly at Charlotte.

Charlotte shifted uncomfortably. She asked Jax, "Is he staring at me? Or am I just imagining?"

"He's staring. At you." Jax tapped his hand against his thigh, looking ready to pounce.

Dayo tried to help break the tension. "Uncle? You remember I introduced you to my friends earlier?"

Ned didn't answer. He kept his eyes locked on Charlotte. He abruptly slammed his book closed and jumped up from the cot. "I got it."

"Got what?" Dayo asked. "Uncle, are you okay?"

Ned pulled a box out from under his cot. He sat on the floor and pulled out several vials and small satchels. The room filled with the smells of unfamiliar herbs.

"It's been quite a while since your uncle had a breakthrough, Dayo." Silvey looked keenly interested.

Charlotte wrinkled her nose. "What is he—"

Ned mixed some kind of concoction in a small bowl. The air began to hold a metal tang. The whole time, Ned kept muttering to himself. Chuckling at random moments. Suddenly, he sprang up and ran towards Charlotte.

Jax stepped forward and put a protective arm out in front of her. "Step away."

Ned's eyes were wild and the shadows from the candlelight danced around his head, creating an eerie glow. He ducked under Jax's arm and pulled on Charlotte's hair.

"Ouch!" Charlotte cried out in surprise.

Ned held up a few strands of hair in delight and squirmed away, back to his corner.

Charlotte rubbed her head and looked at Jax. "Do you think we can sneak away?"

Jax refused to look anywhere but the corner with Ned. He answered quietly, "I was trying to wait until daybreak because we're not exactly in a savory part of town. But I'm beginning to think anywhere is better than here."

Charlotte fought down a wave of guilt. If only she hadn't run into that fruit vendor and caused a ruckus in the market. If only she hadn't panicked when the guard approached them. If only she hadn't insisted on following Dayo to find out about the Underground.

No sense in dwelling on the past. Move forward one choice at a time. Just figure out the next right step. Gran's voice sounded in her mind.

Ned stood and took the bowl to the table.

Silvey stepped away but kept her eyes on Ned. He held the bowl over the candle, and soon the small room filled with the strange smell of metal-tinged smoke.

Charlotte coughed, and her eyes started to water.

"Jax—" she started.

Jax looked at her, worry filling his eyes. He pulled his shirt up to cover his nose, ran to the table, and tried to grab the bowl from Ned. But Ned was surprisingly sprite for being a senile, frail man. He pulled the bowl away before Jax could touch it and then blew on the liquid, creating even more smoke.

Jax ran around the table and reached Ned. This time he grabbed the bowl and flung it against the wall.

But Ned just laughed—more like a cackle.

The smoke had taken a life of its own and circled around the ceiling.

Dayo cowered in the corner near the cot.

Silvey stood, arms crossed, but with a smile on her face watching the smoke. "It's about time, old man."

Ned kept his eyes trained on Charlotte.

Meanwhile, the smoke from the ceiling coalesced into the shape of a lizard, or maybe a dragon? Either way, it had beady red eyes like sparks of fire that also seemed to be fixed on Charlotte.

What manner of sorcery is this? Charlotte wanted to ask. But there was a tingle in her throat. She tried coughing to clear whatever was there, but it only seemed to intensify. Her eyes started watering again, her whole head engulfed in smoke.

"Charlotte!" Jax's voice was distant. "Get it off her!"

She heard Jax shouting as she dropped to her knees gasping for breath. Her pulse raced. She needed something.

Out of instinct more than anything, she reached under the sleeve of her jacket and tapped her gazer. She didn't know exactly what she was looking for, but a little hologram appeared, the one of Jax in the temporal portal.

The light from the hologram was bright in contrast to the rest of the room, and Jax's voice was clear in the video as he read out from the scroll.

"Open your eyes! The one who created the world from nothing is doing something new. Are you seeing it? It's springing forth even now. He causes a river to flow in the badlands. What is impossible for him?"

As the video played, Ned screamed and cowered as the smoke dissipated around Charlotte. She sucked in deep breaths of air.

Jax rushed over to kneel beside her, laying a hand on her back. "Char, are you okay?"

She nodded slowly, steadying her breathing. "What... happened?"

Silvey yelled at Ned asking him the same question.

"We need to get out of here," Jax said.

Charlotte's head was still mushy, but she nodded.

Jax picked up the two packs and handed Charlotte her flyer-board. He grabbed her hand and pulled her towards the front door. They were almost through when a tug from behind snapped Charlotte backward.

"Not so fast, rebels." Silvey glared, her hands holding fast to the flyer-board.

Charlotte struggled against what seemed to be an unnatural burst of strength from the petite woman.

"Leave the board, Char." Jax kept pulling her through the door, his voice taking on an edge.

Charlotte hesitated. How could she lose the board now with nothing to show for it? But one look at Ned pacing the room and the glint in Silvey's eyes, and she made up her mind.

Forgive me, Ava and Lily, Charlotte thought. *I will find another way.*

She shrugged the board off her shoulder, throwing Silvey off kilter. Charlotte took the opportunity and ran with Jax out into the cool night air towards the main street.

Shadows played against the buildings as Silvey shouted behind them.

They ran, keeping to the sides of the buildings. There were more people out and about than Charlotte would have expected, but mainly standing in small groups near bars.

"There has to be a way to get back to the other side of town, other than that main gate," Jax said, picking an alley for them to head down.

At the back of the alley, they encountered a tall, wooden fence. Jax pressed his ear against the fence, then tried to look through a crack in the slats.

Charlotte did likewise. It was too dark to see anything. Her heart was beating so fast she could hardly think, but she did not want to turn back onto the main road again. "Come here," she pulled Jax close to help create a shield as she tapped her gazer.

A small hologram projected a rough map showing the path Dayo had led them through earlier. She tapped again and a dot flashed to show where they were.

"That's close enough." Jax leaned in to get a better look at the map then nodded. "We just need to get through this fence."

Loud laughter spilled into the alley from the main road.

Charlotte pressed against each of the boards in a panic, seeing if anything would budge. But the wood was solid and unmoving, and each slat had been shaped into spikes at the top.

Jax ruffled through his pack. A triumphant smile spread across his face when he brought out the long length of rope. "Never underestimate the power of rope." He knotted the end with deft hands.

He then tossed the loop he had formed over one of the spikes at the top of the wall. He pulled tight, checking the strength of the hold.

"I want you to treat this like climbing a tree back home," he said.

"It's been years since I did that," Charlotte said. Ever since the twins were taken, her focus had been solely on tech.

"Well, let's hope there's some muscle memory in there." Jax squeezed her shoulder. "I'll carry the packs with me and go first."

Charlotte paced nervously, shifting her gaze between Jax as he pulled himself upwards and the end of the alley, half expecting Silvey or crazy Ned to appear. Or Captain Die for that matter.

Maybe it was another Elite captain who had arrived in Portemore, or maybe Silvey was a liar. But Charlotte's gut knew better. They needed to get back on track and find Rapha.

A low whistle from Jax caught her attention. He had reached the top and was using one of the packs to sit on the spikes. He shook the rope and waved at her to hurry.

Charlotte took one last look towards the alley, but there was no movement. She took a deep breath and grabbed onto the rope.

Jax had been kind, or perhaps wise enough, to tie some knots throughout the length of the rope which she was able to use as both handholds and footholds.

As she reached the top, Jax extended a hand to help pull her leg over. She sat on the second pack.

Charlotte seethed air into her lungs from the climb. But as she looked around, she let out a "Wow." The elevated sight of Portemore was breathtaking.

The difference between the two parts of the city was stark. They were coming out of dirt and mud streets with boarded-up buildings and only candlelight or torches available for light. The other side had streetlamps with lights, tech that Charlotte still wanted to explore. While many of the buildings were still only one or two stories, sections of the city were raised to three and four floors.

Jax pulled the rope up, then lowered it to the other side.

Charlotte's breath caught as she looked down. It was a sheer drop into a big channel that had a steady stream of water, likely from the earlier rains.

"I'm hoping the water isn't too deep," Jax said. "I think it's more a drain than a river, so we should be safe... I hope."

"The only way is forward," Charlotte said more to herself than to Jax. "Let me go down first."

Jax opened his mouth, but Charlotte swung herself over before she could over-think anything. She took the smaller pack and strung it over her shoulder. Her feet found the first knot, and she lowered herself, slow but sure. At the end of the wall there was mercifully a little ledge where she found a toehold and didn't have to jump down into the drain. She wiggled her way over a bit to make room for Jax.

He shimmied down in a heartbeat. "Great work finding the ledge." He flashed a smile. He shook the rope loose and slung it over his arm. "I think we're going to need to drop and cross though. Ready?"

Charlotte looked over her shoulder. The drop was about ten feet. She could do this. Jax went first, making a small splash.

Thankfully, he stood, and the water only came up to his knees. She let go of the wall and pushed out. Her fall was less graceful. Though she tried to land with soft knees, she slipped and landed with her butt in the water.

"Ugh. This smells absolutely horrid." Charlotte scrunched up her nose as Jax helped her stand.

"Agreed, let's get out as quickly as we can. I see a drain cut on the other side further down that looks close enough to reach."

Sure enough, only a trickle of water was running through the drain, and Jax was able to jump and reach the edge and pull himself up. He lent a hand to Charlotte.

She let out a sigh of relief as they stood up in an alley on the main city side. Hopefully, far from Silvey and any other crazies.

"We need to find Rapha and get out of this city before Captain Die realizes we're here," Charlotte said.

"Should we head back towards the harbor? There may be more signs of life that way," Jax said.

"Cover me," Charlotte said as she squatted and tapped her gazer to look at the map again, memorizing the route as best as she could.

They made their way quietly down the winding streets, keeping close to the buildings and in shadows.

The clapping of hooves sounded, and they jumped into a nearby alley. A pair of guards rode by ignoring their hiding place.

When they got closer to where Charlotte remembered the square with the gallows, she pulled Jax into a side road so she could check her map again.

She had just pulled up the hologram when Jax yelped.

"Don't move," a female voice with a strange accent demanded, holding a dagger tight to Charlotte's throat.

A guy even bigger than Jax had him restrained with some kind of fancy sword.

"Who are you?" the woman asked.

Charlotte couldn't think straight in her panic. Danger had been finding them at every corner.

Out of nowhere a little monkey ran over and climbed up Charlotte's leg and right up to her shoulder. The monkey chittered at the woman and used its finger to push the dagger away.

In a moment of clarity, Charlotte realized who the monkey was.

"Rapha!" She was overcome with joy. Forgetting the two assailants, she tapped off her gazer and pulled the monkey in for a tight embrace. "Where have you been?"

CHAPTER 21

Captain Die's pulse raced with anticipation as he and his small Elite force sped through the empty streets of Portemore on their flyer-boards.

It was still a few hours before daybreak, and the air held just the right amount of chill.

The rebels landing earlier than expected was perfect, as his time was short.

When the mercenary, Wylder, had approached him earlier in the day to say he had the missing prince in hand, Die knew he'd have to abandon pursuit of the rebels. The safety of the prince was paramount, especially in the eyes of his sister, the Empress. She would never forgive him if harm came to Sonos.

But after the meeting, Wylder came back and reported that Sonos had escaped. Initially, Die had been furious, but now he had his Elites and Wylder looking for both the prince and the rebels, hoping to kill two birds with one stone.

The evening had turned up no leads though, and he had gone to bed frustrated. When the sorcerer had woken him with news of the smoke dragon, Die pulled together his closest officers and moved immediately.

All dark arts served the Emperor, and in the Year of the Dragon, even greater power was released through sorcerers. Smoke dragons were used to attack and snuff out potential threats against the

Emperor and his intents. Die was convinced it was the rebel teens who threatened the Emperor's conquest. He had underestimated them once, but they would not escape him again.

The Elites reached the closed gate which separated the slums from the main part of Portemore. One of his men pounded on the guard door.

Where are the guards? Die thought as his frustration grew.

The door opened a crack, and a guard stuck his head out, hair frazzled as if he'd been in a deep sleep. "What's the meaning of—" His eyes widened as he took in the Elites hovering in formation on their flyer-boards.

While the resident Imperial guards used non-tech weapons and modes of transportation, the Elites had access to flyer-boards and tech-infused weapons.

Die waited impatiently while the guard unlocked and opened the gate. He leaned towards the sorcerer who hovered beside him. "Let me see the map again."

The sorcerer held out his wrist where a holographic map projected from his gazer. A red blinking dot showed the spot where the smoke dragon had been activated; a white dot showed their location. They were close.

After they crossed through to the other side, Die reflexively covered his nose. The streets were still muddy from the rains earlier in the day, and the stench that lingered was a cross between body odors and rotten food.

It wasn't long before the sorcerer stepped off the flyer-board at the end of an alley. He pointed towards a door. "That one," he said.

His senior Elite looked back to Die.

Die nodded. *Finally, we have them,* he thought.

The Elites kicked down the wooden door and entered, electrified swords drawn. One held up a spotlight to flood the room with light.

When Die entered the small room, there was nothing much to survey. A small table in the center took up a large part of the room. A young boy and an old man cowered on a cot in the far corner.

One of the Elites held the tip of his sword against the chest of a scantily clad woman.

The rebels were nowhere in sight.

"Where are they?" Die demanded.

The woman spoke up, her voice dripping with too much sweetness. "How can we be of service, good Captain?"

"The two rebel teens, *where* are they?"

"Two teens? It's just us here," the woman drawled.

Die signaled to the Elite holding the rod, and a current of electricity was released. Her eyes bulged as her body convulsed with the shock.

"Do not test me, woman. Who summoned the dragon? You?" he asked. But the woman did not emit a frequency like his sorcerer. He scanned the room again and looked closer at the old man. He walked around the table and stood before the man and young boy.

The old man scrambled off the cot and prostrated himself on the ground in front of Die. "Oh, great lord, I tried. I tried to snuff them out. I summoned the dragon, and it attacked the girl."

"Where are they then? Why is she not dead?"

"She had a gazer, Great One. She played a video where one of the ancient scrolls was read. I don't know how, but the words... the words. They dissolved my dragon." The man was whimpering.

"It was not *your* dragon," Die said coldly. "All dragons belong to the Emperor and serve his purposes. If the rebels escaped, you have failed the Emperor, even after you were honored with access to one of his own."

Failure disgusted Die. If it's one thing he learned from the Emperor and those in power, it was that the weak would not survive.

"Kill them," Die instructed his Elites as he walked towards the door.

"The boy as well?" one of the men asked.

Die looked back and saw the boy's knees drawn to his chest, staring with two big, frightened eyes. "Let him live and give testament to what happens to those who fail the Empire."

Die walked into the alley, angry but determined. The two rebels were here in the city. He looked up and down, walking towards the main street. "Where did you go?" he muttered.

His Elites joined him shortly after, and his sorcerer stood close by.

"Go and gather reinforcements," he instructed one of the men. "I want to search every corner of these slums before daybreak. They can't have made it far. The gate to the main part of the city is still closed, so they must be on this side. We find them *tonight*."

Chapter 22

— · —

JAX CLEARED HIS THROAT, drawing Charlotte's attention. She was so focused on being reunited with Rapha that she had forgotten all about their assailants.

Two more people emerged from the shadows, and Charlotte backed up to stand closer to Jax with Rapha perched on her shoulder.

"Sibi, what is your monkey doing?" the woman asked while lowering her dagger. Her dark liner accentuated her eyes.

Why does she look familiar? Charlotte thought, racking her brain.

A young boy stepped forward, blonde curls tumbling into his face. He cocked his head at Rapha. "Kairos?"

"Something's coming," a new voice interjected, with what sounded like a strong Pergamum accent. The tall figure who stood beside Sibi was the one who spoke, but he kept his face hidden deep beneath the hood of his cloak.

Charlotte and the rest of the group moved quickly to huddle against the nearest wall and out of the streetlight.

A few moments later, two Imperial guards jogged by on the main thoroughfare heading in the direction from which Charlotte and Jax had just come from—back towards the slums. After they passed, another pair followed suit.

Heat crept up Charlotte's neck, filled with worry. She reached for Jax's hand in the dark and interlocked her fingers with his.

Minutes passed, and no further guards followed.

Charlotte kept her eyes on the street but leaned closer to Jax and whispered. "Do you think they're coming for us?"

"Uhm, *us?*" a strange voice whispered back.

Charlotte yelped. She was holding hands with the strange guy from Pergamum. His hood had fallen back a little, and gold flecks reflected from the blue of his eyes, set in a perfectly framed, olive face. He looked at her, unflinching and... *curious?*

Jax rushed over. "Are you okay?" he asked Charlotte while glaring at the other guy, who adjusted his hood back up.

Why does everyone look so familiar? she wondered.

Charlotte looked back and forth between the stranger and Jax. "Uhm, yeah. I was just confused. No problems." She rubbed her hand against her thigh to calm the pulse of excitement that had sparked.

The large guy who had previously held Jax jogged over to where they stood. *Where had he been?* Charlotte hadn't even noticed him slip away from the group.

He spoke in a strange language to the dagger-lady. Tattoos covered his neck, and when the girl moved her head, similar markings were visible on her neck.

Charlotte leaned into Jax, double-checking it was indeed Jax. "I think those are Kimwaki warriors."

Jax squinted towards the pair. "I think you're right," he said unable to keep the awe from his voice.

After a brief exchange, the girl jogged to the end of the street, moving into the shadows and apparently keeping watch.

"There have been some developments," the warrior said to the hooded guy from Pergamum. "The Imperial guards are all being mobilized towards the slums. Not sure what for just yet, but we have an opening to move."

What are they up to? Charlotte wondered nervously.

"Let's move, then," the hooded guy said. He turned to Jax and Charlotte. "I'm not sure where you're headed, but I suggest getting out of here quickly. And good luck."

That's it? Charlotte thought to herself. She wasn't sure why there was an internal pull towards this group.

"C'mon, Char." Jax wrapped an arm around her shoulder and stepped towards the street. It seemed *he* didn't need to be told to leave twice.

Charlotte hesitated and knelt before the little boy whose gaze was fixed on Rapha. "Sibi, was it?"

The boy nodded, tears in his eyes.

"Thanks for taking good care of Rapha for us. Maybe we'll see each other again." She wasn't sure what caused that last line to pop out.

Sibi rubbed Rapha on the head and nodded again.

The hooded guy pulled Sibi by the hand in the opposite direction.

Charlotte stood and followed Jax to the street, looking behind her as the others disappeared from sight.

Jax pulled her into the shadows just before a group of guards on horseback clamored down the main thoroughfare.

So many guards, she thought.

"Do you really think all those guards are after us?" she asked when the coast was clear.

"It wouldn't surprise me if it is Captain Die behind this. And if so, I'm sure they're all after us," Jax answered.

Charlotte squeezed Rapha's leg for reassurance. "Maybe you could show us which way to go, Raph?"

Rapha hummed happily. Charlotte could feel the vibration in her spirit, calming her nerves.

"Maybe we should wait here for a few minutes," Charlotte said.

"Yeah, I get that feeling, too." Jax nodded.

Charlotte remembered Gran's parting admonition about the power of agreement, especially in uncertain situations. She allowed herself a small smile.

After a few minutes of quiet, Charlotte peeked her head around the corner. The thoroughfare was empty.

"Let's keep heading towards the harbor," Charlotte said, looking to Rapha for any reaction.

The monkey shrugged his tiny shoulders and squeaked softly.

"I'm not sure what that's supposed to mean," Charlotte said, wishing again, that the monkey would simply speak and make things simpler.

"Yeah, let's move," Jax said.

They had just stepped onto the thoroughfare and rounded the corner that led to Woodyard Square when a loud commotion sounded from the center of the square.

There was a flurry of movement on the stage.

"Hey, isn't that where that family was being put to the gallows yesterday?" Charlotte asked. "I wonder—"

"Watch out." Jax nudged Charlotte to the side as he pulled the rope off his belt.

Charlotte yelped as her eyes settled on the guard running towards them. She wished she had some kind of weapon.

Jax stepped out from the wall, swinging the rope in large circles above his head. The guard didn't slow and lowered his spear towards Jax.

Charlotte did the only thing she could think of in the moment and tapped her gazer to shine a bright light towards the guard. It was enough to make him break his stride and cover his eyes with a hand.

In that moment, Jax let the lasso fly from his hand. It made its target and covered the guard's torso. Jax pulled tight and the guard dropped to the ground with a thud.

The Kimwaki warrior who had held Jax earlier in the alley reached them shortly after the guard fell. Electricity sparked in his special weapon, and he touched the end against the fallen guard's back.

The guard convulsed, then held still.

How does someone from Kimwaki have access to Elite weapons? Charlotte wondered.

"Don't worry, he's still alive. He'll just be unconscious for a bit," the warrior said to the hooded cloak guy who had run up behind him.

"Nice trick with the rope," the warrior said to Jax, throwing it back in his direction. The warrior dragged the guard back against the wall.

"You said you thought the guards were after you?" the hooded guy asked Charlotte.

She wasn't sure what to say.

"I'll take that as a yes," he said. "We're heading out of the city if you want to join us."

Rapha hummed.

Charlotte glanced at Jax whose mouth was drawn into a tight line.

"At least these guys are against the Empire," she leaned in to confer quickly with Jax. "For now, that might be the best we can hope for."

Jax's expression remained stoic, staring at the hooded guy.

Charlotte took his lack of disagreement as enough and stepped forward. "We'd appreciate that."

He nodded and led them across the square to an alley off the far corner.

The warrior fell in closely behind them.

In the alley, the family from the gallows was embracing, the father with tears streaming shamelessly down his face. They all had dark golden curls, so Charlotte guessed they were from Salan.

"Thank you for saving us," the father turned to everyone packed into the alley.

An old woman with hair tied back in a loose bun walked to Charlotte and Jax. "Better late than never, my dears."

Charlotte glanced over her shoulder to see if there was someone else the old lady was referring to behind her. "Us?" She asked.

The lady reached out and took hold of Charlotte's hand, then pulled Jax close with her other arm. "You both are pivotal to saving the Mountain Kingdom. I'm glad we got to meet before you go."

CHAPTER 23

THE SOUND OF FOOTSTEPS snapped Sonos' attention from Miss Gemma towards the end of the alley which emptied into the square. A young boy about Sibi's age approached, his hands raised in the air.

"Please, I need help." His dark hair was matted against his forehead, his cheeks stained with tears. Blood stained his hands and shirt. He walked towards the Jamroq girl and dropped to a knee in front of her. "I'm so sorry," he said, his voice just above a whisper.

"Dayo?" the girl asked, her face pale.

Sonos was having a hard time placing her. She had the Jamroq accent. But her creamy skin, soft brown curls, and sharp green eyes were unlike anything he'd ever seen. Her dark-toned companion, on the other hand, looked like what he'd expect from the conquered isle.

She knelt beside Dayo, her voice hard when she spoke. "What happened?"

"Sorry, Miss Charlotte," Dayo whimpered. "They... they came shortly after you left."

"Who came?" Charlotte kept her voice steady, but Sonos noticed her hand shaking.

"The Elites. And a captain."

Taimani made a hand gesture to Taine, then stepped forward towards Dayo as Taine jogged out towards the square. "Do you think you were followed, young one?"

Dayo shook his head. "I know the cracks and shadows of the city, which is how I got here. I thought Charlotte and Jax might go to the harbor, so I headed in that direction."

Jax stood with his arms crossed and narrowed his eyes at Dayo. "Your uncle tried to kill us. Why are you here?"

These two seem to have several people after them. Sonos thought and considered whether it was still wise to keep them as part of the group. But something tugged at his mind. Miss Gemma believed them to be important to the mission ahead.

Dayo hung his head. "I'm sorry. I didn't know he would do that." He looked up at Charlotte with pleading eyes. "But they killed my uncle and Silvey. I didn't know where else to go."

Charlotte inhaled sharply. "The captain killed them?"

Dayo nodded. "Because they failed the Emperor. Or so the captain said." The boy sniffed but stood to his feet.

Sonos' blood boiled. Yet another example of the unnecessary ruthlessness by which his father ruled. *Death for failure?* he thought.

Taine rejoined the group. "The coast is still clear, but we need to get back to the plan and keep moving."

Miss Gemma stepped forward. The young girl from the rescued Salan family held tight to the old woman's hand. "Dayo, you came to the right place. *El* places the solitary in family. And it seems our family is growing quite a bit tonight."

Dayo's shoulders relaxed. "Thanks. I can be a big help."

"Don't worry about that now," Miss Gemma tisked. "Master Sibi, let's get Dayo and our Salanites back to the bakery. Henry, lead the way, and I'll meet you there in a bit."

The big chef who had helped to pull the family from the gallows after the guards were subdued waved for the family and boys to follow him.

Sibi reached up to the monkey on Charlotte's shoulder. "Bye, Kairos... or Rapha."

Charlotte smiled. "He once told me he's gone by many names."

"He talks?" Sibi's eyes went wide.

"Long story," Charlotte said.

Sonos stepped over and put a hand on Sibi's shoulder. He was relieved with how much stronger Sibi was looking but knew the adrenaline would wear off soon. "Sib, you take care of yourself."

Sibi wrapped his arms around Sonos' waist. "Thanks for everything." He looked up, eyes brimming. "You sparked the hope we all needed. I know *El* will show you the answers."

Sonos was still skeptical of all this *El* focus, but they had come so far through so many improbable situations. Sibi was right about hope. Now that the family had been rescued, Sonos felt strangely assured.

All roads seemed to be leading to the Mountain Kingdom. One step at a time.

Taine and Taimani each made a fist and tapped their heart twice towards Sibi.

The boy broke out in a huge grin and returned the warrior salute. He then ran off after Henry and the others, his limp only slowing him slightly.

"Now, for my warriors," Miss Gemma looked around to Sonos, Taine, Taimani, and the two from Jamroq. "Walk straight and true, keep together, and trust the journey."

The monkey perched on Charlotte's shoulder chittered, and Miss Gemma rubbed his head. "And yes, ancient one, until we meet again." With that, she turned and disappeared in the direction of the bakery.

There was something more to that monkey—and to Miss Gemma—than Sonos could put his finger on.

"So, what's the plan?" Charlotte asked.

Sonos pushed the monkey and Miss Gemma to the back of his mind. "First, we need to get out of this city," he answered. "Follow us."

Taimani led the group together with Jamin, one of the burly factory workers from earlier. They walked through the winding streets keeping to the edges of buildings and out of the streetlights.

Sonos caught Charlotte more than once pausing to look up at the lights. When she fell a little behind Jax, Sonos stayed beside her. Her wild hair had a light, fruity scent that distracted Sonos for a moment.

Charlotte scrunched her eyebrows when she looked at Sonos, who kept his hood drawn. It was still too risky to show his face.

He tried to put her at ease and focus back on the light posts. "It's your first time seeing them?"

She nodded. "I love the use of the sun collectors." Her brow furrowed as she touched the pole.

"I didn't realize that islanders would be so interested in tech. I thought they were rather... underdeveloped." He tried to find a polite way to describe the jungle he remembered from his brief visit to Jamroq.

Charlotte snapped her head around to look at Sonos. "We get along just fine," she said with a defensive edge to her voice.

Jax had turned around and jogged back to stand next to Charlotte.

Sonos put up his hands before Jax could say anything. "Just trying to be helpful." *Jealous much?* Sonos wanted to add, but bit his tongue. They had a long journey ahead. Plus, Sonos smiled inwardly when Charlotte stepped slightly *away* from Jax.

She pulled out her gazer, which Sonos was still amazed a non-Imperial from the isles had, and took a quick video of the streetlight before moving on.

The sky lightened with a pre-dawn glow as the sun prepared to make its entry. The streets began to fill with people: vendors pushing carts to the market, workers in leather heading deeper into the city, women carrying baskets of baked goods.

Eventually, they turned a corner and saw a group of people gathering ahead near a large gate in the thick outer wall. Their group joined the long queue, waiting to go through the gate.

In addition to Jamin, the merchant and two women from the bakery joined them. Miss Gemma's followers were all dressed in traveling pants and dark cloaks. Each of the newcomers had two packs each and handed one to Taine, Taimani, and Sonos in turn.

"Supplies as promised," one of the women explained. "I'm a little jealous that you get to go to the Mountain Kingdom. I've always wanted to see Noiz for myself."

Sonos opened his mouth to ask what she knew about Noiz, but shouting erupted further up the line, closer to the gate. He craned his neck, trying to see what the noise was all about.

There were about twenty people ahead of them in the line to exit the city, and others had joined behind. A few merchant wagons were interspersed with those on foot.

Miss Gemma had said this gate would be easy to exit as a steady stream of people would be coming in with market goods, and enough would also be passing out of the city to not make a group their size seem out of place.

But why were the gates still closed now that the sun was up?

"Open the gates!" someone shouted at the guards.

"What's the holdup? It's past sunrise." asked another.

"New protocols today." A guard shouted from where he was perched on a small platform near the gate. "No one's allowed to leave just yet."

Sonos' heart raced. *I'm really beginning to hate city gates.* For the first time since fleeing the palace, he wished that he could simply identify himself and be given unfettered access wherever and whenever he wanted. All this drama and restrictions simply to move in and out of places.

Half of the gate opened to allow those coming into the city to enter, and a stream of wagons laden with goods started to flow through. However, the side of the gate with those waiting to exit remained resolutely closed.

"Let's go! Let us out!" someone shouted.

"We're not prisoners!"

The crowd became increasingly tense and unruly, even as the guard shouted for calm.

A little brown fuzzball scuttled along the ground.

"Rapha!" Charlotte called out from where she stood behind Sonos, but Jax held her back from running after the monkey.

A moment later, Rapha was sitting atop a horse pulling a wagon in the line ahead of them.

"Hey, get outta here!" the farmer sitting in the wagon shouted.

"What is Rapha doing?" Charlotte muttered.

The harness holding the horse clattered to the ground, and the farmer jumped out of the wagon.

"Smart little thing. He's creating a diversion." Sonos tightened the strap of his pack.

Taimani turned her head towards her brother who brought up the rear behind Charlotte and Jax. The warriors sensed the opening, too.

Rapha squeaked loudly atop the horse. For a second, Sonos wondered whether the animal was a red howler monkey in disguise.

The horse bucked and ran, causing even more pandemonium.

"Now!" Taine called from behind, and Jamin cut a path forward for their group.

In all the calamity, the crowd had decided enough was enough, and those at the front had pushed open the other side of the gate.

The guards shouted at the crowd while working to close it. But traffic was flowing both ways now, and it was a mad rush.

Sonos kept his focus on Taimani who was directly ahead of him, not allowing anyone to come between them. Charlotte, Jax, and Taine were immediately behind.

Jamin and his crew kept ahead of Taimani. They kept a tight pack moving together that flowed with the overall stampede.

They reached the gate as reinforcements closed in from the top of the wall.

With horror, Sonos realized the guards were going to drop the iron grating to force the flow of people to stop.

The press of bodies trying to go both in and out of the gateway was crushing. Taimani linked her arm through Sonos' and pulled him through an opening.

Sonos reached behind to grab Charlotte's hand. He caught her wrist just in time. Their gaze locked, as his hood had fallen back just a bit.

Determination flowed through Charlotte's bright green eyes.

Taimani's pull forward helped them navigate the final squeeze through the gate. Even after they cleared the other side, Taimani urged them on. "Keep running! I'll help the others, and we'll catch up."

The iron gate inched downward, and a guard blocked the path of Taine and Jax.

Taimani dropped and kicked the guard in his knees, which gave the other two the chance they needed to drop to their bellies and crawl through.

"Come," Sonos interlocked his fingers with Charlotte. She breathed heavily as they sprinted down the hard-packed road.

The road reached the edge of the forest, and Sonos paused to catch his breath. As he doubled over, hands on his knees, a voice called out from behind a nearby tree.

"Over here." Jamin waved his arm.

Sonos looked back towards the city and saw the warriors and Jax running towards them.

"Taine!" Sonos shouted as an arrow zoomed narrowly to the right of the warrior. Other arrows soon followed.

It was pure chaos as those who made it out of the gates tried to get as far from the gates as possible, and the crowd who had been trying to get in panicked at the sudden attack.

Finally, the warriors and Jax joined the rest of the group inside the forest.

"Change of plans. We're staying off the road and will take the scenic route," Jamin said, leading them deeper into the forest.

No one argued.

As Jax approached, Charlotte let go of Sonos' hand. But not before giving it a squeeze and saying, "Thanks." Her clipped accent made it come out like "Tenks," and Sonos smiled.

"You okay?" Jax leaned in to give her a hug.

Sonos turned and walked ahead to give them some privacy, shaking his head to clear his thoughts.

A little tug on his leg made him jump, and Rapha was soon climbing up to his shoulder.

The monkey chittered and hummed, but if it was supposed to be anything intelligent, it went over Sonos' head. However, a strange sense of calmness enveloped Sonos as he walked forward.

He tapped the pocket in his cloak where his journal was still secure, thinking of the origami trees from his mother, Sah Timur, and Miss Gemma. The collection was growing.

Something more than coincidence and happenstance was at work, even if it wasn't going according to any plan he had envisioned.

Chapter 24

Nervous energy filled Charlotte as they trekked through the forest. The trees were unfamiliar to the fruit trees, bamboo, palms, and other flowering tropical trees she was used to.

The trees here were taller and spindlier, but full of green and the new growth of spring, as Jax had explained. He had named a few of them—beeches, birches, maples, and firs. The only one she really remembered was the Sweetbay, as their papery leaves and cup-shaped flowers offered a pleasant fragrance when they passed.

The sun would not disappear for another hour, but the forest already embraced a cool darkness.

They walked at a pace that was steady, but not too fast. This gave her plenty of time to think.

She rubbed Rapha's head where he was perched on her shoulder. She looked ahead to Jamin and his three companions. She couldn't keep all the names straight, but she remembered the leader and the two warriors, Taine and Taimani.

Charlotte was beginning to recognize a familiar frequency among the followers of *El*. She thought about when Rapha hummed and how it created a sense of peace, affirmation, or confidence. The frequency from people was similar. She felt comfortable, and even familiar with them, as if they weren't strangers she had just met. This happened with people like Sibi, Miss Gemma,

Jamin, and the three with him. It made her wonder how they were all connected.

Did everyone have the *breath* in them similar to what Rapha had done to Jax and her?

But she couldn't make out the warriors and the mystery guy from Pergamum at all. He still kept his hood up, but when they had run through the gate in Portemore, she had caught a glance. He had short, cropped hair which meant he likely wasn't royal as all the nobles wore long, raven hair. But then why did he look so familiar? It's not as if she knew or interacted with people from Pergamum... ever.

"Holding up okay?" Jax stepped beside her as the path widened.

Rapha chittered and adjusted himself on her shoulder.

Charlotte nodded. "I was just thinking, doesn't it rattle you that Miss Gemma was expecting us? And she knew about the Mountain Kingdom? How is that possible?"

Jax shrugged. "It does seem a little crazy because there are so many things that could have happened to *not* have us be there near the square at that exact time."

"Exactly," Charlotte said.

"But in the wider sense, it fits with what we read in the ancient text and what Rapha said. *El* is making a way. And if that's the case, I'm kind of happy it's not going according to what we planned." Jax put on his classic side grin.

"I guess." Every time Charlotte paused to think about the se-quence of events over the past few days, versus how she and her parents had been planning to rescue the twins, her mind got dizzy.

Now, her dad was hiding out somewhere in Jamroq with Gran. She was on this path with Jax and a rabble of people she didn't know. An Elite captain was hot on their heels, and a smoke dragon had almost killed her when they had finally found the

Underground Network. In fact, the Underground may be all but dissipated, now that its leader was dead because of her.

Charlotte gulped.

Every single plan was completely obsolete. She couldn't trace a logical flow to anything, which meant that she also couldn't predict how things may play out. It was a little unnerving.

Rapha stirred again on her shoulder, perhaps sensing her uneasiness.

Well, all plans were gone except for one: follow Rapha, stick together, and save the Mountain Kingdom. But how things were working out was still far beyond what she could have imagined.

Jax dropped behind her as the path narrowed again.

After another hour or so of walking, the moon hung high and bright in the sky. Jamin called for a stop and pulled everyone into a huddle.

"This is where we part ways," he said. "Those heading to the Mountain Kingdom, you'll follow the track heading northwest." Jamin indicated towards a much smaller path, more like an animal track that was barely visible.

Jamin placed a hand on the shoulder of the cloaked Pergamum guy.

Charlotte again wondered what secrets he held. Why else would he continually keep his face hidden?

"Man plans his ways," Jamin said in a voice loud enough for everyone to hear. "But *El* directs his steps. You must not be defined by what lies behind. Instead, keep your eyes always on the road ahead. Walk strong." He directed the last statement at the wider group.

The two women and the big, burly guy all affirmed salutations and encouragement, then followed Jamin down the wide path.

After they were out of sight, the guy in the hooded cloak muttered, "Fight we must," as if to himself.

Taimani tapped a fist to her heart twice in response. "But win we shall."

Jax smiled beside Charlotte, and even Rapha hummed on her shoulder. The words did have a certain ring to them.

Taimani rubbed her hands together. "Okay, then. Next step." She leaned in towards Charlotte, "You have a gazer, right?"

Instinctively, Charlotte put her hand behind her back and stepped next to Jax. "What's it to you?"

Taimani squared her shoulders. "Well, it's not like I've ever owned one, but aren't they supposed to be high-tech and help with navigation and such?"

"We all saw you have one," the hooded guy used a pacifying voice that only served to irritate Charlotte more. "But is it secure? As in, are you sure no one's able to track you?"

Jax crossed his arms and stepped forward in response. "Do you think we're fools?"

Charlotte closed her eyes and took a deep breath. They needed to work together.

Stepping closer to Taimani, she lifted her sleeve. "Can you use your cloak to give some cover?"

Taimani did as instructed, and Charlotte turned on her gazer pulling up a rough map of where they had walked from Porte-more.

"Sorry I don't have a map of the area to overlay and show where we're going," Charlotte said.

"I can help with that," the hooded guy stepped closer forming a tight circle. He pulled a journal from his inner pocket and flipped through some pages until he pulled out a detailed map of the area.

All three dropped to a knee as he flattened the map on the ground.

Charlotte tapped on her gazer, recorded the map, then pro-grammed her previous capture of their path onto the image of the map. In short order, she was able to show an interactive version of where they'd been and the direction of the Mountain Kingdom.

Taimani's brother, Taine, let out a low whistle. Both he and Jax stood above the three on the ground, hovering close to look at the map.

"You're pretty sharp with that tech stuff," Taine said. "Quite impressive."

Taimani stared intently at Charlotte. "In fact, looking at you now, you remind me of two sisters I knew back in the towers..."

"The Legacy Towers?" Charlotte's heart skipped a beat.

Taimani nodded.

Could it be possible? Charlotte wondered. "Twins? From Jamroq?" Charlotte could barely contain her hope.

"Yes, in fact. You know them?" Taimani asked.

Without thinking, Charlotte tackled Taimani in an exuberant embrace. It took a second for Charlotte to feel the knife against her neck, but she just laughed. "You know my sisters!"

Taimani relaxed and shook her head, putting her knife away. "They always did talk about their little techie sister."

A thousand questions ran through Charlotte's mind, but the hooded guy cleared his throat, stepping forward.

"We're about to embark on a path of no return, to try to save an entire kingdom from a ruthless, undefeated army. I think it's time to make a few things clear." He pulled down his hood.

Charlotte placed a hand over her mouth and gasped. His moonlit face was clear as day.

"You're the prince," Jax said, mouth drawn in a tight line.

CHAPTER 25

*A*LL THINGS CONSIDERED, *CHARLOTTE and Jax are taking the news fairly well*, Sonos thought. Unhappy, shocked, but not freaking out.

"What's your intention at the Mountain Kingdom?" Jax asked, eyes narrowed. "You're helping to attack from the inside? Trying to grab the favor of your father from your older brother?"

Sonos took a calming breath. He wasn't used to answering such accusations, but he tried to put himself into Jax and Charlotte's shoes.

"I am not working with my father," Sonos said.

"Are we supposed to call you Highness?" Jax interrupted, his voice growing louder. "Or will you order us to be beheaded for such rudeness?" Jax took a stronger step between Sonos and Charlotte.

"I'm not—" Sonos adjusted his tit-for-tat tone down before continuing. "I'm not going to have you beheaded."

"Yeah, well, forgive us for being a little cautious. We already have an Elite captain trying to kill us," Jax said.

"An Elite captain?" Sonos asked, shocked. The wave of Imperial guards and Elites in Portemore now made a lot more sense. "Which one? And what exactly did you do to capture his attention?"

"It's some kind of big mistake," Charlotte answered Sonos, placing a hand on Jax's arm. "But Captain Die-something was in Jamroq and is convinced that we are traitors involved in some plot to kill the Emperor. As if we'd even have any idea of how to do that. I've never even seen the Emperor in real life."

Jax scoffed and rubbed his forearm. "It's not like the man's immortal."

Taine tensed beside Sonos. "Are you trying to kill the Emperor?" Taine asked.

Sonos knew his bodyguard had no love lost for his father, but years of training to protect the royal family did not just dissipate overnight.

"We are simply trying to be safe... and I'm trying to bring my family back together," Charlotte said, her shoulders sagging just a bit.

There was more to their story, but Sonos believed Charlotte. He ran a hand through his close-cropped hair.

He decided to share the truth of their situation—it might just be crazy enough to believe as they stood in the middle of the forest. "Truth be told, we are all on the run," Sonos said.

"Something else happened at the feast?" Charlotte asked, eyebrows scrunched.

"Not on screen," Sonos answered. "But afterwards, there was an incident."

"An incident?" Jax asked.

Who does this guy think he is? Sonos thought.

Charlotte spoke with a calming voice. "We all saw what happened last year. In fact, the impression you gave that someone from the royal family could think differently gave many of us a spark of hope."

Sah Timur had said something similar about sparking hope. But Sonos was momentarily distracted by how Charlotte's eyes reflected in the moonlight, as soft, wild curls framed her face. Maybe it was her own hope spilling through that sparked such shine.

Then her face changed. "But instead, after the feast last year, you went completely silent, and now we have even more Imperials everywhere."

Sonos had sometimes wondered what people outside the palace and Inner City thought about what happened. It seems he had made some impact, but then it was immediately squelched. "I was put into lockdown for a year. Cut off from everyone and everything. The day I was let out, I interfered with the punishment of a young servant—you met him, Sibi. But even though I saved a boy, I inadvertently killed a man."

"So? Doesn't something like that basically come as a rite of passage for royalty? Killing people." Jax did not relent.

Jax obviously harbors a grudge beyond just me, Sonos thought. *I'm still seen as representing K'Luma and everything my father stands for. But I'm more than that. I am different than the Emperor.*

Sonos stood up straighter and stuck out his chin. "The Emperor may rule in one way, but it doesn't mean it's the only way. The Empress always held true to other values, which I'm only beginning to understand." His eyes softened towards Taine, then shifted to Taimani when he spoke.

"Besides, more than killing the man, the graver action was standing in opposition to a command from the Emperor."

Charlotte muttered something under her breath.

Sonos sighed. "Given that it was my first day out of lockdown, I presumed worse punishment would be applied, and so I ran. At this point, the Emperor may be looking to behead me himself." Sonos paused, struck with the reality of the words he just spoke.

Jax shifted his gaze to Taine and Taimani. "And you two?"

"I am sworn to protect Sonos with my life. An oath I am honored to keep," Taine said. He then stepped a few paces away from the group to keep watch on their wider surroundings.

"And I chose to protect my brother," Taimani said.

Charlotte bowed her head slightly to Sonos. "Thank you for the truth." She glanced at Jax who looked nonplussed.

"You said that you're trying to stay safe and bring your family back together," Sonos addressed Charlotte. "What's that have to do with the Mountain Kingdom, though? Especially if your sisters are in the Legacy Towers."

Charlotte sighed and looked at the monkey on her shoulder. "Rapha needs us to save the Mountain Kingdom first."

"Save the Mountain Kingdom?" Sonos asked. "The two of you and the monkey? Why?"

Jax crossed his arms again. "You still haven't answered what you're trying to do at the Mountain Kingdom."

That was a good question. He wouldn't have envisioned trying to stop Uzoma and the army though. "Trying to find some answers before the kingdom is captured." Sonos decided to leave it there. He didn't want to seem crazy and talk about Timur's instruction to move the mountain without touching it.

"Once you're not trying to attack it, that's good enough for now," Charlotte said. "Let's just all get there first." She waved Taimani over as she took a knee and turned her gazer back on. "Show me again how we're reaching the Mountain Kingdom?"

Sonos knelt beside her, looking at the impressive holographic map. He tapped his finger to the dot above Portemore, indicating where they were in the forest.

"Jamin and his crew are heading to a small village, most likely here." He traced his finger through the forest to the north and east, stopping at a small dot labeled Harmony. The Ti're River and the major city of Riverton lay to the east of the village.

"Taking the main road from Riverton to the Mountain Kingdom would take about a week." He drew his finger in an arc that led from Riverton around the Badlands to the west and south.

"Jamin's sources said the army is expected in Riverton tomorrow," Taimani said.

"It will take them a few days to move all the troops, supplies, and weaponry across, so Jamin has time to make it to the village," Sonos said.

"I hope it's enough," Taimani frowned at Sonos. "We heard many stories of the ravages caused by Commander Uzoma and his forces when they captured Kimwaki."

Sonos hung his head. He knew the ruthlessness of Uzoma and pitied anyone in the way of the commander.

Jax leaned close over Charlotte and used his finger to draw a straight line between where they were in the forest and the heart of the Mountain Kingdom. "We need as much time as we can before the army makes its assault. I say we head straight through the Badlands to the heart of the Mountain Kingdom."

Charlotte used two fingers to zoom into where he had pointed in the mountains. "Noise?" She sounded out the pronunciation of what was spelled as 'Noiz'.

"No-ehz," Sonos corrected. "It's the capital city of the Mountain Kingdom, where their elusive king calls home. Supposedly he holds a treasure trove of gold and gems. The Emperor has long desired to own the mountains."

Charlotte looked up, eyes sharp. "Your dad needs boundaries."

Sonos was shocked to hear someone speak so bluntly, even if he agreed.

Taimani covered her mouth, but a small chuckle escaped. She focused her attention back on the map. "You drew a path through the Badlands," she said, looking at Jax. "You know there's a reason why they're called the 'Badlands', right?"

"I thought warriors weren't scared of anything," Jax said, eyebrow raised.

"It's not fear," Taimani straightened. "But we're not fools."

"It's a wasteland," Sonos explained. "No water, steep slopes of rocks and clay, no vegetation or life."

"That is, unless you believe the stories," Taimani added.

"What do you mean by stories?" Charlotte asked.

Taimani's face was illuminated by the light from the hologram, accentuating her words. "Most people who enter the Badlands are never heard from again. The few that have come out to tell the tale always carry a certain... *darkness* about them."

"What do you mean they carried a darkness?" Jax asked.

"Once, a mighty famed warrior, the Great Osei, took the Badlands for a shortcut in pursuit of his enemies. He was lost for weeks before he showed up wandering the streets of Pergamum, a frail beggar whose tattoos were the only thing to prove who he was.

"For the brief time he was seen, he was in and out of reality, muttering and babbling about living shadows." Taimani's voice dropped as she spoke.

Charlotte shivered next to Sonos. "A few days ago, I may not have believed you. But we've seen one of those living shadows for ourselves. It was a dragon formed out of smoke. It attacked me but the gazer recording destroyed it somehow."

"What kind of recording?" Sonos asked, wanting a possible solution to overcome whatever waited for them in the Badlands.

Charlotte turned off the map and navigated through the videos stored on her gazer. "Here it is."

Jax's voice filled the air as he read from a scroll spread out on an earthen floor: "*This is written for a future hero of El. Open your eyes! The one who created the world from nothing is doing something new. Are you seeing it? It's springing forth even now.*

He causes a river to flow in the badlands. What is impossible for him?"

Sonos had many questions about the source of that text, the monkey, and how all the dots connected. Was it the reference to *El* that defeated the smoke dragon? But he needed to focus on the issue at hand: deciding on the path forward.

"A river in the Badlands," Sonos repeated Jax's words aloud and scratched his head. "I'm not seeing any reference to a river or any body of water for that matter on the map. Just a massive, dead plateau of rocks which eventually runs into grasslands, then the mountains."

Despite Taimani's warning about the shadows, something tugged at Sonos as he stared at the Badlands on the map. It really was a straight line to Noiz and would allow them more time with the Mountain Kingdom before Uzoma and the army arrived.

Sonos was determined to find the kingdom's secrets. He had no interest in gold or precious metals, but how had they withstood the Empire for so long? Where did their strength come from? Was it their king?

"The text did say that *El* was doing a new thing. Maybe the river didn't exist when that map was made," Charlotte said.

Taimani cocked her head. "Yeah, but wasn't that text you found ancient?"

"I guess so," Charlotte said. "But don't prophecies speak about the future? Maybe it was written then, for now."

Rapha hummed from where he sat on Charlotte's shoulder.

"Is he humming something?" Sonos asked.

Charlotte shrugged. "He does that sometimes." Her eyes turned more thoughtful. "Usually when I need a little help with something."

"Despite the risk, I think we need to do everything we can to get to Noiz as quickly as possible. Jax is right with his suggestion," Sonos said.

"I agree," Charlotte said. "And if we're going to confront the Emperor and Uzoma at the Mountain Kingdom, we might as well start facing the shadows now."

Sonos nodded in appreciation. The warriors would not go against his recommendation, and now Charlotte had given hers alongside Jax.

"I'd really like to understand more about these shadows," Jax said. "Char and I already had our first encounter and I'm not looking to get caught unawares again."

Sonos stood and held out a hand to help Charlotte up. "Let's talk as we walk. We've stayed here long enough."

Taimani took lead on the trail as Taine continued to cover their movements in wide circles. Jax stayed close behind as Sonos walked next to Charlotte and explained.

"There's much I don't know, as the real secrets are held by those who practice the dark arts. But all the dragons are connected. The Shadow Dragon appears once in every generation, and it is usually tied to the person with the greatest authority. Hence, the Emperor in this case.

"It's limited to only working within sight of whoever owns it. The powers vary from owner to owner. There are stories of a dragon being able to bolster an entire army with superhuman strength. Sometimes the shadow can physically attack others. When the Shadow Dragon emerges, it also empowers a host of other dragons—smoke, mist, fog. Once the environment is pliable and controllable. Each dragon is limited to operating within its owner's sight, and is strengthened by its proximity to the Shadow Dragon."

"How do you defeat them, though?" Jax persisted.

"Nothing physical works. No steel, no arrows, or the like. There are rumors of certain people who could resist the dragons' power, but the details are fuzzy."

"But you guys were attacked by a smoke dragon, you said. What was it like?" Sonos asked.

"We were in the slums of Portemore. A bad decision, I admit." Charlotte hung her head a moment. "Anyways, an old man, who I believe was a sorcerer of some kind, lit a fire with herbs and metals and a piece of my hair. The smoke came alive and attacked me. I was struggling to breathe and instinctively tapped my gazer. A video came up randomly, it was the same one of Jax reading the ancient text."

"Hmm. I wonder if it was the light from the gazer, or the sound?" Sonos mused aloud.

"Or more likely, the words that were spoken," Taimani said from ahead. "Words have power, especially with things in the unseen realm."

Had Sibi rubbed off on Taimani more than Sonos had seen? Or did Kimwaki have their own version of this unseen realm?

"Words have power," Charlotte repeated under her breath.

Sonos was still a bit uncomfortable with accepting the unseen, or the spirit realm. He had, after all, been raised to accept the Emperor's supreme authority and nothing more, nothing less. But the whispers from his mother over the years grew a little bit louder in his mind.

CHAPTER 26

T HE SUN WAS CLIMBING high in the sky when Taimani nudged Charlotte awake.

Charlotte groaned as she stretched. "Muscles I never knew I had are aching."

They had stopped walking close to sunrise to rest for a few hours.

Rapha scampered into their makeshift camp carrying a small bag of fresh berries and nuts.

"Ah, brilliant monkey," Sonos said accepting his share.

Charlotte acknowledged that Sonos was much less spoiled than she'd expected of someone who grew up in the palace.

Jax rubbed the sleep out of his eyes from where he had slept next to Charlotte. "Hey, I thought we were splitting watch duties?" Jax looked at Taimani.

The warrior was alert and nibbling on a ration bar. "Taine and I covered it last night. We figured you all could use a little extra sleep."

Charlotte for one was appreciative. But Jax stuck out his chest a bit. "We can carry our share, too."

"Don't worry," Taine said as he rejoined the group behind Rapha. "There'll be plenty of time to take on load as we go. Have no fear."

"How long do you estimate until we reach the Badlands?" Taimani looked between Charlotte and Sonos.

Charlotte pulled up the map on her gazer. "I estimate we've gone about—"

"Fifteen miles," Sonos said.

Charlotte looked up from her gazer. "Almost exactly. How—"

"I pay attention to details. Sometimes that includes counting steps." Sonos shrugged.

"Hmm." Charlotte felt a lot more self-conscious. She put a hand to her head to try and assess the state of her unruly hair.

Taimani laughed. It was hearty and unexpected coming from the tough warrior. "I would think those curls are more a statement than a detail, Char."

Heat crept up Charlotte's neck into her cheeks.

Jax sat down next to Charlotte on her sleeping mat. He handed her a small cup of water infused with some lemon balm from his box of herbs. "I know it's not Gran's cocoa tea, but it's at least a little taste of home."

Charlotte smiled gratefully, inhaling the scent. "It's perfect."

"Sorry, did you say cocoa tea?" Sonos asked. "That sounds... revolting. What is it? A mix of chocolate and herbal green tea?"

"Oh, you poor, unfortunate soul," Charlotte said as she stood and rolled up her bedding. "Cocoa tea is taking freshly grated cocoa together with warm milk and bits of spices like cinnamon and nutmeg. It tastes like..." Charlotte paused and closed her eyes. "It tastes like sunshine dipped in chocolate."

"Sounds like a fancy hot chocolate to me," Taimani laughed.

"Cocoa is not chocolate," Jax interjected. "At least not what I've heard others call chocolate."

"Fair enough," Sonos said, rolling up his own bed. "Since we have plenty of time walking, perhaps you can help enlighten us on some more stories from Jamroq. I'm guessing like many things I was taught in Pergamum, I have a lot to learn about our islands."

A spark of anger flared in Charlotte. This was the second time Sonos had made such an arrogant and ignorant remark. Her dad had always insisted that despite the occupation, their homeland would never belong to K'Luma and the far-off Emperor who sat in Pergamum.

"I said something wrong?" Sonos asked, looking at Charlotte's face.

"*Our* islands?" Charlotte repeated, her voice cold. "Do you even hear yourself? You really think you own our home, don't you?"

"Well, I mean, the islands are part of the Empire. There's a lot I don't know about them. I wasn't trying to imply..." Sonos stumbled, clearly caught off guard.

"The first thing you should learn then, is that the Empire doesn't own any island." Charlotte finished stuffing her bedding into her pack and quickly excused herself from the group before she completely lost her cool.

She was still close enough to hear Taine's voice as she walked off. "She's not wrong," the warrior said to Sonos. "Just keep your eyes and ears open. Truth is not always comfortable, but it will set you free."

Charlotte remembered Gran's saying about how freedom is never really free. *But it's always worth fighting for,* she'd add.

"Don't worry, Gran," Charlotte whispered to the wind. "I won't let our family down."

Rapha climbed onto her shoulder. For the first time, the words the Imperial guard had told her when her sisters were taken started to fade. Those words, *No one fights the Empire and wins,* had plagued her with doubts at every corner for years.

But today, here and now, she embraced the mantra she had heard first from Gran, and now from Sonos and the warriors.

"Fight we must," Charlotte said looking at Rapha. She lifted her eyes above the treetops to the bright sky. "But win we shall."

Chapter 27

C APTAIN DIE PACED THE office he had sequestered from the head of the Imperial Guards stationed in Riverton. His sorcerer sat at a small table mumbling some enchantments over a small bowl filled with burning herbs and metals.

Wylder sat behind the desk. He rocked back in the chair and made a show of plopping his feet atop the desk. "Does it always take so long?" he complained.

"Tell me, have you ever tried summoning the dark realm? It's not exactly like hailing through a gazer." Die worked to keep his annoyance at bay. *It's already enough that Baku forced us to work together,* he thought.

It wasn't his fault that the guards at the north gate in Portemore had allowed a stampede, through which Die was convinced the rebels and Sonos had escaped. He had no idea how the two groups had connected, but intelligence on the ground seemed to suggest that they were together when rescuing the Salan family in Woodyard Square.

We were so close! Die thought. *That useless old man had the rebels in his grip. He was blessed with a smoke dragon, and he failed. Wylder had Sonos and the warriors in his grip and failed to keep them safe. The guards were supposed to secure the gates, and they failed. I have fai—*

He didn't allow himself to finish that thought. Failure was not an option.

He didn't remember much of his life from Kimwaki, only the stories his sister would tell him on the few occasions they were together in private. Since being taken at ten, he had been groomed to serve the Emperor as one of the Elites, and he had never failed in his duties. He would not come up short now, especially in the Year of the Dragon.

Metal ground upon stone as Wylder sharpened his knife.

Die sighed and turned to the window which overlooked the town square. The city was bustling as the final battalion crossed the Ti're River. Soon, Commander Uzoma would leave Riverton with his unconquerable troops and special weapon and continue onwards to the Mountain Kingdom. There was no stopping this conquest.

But the safety of the Emperor still lingered. Die balled his hands into tight fists as he considered the futile search for everyone over the past three days. Despite multiple attempts by the sorcerer, there had been no sign from the dark realm as to the rebels or the prince's whereabouts.

Usually, something from the target was required—hair, blood, or the like. That was how the senile, old man from the slums had been able to summon the smoke dragon.

Sometimes strong sorcerers, such as the one with Die, could locate a target without an article once they were in close enough range. But somehow it was as if a covering or force of some kind had been shielding the rebels, and now Sonos, too.

"What makes you think it's going to work this time?" Wylder's skeptical voice echoed off the walls.

"We are exhausting every avenue we can. Guards are traversing the roads, waterways, and every city, town, and village looking for them. And we will consult the unseen realm every day as well," Die answered. "They can't hide forever."

Die spun around as the enchantments grew louder, and a small fire roared to life in the bowl.

The sorcerer continued to murmur, and the smoke began to take shape. It formed a large, crude, rectangular map that hovered above the bowl.

Wylder jumped from the desk and came to stand next to Die. "Is that the Ti're?" he asked, his voice full of awe. He pointed towards a thin, winding, black tendril of smoke on the right side of the hazy gray square.

Die nodded.

A flame flicked upwards and formed a pulsing dot in the middle of the Ti're tendril.

"That's us," Die said.

On the far west on the map, the mountains took shape. A few towers rose near the north of the Ti're to indicate Pergamum.

Die stared at the map. *Where are you, Sonos? Where are you, rebels?* He wondered.

Finally, another flame licked through the map, west of Riverton. Die quickly tapped his gazer and pulled up a holographic map of the mainland, zooming in to the get the scale to match the smoke map. He held his wrist to position his map to overlay the smoke map. The second flame pulsed just outside the Badlands.

"Got you," Die said. *But where are they heading?* he thought. *Nothing could survive in the Badlands for long. And surely, they would realize that the full force of the army was heading to the Mountain Kingdom. Why run there?*

He would figure out their motivations later. Right now, he had their location and would not lose them again. *How many times have I said that?* He clenched his teeth and turned off his gazer.

"Ready the carriers," Die told one of his Elites near the doorway. "We leave immediately. And I want drones dispatched ahead of us."

Chapter 28

It was late afternoon, three days since they had fled Portemore.

Charlotte leaned in close to Jax, arm interlocked through his, as they stood at the edge of the forest. "Can you believe we made this far?"

"I would have never imagined how massive it was when I read that scroll back in the samaan tree," Jax answered back.

Ahead, the Badlands rose like a sprawling fortress. The huge mounds of rock were vibrant colors of red and orange with streaks of white snaking throughout the formations. Even from the safety of the field, the intertwining peaks and crevices formed an intimidating sight.

"Agreed, not at all what I thought they would look like," Charlotte said, wonder filling her voice.

Rapha chittered from her shoulder, shifting his weight from side to side in a restless manner.

Taimani walked over and placed a hand on Charlotte's other shoulder. The two had grown closer and spent many hours talking over the past two days. "For what it's worth, Char, I know we must go and save the Mountain Kingdom. But my end game aside from keeping my brother safe—"

Taine cleared his throat from where he stood next to Sonos and made some kind of intricate signal with his fingers.

Taimani's eyes twinkled and she continued, "As I was saying, my end game is to burn those towers to the ground and free every last prisoner. We will save Ava and Lily after this."

Rapha hummed in agreement.

"Thanks," Charlotte said, truly grateful.

"I want to have as much sun as possible in the Badlands before night falls," Sonos said, his eyes focused ahead. "Shall we?"

He stepped forward, and they fell into their usual formation. Taimani leading from in front and Taine sweeping them from behind.

They were halfway across the field when Sonos suddenly stopped and stared up at the sky.

"What is it?" Charlotte asked. Then she heard it, too. A loud whirring sound from overhead.

Sonos pointed and sure enough, a drone flew over the tops of the trees and headed in their direction.

"Run!" Taine called out.

Charlotte sprinted, needing no encouragement. Her lungs burned even as the drone got closer and louder overhead. It didn't fire any weapons, but surely its presence meant that they had been found.

Charlotte's feet hit the hard ground as they entered the first gully between two large mounds of rock clay.

Almost immediately when passing the rock, sound became muffled. It was like an invisible band was pressed over her ears. A quick glance at the others indicated they were equally confused.

What have we got ourselves into? Charlotte thought.

Taimani grabbed Charlotte's hand, pulling her forward. Rapha clung to her shoulder.

Charlotte looked overhead for the drone, but strangely, it had disappeared.

As she followed Taimani forward, the sound barrier lifted, and it felt like the fuzz was removed from her ears.

No sooner had relief set in, than the earth and everything around them started to shake violently.

Charlotte screamed as she was thrown to the ground.

Chapter 29

"Jax? Mani?" Charlotte coughed and waved her hand in front of her face, trying to clear the air from the cloud of dust.

Someone grunted from nearby.

"Char?" Sonos called out. "I can't see anything."

"Everyone okay?" Taine asked, his muscled form emerging from the dust.

Rapha stood and shook the dirt from his fur, then ran up one of the nearby walls of hard sediment.

Charlotte crawled over to the shape that had grunted. "Jax, is that you?"

"Mmmm," Jax rubbed his head, groaning.

"Is that blood?" Charlotte gasped and rubbed at a red trickle on his forehead.

"I think a rock caught me." Jax took a deep breath.

Charlotte slipped his pack off and dug for his herb-box. "Which herb will help?"

"Hey, let's make sure it's clean, first." Sonos knelt next to Charlotte with a wet rag and reached for Jax's head.

Jax pulled away at first, but Charlotte laid a hand on his arm to calm him down.

"One of my tutors was a trained healer from the Sahemy," Sonos said as he cleaned the cut.

"Look for the orange-colored root, Char. The turmeric." Jax leaned forward as Charlotte dug through his box.

"What in the Empire was that?" Taine asked as he slapped the dust off his clothing.

"Some kind of earthquake, my guess," Sonos said. "That drone wasn't a weapons drone, and I don't even know of anything that could shake the ground without an actual explosion."

A shiver ran down Charlotte's back. These guys spoke so freely of bombs and weapons.

The cloud of dust was settling, and Taimani poked her head from around a nearby corner. *That girl moves faster than lightning,* Charlotte thought. Her respect for the warriors only grew the more she interacted with them.

"I hit the drone with a stone and brought it down," Taimani called, her face covered in dirt. "The field is still empty, so I'm going to retrieve it quickly."

"I'll watch you from the entrance. Things don't feel quite right here," Taine said. He looked at Sonos first.

"Don't worry, we're not going anywhere," Sonos said.

Taine nodded and jogged after his sister.

Charlotte used her pocketknife to thinly slice a bit of the turmeric root. She unwrapped a portion of a ration bar and handed them both to Jax. "Sorry, I know seeping it as tea would be better."

"S'ok. It'll still help." Jax smiled.

Sonos stood, his brow furrowed as he looked around. "Doesn't it feel a little too coincidental that an earthquake occurred the second we stepped into the Badlands?"

"I guess so," Charlotte said. "Did you guys feel that sound barrier when we walked in, or was it just me?"

"Yes! That, too. I've never encountered anything like that." Sonos ran a hand through his hair.

Rapha squeaked as he ran back down the sediment wall. A new wave of dust and loose rock fell on Charlotte.

"Raph!" She called out and spat a strand of hair from her mouth.

Suddenly self-conscious, she quickly pulled her hair back into two buns then wiped her face with the inside of her tunic.

Taimani and Taine returned, and Taimani dropped a fried piece of metal in front of Charlotte.

"I think it had one of those self-destruct modes on it. I picked it up from the ground and it started beeping, then a few seconds later burst into flames. I still brought it back in case you can salvage anything, Miss Tech," Taimani said with a grin.

Charlotte knelt beside the drone, and Sonos looked over her shoulder. "Normally, I'd never turn down or throw away a piece of any technology. But this one's totally crisped, and I'm guessing they have a tracker on it. I think it's safer to leave it behind," Charlotte said.

Taine looked back to where they entered the Badlands. "Okay, I don't know how close the owners of that drone are, and I'd feel a lot more comfortable if we were further into the Badlands and not sitting ducks near the entrance."

"Sonos, do you know the range of those drones?" Charlotte asked.

Sonos frowned. "Tech was not really my strong suit, but based on the size, I'm guessing not more than twenty miles or so."

"Jax, you okay to move?" Taimani asked.

"I think so." Jax nodded and repacked his bag.

Taine offered Jax a hand to help him stand.

"Here, let me carry this a while," Charlotte grabbed Jax's pack and strapped it to her front, since she was already wearing her other pack. She figured Jax would need a little time to catch himself.

By the time Rapha scurried up to perch on her shoulder she was feeling well and true like a pack animal.

Taimani scouted ahead, leading them further down the gully. At every juncture she made choices that seemed at random, with no clear direction or path.

It was hard to keep track of which way they were heading. The mountains or any other landmark were not yet visible, and the rock and sediment walls ran vertically at least thirty feet, sometimes towering hundreds of feet above them. It wasn't hard to imagine people getting very lost in this place.

After putting some distance between them and the entrance, Charlotte called out, "Hold up." Her breath was more ragged than she cared to admit, but it wasn't tiredness causing her to stop.

She dropped the packs on the ground and tapped her gazer. "I was trying to get my gazer to record from the time we moved from the entrance, but something isn't working."

She tapped it again, but nothing. She took off the bracelet to inspect it closer. "It doesn't look like it was damaged in the earthquake. I'm so confused."

"I wonder..." Sonos paced in the narrow gully where they had stopped. "Taine, is your sword working?"

Taine pulled the weapon off his back in a flash, then turned it over and over in his hand. "No. What's going on?"

Sonos tilted his chin. "Remember how we experienced that sound barrier when we first entered the Badlands?"

Charlotte nodded.

"I wondered why the drone didn't follow us inside. I mean, if Captain Die is on our tails, why wouldn't he keep following us and not let us out of his sight?" Sonos' voice grew more excited as he talked. "Add that to your gazer not working..."

"You think there's some kind of technology barrier?" Charlotte asked.

Taine let out a low whistle. "That's some powerful stuff."

"But if that's the case, why didn't Die just lower the barrier to allow the drone through?" Jax asked.

"Now that's the right question." Sonos smiled.

"Because the Empire isn't controlling the barrier." Charlotte's mind swirled at the possibility.

"And that's the right answer," Sonos said. "And if not the Empire, then who?" Sonos looked like a kid with a new puzzle.

"Okay, so it's back to the basics for navigation," Taimani said. "We have about an hour of sunlight left, and we know that Noiz lies to the northwest. That's enough to keep moving for now."

No one disagreed.

Charlotte bent to pick up the packs from the ground.

Jax put a hand over hers, holding it long enough to feel a little awkward. "Thanks for helping, but I think I'm good now."

She nodded, not quite sure how to think about the little touches that seemed to take on more meaning than she was willing to acknowledge right now. Jax had been as close as a brother the past three years, and things were shifting too quickly for her to process since they had set out on this journey.

"Just let me pull out a little something for my headache." Jax dug through the pack and pulled out a green leaf from his herb box. He broke the leaf in his hand and inhaled, then handed it to Charlotte. "Everyone should take a whiff."

She breathed in the scent, a calming wave of lemon and mint mixed with sunshine filled her head. Jax was right, it was just the pop of energy she needed.

Charlotte handed the herb to Sonos next.

"Wow, what magic was that?" Sonos asked, his eyes clear and bright after taking a breath.

"No magic, just what we like to call bush medicine back home." Jax grinned. "This is lemon balm."

Charlotte strapped on her pack and felt wetness seep through. "How is this wet?" She asked, worried that one of the canteens might have leaked.

"Uhm, my pack is wet too," Jax said.

A trickle of water passed through where Charlotte stood.

A trickle of what? she thought.

"Hey, what is—" Charlotte's words were cut short as she traced the line of water further ahead.

There, standing in the middle of the gully, was a massive warrior with a drawn sword. The warrior's dark skin glistened in the sunlight—*or was he glowing?*

"Rapha!" Charlotte hissed as the monkey jumped from her shoulder and made a beeline for the warrior.

"*Na faapefea ona ia oo mai iinei,*" Taimani muttered as she stood, looking ready to pounce, her blowgun in hand.

The glowing warrior paid the monkey no mind as it climbed to perch on his shoulder. He kept his dark eyes fixed on the group. His dark clothing didn't look like any Imperial uniform Charlotte knew. Lines of gold, silver, green, red, and a few other colors crisscrossed down each sleeve. It looked like seven colors in all.

Taine and Taimani made fast and furious hand signals to each other.

Sonos took a hesitant step forward and addressed the unmoving warrior. "Are you here to help us or are you against us?"

"Neither." The warrior's voice boomed. "I have come as the commander of *El's* army."

"If we're on a mission from *El,* and he's commanding *El's* army, doesn't that mean he should be helping us?" Jax whispered to Charlotte.

Charlotte wasn't sure what to think. Having a whole army on their side would certainly be a game changer. But why didn't the commander say he was there to help them then? And why hadn't Rapha mentioned an army?

Her eyes drifted to the ground, and what had started as a trickle by their feet continued to grow into a larger flow of water by the minute.

Taine stepped forward next to Sonos, his knuckles white as he gripped his hooked sword. "You say you are the commander of an army. Where are those you lead?"

For some unknown reason, the intimidating commander turned his head to look at Rapha. They didn't speak, but after a moment, the commander nodded. When he spoke, he pointedly ignored Taine's question. "The earth shook to send you this river."

"Looks more like a trickle to me," Taimani muttered.

The commander continued unabated. "Follow it and you will be protected. Do not stray. Do not turn from it to the left or to the right, and do not be afraid. Be strong and very courageous."

Charlotte sucked in her breath and stepped back.

"Be strong and very courageous," Charlotte repeated under her breath. She looked at Jax, "Just like the words in the journal I read in the portal."

A light emitted from the commander.

Is that right? The light is coming out of him? Charlotte wondered.

Rapha jumped off and stood to the side, watching the commander.

"Those who are with you are greater than the darkness," the commander said, then he shimmered into a million bits of light and disappeared.

"Was that... a hologram?" Sonos asked, stepping forward to investigate the spot where the commander had stood.

"Puts a damper on that tech barrier theory, if so," Charlotte said, deep in thought. She checked her gazer, but still no life.

Taine and Taimani dropped to one knee and placed their weapons on the ground in front of them, bowing a head towards where the commander had disappeared.

Or are they submitting to Rapha, who's just standing in that spot? Charlotte thought, confused.

"Uhm, guys?" Charlotte asked.

After a moment, the two warriors stood.

"That was no hologram. And your little friend is connected to this *El*," Taimani said.

"Yes, that's what I was trying to tell you before," Charlotte said.

"I thought Kimwakis believed—" Sonos started.

Taine waved his hand, cutting Sonos off. "We don't submit to *El*. Our authority is the Great Chief, who is connected to all living spirits of the earth and nature. But it is foolish to not honor a god who showed themselves in plain sight."

"Well, technically he introduced himself as the commander of *El's* army, not *El* himself," Sonos said.

Taimani narrowed her eyes, and he quickly added, "But who's splitting hairs?"

Charlotte knelt in front of Rapha. "You know, it would be nice if you could talk outside of that portal, especially being connected to *El* and all. It certainly would make things a lot easier."

Rapha chittered as he pointed towards the trickle of water and jumped from side to side. The flow continued to increase.

"Remembering what Jax's prophecy said, I really hope that doesn't grow into an actual rushing river with these gullies." Sonos gulped.

"True. But I doubt *El* brought us all this way just to kill us now," Charlotte said.

"What's that?" Sonos asked.

"That *El* probably isn't going to kill us if he's the one who brought us here," Charlotte repeated.

"Sibi said the same thing to us when we were leaving Pergamum." Sonos' face was thoughtful.

"Smart kid. At any rate, I think we should follow the stream," Charlotte said. She glanced towards the sky. "We still have time before sunset. And I can't say I'm looking forward to the night in this place." Her shoulders shivered.

Despite her apprehension, as they walked forward following the water flow, the commander's words ran through her mind. *Be brave and courageous. Those who are with you are greater than the darkness.*

CHAPTER 30

CAPTAIN DIE STOOD AT the entrance of the Badlands, scowling.

Wylder stood beside him and scratched his head.

Twenty Elites spread out across the field.

Die kicked the burned drone which they had found easy enough thanks to its tracker. In the last moments of its live feed, Die had watched the rebel teens along with the prince, Taine, and another Kimwaki warrior run into the Badlands. That was about thirty minutes earlier.

"How long until the new drone is ready?" Die asked the Sah-Elite. He wanted Sonos and the rebels caught before sundown.

The master-techie assigned to his unit from the Sahemy wiped the sweat from his brow as he continued to make adjustments to the drone in his hand. "I don't understand why none of the drones are able to cross over. We told Baku that we needed more time to understand and break through whatever technology is controlling the Badlands."

"The Emperor, may he live forever, waits on no one," Die scoffed. He bit back a further retort, knowing that anger would not motivate one from the Order of the Sahemy. Scientists were meticulous and arrogant on a good day.

"Do you believe the stories of living shadows in this place?" Wylder asked with a mischievous grin.

Die straightened his shoulders and clasped his hands behind his back. "We partner with the dark realm, so if there are any living shadows, I expect them to work *with* us, not against us."

He didn't add that the dark realm in his experience was unpredictable and half as likely to kill as to help on any given occasion. However, this was the Year of the Dragon, so things should be different.

"Ready your men. With or without a drone, we are going in," Die said.

Wylder sauntered off towards his men.

Die walked over to the sorcerer and his senior Elite who stood over the hooded master of the dark arts. The sorcerer was still muttering enchantments.

"Same thing?" Die asked his Elite. "Nothing working?"

The Elite frowned. "No, sir."

"Stay here and hail me if the drone or the sorcerer make any progress. Surely having the weight of the Sahemy and the dark arts should count for something." Frustration threatened Die's cool. They needed to move.

"Battle ready!" Die called his force to order.

The Elites fell into four neat rows of five men per squad.

Wylder and the thugs huddled together to the side, looking every bit the riffraff that they were.

"We move out heading northwest towards the mountains," Die instructed. "Sah will confirm as soon as he has sight of the targets. Comms on frequency forty-eight. Remember that we are rescuing the prince and capturing the rebel teens from Jamroq. Those three must not be harmed. Feel free to neutralize the Kimwaki warriors and anyone else."

A thread of sadness wound its way around Die's heart about killing anyone from Kimwaki, but these warriors had broken a sacred vow to their people and to the Emperor himself. Plus,

Die knew firsthand how dangerous the warriors could be. He was taking no chances.

The Elites thumped their hands to their hearts, their fingers and thumb making a 'K' in salute and agreement.

Die adjusted his earpiece and then activated his flyer-board as the other squads followed suit. Adrenalin and anticipation coursed through him as they buzzed towards the entrance. He led the charge from the front, fearless and determined as he narrowed his eyes and approached the Badlands.

BAM.

Die flew forward in the air as his board seemed to hit an invisible wall at the entrance. He hit the ground hard. His earpiece squawked agonizing static.

Behind him, the other Elites crashed in similar fashion, falling on top of each other.

What a mess. Nothing was going according to plan. Time to go back to the basics.

CHAPTER 31

PALE MOONLIGHT REFLECTED OFF the stream of water as Sonos walked upstream. The trickle that had started mere hours earlier was now a full-blown, babbling brook. The source of the water seemed to be coming from the mountains, assuming they were heading in the right direction.

Sonos was distracted thinking about the prophecy Charlotte and Jax had found, the earthquake, the mysterious commander of *El's* army, and now this flow of water that was well on its way to becoming a river—*in the Badlands.* Not to mention Miss Gemma, the origami trees, and Rapha.

Even Sonos' subconscious had stopped tracking steps and the number of turns they made. All his mental energy replayed the bigger pieces of the puzzle over and over.

"Hey, watch it," Jax yelped as Sonos walked straight into him.

"Sorry, I—" Sonos said, then stopped.

Apparently, everyone had stopped ahead.

"We can't walk all night," Charlotte said, already plopped on the ground next to her pack. Rapha lay curled up beside her.

"I agree," Jax said. "We haven't heard a peep of anyone trailing us, and we need to stop sometime."

"Just because Captain Die hasn't found us yet doesn't mean—" Taine started.

"We know," Charlotte interrupted. Her tone softened as she continued, "Just a few hours to get a little rest."

Sonos knelt on the ground next to Charlotte. "Let's take a breather. Jax, you have any special bush medicine on offer tonight?"

To Sonos' surprise, Jax gave a genuine smile and reached into his pack.

"Not here though," Taimani stopped him.

"What's wrong with here?" Jax asked.

"By the body of water that is leaving a trail as obvious as breadcrumbs?" Taimani crossed her arms.

"She does have a point," Taine said.

Rapha scrambled on top of the pack and chittered at Charlotte.

"I don't think Rapha agrees," Charlotte said.

"All respect due to one connected to your deity, but in cases like this, I prefer to trust my instincts which have been trained over many years. We can pick the river back up in the morning, but it's another matter making camp here." Taimani's tone became more resolute the more she argued.

"That commander from *El's* army was pretty adamant that we do not stray from the river," Jax said, unmoving by Charlotte's side.

"We're not straying from the river, we're just not camping beside it," Taine said. "I agree with my sister."

Sonos turned to Charlotte and Jax. He knew the warriors would not change their minds, and he didn't want the group to split up. "I know it feels funny leaving the river that came to us quite dramatically, but Taine has saved my life more times than I care to admit. Kimwaki instincts are rarely proven wrong. We'll find the river again in the morning, I promise."

Charlotte glanced once more at Rapha, then slowly shook her head. "Sorry. But I got in serious trouble the last time I didn't listen to Raph. We'll stay put and see you in the morning. Though I still don't think you should go."

Taine put a hand on Sonos' shoulder. "Your safety is paramount. We'll come back in a few hours."

Sonos drew his mouth in a tight line but stood with the warriors. Gone were the days of commanding others from his position of royalty. But arguing with either group here would be futile. And Taine and Taimani had more than proven their worth during this journey.

Taimani led the way down the gully and away from the river at the next turn.

"Let's not go too far," Sonos said.

Taimani turned her head around long enough to roll her eyes.

"Sound seems to travel strangely in this place, but hopefully we'll hear any commotion," Taine said. "We need to get far enough away to not get caught if Die does show up though. You, of all people, must know how dangerous he is."

Sonos grunted. A knot in his stomach continued to lodge its disagreement with the decision to leave Charlotte.

Clouds passed over the moon, throwing the terrain into deeper darkness. They continued to walk, taking each turn in utter silence. The quiet was deafening, as no other signs of life were in the place. No rustles, no wind, no birds, no running water. Only their footsteps on the dirt and loose stones.

The only thing that seemed to move were shadows made by the moonlight. Sonos fought against his imagination spiraling into one of Taimani's stories.

Just as he was about to insist that they had gone far enough, it was half a mile by his count, Taimani stopped in a narrow crevice. It was wide enough for two across to stand side by side, but not much more.

"This is as good a place as we will find. Not too wide and hopefully far enough away from the river, that they won't find us in the dark," Taimani said.

Sonos slipped the pack off his back and sat against the rock wall.

Just a few hours, then we'll go back, he reminded himself.

The thought barely crossed his mind when the entire place went pitch black. Sonos looked at the sky to see if more clouds had covered the moon, but he could no longer see anything. The rock walls, Taine, Taimani... had all disappeared. He held a hand in front of his face and saw nothing. It was as if a deep shadow had descended like a blanket.

Shadows.

A chill ran down his back.

"Taine!" he tried to call out, but it barely came out as a hoarse whisper. An invisible force constricted his throat.

A gurgling sound came from nearby.

Sonos tried to stand, but his body was pinned against the wall. He couldn't move. It was as if something was pulling him back into the rock wall.

Panic surged, even as Sonos struggled to breathe.

Think, Sonos, think.

He worked to focus his mind. What did Charlotte say about defeating that smoke dragon? Words... words have power. That was something Taimani had said. But what words?

The only thing he could think of was what the commander from *El's* army had told them before he disappeared: *Those who are with you are greater than the darkness.*

He grabbed at his throat, fighting against a shadow he couldn't see. He whispered between gasps, "Those who... are with... us... are greater... than... the darkness." *May* El *help us,* he added in his mind.

The tightness faltered just a little and Sonos gulped a big breath.

"Those who are with us are greater than the darkness," he said a little louder.

The constriction on his throat grew fainter. He leaned forward coughing.

"Those who are with us are greater than the darkness!" Sonos shouted this time.

The faintest glimmer of moonlight shone through the shadow.

Another saying flashed through his mind. "Fight we must, but win we shall!" He looked around the crevice, the squirming outlines of Taine and Taimani slowly becoming visible.

"You are defeated, shadow!" As the words slipped through Sonos' mouth, they felt spurred from a different place. A place beyond his conscious thought.

The shadow finally lifted allowing the moonlight and stars to once again illuminate the crevice.

"Taine!" Sonos ran to the warrior who was doubled over, coughing and struggling to catch his breath.

"Taimani..." Taine whispered.

Sonos turned and ran to another form who lay crumpled on the ground. "Mani!" He shook her unmoving body.

After a few seconds, she gasped for breath. Her eyes staring outwards held an unfamiliar look of fear.

"Mani, it's okay. It's gone." Sonos held her shoulders and focused her gaze on him.

Slowly, her shoulders relaxed, and her breathing resumed to a normal cadence. The fear never quite left her eyes though.

Taine stumbled over to them. "How did you stop it?" he croaked, labored breaths coming between his words.

"Words have power, I remembered from Taimani," Sonos said. "And I just called out the last words I remembered from the commander of *El's* army."

"River. Back to the river." Taimani sat up. "Now."

"Agreed," Taine said, his strength returning. "I would much rather fight an enemy we can see versus a living shadow like that."

Sonos and Taine helped Taimani to stand. There were no visible bruises or marks on her body, but she was shaking as they moved forward. She must have taken the brunt of the attack, or perhaps fought back the fiercest, knowing her.

Taine stayed by her side, draping her arm over his shoulder.

Sonos led the way back to the river keeping as far away from the walls and shadows as possible. Finally, he heard a trickle of water as they turned a corner.

"We made it, Mani," Taine said softly.

Sonos had never heard Taine take a gentle tone with his fierce warrior sister. It was unnerving.

Taimani walked stronger, but her eyes were distant, and she kept her arm around her brother's shoulder.

The stream had grown in size since they left it—or maybe it was Sonos' imagination. But what really gave him pause was a large tree that had sprung up out of nowhere.

"How?" Sonos' jaw dropped.

"What in the Empire..." Taine was similarly speechless.

As they drew closer, Jax jumped up from where he sat near the trunk. "What happened?" Concern spilled through his voice as he ran forward to help Taine.

"Long story. But it seems we could ask the same here," Sonos answered. "Where did that tree come from?"

Charlotte stood and stretched from where she had been laying down. She rubbed her eyes, her unruly hair sticking out.

"Hey, you're back," she said with a sleepy smile. Then her gaze drifted past Sonos to the others and her eyes went wide. "Mani!"

Charlotte helped sit Taimani down, propping her back against the tree.

Rapha jumped off a branch and swung down next to Taimani. He laid a hand on her arm and started to hum.

"What's he doing?" Sonos whispered to Charlotte, not wanting to disrupt the moment.

"Dispelling the darkness," Charlotte answered, her eyes fixed on Rapha.

"Huh?" Sonos was confused.

Charlotte turned to look at Sonos, her green eyes thoughtful. "You know how gazers can tune to specific frequencies?"

Sonos furrowed his brow. "When I think of frequencies, I think of the earpieces that allow Elites to communicate on a specific channel."

"Exactly. Well, this is like helping to get Mani back to our channel." Charlotte bit her lower lip. "Or is this too techie an explanation? Sorry. My mind sometimes works a little differently."

Sonos smiled. "I get the gist of it."

Jax and Taine had been conversing quietly to the side.

Taine walked over to where Charlotte and Sonos stood near Mani. "Thank you, Char, for helping Mani."

"Thank Rapha." Charlotte inclined her head to the monkey who was now curled up in Taimani's lap. Both were fast asleep.

"Either way, I'm grateful for *El*'s kindness," Taine said. "Jax and I will keep watch for a while. I'm going to scout a bit, just to ensure no one is close.

"And don't worry, I'll stick close to the river," he added with a grimace.

Charlotte sat near Taimani, her back also against the trunk. "Jax, make sure to wake me so you can get some rest too."

Jax nodded, then looked at Sonos. "I'm glad you guys made it back."

Well, that was unexpected, Sonos thought. Then added, "Me, too."

Sonos sat a little distance from Charlotte, resting his pack against the sediment wall. His mind was full of questions, not the least of which was the whole concept of frequencies as Charlotte had explained them, in the unseen realm.

Even more than the spirit realm though, Sonos thought about his Uncle Diekololaoluwa. Granted, his interactions with Die had been very limited over the years. His most vivid memories were ones of Die doing everything possible to please and impress the Emperor.

Did he think it would earn him freedom or any favor in the end? Sonos thought, but he knew better.

Sonos didn't believe his uncle would try to kill him, but none of the others would be safe. He needed to get the Elites off their back.

Moral suasion would not change Die's course, but Sonos hoped that Die's loyalty to family and love for his sister ran at even a fraction of what he saw between Taine and Taimani.

An idea formed in his head, and he pulled out the origami tree Miss Gemma had given him. He unfolded and scribbled a note on it, planning to leave it in the tree before they left.

More than once his mother had joked that Sonos got his power of observation from her brother. If that was the case, this plan should work.

CHAPTER 32

"THEY'RE GONE AGAIN," THE sorcerer said, cowering away from his bowl of incense and smoke.

"You don't think... They didn't hurt the prince, did they?" Die narrowed his eyes.

"The shadows are unpredictable in this place. I felt the attack, but something stopped it." The sorcerer wrung his hands, his eyes downcast.

Die paced the narrow space in the gully, frustrated and angry. Their pace was woefully slow. Twice, the groups had been separated, and it took painstaking hours to find each other. Now, in an effort to use the dark arts to locate Sonos and the rebels, the sorcerer seemed to have actually launched an attack with the shadows.

Cursed, unpredictable dark realm, he thought.

"Take a squad and send this man back to the field with the Sah," Die instructed one of his senior Elites. "And do *not* activate the shadows again. Focus everything on breaking this tech barrier."

It was impossible to navigate through this maze coherently without technology. He finally assented to give the other squads a rest, and they would regroup at daylight. It would also give the scouts a chance to scour the area without the groups completely losing each other.

A few hours later, one of his seniors woke him. Die glanced at the sky, the moon had disappeared, and the sky glowed faintly with the impending dawn.

"I think we found something," the senior's voice was urgent. "One of the scout teams discovered a stream of water."

"A stream of water in the Badlands?" Die wondered aloud.

"Exactly. It must mean something, no?"

"Ready the squads." Die commanded.

He remembered words from his sister written in one of her little origami trees years ago: *E leai se mea fa'afuase'I, na'o le fa'amoemoe.*

"There is no coincidence, only purpose," Die muttered under his breath. Die might have burned every note, but the words were never forgotten.

CHAPTER 33

—·—

RAPHA SWUNG DOWN FROM a low branch in the tree, landing on Charlotte's shoulder.

Charlotte yelped. "Hey, no need to scare a girl, eh?" She chided the monkey. She had been standing already, trying her best to keep alert while on watch.

Rapha chittered loudly in response, bouncing from foot to foot.

"Shh, you're going to wake the others." Charlotte tried to calm him down. She looked at the sky, which was still dark, with no signs yet of the sunrise.

Rapha ran over to Jax, climbing onto his chest.

"Huh?" Jax sat up straight, his hand already grasping a dagger.

"Sorry," Charlotte knelt next to Jax. "You still have some time. I don't know what's gotten into Raph."

She turned to see Rapha jumping from Taine to Sonos, waking them as well. In a matter of moments, everyone was wide awake.

"What happened? What's the problem?" Taine stood, hooked sword in hand.

Charlotte glared at Rapha. But good sense started to prevail. This was Rapha. Something *was* likely up. "I think we need to move."

Taimani stood and stretched. "My memory of last night is a bit hazy, but I think I owe this monkey my life... or at least my sanity.

If he's telling us to move, you don't need to tell me twice. What are you all waiting for?"

Taine pulled his sister close, touching foreheads. "Glad to have you back, Mani."

Charlotte smiled at the sibling affection. It reminded her of moments shared with Ava and Lily. Before a well of emotions could break through, she pushed the thought back. Instead, she stuffed the bedding in her bag.

Sonos knelt beside the stream, filling his canteen.

Charlotte joined him. She cupped some of the cool, refreshing liquid in her hands and splashed her face.

"You have some kind of protection, or special bond with Rapha, don't you?" Sonos asked.

At first, Charlotte thought he was being accusatory, but then she saw the curiosity in his eyes. "Yes. I can't say I fully understand it, but before leaving Jamroq, Rapha breathed on both me and Jax. He said it was necessary to be connected for the mission."

Rapha hovered by Taimani near the tree. They had really bonded.

"Last night, when the shadow attacked, I spoke the only words I could remember from that commander of *El*'s army. I think that's what saved us," Sonos said.

Charlotte nodded; she had felt the same about the video of the prophecy stopping the smoke dragon.

"But I want more," Sonos said. "I want a direct connection to Rapha and his unseen world."

Charlotte raised an eyebrow. "You're sure? I mean, I don't think there's any way to get rid of the connection once you have it. And I must warn you, that things don't always go according to how *you* want or plan."

Sonos let his eyes rest on Rapha. "I don't want to wander and rely only on what I know or can see with my eyes. Miss Gemma talked about how my mother helped prepare me for this quest. I can see that now. And I think this is something I need to do. It's something I *want* to do."

As if hearing them, Rapha scampered over to the river, and Sonos knelt in front of him.

Rapha placed a small hand on Sonos' forehead and took a deep breath.

"Don't worry, it doesn't—" Charlotte's encouragement was cut short as Rapha blew out.

Sonos closed his eyes, and his whole body seemed to relax as he exhaled.

Charlotte remembered that crisp feeling of calm and peace mixed with assurance.

When Sonos opened his eyes, he bowed his head to Rapha. "Now, let's see where this road... well, this river, takes us."

Jax walked over and offered a hand to help Sonos up. It wasn't necessary to stand, more a gesture of friendship and community. They offered each other a small smile but didn't say anything more.

Charlotte caught Taimani's eye, and they both shared a similar moment. What a difference a night in the Badlands had made.

"Taine?" Sonos asked.

"I'm good," Taine answered, holding both palms in front of him. "After all, I think one of us should keep our senses as-is, just in case."

Charlotte wanted to say something, but then she remembered her own first reaction to Rapha in the temporal portal. If it was meant to be, Taine would find his own way and time to connect to *El* and the unseen realm.

Rapha went back to chittering and jumping from foot to foot.

Charlotte grabbed her pack, as did the others, and headed out.

Taimani set the pace from the front; Rapha perched on her shoulder.

Taimani was still a little worried about any lingering effects from the shadow, and Rapha seemed happy to keep close to her side.

As they walked in silence, the sky turned a lighter shade of pink as it warmed with the soon-to-come sun.

Every so often, Taine would jog up beside Taimani, and they would talk in low voices.

"Char, has Rapha said anything more to you about any danger or why he got us up and moving?" Taine asked. "I keep checking behind us, but there are no signs that anyone is closing in."

"He doesn't really speak like that." Charlotte shrugged. "It's more like I've learned to sense generally what he's trying to communicate. And sometimes I can hear frequencies—like when something resonates and agrees, or when something is dissonant and doesn't sound right."

Taine grimaced. "I'm not sure I get that. But just let me know if you hear, or sense, anything more, please."

"Of course."

The sky turned red with the sunrise and soon enough, the sun was blazing in the sky.

After traversing a particularly long ravine, the river took a sharp left. As soon as Charlotte turned the corner, her breath caught.

Jax peered over Charlotte's shoulder and let out a low whistle. "Well, this should get interesting."

Charlotte agreed.

The river poured out from the mouth of a cave. Calling it a cave was generous. It was more like a crevice that was barely large enough to squeeze into.

"Char, you're sure Rapha isn't upset with us for leaving last night and leading us into a death trap, right?" Taine asked from behind.

Charlotte frowned. "In case you forgot, he helped your sister last night. And no, I don't think he brought us this far just to kill us."

"That seems to be a recurring response," Taine muttered.

"Shh," Sonos put a finger to his mouth, his eyes intense. He pointed to his ear.

There it was... the sound of loose rocks dropping from the way they had just come.

Taine and Taimani both jumped to warrior stances, weapons flashing to the ready.

"A scout. Up there," Taimani looked in the direction of the nearest peak of sediment rock.

Charlotte caught a flash of movement before it disappeared.

"Quickly," Taimani said ducking into the mouth of the cave, following where Rapha had already gone. "And stay close."

Charlotte followed, her heart in her throat.

After crouching for some time as they moved through the steady stream of water, the cave opened up into a large cavern. Rays of sunlight streamed in from small holes in the high ceiling, giving just enough light to see.

The cavern was huge—Charlotte estimated a three- or four-story building from Portemore could easily fit there.

The river flowed along a ledge that ran along the left side of the cavern. Water poured through tiny tributaries that seeped through the porous walls of the hard sediment. A narrow ledge just wide enough to walk on ran a few feet above the water.

Taimani pulled herself onto the ledge. "Seems to hold okay," she confirmed. She extended a hand to help Charlotte climb up.

Once on the ledge, Charlotte took a deep breath. It was a long fall to the cavern bottom.

"Keep your eyes on me, Char." Taimani gave her hand a squeeze.

"You got this," Jax whispered from behind.

The confidence was contagious. Charlotte kept a hand on the rock wall as she took one slow, small step after the other. She kept her eyes fixed on Taimani's back.

Sweat trickled down Charlotte's neck, and her legs trembled from taut muscles. Each minute seemed to stretch for an hour as they walked, but she kept moving forward.

"Almost there," Jax finally said.

After a few more excruciating steps, Taimani was able to crouch down and jump a short distance to a floor similar to where they had entered. Another tunnel led deeper into the waterway.

"You'll have to jump a bit," Taimani said.

Charlotte took a deep breath again and bent her knees. Right before she was about to leap, shouting erupted from the direction they had come.

"Now, Char!" Taimani urged even as she pulled out her blow gun and darts.

Charlotte jumped, heart pounding.

Jax, Sonos, and Taine were moments behind her.

"We need to create a diversion," Taine said as more Elites poured in.

"How about a way to stop them?" Jax offered. "I have an idea of how we can cause a break in the ledge." He dug in his pack and pulled out his rope.

"Sonos, you and Char follow Rapha and get out of here," Taine said. "We'll catch up."

"But—" Sonos started.

Charlotte felt the same. Splitting up was rarely a good idea.

"No time to argue. Go!" Taimani echoed her brother's words.

"I'll find you, Char, don't worry," Jax pulled her in for a quick embrace.

The first Elite stepped onto the ledge near the entrance.

It was enough.

Sonos grabbed her hand, and they followed Rapha into the depths of the cave.

<h1 style="text-align:center">CHAPTER 34</h1>

THE LIGHT THAT HAD poured in through the ceiling of the cavern quickly disappeared, as Sonos and Charlotte followed Rapha into the tunnel.

Sonos could only hope that the breath from Rapha would save them from another encounter with the shadows. He shivered at the thought.

Soon after they started down the tunnel, Rapha took a sharp left, tugging on Sonos' leg so he didn't follow the wider tunnel forward.

"Why are we leaving the main tunnel?" Charlotte whispered from where she walked directly behind.

Sonos held her hand. "Rapha wants us to go this way."

One of the small tributaries of water trickled at their feet as they moved forward.

"Doesn't it feel like we're walking in a circle?" Sonos asked after they had been walking for some time.

"I guess," Charlotte said. "But the lack of light has my sense of direction totally off."

A loud crash sounded to their left.

"That sounded like an avalanche," Charlotte said. "Maybe we should turn back?"

Rapha chittered urging them forward.

"It was probably just Jax destroying the ledge, like he said," Sonos said, interlacing his fingers and squeezing her hand.

He felt her anxiety, but Rapha was still moving ahead, and he was resolute to follow. Thankfully, Charlotte moved forward with him.

Muffled sounds of men arguing drifted towards them, as small shafts of light seeped through the porous wall. It was almost as if they were walking in a huge snail shell, with just a thin layer separating them from the other side.

Charlotte seemed to relax with the bit of light.

They walked a little further, and a hole in the wall near the floor opened, wide enough to see the Elites' boots.

Sonos sighed. The small bit of hope he had in leaving the origami tree for Die withered. There was no stopping Die's pursuit.

Unless... But could Sonos really kill his uncle? Could he kill anyone, deliberately? The servant whose life he had accidentally taken, still haunted his dreams. How could he take such drastic action intentionally?

Rapha sat calmly by the opening, waiting.

Surely Rapha didn't expect his first act as a follower of *El* to be murder.

"Those cursed warriors. We must find another way to cross. Sonos and the rebel girl already fled." A familiar voice sent a chill down Sonos' spine.

"That's Captain Die," Charlotte put her mouth right next to Sonos' ear and barely made a sound, her body tense.

He nodded. "I know."

An idea suddenly formed in his mind. He glanced at Rapha who still sat calmly by the opening. Sonos dropped to his stomach, careful not to make a sound in the water that continued to trickle at their feet.

He confirmed that it was Die right in front of the opening. The Elites continued talking, and Die shuffled his feet, as if pacing.

Sonos pulled a small dagger from his cloak.

"What are you doing?" Charlotte hissed.

Sonos ignored the question and kept focused on his uncle. It was now or never. If Die moved too far away, he'd have nothing.

Without over-thinking, Sonos stuck out his arms and grabbed hold of Die's cloak. His pulse raced, but he focused on the task at hand. With deft hands, he cut a large swath of Die's cloak.

Let's hope it's enough, Sonos thought. He pulled back his arms and tucked the cloth and dagger back into his cloak.

"What was that?" Die called out.

Charlotte's eyes went wide as she held her breath and locked eyes with Sonos.

"What was what?" Another Elite asked.

Shadows from the men moving played against the streams of light on their side of the wall.

"Never mind, it was probably nothing," Die said.

Rapha touched Sonos' leg and pointed back the way they had come.

Sonos pulled Charlotte close so they could follow.

Her eyes showed pure confusion, and he couldn't blame her.

When the muffled voices died down and the darkness had again enveloped them, Charlotte asked, "What was that about?"

"Captain Die is my uncle," Sonos answered.

"What?" Charlotte gasped.

"My mother's brother. Both were taken from Kimwaki after the conquest."

Charlotte was silent, and it was too dark to see her face. "I knew about the Empress, but I didn't realize her brother was taken too. I'm sorry."

"That he's my uncle?" Sonos asked.

"No, not that," Charlotte said squeezing his hand. "I'm sorry they were both taken from their home and their people. But why is he trying to kill me then? Shouldn't he be more... sympathetic?"

Sonos sighed. "People handle oppression differently. Die was put through total and complete re-education and training during his very formative years. While my mother found her own small ways to nurture the seed of her beliefs, Die took another path.

"I'm sorry for the pain he's caused, but a part of me still holds out hope," Sonos said.

"Hope," Charlotte said. "The thing you seem to have in abundance." She muttered the last part as she kept hold of his hand in the darkness and walked forward.

After a few steps, she stopped again. "But what was that thing with cutting his cloak?"

"An idea. We'll see if it works soon enough," Sonos answered.

Charlotte grunted but started walking again.

Soon enough, they exited the tributary and were back in the wider tunnel.

Sonos pulled her towards the right, heading back to the cavern. "I'm not seeing signs that the others came out of the tunnel yet. Let's go check on them."

His eyes adjusted as light streamed in from the cavern ahead. Dust filled the air, and he coughed as they entered the vast room.

"Over here," Taimani said from where she knelt next to Jax, who was sitting propped up with his back against the wall.

Taine crouched nearby, keeping his eye fixed on the entrance of the cavern, even though there was too much dust to see clearly.

"Jax! What happened?" Charlotte ran over to him.

"We just pulled him out of the rubble," Taimani said. "His leg got caught in a small avalanche. I think his ankle may be broken." She had stripped one of the tunics and was wrapping his ankle.

Jax moaned and Charlotte placed a hand on his forehead. "Hey, I'm here. How can I help?"

He pointed to his mouth which was full of something, most likely from his herb box. "White willow bark," he said through his mouthful.

Sonos knelt nearby. "Do you think you'll be able to move?"

Jax wiggled his toes and bent his good leg and nodded.

"I made it as stable as possible with the materials we have," Taimani said. "Let's help you up."

Sonos waved Taine over to help Taimani and Charlotte with Jax.

Rapha climbed over onto Jax's shoulder and hummed.

The dust was clearing. Time to move.

Sonos exhaled and stepped forward to the edge of the cavern, ignoring the whispers from the others calling him back.

"Diekololaoluwa!" Sonos' voice rang clear and strong across the cavern.

A tall figure straightened and stepped forward into a ray of light that shone in from the ceiling on the other side of the cavern.

"Let us go!" Sonos shouted.

Laughter answered him. "It's not too late, Highness. Surrender, come back, and those with you may be shown a merciful death."

The warriors cursed from behind him, but he signaled for Taine and Taimani to keep back.

Sonos dug in his cloak pocket and pulled out the scrap of cloth, extending his arm and holding the black material with red and golden trim. "It is not for us to surrender, but for you.

"I extended you a warrior's mercy when you didn't even know it. I cut this cloth from your cloak, when I could have done much more." It brought Sonos no pleasure to cause his uncle shame, and he hoped in the end, the mercy wouldn't kill his uncle. He knew the cost of failure instituted by the Emperor.

In a flutter of motion, Die pulled off his cloak and inspected it. He must have found the cut because he hung his head and dropped to one knee.

The Elites around him slowly backed away.

Sonos took a deep breath, and some of the hardness dropped from his voice. "There is a better way than my father's rule. I am determined to find it. Even if you don't join me, in honor of mercy shown to you, do not pursue us."

Captain Die kept his head down and made a fist, tapping his heart twice.

Sonos was relieved to see his uncle use the salute and not the K'Luma signal. Maybe his uncle would find a way after all.

He then turned to the others. "Let's go before any of the other Elites decide to find a new leader."

CHAPTER 35

C APTAIN DIE REMAINED ON one knee; head bowed.

"I'll take the men and give you five minutes," his second in command said. There was no pity in the Elite's voice, it was purely tradition that allowed a man of Die's stature to fall on his own sword instead of being killed for failure in a mission.

The other Elites filed out of the cave. They would regroup and continue pursuit another way. Wylder had already split his men away at the mouth of the cave. He had insisted they'd find another way around and cut off Sonos on the other side.

But these Badlands were not normal topography. Strange things were in control: tech shut down, a mysterious river appearing, the tree, the dark realm having a mind of its own.

Die was confident something was working with Sonos and the rebels, and against those who sought to stop them.

In his fist, he held the crumpled origami tree he had found in the strange tree by the river. In the note, Sonos spoke of hope and a better future.

Over the years, the Empress had dropped hints of a plan to free her people—their people. She had never given up hope, and somehow, she had instilled this same dream inside of Sonos.

Die remembered the haunting question Charlotte had spit out during the interrogation in Jamroq. *"What choice did we have?"* What choice did *he* have? For so long, his very life and existence had been defined by the service and value he brought to the Empire.

But was there another choice?

He stood and unstrapped the hooked sword from his back. The tech infusion was of course not working, though the metal still caught rays of the sun, shimmering as he turned it in his hand.

He was at a crossroads.

At his moment of failure, he finally felt free of the fear that had gripped him for so long. If Sonos and the Empress could find a way, so would he.

"It is time," a raspy voice said from nearby.

Die turned his head, frantically looking for who was with him. "Who's there? Sonos?"

A little dragon lizard scurried out of the small stream of water to what remained of the destroyed ledge.

"Follow me," the raspy voice seemed to come from the dragon lizard.

How could that be? Die wondered.

The lizard inhaled a deep breath, its scaly throat puffing out, then blew out, white smoke covering the hard sediment wall of the cave. Rocks crumbled away, creating an entrance just large enough that Die could crawl through. The lizard turned its head to glance once more at Die, then scuttled through the opening.

Die made a choice. A choice he had waited his whole life to make.

Curiosity, infused with hope that this was not the end, propelled Die forward.

He pulled himself onto the ledge and into the crawl space to follow the dragon lizard.

CHAPTER 36

HOURS OF PAINFULLY SLOW progress, mainly in darkness, had Sonos' nerves taut. They followed the stream, their boots forever splashing in water.

Sonos helped Taine to prop Jax up between them and hobble along.

Rapha chittered and hummed, moving from person to person.

At any moment, he expected to hear the Elites running up behind them, or maybe Wylder had tracked them down and would surprise them from the front. There were too many enemies to count.

Just when his thoughts were turning dark, they turned a corner, and a sliver of bright light shone in the distance. Was that an exit?

Sure enough, the light continued to grow brighter and bigger as they moved forward. It finally coalesced into a crevice wide enough to squeeze through.

"We made it!" Charlotte put a hand over her heart and exhaled.

Taimani and Charlotte went through first.

Sonos helped Taine to navigate the small opening with Jax. As he stepped into the crevice, the air thickened and sound became muffled. Even the light turned a little hazy.

But as soon as he stepped fully through, the air cleared, and he was greeted with a panoramic, breathtaking view of the massive green and golden-hued mountains and a vast open field in front of them.

Sonos was captivated by the sheer massiveness of the Mountain Kingdom. *It's one thing to read about the mountains in stories or even see videos. But to see the magnitude, the height, and the breadth of such mountains. Stunning,* he thought.

The silence of the group was startled by a new voice coming from behind. "Well, it's about time you guys made it! I was starting to worry."

The speaker was a short, bald man, dressed in a thick, fur-lined coat. His pale skin stood in contrast to his dark eyes and a full, black beard.

Taimani and Taine pointed their weapons, leaving Sonos to hold Jax up on his own.

Electricity hummed once again through Taine's hooked sword, giving off a faint blue glow.

The man spread his arms and dropped his head in a bow, unfazed. "I'm here in peace. My name is Tuvo, and I'm here to escort you to the king. We've been waiting."

CHAPTER 37

— • —

CHARLOTTE PULLED HER JACKET closer, fighting to keep the cool wind from reaching her skin. Rapha curled into a tight ball on her shoulder.

"Okay, this should do it," Jax said pulling the last knot tight. A little color had returned to his cheeks from the ashen look he had taken on when they were in the cave.

Using a long branch Taine had cut from a nearby tree, Jax had created a makeshift carrier. He sat on a sleeping blanket that was tied to the pole, and when Taine and Sonos lifted either end, Jax hung as if in a hammock.

In no time, Rapha scrambled from Charlotte's shoulder to take shelter in the hammock with Jax.

"I see how it is, Raph." Charlotte walked next to the hammock as they started following Tuvo across the plain.

Taimani walked behind the group, in Taine's normal spot. Every few minutes the warrior turned her head to scan behind them and watched the sky above.

Charlotte couldn't blame her paranoia.

She inhaled and tried to enjoy the calm; however momentary it might be. It was a beautiful afternoon, clear blue sky, sun shining. The stream of water they had been following in the Badlands, cut through the field. As best as Charlotte could tell, it was coming from the mountains. The water sparkled blue against the grass that rippled its green tendrils.

But a biting wind came straight off the mountains. Probably from the highest peaks.

"How can you be so bundled up?" Sonos asked, from where he carried the pole near Jax's head.

Sonos' cloak was hanging open, and there was even a small trickle of sweat rolling down his temple.

"How can you be *sweating* with this wind?" Charlotte asked in response. "But seriously, I think the sun works differently away from the islands. This time of day back home, we'd be roasting. Here? No matter how the sun shines, it's just not *warm*."

Tuvo laughed, looking back. "Yes, we're a long way from the islands. Just be glad it's spring and not winter." He turned back around and hummed as they walked along.

Charlotte recognized the now familiar frequency when Tuvo spoke. It was as if her heart had developed a tuning fork, and certain people simply resonated at the right pitch. She was still trying to figure out exactly how it worked. She tapped her gazer, thankful she could do that once more, and recorded their path. As she did so, she projected a small holographic map of the area from the snapshot she took from Sonos' physical map.

"How do you suppose we covered so much ground in the Badlands? I was sure it would take us several days to make it through." Sonos said.

Charlotte bit her bottom lip, deep in thought. "Jax, do you remember how time operated differently for us in the forest after we stepped out of that temporal portal in the hollow?"

Jax cracked his eyes and nodded slowly. "I left with Rapha and made it back to the house with time to spare. Meanwhile, you were hours later and practically missed the feast."

"Yeah. Traveling with Rapha doesn't always walk straight," Charlotte agreed.

"Walk straight?" Sonos asked.

"Meaning it doesn't necessarily follow logic or make sense," Charlotte explained. She tapped the gazer off but continued to muse as they walked.

"Tuvo, you didn't explain yourself earlier. How exactly did you know we'd be coming?" Taimani asked, jogging up to walk alongside the short man.

"Well, we didn't know *who* exactly would be coming. But King Mason had a dream that *El* was sending a beacon of hope before the army arrived. Given that the army is only a day or so out, we're getting close to the wire. And given that you were unlikely to come from the main southern road like the army, we guessed it had to be either through the Badlands or from further north.

"There's another scout we sent to the north, just in case. But when the earthquake opened the stream to flow from the mountain out to the Badlands, I was almost certain you'd be coming through that crevice where the water flowed."

Charlotte wondered whether it was the same earthquake they had experienced when stepping into the Badlands. It must have been.

"You said the army is only a day or so out?" Taine asked, adjusting the end of the pole on his shoulder.

"Yes," Tuvo nodded. "I had a runner check in on me this morning to see if there were any updates. He said that the army is close. Scouts also say they are carrying some huge, covered weapon."

Tuvo raised an eyebrow at Sonos, and Charlotte wondered if the man knew it was the prince he was talking to. The Mountain Kingdom was reclusive, but she assumed they would have a network of informants and access to K'Luma broadcasts.

Neither Tuvo nor Sonos said anything further, and they continued to follow the stream as it led closer and closer to the mountains.

At one point they stopped for a break, and Jax dug into his herb box to pull out some lemon balm. He broke off a few leaves and passed them around.

Charlotte took one whiff and enjoyed the instant head-clearing and refreshment.

"Has no one ever thought of bottling this somehow and making a fortune?" Sonos asked.

"Bottle it for who?" Jax asked. "We have all we need. And if Imperials understood the real value of something, I'm guessing it wouldn't be ours to make a fortune off anymore."

Sonos' cheeks flushed red, but he didn't argue.

They continued the trek across the vast field, regularly switching off who carried the pole that held Jax's makeshift hammock. Charlotte was relieved when they finally reached the bottom of the mountain in the late afternoon.

The stream of water intersected with the main road which ran from north to south along the base of the mountains.

A shiver ran down Charlotte's spine thinking of the army that would be marching soon.

Tuvo led them north on the road.

They rounded a bend, and the entire mountainside burst into an explosion of color. Brightly colored wooden structures lined an upwards-winding road like flowers. The structures looked like small shops. People freely moved in and out, carrying bags and packs.

"Whoa." Charlotte whistled under her breath.

The place was brimming with life.

Rapha scrambled out of the hammock with Jax and climbed onto her shoulder.

Tuvo called out to a man nearby who was leading a donkey pulling a small cart. He arranged for the man to carry Jax in the back of the cart.

Jax moaned as Taine and Sonos helped to situate him from the hammock to the cart.

"I've sent a runner to have the healers ready to receive you as soon as we arrive," Tuvo said.

"Almost there," Charlotte leaned over the cart and squeezed Jax's hand.

"Almost there," Jax repeated, his eyes closed.

The road narrowed as it led further up the side of the mountain, at points becoming wide enough to allow only one wagon to pass through at a time.

"I guess you don't get a lot of two-way traffic on this tight road?" Sonos asked Tuvo.

"There are little places to pull off and let other wagons squeeze pass. After a while, I suppose you just get to know the dance of the road." Tuvo shrugged.

Everyone hustled on the winding pathway, seeming to be in a hurry to finish their business. But they still found time to wave and call out greetings to one another in friendly and helpful tones.

Charlotte considered the relative ease of the people versus the savagery of the coming threat. Didn't they know the army was coming?

"We're out of grain, sorry," one of the vendors told a woman as he shuttered the window of his bright red shop. "But I think Simon still has some left. He's the green shed just up past the pine tree."

The woman thanked him and scuttled around Charlotte to rush ahead.

Charlotte looked around and saw plenty of pine trees interspersed along the way. She hoped the woman would figure out which one the vendor meant.

Charlotte thought about making a joke with Jax—many folks on Jamroq gave directions in a similar fashion with ambiguous landmarks. But when she glanced at the cart, Jax had his eyes squeezed shut and fists balled tight. He was clearly in a lot of pain. She hoped the healers here were skilled.

It took over an hour of walking along the path, zigzagging up the side of the mountain, to reach the entrance of a cave. The entrance itself was nondescript because the pathway continued after the entrance to the cave, and the rows of shops continued as far as Charlotte could see.

Tuvo led them inside the cave, the man with the cart pulling Jax close behind. Torches along the wall provided clear lighting as they walked.

Charlotte was thankful for the shelter from the wind but kept her jacket pulled tight, longing for warmth.

An older man called out from behind, as he was shooing some chickens ahead of him. Charlotte jumped against the wall as they passed.

"Folks are preparing for the impending arrival of the army," Tuvo explained. "Springtime is usually when everyone loves to be out on the mountain for as long as possible, but right now, everyone is getting ready to hunker down inside for some time."

The narrow hallway soon opened into a huge cavern, easily a hundred times the size of the one they had seen in the Badlands. A wide staircase carved from the rock led from where they stood all the way down to the floor of the cavern, maybe a hundred feet below.

Down below was a mass of activity. Women stood over cooking fires, long rows of tables were being cleaned, and kids kicked a ball in one of the far corners.

Rapha jumped from Charlotte's shoulder and scurried down the wide staircase, heading off to explore.

A more gradual sloping path ran along the outer walls of the cavern, circling down to the base. Along the pathway, there were brightly colored curtains covering entrances that people would come in and out of.

"Welcome to the Noiz, core of the Mountain Kingdom." Tuvo smiled and gazed over the cavern.

"Never in my wildest dreams did I imagine something so... massive, inside the mountains," Charlotte said.

Sonos ran a hand through his hair. "I know. We were told stories of primitive people who lived in caves. I never imagined such expanse."

Charlotte grimaced. *Does he really not see how arrogant his comments are when talking about anywhere outside of Pergamum?* she thought.

"Most of the people of Noiz live here in the grand cavern. The curtains along the sloping path lead to individual living areas. The kitchen, dining, and cleaning areas are all common—plus, what you see happening in the hub." Tuvo gestured towards the center of the cavern.

Two women in long white robes approached the cart which held Jax. They waved over two young men who carried a stretcher. They handed Jax a steaming mug of liquid.

Charlotte was relieved he was getting help.

Jax looked around after he sipped, life once again sparking in his eyes. He rested his gaze on Charlotte. He beckoned her over as the women inspected his broken foot.

"Bush tea." He smiled over the brim of the cup, then took a deep breath, inhaling the scented fumes.

"Looks like you're in good hands," Charlotte said, leaning close to catch a whiff of the mint from the tea. "Don't give them too much trouble, and I'll come find you later tonight."

He smiled, and his eyes softened. "We made it, Char."

"We did," She squeezed his hand. Her mind flitted to her dad and Gran, hoping they were both still safe as well.

The two women shooed Charlotte away and directed the boys to help Jax out of the cart and onto the stretcher.

Jax winked at Charlotte as they carried him away.

A thought flitted through Charlotte's mind about what they would do when the army arrived and Jax was still immobile. But she could only keep taking one step at a time.

At least here, they stood a better chance than facing Captain Die and his Elites alone in the Badlands.

She wondered what happened to Die after they left the cavern. Even though he had terrorized her and Jax, and destroyed her home, there was a small part of her that hoped he would find a path truer to himself and his roots than the Empire.

"Follow me. The first stop is to see the king." Tuvo led them on a wide ledge that formed an upper ring for the hub.

As they walked, they passed hallways that were guarded by a pair of sentries dressed in various colors. Each of the guarded hallways was outlined with a specific stone or jewel. One was emeralds, and the guards were dressed in a deep green. Another entrance was covered in sparkling diamonds, and the guards wore a stark white uniform.

"I'm guessing these hallways lead to where the nobles live?" Sonos asked.

"Correct. Though we don't call them nobles. There are seven members of the Leadership Council, which is headed by the king. After the king passes, the Council elects a new king from one of the families."

"Electing a ruler? We used to do that in Jamroq before..." Charlotte hesitated, looking at Sonos. Those history lessons had been part of her father's banned teachings.

Red crept up Sonos' neck above his cloak.

Charlotte kept from saying anything more. She was glad he had the decency to blush, though.

Tuvo stopped before a hallway where the guards were dressed in midnight black. Charlotte touched the rocks that lined the curved walkway, entranced by the way the black rocks shined like glass. They vibrated slightly, and her mind flashed back to the obsidian on the scrolls from the temporal portal.

"Obsidian," Sonos said, studying the rocks and laying his hand against one. "Amazing."

A family passed by them, leaving the hallway and chatting loudly.

"It's not fair," a young boy cried to his parents.

"Prince Malachi was right," the dad answered. "We'll continue practicing after things settle, and you can try out for the defender school again next year."

The father gave Tuvo a nod in greeting before continuing back out to the main cavern.

"You train your warriors from young?" Taimani asked Tuvo.

"Not as young as Kimwaki, from what I've heard, but yes, we allow training from age twelve. Some try to join early like that eager boy, but that requires special permission from the king."

They walked down the hallway and entered a large room with obsidian pillars. Charlotte gazed around the room in astonishment.

The throne, made of the same beautiful black stone, was situated on the wall opposite where they entered. Leading to the throne stood six large stone pedestals. Next to each pedestal stood a guard from each of the other ruling families, and atop each pedestal stood a massive carving from the respective stone or gems of that family.

As they walked towards the throne, Charlotte paused at the first pedestal. The emerald was carved into an exquisite tree that stood at least three feet high. Individual leaves had been honed with such detail that Charlotte stood on her toes trying to get a better look.

Taimani nudged her as she passed. "Focus, Char. Come."

They approached the throne as someone around Charlotte's age finished listening to two petitioners. He was dressed in a crisp black uniform with stripes of all the other family colors crisscrossing down his sleeves. Something was familiar about that uniform. He had deeply tanned skin, which Charlotte found ironic given that they lived underground.

"Do you think that's the king?" Charlotte leaned over to ask Sonos. He looked so young to be king.

Sonos shook his head. "I heard the boy we passed in the hallway mention something about a prince. That's my guess. But he's wearing the same uniform that the commander of *El's* army had on."

Oh! That's why it looks familiar, she thought. *But what did* El's *army and the Mountain Kingdom have to do with one another?*

The prince looked up and caught sight of Tuvo and their group. He smiled broadly and dismissed the men standing in front of him. "Reports acknowledged. Please continue with preparations. My father will return to address the Leadership Council later this evening." He jumped down from the platform and jogged over to Tuvo.

"You came! And just in time, too. So, they came from the Badlands? From the stream? Or is it a river now?" The questions spilled out from the prince.

Sonos put his hands to his side and bent at the waist.

Charlotte was unsure of courtly protocols and, in a panic, simply followed Sonos' action.

The prince waved his hand casually. "No need. Save it for the king, if anything. Though Father isn't fond of too much formality.

Anyways, I'm Malachi. Feel free to call me Kai. We've had our scouts waiting for over a week, ever since my father received word—"

"Sorry, you received word about us?" Sonos interrupted the prince's outpouring.

"Yeah, you know. My father had a dream. Anyways, you're a strange group. From many places? I didn't expect that. And you look familiar." Kai cocked his head looking at Sonos. "Sorry, I know I talk a lot."

Rapha chose that moment to run across the throne room and scamper up to his resting place on Charlotte's shoulder.

"And oh! You have a *monkey*." Kai reached a hand towards Rapha.

Tuvo took the opportunity to speak. "Highness, they have named this one Rapha. And may I present to you, Charlotte King from Jamroq, Taine and Taimani Folaou from Kimwaki, and Prince Sonos K'Luma of Pergamum."

All eyes turned on Tuvo, and Charlotte's mouth hung open. How had he gathered all this information? They had surely not shared this level of detail over the last few hours.

"There is one more," Tuvo continued. "Jaxtyn Holston from Jamroq is being treated by the healers."

"Impressive group," Kai said and raised his eyebrow. "You've almost left me speechless." He laughed. "At any rate, my father and sister will return from the deep cavern soon and there will be much to discuss. I'll show you where you can freshen up and then we can talk over the feast."

"Feast?" Charlotte asked. "Before the army comes?"

"Ever since the king's dream, the whole of Noiz has been fasting from sunup to sundown, praying to *El* for your safekeeping. A feast of thankfulness is sure to be held, and tomorrow we will fight. There's a saying, Fight we must—"

"But win we shall," Sonos finished.

"Yes! You know it." Kai smiled.

"A wise, young friend taught us along the way," Sonos answered.

Charlotte's spirit hummed inside of her, alongside a feeling of something she finally allowed to spring forth: hope.

CHAPTER 38

SONOS STRAIGHTENED THE KNOTTED collar of his tunic. The fabric was made from thick linen, but he had been given a soft, airy fleece to wear underneath. The whole outfit matched the obsidian of the king's house color.

"The neck's a little tight," Taine said, adjusting the knot in his own tunic, then tightening the strap of his hooked sword. "Have I said enough how uncomfortable I am going to a feast where we haven't been able to scout properly."

"Have you forgotten that we look like the enemy?" Sonos asked. "We need to tread very lightly here."

Tuvo knocked and stuck his head into the guest room. "Ready?"

Sonos nodded and they followed Tuvo down the hallway.

Charlotte and Taimani waited outside of their room, not far away. They both stood in long, form-fitting black dresses with a similar knotted collar and long slits in the skirts.

"Did you guys have the little waterfall shower too?" Charlotte asked, her eyes sparkling.

A pleasant, fruity scent drifted towards Sonos.

Charlotte's hair was pulled back in an intricate braid, though a few rebel curls framed her face. She reminded him of the Empress in this moment, full of confidence alongside grace and poise.

"Uhm, what? Showers? Oh yes," Sonos stumbled over his words. "Tuvo, who designed this place? I've never seen anything like it." He shifted his focus.

"We've been here for many generations; some would say it's even older than Pergamum. We have a dedicated group of engineers who are constantly upgrading and improving the place." Tuvo smiled and added, "My daughter has just been accepted into their newest cohort, in fact. But come, we must be on our way. The king appreciates timeliness in all things."

Tuvo led them through a small maze of torch-lit hallways and back towards the main throne room.

They passed a pair of young serving women dressed in dark grey uniforms. The women stepped to the side of the hallway and gave a slight bow of the head. But instead of keeping their eyes downcast and trying to keep unnoticed as servants did in Pergamum, these women made direct eye contact and smiled. Their eyes were curious, but they didn't speak out of turn. Tuvo kindly acknowledged them and kept everyone moving along.

Sonos might have thought the pair of women were some special maids or perhaps even concubines, but the same interaction happened twice more with different servants.

There was rank and order, but no underlying fear and intimidation which Sonos had always despised. Sibi would love this place, Sonos smiled at the thought.

Eventually, they exited the obsidian quarters and stepped out onto the ring overlooking the great cavern, the Hub, as Tuvo had called it. The place was alive and swarming with people. People of every size, shape, and color.

"The king eats with the masses?" Sonos asked, trying to take it all in.

"Not all the time," Tuvo answered, leading them to the wide staircase. "Each ruling family has their own dining and living quarters separate from the Hub. However, once a month everyone eats together—and on special occasions, like today."

Curious looks greeted them from anyone who passed by, but always with a smile or shy wave.

A little boy ran up to Tuvo. "Are these the people who the king dreamed about? What are their names?"

"All in good time, little one. The king will introduce them. Now run along." Tuvo tapped the boy good-naturedly on the shoulder.

"I don't like this," Taine whispered beside Sonos. "A mass of people and complete freedom of movement. It's a security night-mare."

"And you suggest what? Running out now?" Sonos asked.

Taine frowned. "Don't tempt me. You do realize that Tuvo knew exactly who all of us were?"

Sonos had to admit that his stomach had dropped earlier when Tuvo introduced them to the prince by full name. Nonetheless, they had come too far to turn back now. And based on what he was seeing thus far of the Mountain Kingdom, he most certainly wanted to meet the king who ruled it all.

When they reached the base of the cavern, Sonos was amazed at how everyone intermingled. The ruling families were dressed in the solid colors of greens, blues, whites, and reds that represented their houses. However, they stood in groups that were a mix of not just colors, but with the dark grays of servants and the colorful patterns of normal citizens as well.

Tuvo led them to a table on a raised platform in the middle of the cavern. Prince Malachi ran down to greet them.

"Come, meet my father," he said enthusiastically.

King Mason was tall with broad shoulders that showed signs of more than just sitting around a throne all day. Instead of a crown, he wore a leather band over his thick, black hair with an obsidian pendant that hung down on his forehead. Both the king and prince wore black jackets, but brightly colored stripes adorned the sleeves, matching all the other house colors.

Sonos marveled at the representation and inclusion displayed by the rulers. K'Luma thrived on a constant power struggle to prove strength—led first and foremost by his father. Giving way to any other family would have been considered weakness.

King Mason stood as Tuvo led the group forward, inclining his head in a way Sonos had never seen his father show respect to anyone. "Welcome to Noiz, heart of the Mountain Kingdom, people of *El*."

Not sure exactly of the protocol in this different environment, Sonos simply held his arms against his side and bowed from the waist. Charlotte and the warriors followed suit. "Thank you for the warm welcome."

Charlotte yelped as Rapha scurried over from wherever he had been gallivanting and climbed up her shoulder.

King Mason laughed—a deep, genuine belly-laugh. "Ah, I see you've brought a friend." He reached out a hand to rub the monkey's head. "Mmm, very good, indeed."

A young woman with long, dark hair and an obsidian pendant on her forehead nudged the king. That must be the princess.

King Mason looked up and smiled. "Ah, yes, Lenora, the last of the warriors has arrived."

Sonos turned and saw Jax being wheeled forward in a chair, his ankle wrapped, but overall looking much better than when they had left him with the healers earlier.

Charlotte ran over to him. "Jax! So glad you made it."

"Me, too. The healers here are amazing," Jax said. "You look great," he added in a much softer tone.

Sonos watched a slight flush reach Charlotte's cheek, then she turned and walked back to sit on Sonos' other side.

A small ramp had been set up to the platform, and a young man dressed in white pushed Jax forward. After everyone was situated, the healer and Tuvo both disappeared into the crowd.

The king waved everyone to their seats at the table. In a well-ordered manner, the entire cavern moved to follow suit and sit as well.

While the head table sat in the center of the Hub, the other six houses were on similar, slightly elevated tables positioned around the periphery of the cavern. It reminded Sonos of creating a hedge of protection around the people.

The king, Malachi, and Lenora sat across from Sonos, Charlotte, Taine, and Taimani. Jax was positioned next to Lenora at a slightly odd angle as his foot was elevated.

A flurry of servants came and brought steaming bowls of stew and freshly baked bread, along with steamed cider.

"What kind of stew is this?" Sonos whispered to one of the servants. He hoped it wasn't anything crazy like cowheel or whatever that was Miss Gemma had made.

"Venison and vegetable, sir," the servant responded.

Sonos' stomach grumbled, ready to inhale the food, but he looked around and realized that no one was eating, even at the other surrounding tables.

A servant walked over and bent near to the king, whispering something in his ear. The king nodded in response, then stood, grabbing a loaf of bread in his hand.

"Good people of Noiz, heart of the beloved Mountain Kingdom. Even as the army of K'Luma presses closer to our gates, *El* has been faithful. As promised in a dream, he has brought us hope. A spark that will serve as a catalyst for securing our future." The king scanned those around his table, torchlight dancing in his eyes.

He then continued addressing the people, "Our defenders are well prepared and will step out bravely to defend our home. As the battle rages, the Inner Sanctum has been prepared and stands ready to hold all those not fighting for as long as needed. After we break bread together, you will follow your assigned group leaders, taking only what you can carry. Go forward with courage, in the name of *El.* He will not forsake us, and we will not be broken."

A roar of agreement rose from the people and reverberated off the walls of the cavern.

The king held up the loaf of bread and tore it in half. In similar fashion, at each table in the Hub, a person stood and did likewise. Then the king, walked around the head table, giving each person a chunk of bread.

A king acting as a servant? Sonos wondered.

"Our customs must seem strange to you," King Mason said, "But here in the Mountain Kingdom, leaders exist to serve the people."

"Certainly different than K'Luma, you are correct," Sonos answered.

"I couldn't help but notice that you seem to have people of every race here," Charlotte said between a mouthful of bread.

Even more so, Sonos couldn't place how ethnic backgrounds seemed to play into rank and power. Some of the ruling families were led by persons paler than the king, some were tanned, some were dark skinned, and he had also heard various accents as they had walked through the hub earlier.

Lenora spoke from where she sat next to Jax. "M-my fa-father calls the M-Mountain Kingdom a sanctuary."

Royalty with a speech impediment, Sonos observed. And yet she was not hidden away. In fact, the king and Malachi didn't seem in any way uncomfortable when Lenora spoke.

Taine, on the other hand, was stiff and on edge since they had entered Noiz. "Sanctuaries can often become a dangerous place when positioned next to an Empire like K'Luma," Taine said.

"*El* protects those who are his," the king said, unfazed. "Our doors are open to those he calls. Imagine the power of one who can bring together a prince of K'Luma, a genius from the isles, and their mighty companions." He grinned.

When Sonos first heard Sibi's similar insistence that their odd group had been brought together by *El*, he remembered being dismissive and skeptical. But now, something felt different. Something in the king's words resonated with Sonos.

They were interrupted by an older man dressed in crisp black fatigues, with a golden line running across his shoulder.

The man bent down near the king, speaking softly.

The king's brow furrowed. "Please excuse me," he said to the table as he stood. "Continue without me. I'll return soon. Malachi, come with us."

Malachi jumped up from the table and followed the men to a hallway that led out of the Hub.

"Don't worry," Lenora smiled from where she sat next to Jax. "Th-they're just fi-finalizing with the defenders."

"Where will all the people go during the attack?" asked Taimani. "Surely, you'll not keep them all here in the Hub like sitting ducks."

"No. Our engineers and... construction teams worked nonstop. To build th-the Inner Sanctum, deep in the heart of the mountain." Lenora spoke with a quiet confidence, even though her words took long to come out. "E-everyone who is not a defender or essential will move there after the feast. Th-they'll stay until things are safe."

"Isn't that a little presumptuous? Assuming things will be safe?" Taine asked. The warriors were relentless and clearly not comfortable.

"Surely there's nothing wrong with hope," Jax spoke up, eyes narrowed at Taine.

Charlotte, who had been quiet since the king left, also looked defensive of Lenora, shooting a similar glare towards Taine.

"We don't mean to be harsh," Taimani said. "But my brother and I have lived through what happens when the Emperor and Uzoma come to take over."

Lenora bowed her head respectfully. She then made a hand signal which reminded Sonos of how the warriors communicate.

A sharp look passed between Taine and Taimani, but Taine leaned over to Sonos. "It's not the same. I'm not sure what she said."

Tuvo's short form moved deftly through the tables as he stepped up to the head table.

"T-tuvo will help t-to translate. We have much to discuss." Lenora explained while signaling to Tuvo.

Tuvo slid onto the bench on the other side of Charlotte, watching Lenora intensely. "You're up first, Miss King."

A group of children nearby let out a cry, and Sonos turned to see Rapha run away and swing up into Charlotte's lap.

She rubbed his head and exhaled. "Call me Charlotte, please."

Tuvo continued, watching Lenora's hand signals and translating them into words. "Lenora says their intelligence has confirmed that a high-tech weapon is intended to lead the assault against Noiz. A heavy-duty machine that operates like an old-time catapult." Tuvo leaned forward to look at Sonos. "You have any insight into that weapon?"

"I heard rumors of a game-changing, land-based weapon in development, but it must have come to fruition during my lockdown," Sonos answered. He wished he had more to offer to the discussion, but the Sahemy often kept those projects to a very close circle that lived in special housing and were never allowed to leave—even to visit family—when working on a project.

"I'm surprised *you* have knowledge of such a weapon," Taimani addressed Lenora.

"N-not much," she answered, then continued signaling to Tuvo.

"The most we have learned has only been since the weapon has been in transit from Pergamum," Tuvo explained. "But we do understand that it's a tech-driven machine, which means that it should be able to be controlled by..." He reached out and tapped Charlotte's wrist, which was covered by her long sleeves.

Still, Charlotte reached her left hand to cover the wrist where she wore her gazer. Her mouth hung open. "And I'm supposed to figure out how to control it by tomorrow morning?"

"Well, at least how to stop it or turn it off," Tuvo shrugged.

"Char, we can—" Jax's tone was calming, he must have sensed Charlotte's panic.

"I can't do it without being at least within range of the weapon. Tech doesn't work in isolation." Charlotte's voice was high-pitched.

Sonos felt the bench shaking and noticed that both of Charlotte's feet were tapping nervously. Without thinking, he reached out to take her hand under the table.

At first, she jolted and turned her head, but then she bit her bottom lip and squeezed his hand tightly. At least her legs stopped shaking.

A soft murmur went through the crowd and the king, Malachi, and general returned to the head table.

King Mason returned with the intensity of a warrior on the eve of battle. But he was gentle as he laid a hand on Lenora's shoulder. "You finished briefing them?"

"J-just Charlotte."

The king looked at Charlotte. "Be brave and courageous, *El* will help your efforts with the machine."

Charlotte clutched Sonos' hand tighter. "Be brave and courageous. It's just like what the journal said," she whispered.

The king shifted his gaze to Sonos. "As for you, you must confront your father."

Sonos swallowed. He knew he would have to reach his father somehow. But what he would do when he got there, only *El* knew.

Was there a way to move the mountain without touching it? Sonos had assumed the mountain referred to the Mountain Kingdom. But what if the mountain was his father? He had to do the impossible, but not in his strength. Sonos glanced down to see Rapha's gaze fixed on him.

Rapha's eyes softened, and he patted Sonos' leg, as if content that Sonos understood.

The king's eyes narrowed, but his voice was soft when he spoke, looking at everyone in turn around the table. "I don't know the exact plans to instruct you on details, but each of you has been brought here for a purpose. Do your part, but remember—you are only the sparks, do not try to bear the burden of the fire."

The king raised his arm above his head, in some kind of signal.

A loud *boom* sounded from the upper ring of the cavern, which was lined by defenders. In unison, they slammed the edge of their shields in response.

"Fight we must!" King Mason shouted, his voice sounding loud and clear.

"Win we shall!" The cavern walls reverberated as the people and defenders alike answered.

A flutter of activity began in the Hub as group leaders held up color-coded placards, calling people to follow. Servants in gray were already collecting and cleaning up from the meal.

The movement was carefully managed, with no one panicking or being left behind.

"Jaxtyn, you will go with Lenora into the Inner Sanctum. You are in no shape to fight, but you can help give encouragement to others and take time to heal," the king said.

Jax opened his mouth to protest, but the king held up a hand.

"I will go with Char and help cover her as she disarms the weapon," Taimani stood.

Jax's eye flowed with hurt and disappointment, but he nodded towards Taimani. "Thank you."

Charlotte jumped up from the table, Rapha scampering up her shoulder. "We have no time to waste. Tuvo, you said the defenders can get us close?" She was more focused than Sonos had ever seen her.

"Of course," Tuvo nodded. "It is not far, and there are secret tunnels through the mountain that will get you close to the weapon. I will take you there myself."

Sonos and Taine stood together.

"It looks like it's you and me, back to the heart of things," Sonos said. "I am certain my father will have set up a battlefield tent in the field nearby. We should make our way there."

Charlotte paused, grabbing Sonos and Taimani and nodding towards Taine as she pulled them over into a huddle around Jax.

"This is it," she said. "The moment we were brought together for," her voice held a nervous energy, but her eyes burned with resolve.

Rapha hummed from her shoulder.

"I wish we had a clearer picture of what exactly to do," Charlotte continued, "But we have to trust the process that got us here. We have to have hope." Her eyes softened towards Sonos when she spoke the last part.

Lenora spoke from where she stood behind Jax.

"D-do not worry. The heart has eyes that th-the mind cannot see."

The unseen realm, Sonos thought.

Before they parted, Jax dug into his cloak and handed something to Charlotte. It looked like a small ball, or maybe a big nut.

"I'm not sure what may be on that weapon, but something tells me you may need this," Jax told Charlotte.

She leaned in for a last embrace, "You keep safe. Remember, you're helping me with phase two of this journey."

"I wouldn't dream of missing it," he held her gaze until Charlotte turned to leave with Taimani.

<h1 style="text-align:center">Chapter 39</h1>

C HARLOTTE TOOK A SLOW, steadying breath and balled her hands into fists to try and curb the wave of fear that washed over her.

After a dizzying amount of turns in black hallways, Tuvo had opened a hidden crack near the base of the mountain and deposited Charlotte and Taimani outside.

"That way," Tuvo pointed towards a massive dark lump. He placed a hand on each of their shoulders, gave a squeeze, patted Rapha on the head, then disappeared back into the mountain.

It wasn't the mound that gave Charlotte heart palpitations though. Rather, it was what looked like thousands of campfires. General Uzoma must have brought every living, breathing soldier with him on this campaign.

"There are so many," Charlotte whispered.

Rapha shifted on her shoulder.

"I only see one," Taimani said. "You're seeing more weapons?"

"Not the weapon, Mani." Charlotte shook her head. "But look how many soldiers. Even if we destroy the weapon, how can we hope to stop an army this size?" She was thankful Jax was recovering in the safety of the Inner Sanctum.

"Focus on our mission. Don't stress about all the other stuff." Taimani's voice was confident, but not unkind. "Now, what do you need?"

Charlotte pulled the dark scarf over her nose and mouth, trying to keep the cold at bay. "When I was on the boat with Jax, I saw the captain control the motor I fixed with his gazer. I'm hoping to do the same with this, assuming the weapon is motorized as Malachi said."

"Great. So, you just tap a few buttons and—" Taimani made a *poof* signal with her hand.

"Not quite so easy. We need to get close to the motor," Charlotte said.

"How close, exactly?" Taimani raised an eyebrow in the waning moon.

"Close enough for me to touch," Charlotte answered.

"Best we get moving then." Taimani didn't skip a beat or complain. "I estimate we have about five hours until sunrise. That should be enough time, right?"

"Uhm... sure." Charlotte didn't bother to point out that it took her three days on the ship to understand the motor well enough to get it working. And she hadn't exactly built a gazer-control for a motor before. She just knew it was possible.

Charlotte turned her head to look at Rapha. "Hoping you can give some help here," she whispered.

Rapha responded by finding an opening at the top of her jacket and climbing inside.

When Charlotte let out a soft yelp, Taimani shot a warning glare. "I hope I don't need to remind you of the need for stealth."

Charlotte bit her bottom lip and shook her head.

Taimani checked the blowgun tucked under her sleeve and tapped the darts strapped to her thigh. "Let's go then."

As they drew closer to the covered weapon, Charlotte realized the reason it was left apart from the campfires was that the weapon was on the roadway, and the troops were camped a short way off in the fields.

Malachi had shared that the weapon was made in the image of a dragon, and Charlotte could see the narrow head, a round body under the covering, and a long tail stuck out the back.

Taimani held up a fist and hunkered close to the ground beside a large rock.

Charlotte stooped beside her, holding her breath.

Rapha squirmed inside of her jacket, and Charlotte rubbed his head hoping to signal that he needed to remain still.

A few moments later a pair of guards crossed in front of them on the road. They were making a circle around the weapon.

After they passed, Taimani tapped Charlotte's knee, and they scurried across to the dragon. Taimani lifted the cover, and they both climbed underneath.

There was no light, but as Charlotte's eyes adjusted, she was struck by the massiveness of the weapon. Metal siding made up the body. Charlotte ran her hand over the smooth iron and knelt at its base. Thankfully, the covering reached the ground, but she needed to figure out how to get a closer look at the motor.

Rapha scrambled out of her jacket and squeezed under the machine.

The dragon was mounted on some hover pads that would lift it when being transported, but stationary as it was, there was only just enough space for Charlotte to squeeze under on her back.

As Charlotte moved further under the belly of the dragon, Taimani followed.

"Let's make this quick, please," Taimani dared to whisper.

Charlotte turned to give Taimani her best deadpan look, but the effect was likely lost in the darkness.

The cold was biting, but Charlotte pulled off her gloves and tucked them into her belt. She was just able to reach her hands above where she lay to inspect the motor closer.

The titanium gears and pipes reminded her of the motor from the ship. It was certainly built by the Sahemy.

She tapped her gazer, keeping the lighting on the dimmest level possible and praying that the metal sides of the dragon together with the thick blanket covering would be enough to keep any light from escaping.

Rapha lay calmly on his back to her one side, and Taimani shifted on her other side.

Charlotte scrolled through the coding that projected from her gazer. She needed to find a way to sync the main controls of the motor to a basic control panel program on her gazer.

But first, she needed to figure out exactly what this weapon was supposed to do. Malachi's intelligence on the details had been rather sparse.

Voices outside on the roadway froze Charlotte's thoughts.

Taimani tensed beside her.

Soon enough, the voices passed and became more distant.

Charlotte exhaled. She put the gazer on her belly so that she could use both hands to type into the hologram. Using some of the base program she had made when fixing the ship's motor, she was able to connect into the dragon's controls.

The Sahemy were arrogant, believing their programming to be so secretive. They didn't realize that their pride had created a weakness in that the same backdoor could be used over and over.

Charlotte was happy for their consistency. But getting into the network was one thing. Understanding and writing code to control the specifics of a motor was something else.

As Charlotte scrolled through the commands and schematics of the dragon, she sucked in a sharp breath.

Taimani turned. "You got it figured out?"

"Not how to control it yet..."

Taimani sighed.

"But this isn't some simple catapult that will be throwing rocks or debris. They plan on launching some kind of... chemical into Noiz."

Taimani cursed under her breath.

Charlotte reached to grab Taimani's hand. She was well aware that chemical warfare was the thing that had finally defeated the Kimwakians after a grueling battle. And its use on the warriors had been devastating.

The amount of chemical and the range that the dragon had was astounding. Realization set in that Uzoma and the Emperor were not just attacking the Mountain Kingdom, but they were seeking to destroy it.

Anger boiled up in Charlotte, and she went back to the hologram. "Don't worry, we will stop this dragon before it comes to that."

Charlotte thought about Ava and Lily in the Legacy Towers. She thought about Taimani having been locked up before. Indignation welled up in her bones thinking about how the Emperor was determined to kill, steal, and destroy in order to build the K'Luma Empire at all costs.

Her fingers flew across the hologram as the lines of code ran with lightning speed. Her mind was on overdrive, the commands and prompts coming almost effortlessly.

At some point in time, she felt Rapha's small hand against her arm. He was humming softly. But even Taimani hadn't made an effort to try and quiet him. They were in a flow.

Charlotte wiped her eyes, the line of code momentarily blurring. How long had she been going?

"Char," Taimani whispered. "We're running out of time."

Feet scuffled on the roadway, and a trumpet blew. The soldiers were moving into formation for battle.

CHAPTER 40

THE EARLY SPRING BREEZE reminded Sonos more of the winter gone than the summer coming. He pulled the collar of his cloak a little tighter, wondering how Charlotte was faring in the cold. He glanced down the road at the covered weapon Malachi had told them about.

"You think they'll be able to build something to control that dragon in time?" Sonos asked Taine, who stooped behind a large rock watching the road.

"We have enough on our plate getting to your father. I can't worry about the others," Taine answered sharply. He stole a glance towards the dragon all the same. "But if it's possible, those two will make it happen."

Sonos glanced at the sky. They were still in the hour before the sun would begin to peek from behind the Badlands.

A deep rumbling filled the sky, and flares lit up a circle in the field between the mountain and the Badlands.

"He's here," Sonos said, a knot forming in his stomach. A fleet of four K'Luma Carriers zoomed in from the north.

There would be just enough time for his father to settle in with Commander Uzoma, and they would likely attack at daybreak, as Malachi had predicted.

"You sure about this? I still don't agree with us splitting up," Taine said.

Sonos looked across the road to where large tents had been erected in the middle of the field to form the battlefield head-quarters.

"They would kill you on sight without hesitation. You know that," Sonos said. "We're sticking to the plan, and I will meet you where the river enters the Badlands."

The plan, he thought.

Sonos tried to replay in his mind how he would confront his father and convince him to hold negotiations with King Mason before attacking. But he knew his father had no intention of backing down. The year of the dragon was not about peace, it was about conquest.

"Fight we must," Taine said, placing a hand on Sonos' shoulder. He must have sensed Sonos' hesitation.

"But win we shall." Sonos let the words sink into his spirit. "I'll see you on the other side."

"I'll be there," Taine assured him.

Sonos squared his shoulders and walked across the road into the army encampment. He spread his arms in a non-threatening way.

It didn't take long for a soldier to shout and come running.

Soon, he was surrounded by a squad of soldiers pointing spears and electrified swords.

"Take me to my father," Sonos said in his most princely voice.

Trumpets blew across the camp.

The sky was starting to lighten ahead of the sunrise.

The face of the most senior soldier flashed with surprise, then recognition. He barked an order to a young boy who hardly looked old enough to wear a uniform. The boy went running.

"Follow me, Highness," the soldier said, leading the way towards the large tents.

CHAPTER 41

"YOU NEED TO HURRY." Taimani's voice bordered on panic.

Thankfully, Rapha was still calm and softly humming by her other side.

Charlotte furiously typed out the final codes and commands, double-checking her work every minute. There was no room for error, and they would get no second chances.

The sun was rising. It peaked through the bottom of the covering.

Voices of soldiers surrounded them on every side.

Charlotte had no idea how they would escape if—no, after—she got the control program to work. She tried to focus.

"Char..." Taimani said again.

"Almost." Charlotte looked back over her work, gnawing on her bottom lip.

"Prep the dragon," a loud voice shouted.

"Okay. I think I have it," Charlotte whispered. "I programmed the dragon to self-destruct, just like the drone did when it was chasing us as we ran into the Badlands." Charlotte glanced at Taimani. "I just need to do a small test and turn it on."

Taimani nodded.

Rapha gave Charlotte's arm a squeeze.

Charlotte pulled up the program on her gazer.

"Once I know it works, we need to run as far from here as we can."

Just then, the cover to the dragon was pulled off.

Charlotte thought her heart might beat out of her chest as adrenaline raced through her veins. *Focus,* she could hear Jax's voice in her head, just as he had encouraged her every day since Ava and Lily had been taken. She narrowed her eyes and typed in the command.

The hover pads vibrated to life underneath them.

Charlotte did a silent cheer, relief warming her frozen hands.

Shouting and confusion erupted from the soldiers outside.

"Who turned that on?"

"We weren't ready!"

"What's going on?"

Taimani tugged at Charlotte. "Let's go."

Charlotte activated the timer and tucked her gazer securely into the motor with a pang of sadness. It had served her well and reminded her of Gran and her family. *Eyes forward,* she thought. "We have ten minutes."

Charlotte didn't know exactly what would happen when the dragon self-destructed, but she surely didn't want to be close when it happened. Who knew what kind of chemicals were inside.

Taimani edged herself towards the opening.

Rapha squirmed out to the other side of the dragon, the one facing the army camp, and started making a ruckus.

Feet pounded and voices shouted as soldiers ran towards where Rapha had exited.

Taimani quickly squeezed through and squatted low beside the opening.

Charlotte slipped out, thankful for Rapha's diversion. Her mind raced over a thousand possibilities of what could happen next, but she willed herself to focus on simply getting far from the dragon and the imminent explosion.

Taimani pointed towards a large rock on the other side of the road near the mountain, and they both sprinted.

No sooner than Charlotte took a big gulp of air, a soldier in full uniform stepped around the rock, his two short spears glowing with electricity.

In less than a breath, Taimani had loaded a dart into her small forearm blowgun.

"Don't move," another soldier said from behind.

They were trapped.

Taimani cursed in her native tongue.

Nine minutes and counting. Captured or not, their bigger problem was needing to get away from the dragon.

"Who are you?" the soldier with the short spears asked.

"We are trying to escape Noiz and get away from the fighting," Taimani answered.

Charlotte was proud of her quick thinking.

"Running towards the army doesn't seem like a way to avoid the fighting," the soldier responded.

"There aren't many options when the army is taking up the whole road," Taimani retorted. Her fingers twitched towards where she stashed her darts.

For a moment, Charlotte thought Taimani might pull it off and take both soldiers out so they could run. But it seemed that the soldiers had the same thought.

One tapped Taimani with his long spear and sent an electric shock through her. Taimani convulsed and fell to the ground.

"Stop it!" Charlotte cried out. She knelt beside Taimani. Thankfully, the warrior was still conscious, albeit dazed.

Charlotte fought down the flashing images of her parents and the wave of anxiety that threatened her now.

The soldier with the two short swords bent over and disarmed Taimani, taking the stashes of darts along with the blow gun.

Taimani was still paralyzed but muttered under her breath.

"She'll be able to move in a bit, and we'll take you both for inquiry," the soldier said.

"A bit?" Charlotte repeated. Her mind was ticking. They were probably down to eight minutes left. She pulled Taimani's arm around her shoulder. Even though the warrior was more than a head taller, she tried to encourage Taimani to move.

Taimani must have felt Charlotte's urgency as she stood on shaky legs.

"She's moving. Let's go," the soldier said. "I don't want to miss the start of the assault."

He led Charlotte and Taimani back across the road and towards the army encampment. He paused a moment to call a young boy over.

After receiving his instructions, the boy went running into the camp.

Charlotte stole a glance at the dragon.

Sahemy dressed in red cloaks surrounded the weapon, gazers projecting holograms as they gesticulated wildly. Charlotte allowed herself a smile as she confirmed that the hovers were still on, and it seemed as though the Sahemy had not gained control.

"Keep moving," the soldier behind them urged them on.

As they moved across the field towards a large grouping of white tents, Charlotte fought the urge to run as far away as possible. But she also wanted the dragon to self-destruct before the Sahemy found a way to break through the security of her program.

Only a few more minutes.

Chapter 42

Sonos neared the command tent. He recognized Ade's body-guard watching the entrance along with a handful of other Elites. The Emperor's personal protection would be stationed inside, never out of sight of his father.

He knew the runner would have already informed those inside of his presence. He rehearsed in his mind the first words he would speak.

"Well, well, well. Look who we have here." Wylder sauntered out of the front entrance of the tent.

Sonos' heart skipped a beat.

"You're... you're working with my father?" His mind raced to put the pieces together.

"Let's just say, things have a way of coming together." Wylder's smile never reached his eyes, and his arrogant tone made Sonos second guess himself, yet again. "In fact, I hear the head of the Imperial Guards may have an opening after your... *uh—uncle, wasn't* he? —fell on his sword."

Sonos winced. He had hoped Die would have simply given up pursuit. But he should have known better. He prayed his mother would forgive him.

"Mmm, just in time." Wylder once again spread his lips into a malicious grin.

Sonos tracked Wylder's gaze to where two Elites were approaching with two prisoners between them.

"Char," Sonos choked, recognizing her short, slim frame and wild curls.

Charlotte's eyes darted all over.

Taimani's tall form walked rigidly beside her.

If they are here, did that mean the dragon was still a threat? Sonos wondered.

Sonos stepped forward towards them, but Wylder placed a hand on his shoulder pulling him back.

"Not so fast, *Highness.*" He spewed the title with blatant disregard.

Sonos opened his mouth to argue but was interrupted by a massive *boom* that shook the ground and echoed off the mountain.

Sonos dropped to the ground as shouts erupted around the camp.

"Secure the prisoners!" Wylder's voice rose above the chaos.

An Elite pulled Sonos to his feet.

Charlotte and Taimani were brought to the entrance of the tent as well.

A massive pillar of smoke billowed about half a mile away on the far end of the field. It seemed to come from the base of the mountain, not high up near the entrance to Noiz, which meant it was from the road. That would mean...

"The dragon?" Sonos mouthed to Charlotte.

She gave a slight nod and couldn't hide the look of relief that flowed through her eyes.

Wylder kept a tight rein on Sonos, Charlotte, and Taimani, apparently determined not to lose them in the commotion. "Inside to the Emperor, now," he commanded the Elites.

Inside the tent was just as chaotic as the outside. A large table spread with maps stood in the center of the room. His father was shouting with his back to the entrance when they entered.

Ade stood nearby with his hands clasped behind his back, head held high. A hologram of Baku projected from a gazer placed on the center of the table. A dozen other senior officials conferred with runners, soldiers, and Elites as they tried to ascertain exactly what was happening.

In the midst of the frenetic activity, Sonos bent from his waist into a bow towards his father as the two guards dropped to their knees.

"Sonos," the Emperor turned and spit out his name as if it was venom.

Having been acknowledged, Sonos was able to stand straight. He kept his eyes downcast and didn't move any further. His hands trembled, and he held them tight against his side. How could he possibly negotiate anything with his father?

Charlotte was brought into the room and shoved into a prostrate position next to Taimani who was already prone. She let out a small yelp as she was shoved down. It was enough to draw his father's attention.

He walked towards Charlotte. "This... *girl*? She is the one who destroyed my weapon, my dragon?"

Charlotte started to raise her head, but one of the Elites quickly shoved her face back into the dirt floor.

Now, I need to say something to help her, Sonos thought. He licked his lips and opened his mouth to speak.

His father was quicker. "She is yours, General Baku. I want you to find out exactly what she did and how. Use any means. The Kimwaki escapee will also be at your disposal." His eyes would have bored holes into Charlotte if they could.

"Yes, Great One," Baku's mouth twitched upward through the hologram. "Wylder will bring her via Carrier."

"Father, I..." Sonos stuttered as he scrambled to say something, anything.

"As for you..." The Emperor glared at Sonos. "Be thankful you are not going with her, yet." He looked at Wylder. "Get them all out of my sight."

Elites grabbed onto Sonos.

"Wait," Sonos said. He couldn't fail so completely now.

His father ignored him and conversed with Ade and some other officials at the table.

Wylder pulled at Sonos' shoulder.

"Wait," Sonos said louder, shaking off Wylder's hand.

The Emperor turned ever so slowly back to face Sonos. "What did you say?"

A cool breeze fluttered into the tent, stirring the maps behind the Emperor. Perhaps it was silly, but it gave Sonos courage. Wind from the mountain, from a place beyond this tent, from *El*.

"It stops here, Father." Sonos kept his gaze locked on the Emperor, refusing to look elsewhere lest he lose his nerve. "All the questions I dared to ask before. All the times I looked for a better way. Well, I have found *El* and his people. You may not have the Mountain Kingdom."

Where did that come from? Sonos wondered. The last line had just popped out.

All eyes were fixed on Sonos.

"Get out," his father narrowed his eyes as he enunciated each word with force.

But resolve now pulsed through Sonos. He squared his shoulders and prayed inwardly. The words flowed from his spirit through his mouth. It wasn't conscious thought from his brain. "Your pride, lust for conquest, and oppression of others, stand in judgment against you. *El* has seen and now speaks. For seven years you will be confined to live in the Badlands as if a wild beast, until you raise your eyes and acknowledge *El* as sovereign over all the kingdoms and all the empires of the entire earth."

Sonos' heartbeat pounded in his ears.

The room fell completely silent. Even the noise from outside the tent seemed to have stilled.

The Emperor broke the tension with a laugh. Perhaps it was more of a cackle. Sonos had never heard his father laugh before in his life, and the sound was strange, almost maniacal.

"You are truly mad, Sonos, and you will join your little friends with General Baku. You are no longer my concern." His father pulled his mouth into a tight line. "Even without the dragon, the Mountain Kingdom *will* be destroyed."

He turned to his officials and ordered for the largest and most powerful bombs to be catapulted against the mountainside. "Close up every entrance, flatten every structure, let every single follower of *El* be destroyed. We will dig out the gold another time."

"No," Sonos gasped.

Charlotte's hand flew to cover her mouth, and Taimani's eyes narrowed with anger practically spilling out in waves.

Baku's soft voice spoke through the hologram. "If the dragon was indeed destroyed, might I remind everyone to wear your air purifiers. We wouldn't want any of those chemicals affecting our own."

The officials slipped slim masks over their nose and mouth and ran from the room to carry out the Emperor's instructions.

Wylder tugged Sonos towards the exit, but the Emperor turned.

"Perhaps before taking them to Baku, they can remain to see the destruction of the Mountain Kingdom firsthand." His eyes flickered.

Wylder nodded and instructed for the three prisoners to be placed on the floor, out of the way. The Elites slapped purifiers over their mouth and nose. "Can't have you dying before we reach Pergamum, now can we?" Wylder smirked.

Soon, only Wylder, the Emperor, Ade, and the hologram of Baku remained, along with the Kimwaki bodyguards.

Sonos hung his head with the weight of his failure. *What had he done wrong?* The words he had spoken had come from somewhere other than his brain, he knew that. And they felt so powerful being said. But to what end? Would his father only be judged after the Mountain Kingdom was destroyed?

Lenora's parting words came back to Sonos' mind. *"The heart has eyes that the mind cannot see."* Sonos closed his eyes, trying to take his focus out of the room. *Where is the bigger picture, the unseen realm?* he thought.

Another breeze blew in from the doorway, causing Sonos to shiver, but his head remained down. He couldn't even look at Charlotte or Taimani.

"Father!" Ade's voice snapped Sonos from his stupor.

A dark mist covered the Emperor. Ade ran forward, waving his arms to try and dispel the mist. The form of his father could barely be seen, writhing in the thick cloud that had formed.

The guards in the room split. Half running to defend the Emperor, the other half moved in towards Sonos, Charlotte, and Taimani.

Wylder kept his spear trained at Sonos, dark eyes fixed as if accusing Sonos of bringing the mist.

I wonder...

"Emperor?" Baku's holographic image leaned forward. "What's happening?" Baku's eyes flashed towards Charlotte, but she was just as wide-eyed and confused.

Ade yelped and jumped back from the cloud as a growl erupted and a long, hairy arm thrust out.

Slowly, the mist dissipated, and what was left looked more like a beast than a man. Long, shaggy hair covered the Emperor's body. Or what used to be his body. His fingers and toes were elongated with claws now protruding. His face remained, albeit covered in hair. His blue eyes carried a wild look. He let out a deep, guttural cry and scampered from the room on all fours.

"Follow him!" Ade commanded the bodyguards.

The warriors ran.

"You, too!" Ade shouted at Wylder. "My father is more important than these worthless fools."

Wylder hesitated but looked at Ade and Baku and followed the other Elites out.

"You," Ade hissed at Sonos. "What have you done? Who have you become? This... this *foul* magic from the enemy? On your own blood?"

"I—" Sonos wasn't sure where to start.

Ade cut him off. "You are no longer a K'Luma. The Emporer's orders will stand. The Mountain Kingdom *will* be destroyed. Baku will deal with you after Father is recovered and restored." Ade turned to his bodyguard. "Get them out of my sight."

The few remaining Elites hesitated. Ade wasn't thinking straight. Plans started to form in Sonos' head once more. They had an opening.

"Highness," Baku tried softly.

"Enough," Ade screeched. "I want my father back here, and I want the Mountain Kingdom destroyed. And I want these traitors out of my sight." Ade was pacing the room now.

Did some remnants of the mist land on him and make Ade irrational and crazy, too? Sonos wondered.

Taimani caught his eye and nodded towards the exit.

Together with Charlotte, they scrambled up and quickly moved towards the tent flap. Elites followed behind them.

Sonos caught Taimani's eye for the briefest second before she dropped her gaze. It was enough for Sonos to confirm that she was ready. Ready to make a run for it.

Outside the tent, chaos abounded. Soldiers who had not been quick enough with the gas masks lay writhing on the ground, crying out in pain. Soldiers and officers alike were running and shouting, often giving conflicting orders.

A burst of lightning broke through the early morning sky, followed by a loud clap of thunder mere seconds later.

In all the confusion, a small movement from the outside of the tent flashed, and all of a sudden Taimani had a hooked sword in hand, and Rapha was climbing up onto Charlotte's shoulder.

Taimani engaged the two Elites in an instant.

Meanwhile, the heavens opened, and rain started pouring down in buckets.

Sonos wiped his eyes and scanned the ground. He found a short spear that he grabbed from a downed soldier and ran to join Taimani.

She had already dropped one of their guards and was engaging the second.

Sonos threw the spear near the guard's feet, causing him to become unbalanced. It was all Taimani needed to land a blow and knock him out as well.

The pelting rain made it hard to see or hear, but Charlotte grabbed Sonos' hand and yelled at Taimani. "Follow me!"

CHAPTER 43

CHARLOTTE WIPED THE RAIN from her eyes, searching for the brown bundle of fur. A thrumming in her right ear shifted her gaze, and she caught sight of Rapha again.

"Come on." She gripped Sonos' hand and confirmed that Taimani was right behind them.

The camp was mostly empty as the soldiers had gathered near the road for battle. Those that remained were a mix of confused and hurting.

She grimaced as she almost tripped over a soldier writhing on the ground, reaching out for anyone who passed.

Charlotte hoped that Jax was safe inside the Inner Sanctum and far from the dragon's chemicals.

A loud crack of thunder shook the ground under their feet.

Charlotte ran after Rapha with renewed energy.

The rain and wet terrain made it difficult to keep upright. Not to mention the contraption that covered her nose and mouth, preventing her from gulping as much as air as she wanted.

"The river!" Sonos shouted above the rain. He pointed ahead of them.

Rapha was jumping and waving his arms waiting by its banks. He took off running towards the Badlands as soon they neared.

"We're about to have company," Taimani warned from behind.

Charlotte followed her gaze. A soldier with a pair of Elites pointed in their direction.

"Run!" Taimani bellowed and adjusted her grip on the hooked sword.

Charlotte sprinted along the river towards the Badlands.

Sonos kept by her side, even though she was sure he could have run much faster.

Shouts from the Elites grew closer, their footfalls splashing on the wet ground.

Charlotte didn't dare turn around. She kept her eyes forward, all energy focused on getting into the Badlands.

When they finally reached the high dirt walls, Sonos ran first into the narrow crevice.

Charlotte was on his heels while Taimani held back a few paces to give them a buffer from the incoming Elites.

A bulking form shoved past Charlotte as soon as she was through the crevice and ran back towards Taimani.

"Taine!" Sonos cried out.

"Stay inside!" the warrior shouted, his hooked sword glowing blue. "I'm getting my sister!"

Charlotte's ears buzzed as they passed through the invisible haze.

The crevice opened into the cave-like tunnel they had come through just the day before. She doubled over, trying to gulp as much air as possible through the mask.

A thrumming zoomed over Charlotte, snapping up her head.

"What the—" Charlotte flailed her arms.

"Are those... bats, just circling in the crevice?" Sonos had a bewildered look on his face.

Sure enough, a cloud of bats flew into the narrow crevice and stayed there, circling in the storm.

Taimani and Taine sprinted into view, finding a way to break through before the bats became almost solid in the entrance.

"They won't hold your pursuers off forever," a deep voice rumbled.

Charlotte scanned the tunnel.

Further ahead, a ray of sunlight shone through on the dark form of the commander of *El's* army.

Rapha sat perched on his shoulder.

They seemed oddly far away, but as Charlotte took a step forward, she realized why. A chasm in the floor separated them. How were they supposed to cross?

Violent coughing from nearby shifted Charlotte's attention to Taine. He was doubled over on the ground, gagging.

"I think some of the chemical got to him." Taimani cursed in their native tongue. "Why didn't he listen and just stay in here?"

Charlotte knelt beside Taine, checking his vitals.

Taine's pulse was racing, his eyes unfocused.

"Oh!" Charlotte exclaimed as she dug in one of her pockets. She remembered the cola nut Jax had handed her before they left Noiz.

"What will that do?" Taimani asked.

"We call this bizzy back in Jamroq." Charlotte looked around and found a sharp stone on the ground. She grated the nut directly into Taine's mouth, then forced him to drink some water.

It took less than a minute for Taine's color to return and his eyes to focus on Taimani.

"Unbelievable," Sonos said. "The Sahemy healers have nothing on your bush medicine."

Charlotte smiled.

"It's time," the commander called from across the chasm.

Charlotte refocused her attention. "How exactly are we supposed to cross?" she asked.

The Elites shouted from the other side of the entrance. They were close to breaking through.

"Jump!" the commander answered.

"Jump?" Charlotte eyed the distance across. *Maybe?* she thought. It looked impossibly far though.

Taimani and Sonos stood on either side of Taine. He was standing on his own, but how could they all make it?

Rapha chittered and flailed his arms.

Charlotte looked at Sonos, trying to gauge his state of mind.

"What was that thing you and Sibi both said? That *El* didn't bring us all this way just to kill us?" Sonos asked. "And I'm not seeing any other options."

Charlotte took a deep breath and bent her knees.

But just as she was about to jump, the first Elite broke through the cloud of bats.

Taimani moved with lightning-quick reflexes to deflect a spear the Elite had thrown.

Both Taimani and Taine stepped forward to engage the two Elites. Metal clashed against metal. No electricity pulsed through the swords in the cave, but light reflected off the fast-moving weapons.

Charlotte glanced at Sonos, trying to figure out how they could help.

Taine knocked out his Elite and moved to help Taimani. But then a third figure with a floppy hat ran into the cave and made a beeline for Sonos.

Sonos cried out, and Taine dove in between the newcomer and Sonos, a feathered dart sticking out from his arm.

Taimani screamed a battle cry that echoed off the walls and dropped the remaining Elite. She threw a dagger and knocked the blow gun from the floppy-hat man's hand.

Sonos ran towards Taine, but Taine shouted.

"Go!" Taine locked eyes with his sister even as he lay still on the floor. "Get him to safety, now!"

Another Elite burst through the crevice.

Taimani's eyes narrowed.

In her hesitation, Charlotte grabbed Sonos and ran towards the chasm. They needed to get to Rapha.

Taimani ran up beside them.

This time, there was no pause. All three took a giant leap together.

A tingle washed over Charlotte mid-air. Panic gripped her. *Was I wrong? Is this the end?* But then the hard, dirt ground caught her, and she rolled as best as she could to soften the landing.

They made it.

"You okay?" Sonos asked Charlotte.

"I think so," Charlotte said, dusting off.

"Where's Taine?" Taimani cried out.

Charlotte squinted back across the chasm, but it was completely blurred and dark. *What?*

"Peace, be still," a familiar, mellow voice said.

"*E fa'apefea 'ona 'outou fa'amoemoe 'ou te nofo filemu?*" Taimani wailed.

Rapha stood, and laid a hand on Taimani. "Taine is on a different path, but he is not lost."

Charlotte felt a lump in her throat—knowing how Taimani must feel, watching her brother be taken by the Empire. She added one more name to the siblings they would soon rescue.

"You do talk," Sonos whispered, eyes wide. "Where are we?" He looked around the cave.

Taimani slumped to the ground, staring at the chasm.

"My guess is another temporal portal," Charlotte said.

"Mmhmm." Rapha nodded.

"But what about Jax?" Charlotte asked. "And the people of Noiz? Aren't they still under attack? Surely, we can't leave them, too?"

"They are protected in the Inner Sanctum," Rapha said. "The army will not reach them there, try as they might."

Charlotte allowed herself a smidgen of relief, but she was feeling antsy. This was not a calm after the storm. In fact, it felt more like saving the Mountain Kingdom had really just been like kicking a beehive.

"As for us, there is work yet to be done and a promise to uphold." Rapha looked pointedly at Charlotte. "The journey has only just begun."

Charlotte glanced at Sonos. His crestfallen face reminded her of what it was like to leave her dad and Gran behind in Jamroq.

Taimani's slumped shoulders looked to hold the weight of the world, or at least her brother.

Charlotte took Sonos' hand and knelt beside Taimani, placing her other hand on the warrior's shoulder. "Be bold and very courageous," she repeated the words from the ancient journal. "We will get our loved ones back and burn those towers to the ground. *El* knows the end from the beginning. Fight we must, but win we shall. We have hope."

END OF BOOK 1

ACKNOWLEDGMENTS

"If you want to go fast, go alone. If you want to go far, go with others." This African proverb captures the heart and soul of my author journey.

So often, writing is a solitary venture. Staring at a blank screen, writing for hours on end, toiling to bring an idea to life. Quite frankly, although I've been a reader all my life, I never knew what it would take to turn a basic storyline into a novel with characters, plot, pacing, dialogue, and all the million little pieces required for a finished novel.

But we're here! And please indulge me a few acknowledgments to those who made this possible.

Firstly, I want to thank you, dear reader. Without you, everything is for naught. I hoped you loved the story and felt connected to Charlotte, Sonos, and the rest of the gang. But more than anything, my deepest wish is for the words to inspire, give hope and make you think.

As an indie author, one of the greatest ways you can help support and ensure that more stories like this come to life is to leave a review. Every single rating and recommendation does a lot to help spread the word, improve rankings and help this book reach a wide pool of readers. I'd love to connect on social media, and if you're able to engage and spread the word to your own networks, those efforts also mean a great deal! You can find links and contact info on my website: www.heidialert.com

While I took great liberties in the storytelling, the unseen realm is real. The core of this story, inclusive of the title, is linked to my Congress-WBN community. You'll also see inspiration from Moses, Joshua, and Isaiah, just to name a few. I hope those who know the "thing behind the thing" enjoy all the references that you know and love!

You may have also picked up multiple references to the Caribbean—especially Jamaica with flavors from Trinidad & Tobago, where I lived for eleven years. Jumping oceans to the Pacific, Samoa was the inspiration for Kimwaki—I simply love their language.

I already named my family in the dedication, but I must again acknowledge them here. Gordon, aside from being my best friend and confidant, you are my biggest supporter and champion. You were the first one to read my rawest attempt and the last to read my final version before going off to the editor. You were my developmental editor and helped ensure all the characters had an arc, not just a two-dimensional journey. Our life together in Trinidad & Tobago was infused with your own Guyanese-Jamaican roots and helped make this story all the richer.

Zakyla, it was your drawing and naming of Charlotte that first inspired the main character for this story. Your avid reading also gave this mama a deep-seated desire to provide clean fantasy options for you, and others like you, to devour. I can't wait to read your own book one day!

Zhaun, whether you meant it as a challenge or not, your declaration that "I'll read the book after you sell a million copies," helped me to think and dream bigger. Thank you.

To my alpha readers who stuck with the story through the earliest version on Scrib, thank you! Special shout-out to Kathryn Elliott and Kalten Browning! Even in those rough chapters, you saw what was possible.

To my weekly writing group, Mosaic, who walked with me through the grueling rewrite of version two. Thank you, Richard Ince, Shala Alert, and Gordon Alert.

To my beta readers: even though it was more polished than versions one and two, it was still quite rough around the edges. Notwithstanding, you found a way to both encourage and challenge me. Kevin Khelawan, Ruth Rudden, Kalten and Allison Browning - thank you!

Sara Coombes, you are my editor extraordinaire. Thank you for the extra time to fix the final holes and rewrite the last chapter about 20 times. Your flexibility and collaborative approach were wonderful to bring the final polish to the book.

My dear Alert ones... Grayson, Shala, and Koen, you worked magic, passion, and grace to come up with an amazing cover. Koen, I love that you made your voice heard and became a champion of the book! Thank you all for putting your fingerprints all over this venture—it's better because of all three of you.

Special mention to Ilya Spencer who also played a part in the journey to a finished product.

To my Gilliland crew: Mom and Dad (a.k.a. Mr. and Mrs. Kim), Crystal, Brock... you guys are my rocks. You've always believed in me, encouraged me, and loved me through every up, down, turn, and phase of life. Thank you! Special shout out to Becky, Josh, and all my Pittsburgh nieces: Molly, Emily, Addy, Leah, and Lib. Love yinz!

To all my friends and family, too numerous to mention each by name, who spoke life and encouragement along the way—thank you for being part of the process in every way both big and small.

Lastly, to my roots and community: Elijah Centre. Plain and simple, without you, this book would not exist. You are the heart, soul, and spirit—the essence—of both the story and the author. This is for you, with all of my love.

HEIDI ALERT

Days are spent in the corporate world, but the midnight oil burns brightly with stories that need to be told.

Originally from Harmony, PA, a country suburb of Pittsburgh, a winding journey led across the U.S. and eventually to Trinidad & Tobago in the Caribbean for eleven years. Heidi now calls Atlanta, Georgia, home, together with her Jamaican husband, two teenagers, and rescue pets.

She holds a bachelor's in marketing from the University of Pittsburgh and her MBA from Georgetown University.

Connect on IG @heidialert or visit www.heidialert.com.